So 5 Minutes Ago

V VILLARD / NEW YORK

So 5 Minutes Ago

A NOVEL

HILARY de VRIES

Copyright © 2004 by Hilary de Vries

All rights reserved under International and Pan-American Copyright Conventions. Published in the United States by Villard Books, an imprint of The Random House Publishing Group, a division of Random House, Inc., New York, and simultaneously in Canada by Random House of Canada Limited, Toronto.

VILLARD and "V" CIRCLED Design are registered trademarks of Random House, Inc.

LIBRARY OF CONGRESS CATALOGING-IN-PUBLICATION DATA
De Vries, Hilary.
    So five minutes ago: a novel / Hilary de Vries.
        p.   cm.
    ISBN 1-4000-6138-5
    1. Women public relations personnel—Fiction.
    2. Hollywood (Los Angeles, Calif.)—Fiction.   3. Motion picture industry—Fiction.   4. Public relations firms—Fiction.
    5. Celebrities—Fiction.   I. Title.
    PS3604.E89S6 2004
    813'.6—dc22   2003059601

Villard Books website address: www.villard.com
Printed in the United States of America on acid-free paper
9 8 7 6 5 4 3 2 1
First Edition

Book design by Victoria Wong

For Ruth, who always wondered what it was like,
and Michael, who knows all too well.

And you may ask yourself . . .
well, how did I get here?

—Talking Heads, "Once in a Lifetime"

The Rules

It would have made it a lot easier. Knowing what I know now. But as Glinda the Good Witch said to Dorothy, you had to find these things out for yourself. After my first three years as a Hollywood publicist for some of the biggest and not-so-biggest stars, I've learned a few handy rules any girl needs to get by. Feel free to take notes. Or just sit back and watch. Like a car crash in slow motion. Or the Wizard frantically pulling the levers behind the curtain.

Get your hair professionally blown out before hitting the red carpet.
Never take any call you can return.
Never say no. Always "Take a pass."
Never expect stars to be your friends.
Never expect stars to acknowledge you exist.
When in doubt, wear black.
When in doubt, stay in the closet.
No one cares what you think.
Everyone cares what you look like.
Cheekbones are the new tits.

Butts are the new tits.
Lie about your age. Everyone does.
Lie about your prescription drug intake. Everyone does.
Lie about your yoga obsession. Everyone does.
Never let them see you sweat.
Never let them see you smoke.
Never let them see you drink. At least not at lunch.
Never eat if you can avoid it.
Never read anything. Except the weekend grosses and the tabloids.
Hollywood is all about numbers, no matter what you've heard.
Hollywood is all about rumors, just like you've heard.
Boys rule.
Girls never rule.
And they hardly ever win.
Except now.

So 5 Minutes Ago

1 | Down the Rabbit Hole

Before dawn and already I'm off to a bad start. But then I could have guessed as much when I forgot to close the window last night and got jolted awake at 5 A.M. by the sprinkler system rattling to life. Sometimes, depending on my mood, if I can be said even to have a mood at 5 A.M., the sound of running water can be reassuring. Like a stream or a bath being drawn. But this morning it sounds like nothing so much as a bursting pipe. A taunt to my inability to bring anything to heel.

Not my job as a senior publicist to some of Hollywood's lesser celebrities at DWP, a legendary if fading publicity agency. And certainly not Los Angeles, where I—raised in Philadelphia's custardy Main Line—inexplicably found myself three years ago. My house with its dyspeptic sprinkler system is the least of my worries.

For one thing, it's Thursday, which means the dual reveille of sprinkler and garbage truck. Just when I'm drifting off again, the city's sanitation department begins its weekly assault, grinding along the street running below my modest but nonetheless desirable rental in the hills, followed by a second, noisier pass by my front gate.

"Thursday," I groan, rolling over to peer crankily at the bed-room wall, which looks, in the dim, coffee-colored light, like it could stand a paint job. Thursday. Another weekend fast approaching with no plans unless you count a screening Friday night and a meeting with a stylist on Saturday. Maybe I can fill the hours looking at paint chips or something.

Thursday, I realize with a thud, the kick of adrenalin as my heart lurches back to its usual wracking pace. This isn't just any Thursday with its annoying staff meeting, everyone sitting around waiting to carve one another up over nonfat vanilla lattes, but the Thursday of my big client meeting.

With Troy Madden.

Troy Madden. I haven't even signed him yet and already he's a problem. Actually, Troy *is* the problem, which is why he's in the market for a new publicist. Someone to solve the problem of his just-back-from-court-ordered-rehab career reentry. Someone lower down the food chain. Someone like me. Which is why I'm taking a meeting with him in about—I roll over and attempt to focus on the silver-plated clock on my bedside table—six hours. With a sigh, I kick off the duvet and slide my feet to the sisal carpeting, which I notice, irritably, could stand replacing.

Staring at myself in the bathroom mirror, I mentally clock the distance I have to travel to go from how I look now—an over-worked, underachieving single woman in her early thirties who could use a haircut and a boyfriend—to the kind of polished, savvy professional I'm supposed to be a few hours from now. No-body looks their best at 7 A.M., no matter how many models were photographed in tangled bedsheets and dirty hair during the Slept-in Chic phase, which, if I have the chronology right, fol-lowed the Heroin Chic phase. I have Italian sheets, but they do little to erase the fact that 1.) I hate my job even though I'm fright-eningly good at it, 2.) I hate my life because everyone thinks I have the most FABULOUS job and no one wants to hear *anyone* com-plaining about mopping up after stars, and 3.) I went to bed too late—which meant I had my requisite two glasses of white wine too late—after a screening, another relentlessly unfunny De Niro comedy that just makes you want to kill yourself.

Now, bleary eyed and grouchy, I have to come up with a game plan before my meeting with Troy this afternoon. Actually I should come up with a plan for the rest of my life. Like, what happened to my goal of becoming a top magazine editor by age thirty-five? Or my marriage? Like, where did that go?

I snap on the shower and pray the steam helps clear my head, if only about Troy. We at DWP specialize in resuscitating down-and-outers. Or at least we do now. At one time, DWP was the Tiffany's of PR firms. But that was before my time. Now, we're like Jesus working the crowds at the pool of Bethesda. Careers on the slow fade? A little trouble with the law? Can't quite claw your way onto the B-list? The aging pretty boys. The actresses who spend more time at the dermatologist than at auditions. You've come to the right place. My bosses like them as clients. Their names still sound classy—like Sally Field and Cybill Shepherd, who everybody joked was the Old Maid, the card nobody wanted to hold—their fees are lower, and because they seldom have anything to promote, the workload is nothing. Just some handholding, the publicist's equivalent of phone sex. Even the company's acronym, after the partners—Davis, Woolfe, and the long-departed Peterman—is identical to that of the city's utility company, the Department of Water and Power.

Troy is perfect DWP material. After his little stay in rehab—actually it was three stays, including swanky Promises out in Malibu, but nobody besides the judge was really counting—he needs to get back in the game. Recapture his heat, his wattage. He had plenty at one time, like three years ago, which makes him positively Paleolithic here. In L.A., you age faster than anywhere on the planet. In fact, Hollywood years are almost exactly the length of dog years. With an average life span about that of a dachshund or a Great Dane, you can expect to be professionally dead in fifteen years. Give or take.

Take Troy. At twenty-nine, or so he says, he still has a few miles left on him, even if he has tumbled from his *Vanity Fair* cover heights of a couple years back, when his dark eyes and cocksure grin had caught the eye of every gay director in town. Before he'd made a single studio picture, Troy had been crowned the new Steve McQueen. But that was before his last movie tanked—"*Blow Your Mind" Games,* a low-budget, pseudodocumentary horror flick about a reality show, a kind of *Blair Witch*-meets-*Survivor*—and before his run-in with the Portland cops when he was caught with a bong in a suite at the Heathman Hotel. Later there was some DUI incident in the Palisades, actually two of them, which meant Troy spent the better part of a month in the Beverly Hills court-house. Then came the trio of rehab stays.

Now, nine months later, Troy is back, itching to get back in the game. And I—as the youngest and newest member of the DWP team—am the designated hitter. "You're the girl to land Troy," Suzanne Davis, my fifty-something boss (the *D* of *DWP* and one of the firms two remaining founding partners), had said, pausing for her usual nanosecond in my office before disappearing down the hall, a blur of one of the white Armani suits she always wore. "You're the one who knows how to recycle the Gen Y crowd." *Recycle?* Like I'm doing something good for the planet.

I step from the shower, grab a towel, and head into the kitchen. Troy might need a comeback campaign, but I'm in serious need of coffee. He's already heard Hollywood's death rattle. A TV producer with a network deal called his agent sniffing around about Troy's post-rehab availability to shoot a pilot about a divorced dad who becomes a foster parent to a pair of Hispanic twins. "Cute kids, like Elian Gonzales," the producer said. His agent naturally passed, but when Troy heard about the offer he panicked and fired everyone except his lawyer, an old friend from Iowa State, where the two of them played baseball until Troy started shooting too many beer commercials in Chicago to make it to class, let alone practice. Now, a few months after the sitcom scare, Troy has new representation, a slate of meetings around town. And me.

I'm no closer to figuring out Troy's life or mine when I arrive at the office.

"Hey, want coffee? I'm going out," Steven says when I stagger in, snagging my heel on the ratty carpeting.

"Yeah, and find out why we still have these shitty offices when there's so much money in this town."

"Speaking of that," Steven says, rolling his eyes, which is his way of saying, *We have to talk. In your office.* A former top shoe salesman at Barneys (it was actually amazing how much they could earn), now the heir to his former lover's not-insignificant fortune—well, he was an entertainment lawyer before he died of AIDS—and inexplicably my assistant, Steven has many skills, but reading my moods and watching my back are two of his best. He's also a dead ringer for Paul Rudd, which makes him very popular around the office.

"No shit, it happened today?" I say, grabbing him by the arm and all but yanking him into my windowless office—cubicle is more like it—with its stained beige carpeting and chipped plywood desk.

Even before he can blurt out the news, I know what's coming. We are officially BIG-DWPers. Or as Steven puts it, "Big Dwippers."

"I'm not even going to ask how you know this before I do."

"That would be like trying to explain matter and antimatter or why I'm still in touch with my old boyfriends—including the one who writes for *The Wall Street Journal*—and you're not," Steven says, sinking into my chair and putting his feet on my desk. "Let's just say Suzanne et al finally got their cherry popped BIG-time."

"Shit," I say, sinking into the room's only other chair, a grotty gray thing with the stuffing poking out the back.

The rumors had been building for weeks. BIG was buying us out. Or maybe it was a merger. Hard to tell with so many agencies mating like rabbits and turning out acronym-crazed mutants ready for listing on the NYSE or NASDAQ. PR agencies used to title themselves like law firms, with a string of pretentious last names. Ego, Superego, and Id. But ever since the almighty PMK had been bought out and/or merged and was now PMK-HBH and owned by some big international ad conglomerate, the "praiseries," as the trades still called us, had thrown in the towel and were aping the big boys, the *real* agencies: CAA. ICM. ETC.

"Don't tell me. D-W-and-P can now retire?"

"Well, P's dead, as you may recall, but yes, Woolfe is said to be heading for the door even as we speak," Steven says. "But you lesser mortals get something."

I know better than to let my expression change.

"BIG new offices. And a new contract agreement. Oh, and punch and cookies will be served in the conference room this afternoon."

I resist the urge to bury my head in my hands.

"When do we move?"

"Not soon enough, judging by your tone of voice a few minutes ago," Steven says, heading for the door, having decided he needs coffee even if I don't. "A month. I think. Look," he says, staring at me with that look he gets sometimes. Like I'm supposed to throw him a ball or something to fetch. "Think of it as a whole bunch of new people we can make fun of."

"Thanks," I say, giving him a feeble wave, aware that my sucky day just got even suckier. "Yes, go to Starbucks. And get me a latte."

I drop into my chair and try to focus on my call sheet. The usual endless blizzard. Editors. Studio publicists. The New York office. A bunch of squawking baby birds demanding daily feeding. But I'm too distracted to call anyone. The BIG buyout means BIG changes. DWP may have seen better days with its mostly aging client list—okay, we still had a few stars like Carla Selena and the Phoenix, who Suzanne handled, and I had my young up-and-comers—but it was small, owned solely by the partners, and staffed totally by women (except for Stan Woolfe in New York and all the gay assistants), which meant it was slightly less Borgia-like than the rest of Hollywood. But now it was history. Now, I'm a BIG-DWPer.

As far as I can tell, the biggest dwip is one Doug Graydon, ex-Sony marketing head who bought the upstart boutique agency B.I./PR—transforming it into BIG—with his golden parachute and some private financing. Word is he's looking to build up the agency—acquiring DWP was just another piece of the puzzle—and cash out big-time, selling to some ad agency back East. Word is G had also had a weave, had his eyes done, and had engaged in a little elective surgery on his last name as well. As in no longer née Grossman. Jesus, who didn't want to be Jewish in Hollywood? Or New York, for that matter? All I know is, the few times G rolled through our offices looking like a real estate agent kicking the tires of a tear-down, he loved the sound of his own voice and had a major thing for hiring all the blond MAW's—the ubiquitious model-actress-whatevers—to populate BIG's offices, which are, I realize, about to become my offices.

I reach for the trades in my in-box to check for news of the deal. Nothing—which means it will be tomorrow's front page. Today's headlines are not much more cheering. NETS LEAK AS RATINGS HEMORRHAGE. POLICE DOG WHO DIED AT WTC HONORED. STUDIO CHIEFS BRACE FOR BODY BLOW AT B.O. I imagine another headline: PRAISERY AGENT WANTS OUT—NOW! "HOLLYWOOD WORSE THAN I FEARED!"

God knows I hadn't felt this way when I first stumbled into Hollywood the way Alice fell down the rabbit hole—by accident and a surfeit of curiosity. A friend of my mother's back in Upper Darby had a son who'd started a production company with a few college buddies—Yo' Flicks—which needed help around the offices in New York. I'd spent the seven years since graduating from Brown working as an assistant editor at a couple of the lesser women's mags before quitting to get my master's in creative writing at NYU. I got my degree, but I'd also gotten married to one of my classmates, Josh Davidson, a former Smith Barney analyst who had a passing fancy of becoming a playwright—a marriage which lasted about as long as my dreams of becoming a writer. Marrying and divorcing Josh was, as my mother said when I called to tell her I was engaged to the son of a doctor from Williamsburg ("Oh, I love Virginia," she'd said before I pointed out her geographical mistake: Williamsburg as in *Brooklyn*), my little moment of "going native."

The one thing I kept was Josh's name, because it was less embarrassing than to give it up and go back to being Alex Bradford, who grew up on baloney sandwiches and went to Sunday school. I also kept it because now everyone thought I was Jewish. Like I was already in the club. Working at Yo' Flicks, where all the partners had bar mitzvahed in the same year, Alex *Davidson* fit right in, even if I only answered phones, helped out in casting sessions, and planned a few parties—like the premiere for their documentary *Wassup Wheels*, about a group of extreme skateboarders from Bed-Stuy.

That film put the company on the map after Spike Lee, one of the executive producers, mentioned the movie during an appearance on *Charlie Rose* to talk about the Knicks. DWP was helping promote the premiere—sort of pro bono because one of the publicists was the aunt of one of the Yo' Flicks partners. It was February, Black History Month, and Nike had been a cosponsor of the party held at Mr. Chow because a lot of rappers actually ate there. At the party, a bunch of DWP publicists showed up, including Stan Woolfe (the *W*, I realized later, and the agency's reigning éminence grise), who, after a couple of martinis and under the impression that the party had been all my doing, offered me a job. I'd had just enough martinis myself and was also feeling just miffed enough when I saw all the Yo' Flicks partners high-fiving each other at the bar when Dr. Dre walked in (totally coincidentally, because he was a Mr. Chow regular) that I turned to Stan and in his bleary eyes saw my own office, a six-figure salary, and a ticket out of Yo' Flicks and said, "Yes." It actually felt more moving than when I agreed to marry Josh, but then the whole tent-and-rabbi thing had been a lot more out there than Mr. Chow.

Now, three years later, here I was, feeling not only like I'd fallen down the rabbit hole but had somehow gotten wedged. Stuck. All the casual *whatevers* of my twenties, the endless horizon of my postcollegiate future had given way to this fluorescent-lit cubicle where I was depressingly in my thirties and even more depressingly a publicist, for real.

Publicists, as I've learned all too well, are at the bottom of the Hollywood food chain. Not because most of them are women, and overweight at that, or young gay guys (there're just too many powerful gays in Hollywood for that to be true), but because power in Hollywood, like Wall Street, is tracked solely in earnings. Publicists are lowlifes because, unlike agents or managers, they don't generate income, only exposure. It doesn't matter whether you represent Brad Pitt or the Olsen twins. Stars pay publicists like they pay a monthly insurance bill, annoying but necessary coverage in case of disaster. Agents get stars work. Managers get stars work *and* hold their hands. But a publicist is one notch above a maid. Or a nanny. The only people we outrank are journalists, and they don't register on Hollywood's seismograph. And the real proof of our stupidity is that we don't even generate real income for ourselves. Nobody, except the few senior partners in those PR agencies big enough to be acquired by a bigger agency, ever gets rich.

Sure, in a better world, we'd be as highly paid as lawyers, given all the lying we do on behalf of our clients. A star in rehab is "taking some time off." If a star's movie doesn't open, he's "trying to push the envelope." A star who loses his production deal is "transitioning." A star found naked wandering Sunset Boulevard, disoriented in a cornfield, or picking up a transvestite in a hotel lobby is "suffering from exhaustion."

But, in reality, being a publicist put me in the Hollywood food chain somewhere around the level of zebras. Too many of us thundering around in circles, stirring up dust, and generally behaving as noisily and annoyingly as the carnivores expected us to. All I had to do was try not to get eaten.

I toss the trades aside and turn on my PC. E-mail. Such a great time-suck even if most of it's just a duplicate of my call sheet, except for the scary gang message from Suzanne marked URGENT. There are also two from Rachel flagged FUCKING UNBELIEVABLE and STILL FUCKING UNBELIEVABLE. Rachel Chapman's one of my closest friends largely because she's a publicist and moved out from New York the same time I did. Although she made the jump to the studios, working as a publicist at Fox, she inhabits a no-less-demeaning circle of hell than I do, and her ambivalence about this industry outstrips even mine. I click open hers first.

To: Alex Davidson
From: Rachel Chapman

*&#$!!}-BIG. CALL ME!

The second message, sent two minutes later, is only slightly less hyper.

To: Alex Davidson
From: Rachel Chapman

GET YOUR HEAD OUT OF THE MICROWAVE AND CALL ME—
ON YOUR CELL IN CASE G ALREADY HAS THE PHONES
TAPPED.

At least I'm not the only one who's paranoid about this merger. About working for G. I decide to live dangerously and click open Suzanne's.

To: The DWP Staff
From: Suzanne Davis

As you know, the partners of DWP have accepted a most generous offer from our friends at BIG. Of course, this will mean many changes for us all, changes that will be discussed in greater detail in the coming days. But I speak for all of us when I say this is the beginning of a truly remarkable new chapter in our company history.

Meanwhile—and I cannot emphasize this enough—all DWP publicists are to avoid talking to the press. Doug and I are sending out a press release outlining the deal to the media outlets as well as our clients and studio liaisons. In the future, all corporate communications must be cleared in advance with one of the senior partners. Meanwhile, please join me and Doug in the conference room at 4 P.M. for champagne and cake. SD.

I log off, too depressed to even troll the wires. I can already hear a high-pitched buzzing outside my door. The nursing home on High Alert. I'll need more than caffeine to confront my colleagues today. I punch up Rachel on my speed-dial.

"God," she snaps when I reach her. "Did they put you under house arrest?"

"That'd be BIG of them," I say, pointlessly. "No, just trying to get my bearings. Tell me what you've heard."

"What *I've* heard? What have you heard? You know G cleaned house when he was at Sony?"

"Yes, even *I* know that." I'm starting to get depressed all over again. "I'm just trying to figure out if we still get to play by Suzanne's rules."

"Are you serious? You're the ones who got bought out. Shit, Suzanne probably won't even be there in a year. Two at the most."

"See, you *have* heard something," I say irritably, yanking my hair into a ponytail and anchoring it with a pencil. Most days I loved Rachel's no-bullshit attitude. But not today. "All *I* know is they're still working on the contracts, we haven't even seen the new offices yet, and I have my first meeting with Troy this afternoon. But there's cake and ice cream at four."

"Oh God," Rachel says, and I can tell she's trying to be sympathetic. "Look, I'll make some calls. There's someone I know at Sony who survived G's reign of terror. I'll call you in a bit."

"Nonfat with an extra shot." Steven parks the familiar green and white paper cup (grande) on my desk. "What'd I miss?"

"Nothing," I say, peeling off the lid and immediately burning my tongue. "Just read Suzanne's e-mail and was deciding which 'media outlet' I was going to call."

"I have Richard Johnson's number on speed-dial."

"We all do. So, what's the mood in the hive?" I say, nodding in the direction of the hall. "Am I the only one who's going to miss little Camp Estrogen Patch?"

"What can I say?" Steven says, taking a slug of cappuccino. "Size matters. They want to be BIG."

I love Steven. He can't write, but no one can in Hollywood, and he's incredibly disorganized, but he makes me laugh, which hardly anybody does out here. An entire industry devoted to entertainment and nobody has a sense of humor. But Steven can get me to laugh. Like that week after I hired him and he started answering the phone in an English accent, which pissed off Suzanne—not because his accent was obviously fake, but because the craze for English assistants was about five years out of date. Then there was his Anna Wintour phase, when he wore sunglasses for a week to celebrate the fact I got *Vogue* to do a story on one of my creakiest clients, a director who hadn't had a hit in years but who was good friends with Tom Ford. I also love Steven because even though he inherited a pile from his lover, and lives in a fabulous house up in Coldwater Canyon, he still comes to work every day.

But I draw the line at pity.

"I can't be the only one who doesn't want to have a boss who's shorter than me and wears a rug."

"Look, you knew you were the odd man out when you joined this aging sorority," Steven says, launching into his get-a-grip speech that he uses on me when I'm feeling sorry for myself. "With any luck you'll get a nicer office, colleagues your own age, and you'll just deal with the new contract. Besides, none of the clients are going anywhere. They're not that ambulatory."

He had me there.

"You're right. The clients aren't going anywhere," I say, taking another hit of coffee.

"With our client roster we actually need to stock the office with a defibrillator. Just like the airlines."

"You can be in charge of shaving their chests, since you're already the expert."

Steven waves me off. "We can roam Hollywood just waiting for stars to have a breakdown and then revive them. Courteney Cox is having a panic attack because Jennifer Aniston is having a bigger career than she is. John Travolta is having a breakdown because all his movies, not just the ones about Scientology, are tanking."

"Hey, I like John Travolta."

"Of course we'd have to have a special vigil outside Charlize's house for the time when everyone wakes up and realizes she's just a talent-free ex-model."

Steven has hated Charlize Theron ever since she was mean to him at a photo shoot. Actually, she'd been patronizing and bossy, which didn't actually count as mean in Hollywood, but Steven was still miffed that she'd called him Steve and asked him to walk her dogs.

"I still can't believe she did that," he said.

"Her assistant was busy yelling at the caterer for putting too much pasta in the vegetable salad."

"I'm waiting for the day when Charlize goes into cardiac arrest because Harvey Weinstein stops returning her calls."

"Stop. We could do this all day."

"Let's, and then we'll go for drinks."

I'm starting to get annoyed.

"Okay, forget the clients and forget BIG for a minute. I need ideas for my pitch to Troy this afternoon. I mean, I have to land this guy before I can fix his image problems."

"Well, what's his movie?" Steven says distractedly, picking up *Variety*.

"He doesn't have one. Not yet. That's the problem. Remember *"Blow Your Mind" Games*?

"I still think the only thing wrong with that was the title. I mean, anyone looking at Troy isn't thinking about blowing his mind."

Now I'm *seriously* annoyed. "This town is filled with a million pretty boys but it doesn't mean they can open a movie."

"Okay, okay," Steven says, dropping *Variety*. "But shouldn't his new agent land him a movie and *then* you can promote him? I mean, even Demi Moore knew enough to stay out of sight until CAA conjured her comeback."

"Thank *you*," I say, grabbing the *Variety*. "But in these troubled times, we need all the clients we can get, even if we have to fake it."

"Okay," Steven says with a sigh. "You know the drill. Just call some editors. Tell everyone he's been writing a novel. He's just back from an ashram. Or Nepal. Call *US*. They'll do a story on anybody. Will he talk about his time in rehab? Or call *InStyle* and stick him in some rental house in the hills with some borrowed dogs and framed pictures of family members. He has a foster child in Uruguay!"

"I know, I know," I say, waving him off and pulling on my headset to attack my call sheet. "I just have to convince this guy he won't wind up like Luke Perry."

The rest of the morning is chewed up with calls. I confirm the stylist appointment for Saturday, turn down an editorial request from *My Generation*, AARP's new "celeb" magazine, and another one from *Reader's Digest*—deftly fielding all queries about BIG. I hear myself using *synergy* a lot. I spend a half an hour going through an arduous cover negotiation with *Marie Claire* for their "aging" issue, followed by a conference call with a studio marketing exec about their fall release schedule, which amazingly includes a few of our clients.

When Peg, Troy's manager, calls at eleven-thirty to say Troy can't make the meeting at lunch but wants to meet at seven at the Chateau, I am both annoyed and relieved. At least I have a few more hours to come up with a game plan. Or a few more hours to put off coming up with a game plan.

I have Steven order my usual take-out Cobb salad and iced tea and spend lunch going over my pitch. After staring at his credits long enough, I decide Troy needs to lose the sex-stud image and go for steady and reliable. Like Rob Lowe did with his comeback-from-the-sex-scandal gig on *The West Wing*. And Robert Downey, Jr.'s return from the Big House, playing the doe-eyed swain on *Ally McBeal*. It's perfect, a new image but not that much of a stretch. Playing a Gary Cooper type will also help solve Troy's off-camera tendencies to blurt out whatever crosses his pot-addled brain.

I've even gone so far as to work up a mock photo shoot: ranch, blue jeans, pickup truck, and lots of animals. Make that baby animals. Lose the girls in short cutoffs and their dazed "do me" gazes, and stick Troy on a hay bale holding a lamb or a calf. Might be a nightmare to actually shoot, but that isn't my problem. If only Westerns were still hot. Still, it could work. Troy—the Classic American Hero.

Hey, it worked for Tom Cruise—and talk about baggage.

2 | ... and Farther Down

I'm feeling very on my game when 4 P.M. and the BIG staff meeting rolls around. When Steven and I wander in at exactly four-ten, the room is packed. Amazing, since these command performances usually elicit a flood of no-shows. Suzanne and G are nowhere to be seen, but among the denizens there's the usual flouncing of hair and nervous sidestepping of mules and the hissing sound of Diet Cokes being pried open. On the conference table there's a giant sheet cake decorated like *Variety*'s front page with the headline BIG DEAL FOR BIG-DWP in black icing. At least there aren't any balloons.

"I forgot to wear my estrogen patch," Steven hisses, scanning the crowd.

"Be a good boy and work the room," I say. "I'll get you a Coke."

I thread my way to the table, murmuring the usual pleasantries as I squeeze between the bodies. Control Freak Sylphs and Earth Mother Endomorphs and almost all of them north of forty, which in Hollywood is a citable offense. I'm five-five, weigh 125, still have the same unruly brown hair God gave me (plus a few non-God-given highlights), and am at least a decade younger, so where I fall in this house of cards is anybody's guess.

"So, I hear ten years is the cutoff for equity positions," Sandy says, right at my elbow, startling me so I spill my Diet Coke. Sandy's one of the lifers. Blond, and radiates steely self-interest. I trust her as much as I trust Martha Stewart. I'm about to launch into my "synergy" speech when I hear another, friendlier voice at my back.

"Howdy, stranger."

It's male, straight, and not wholly unfamiliar. I try vainly to place it but, given my surroundings, I give up and turn in its direction with a smile plastered on my face.

Charles. *Charles!* Jesus, what is he doing here, not that I don't welcome a friendly face. A longtime DWP publicist out of the New York office, Charles is Stan Woolfe's most trusted deputy and the office's most senior agent after the founding partners. I met him during my first weeks at DWP when I worked out of the New York offices on West Broadway before moving to L.A. He seemed nice enough, but those weeks had been a blur and I can't recall thinking much about him one way or another. I can't even recall if he's married, although given that he looks to be in his early forties with a few creases around his startling green eyes and some rather stylish streaks of gray in his dark brown hair, one would assume so. I haven't seen him in almost three years and, frankly, have no memory that Charles was so . . . so . . . well, *comforting*-looking.

"I see, Ms. Davidson, you're one of the last to arrive. As usual," Charles says with a grin as large as my own. "This won't do. Not when there are BIG people waiting. So to speak."

Jesus. A good-looking straight male *and* a sense of irony. How could I have been so oblivious to Charles back in New York? Maybe it's another Hollywood miracle. You become so inured to all the mutant males here you forget there are actually nice guys in the world. Nice guys who smile at you without it seeming like a come-on and whose starched blue shirt and soft brown herringbone jacket and green rep tie—Christ, a tie? When's the last time I saw one of those?—make the world seem worth living. Like a weekend sail off Nantucket. Or opening presents on Christmas morning. Or a cab ride through Central Park during one of winter's first snowfalls.

"Yes, well, I don't suppose I could convince you I got lost," I say, and I feel my cheeks flush.

"Actually, I think you took a wrong turn off Broadway," he says, his smile deepening. "By the way, how is Hollywood treating you?"

"About the way it treats anybody. With great indifference."

"That's not what I hear," he says.

I'm about to ask him what he means, what *exactly* he means, and of course why he happens to be here and not in New York, when there's a commotion at the door. Suzanne and G, looking like the bride and groom. Except she's taller. There are also two blondes. Bridesmaids. Or maybe G's bodyguards.

"Thank *yew*—everyone—for such a great turnout," Suzanne says, quickly moving to the center of the room. She's in another one of her white suits, and with her short, gray-blond hair and Southern drawl that she refuses to lose, she could pass for Tom Wolfe.

Great turnout? Yeah, like any of us could have not showed for this dog-and-pony show?

"I know a lot of *yew* have already met Doug," Suzanne drawls on. "But we wanted to officially welcome all of *yew*—all of *us*—to BIG-DWP."

There's a brief round of applause followed by a buzzing that I realize is G addressing the crowd. I have to stand on my toes to see him. With his big head, tiny body, and orangey Bob Evans tan, he looks like Mr. Potato Head. Only with a better tailor.

"I look around this room and I have only one question," G says, a smile gripping his face. "How did I get so lucky?"

Lucky? G is being unbelievably patronizing, but a titter of laughter sweeps the room along with a few self-conscious glances. I look over at Charles to see how he's taking all this but his face is unreadable. Well, he's been a publicist longer than I have.

G runs a hand over his hair and plunges on. "I mean, I look at this group of amazing women," he says, turning to Suzanne, who's grinning like an idiot, "and I wonder why we didn't join forces before. Can anyone tell me?"

There's an awkward silence like he's actually waiting for someone to answer him. "Well," G finally blurts out, raising his plastic glass of Coke. "All I know is we're going to make one beautiful agency."

There is a smattering of applause and I feel a hand creeping across mine for the Coke I'm holding.

"Word is you get nada," Steven breathes into my ear. "Too new."

"Already heard that piece of good news," I say, yanking the Coke back. "Equity cutoff positions or whatever they're called."

"Well, have you heard the contract's a killer?"

I whip around.

"Publish or perish, my dear."

"We're already on commission," I whine.

"It's the BIG new way. More commission, less salary. And you gotta make your quota."

"Great. Suzanne gets to retire and I get a quota."

"Well, she's not exactly retiring," Steven adds, dropping his voice. "Not yet, although Stan's supposedly leaving by the end of the month. Taking his money and running. Suzanne's sticking it out."

"Because she loves the business so much?" I can't imagine staying in Hollywood if somebody pressed half a million into my hand. Or whatever Suzanne's getting for selling the company she cofounded to G.

"Think it's some future deal G has cooked up. The longer she stays, the more money she gets, or more equity. I don't know. Don't go by me."

"Why not? You're the one with your own portfolio," I say. "I just have Barneys bills and a lease."

"And your new contract!" Steven says, flashing me his best fake smile.

G is nattering on, but I've heard enough. Or at least enough to know Suzanne isn't the only one whose cherry just got popped. My three-year introduction to Hollywood is officially over. This is The Show, like it or not. When you break it all down, all the bullshit, all the covers, the photo shoots, the premieres, the schmoozing and the lying, it all comes down to a sleazy guy trying to sell you something.

When G finally quits buzzing, the room erupts into the chaos of exiting and a mad rush for the cake. "I'm going to forage," Steven says, plunging into the crowd.

"So, as I was saying," Charles says at my elbow, startling me. "Congratulations on being a member of the BIG new team." His tone is difficult to read, but it seems, or perhaps it's only wishful thinking on my part, to be entirely ironic.

"Thanks ever so much," I say, aiming for the same barely detectable irony. "So you're here because . . . ?"

"Actually I'm in town for the transition," he says, taking my elbow and steering me into a slightly less crowded corner of the room. "I'm making the rounds of our publicists, easing them into the new agency, as it were. Which means I have to schedule some time with you."

He gives me a knowing look and I realize I know next to nothing about him other than he looks totally out of his element. Like he should be on a boat. Or in a Ralph Lauren ad. He's also not wearing a wedding ring, I notice. Perhaps I'm not the only one whose life took a wrong and unexpected turn.

"Shouldn't you be in a law office somewhere? Or Boston?" I blurt out and instantly regret my familiarity.

He gives me a quizzical but not wholly unpleased look. "I'll take that as a compliment," he says. "Meanwhile, given my current corporate duties, when can you pencil me in?"

"Uhm, I'm sure I have some time this week," I say, fumbling for my Palm Pilot, when Steven reappears bearing two paper plates of cake. "For those of us not on Atkins," he says before catching sight of Charles. "Oops, sorry. I didn't realize you were entertaining."

"Charles, Steven. Steven, Charles," I say, giving Steven a "Can we please do the sugar thing later?" look.

"Good to meet you," Charles says, extending a hand while Steven fumbles with the plates.

Out of the corner of my eye, I see G and Suzanne threading their way through the crowd in our direction. Oh, great. *"Chahles,"* Suzanne drawls at top volume, waving him over. *"Chahles."*

"I think Blanche and Stanley have you on their dance card," I say, nodding in Suzanne's direction. Charles gives me a slow smile and I have a sudden urge to grab his green tie and never let go.

Instead, I opt for the door, making noises about finding him later. After G and Suzanne. After my meeting with Troy. After I return to the land of the living.

It takes me most of the drive to the Chateau to get my head out of G and into Troy. Actually, it takes most of the drive to get my head out of Charles and into Troy. How had I been so oblivious to him back in New York? And how long is he going to be in L.A.? I have to give this some serious thought. After I dispatch Troy.

But when I hit the Chateau's lobby, Troy—typically—is nowhere to be found. What now? Sit and order a drink? That bespeaks confidence and a certain casualness and God knows I could use it. Might even put Troy at ease. Or maybe it's *too* casual. Not enough deference to his place in the pantheon. Oh Christ, who knows what his place in the pantheon is? He's the one in need of help. He's called the meeting. *Sit.*

I'm eyeing the room, which is filling with insouciant actor types looking like they have too much money and too little sleep, when Troy ambles in. Three trips to rehab but he still has the right look—jeans, leather jacket, 5 percent body fat. He's also nibbling a half-eaten apple and he has his dog, the requisite foundling from a pound, tugging at his side. The whole thing screams, "cute but dangerous." I hate it when they bring their animals. Animals are worse than cell phones. But that's the rule: celebrities are never alone, even when they're alone. I once saw Marisa Tomei do a week's worth of shopping at my neighborhood market while talking on her cell, timing it so she said "Okay, call me," at exactly the moment she pushed away from the checkout stand.

"Hey, meet Miss Sue," Troy says, when his dog, some Labrador or pit bull type, sticks its nose in the direction of my thighs. *Thank you!* I turn quickly so the dog leaves its wet nose imprint on the side of my black Darryl K pants and not my crotch. "Hey, Troy," I say, standing and extending a hand. I love doing that. Actors are so unused to being touched. Like they're the Queen of fucking England: Look but don't touch. Troy studies me for a second before he shoves the apple into his mouth and extends a slightly sticky paw. "Well, hey, and, hey, thanks for meeting me."

I lead the way to a corner of the lounge where we sink into a sofa, one of the hotel's over-upholstered Victorian things that just swallows you. Why can't the Chateau just have normal tables and chairs instead of this trick furniture? The couch is so deep, I have to wedge a pillow behind my back just to keep upright and, even so, my feet barely reach the floor. I'm still wrestling with the cushion when a spike-haired waitress rolls up and Troy trots out his laid-back famous-actor number. "She'll have a white wine," he says, nodding in my direction, "and I'll have a beer and you know," he says, winking at her, "that'll be it."

I press my toes into the carpet, trying to get enough traction between the floor and the cushion to remain upright. "So," I say brightly when I finally find my balance. "Tell me what you're looking for from us."

Even before he speaks, I know how this will go. That he's looking to make changes, that he needs to rethink his image, and that he needs to feel a more personal connection to his publicist, "his people," than he'd had over at Baker, Osterlund and Beadle— BOB, as it's known—one of DWP's competitors. The public, he will say in his gosh-and-golly Midwest accent, has the wrong idea of Troy Madden. The wrong idea "after all that's happened."

"I'm hoping you can help me correct that," he says, reaching forward to fondle Miss Sue's ears and giving me a wry smile.

I can help little Troy Madden or I can turn the page.

I take a sip of wine and dive into my spiel—that DWP, or rather BIG-DWP, is the kind of agency that takes a personal interest in its clients, that not only do we preserve a kind of trust among our client base, some of the most venerable in Hollywood, but we maintain one of the best, even an *intimate* relationship with editors. I'm rattling along nicely, only mildly distracted by Troy's lazy grin and the suggestive way he plys Miss Sue's ears—when I have a sudden and awful thought. Troy expects me to sleep with him. Or at least to *want* to sleep with him.

"I like what I'm hearing," he says, leaning forward, his smile widening.

I can feel my face flush. *Fuck.* I should never drink, even a glass of wine, when meeting a new client. "Well, I'm glad," I say, lunging for the glass of water thank God I'd thought to ask for. "Because I know Suzanne and I—" I pause to gulp—"and of course we've talked to your lawyer, Tom, about this, and we're pretty much"—I gulp again—"on the same page."

When I finish draining the glass, I realize Troy is grinning at me. "Can we get you another, ah, water?"

Actually, he's one step short of laughing as he turns to look for the waitress. *Oh, get a grip;* visions of my bonus disintegrating. Whenever I get rattled by an actor's sheer physical presence—the one thing any of them has if they're worth their salt—I just remember my years at Brown. By Hollywood's usual yardstick I come up a loser 99.9 percent of the time. The rock-paper-scissors rule is celebrity beats an executive; an executive beats talent; and everyone beats a publicist or a journalist. But in my book, brains always beat sex appeal. They could even beat heat. Well, most of the time.

"This is what I'm talking about," I say, suddenly dropping my voice and leaning toward him. Troy swivels back in my direction with a slightly startled look. "You've got all this going for you," I say, waving vaguely, "and it's not being put to its best use, shall we say. I mean, don't you think people have gotten the wrong idea about you, because of things you have done? I mean, not that you did them on purpose, but just unconsciously, the way a kid might react. Instinctively."

I pause to let this nonsense sink in.

"I mean, the movies have been their own choices—some better than others—and no one is blaming you for them," I say, plunging on before Troy can answer. "But we're talking about a whole that's bigger than the sum of the parts."

I lean back. "I want you to think of it . . . as *us*—as a partnership, overdue to say the least, but one that will, in the long run, go a long way toward rectifying all that."

I have him. Troy has no idea what the hell I'm talking about. I don't even need to trot out the hay-bale photo shoot idea. Glancing at my watch, always a nice touch—not even an hour—I decide to wrap it up. Take a second meeting at lunch with his manager and close it then. "Look, I don't to want to overwhelm you, not at our first meeting," I say, reaching for the check. "We'll sit down next week—I'll work it out with Peg, come up with a game plan that not only makes sense to you but includes you in a way that I'm not sure you've been included before."

I give Miss Sue a farewell pat and flee. When I hit the safety of the Audi, I punch up Rachel's number on my cell.

"He doesn't, does he?" I say when Rachel picks up. "Expect me to sleep with him?"

"Who are we talking about? G?"

"Sorry. Troy. I just came from my meeting, which seemed more like—"

"A date?"

"If I was a call girl."

"Hey, it's his way of marking his territory," Rachel says, laughing.

"This isn't funny."

"Think of it as his own little fraternity initiation," she says airily. "Go out for dinner and see what happens. God knows you need him as a client. Has he tried to put the moves on you yet?"

"Unclear," I say, trying to sound suddenly bored with the whole thing. Technically, petting his dog's ears doesn't count as *moves* per se. Still, I know when I'm being hustled. "But you'll be the first to know."

I'm about to tell Rachel about Charles—any sighting of an available heterosexual male is always noteworthy—when I think better of it. Besides, Rachel's on a tear.

"Think of Troy as your first scalp on your BIG belt," she says. "By the way, the word is he's a beast who needs to be fed. Unless you happen to be twenty-six, blonde, and brainless."

"Who? Troy?"

"G. The word from my Deep Throat is that he jumped from Sony before he was pushed. I mean, what VP leaves a studio to handle talent? He took his severance and bought his way into B-I. Now the word is that he's on the make for a buyer for the whole company. Look, he'll be gone in two years. Or less, depending on what happens. Just keep your head down. And, whatever you do, don't forget his birthday."

"His birthday?"

"Apparently it's a national holiday. By the way, I saw Carrie Fisher buying shoes at Fred Segal."

"Oh yeah?" I say, seriously interested, or maybe just happy to stop talking about G. That's the thing. You represent stars, know way too much about their lives, mop up way too many spills, but you still get worked up if you see them around town. Like sightings of native wildlife. "How'd she look?"

"Like she was off drugs."

"Legal or illegal?"

"Illegal."

"Too bad," I say.

"Yeah. She was pretty cute when she was thin."

"Weren't we all," I say, turning west on Sunset, suddenly anxious to find Charles.

3 | Just Shoot Me

The Dwarf—line 2.

The Amtell rattles to life. Peering over my Starbucks latte—nonfat with an extra shot—I type back, *Que?*

Things are looking up. Or I am trying to *believe* things are looking up. I've gotten my first look at our BIG contracts—publish or perish is right—but Suzanne is promising to run interference and give us a graduated quota. Whatever that means. We've also done our drive-by of the new offices and Steven is right: they *are* better. Orchids. Aeron chairs. Brand-new computers. Scented candles in the bathrooms. All the stations of the cross. Which is how I'm trying to think of G. Just another ass to kiss. Steven has already dubbed him the G-string.

I've also signed Troy, my first kill as a BIG-DWPer. And I haven't even had to have sex with him. At least not yet. Actually, I'm too busy to *see* Troy. That's the beauty part. Unless you have to serve as their walker at a junket or an award show, you never really *see* the clients or even speak to them. You just call their personal assistants.

The only bad news, and it technically isn't *bad*, just disappoint-

ing, is that I've had to make and break my lunch date with Charles
something like five times in two weeks. (Twice on my part, twice
on his, and once when Suzanne big-footed our plans and dragged
him to some award luncheon.) Other than a few chance encoun-
ters in the office hallways, I've logged zip quality time with him. Or
HRH, as Steven has dubbed him.

"So HRH is another no-show," Steven said, when our lunch
was canceled for the second time.

"His Royal Highness?" I didn't often miss Steven's acronyms
but he had me this time.

"The Human Resources Hunk. And don't think you're the only
one who's noticed."

What was I thinking? Of course I wasn't the only sex-starved
workaholic clawing the DWP walls. Back in New York, Charles
may have been just another good-looking, slightly preppy guy—
B+ material—but in L.A., a WASPy heterosexual male with a
sense of humor and his natural nose approached deity status. Of
course, others were hot on his trail.

Actually, after our third broken lunch date, I'd resolved to put
him out of my mind. Charles was just a colleague. Nothing more.
Besides, he worked out of the New York office, where, presumably,
he would be returning once his visit to Oz was over. Whenever
that was going to be.

Besides, I really was busy with work. I was also taking Spanish
lessons every other Wednesday in a belated if unchic attempt to
communicate with all the Latinos who come with life in L.A.
Housekeeper, gardener, pool man for the diminutive hot tub that
burbled out on my patio, although technically the pool guy didn't
count since he was from Encino, a dropout from UC–Santa Barbara who showed up stoned half the time. It would take more than
Spanish lessons to communicate with him. Technically, nobody in
my gene pool spoke Spanish. Like nobody in my gene pool ate
bread. Still, life would go so much more smoothly if I could do
things like explain how to work the washing machine to my
Guatemalan housekeeper.

"It's not like you need to learn the whole language," Steven said. "Just a few key phrases. Like, 'Please put out that fire,' or, 'Can you stop the flooding?' "

El Dwarf . . . ! The Amtell rattles again.

I put down the latte and type back, *What fucking dwarf?!!*

The Amtell is such a dinosaur. Everyone else in town has instant messaging—IM—to deal with calls, but DWP is still stuck in the Stone Age. Along with our Haitian-cotton sofas, stained Berber carpeting, and metal-framed posters of movies from the seventies—*Norma Rae* anyone?—we have the most antique communication equipment. In addition to our balky PC's that are forever breaking down, we still use the stupid Amtells on our desks to communicate with our assistants. Like big walkie-talkies that are just up a notch from screaming. The only good thing is that they do foster their own coded language. After my meeting with Troy, Steven billed him as "succubus" on the Amtell until I pointed out that was a sexually depraved *female* demon. *Okay, "succu-boy,"* Steven had typed back, adding for good measure that Troy's lawyer was now "succu-boy's DA."

"You know—the Dwarf!" Steven says, suddenly appearing in the doorway. "The one you met at the party last week? The one who said he was looking for representation?"

"Oh, *that* dwarf. Put him through."

Dwarves were hot. You couldn't go to a party or a premiere without running into at least a couple of them. But then L.A. has always had a thing for freaks. First it was boobs. Now it's cheekbones and butts. Even guys aren't immune. Not with every male in town sprouting a forelock like Elvis. Why not dwarves? At least it was a new way to make studio execs, all those tiny, intense guys with their manicures and Gucci loafers, feel like big men.

"Hi. I was hoping to hear from you," I say, picking up. Normally I would have said something like, *What can I do for you?* But my client list is dwarfless at the moment and with my BIG new contract hanging over my head, the dwarf is an easy way to feed the beast. A former Disneyland employee (he was Donald Duck in the parade), the dwarf is a SAG member who's had a walk-on in a Coen brothers comedy, done four episodes of *Jackass*, and gotten all the way to first callbacks on the latest *Austin Powers*. How hard could it be to drum up some coverage? Convince *Vanity Fair* to do some photo spread in their annual Hollywood issue? Put him and a few other dwarf actors in a circus setting and get Steven Meisel to shoot it? I set up lunch with the dwarf and hang up. When I finish the call, Steven sticks his head around the corner.

"Six more and we can call you Snow White."

"I was hoping you'd say that."

"Meanwhile, in another part of the enchanted forest, am I going to the photo shoot or are you?"

"Which shoot?"

"Troy and the Babes in TV Land."

"It's the day after tomorrow," I say. "And yes, I am going. The day after tomorrow."

"Actually, *TV Guide*'s photo editor called and they had to move it to today. Some scheduling mix-up."

"What!" I'm seriously pissed. Two days ago Troy's shoot was all set. Now, apparently, it's all fucked, and I've spent hours on the phone with the magazine setting up the story after Troy's manager wrangled him a guest-star stint on one of the hottest new drama series—an anorexic chick law show that I can't bear to watch but that has become the "flash point of the postfeminist cultural zeitgeist." Or that's how *The New York Times* put it.

Normally TV is no-man's-land for movie stars. But ever since Michael Douglas and Matt Damon went on *Will & Grace* and Brad Pitt carried the flag for Jen by doing an episode of *Friends*, stunt casting, as it's known—especially for a highly promotable sweeps episode—no longer means your career is coding. So Troy is easing back into the public eye via prime time. At least it gives me something to promote until his next movie comes along. Besides, one of the series' stars, Val Myers, an ex-Broadway chorine who

plays one of the nerdier women on the show (which means she actually weighs what a five-eight, thirty-three-year-old might weigh)
is already one of my clients. The shoot was to have been an easy
twofer for me: Troy would have an hour or so at the same shoot for
the magazine's cover story on Val and her two costars.

"When did we find this out?" I snap, knowing I'll have to rearrange my whole day and I *hate* baby-sitting shoots, the endless
fussing with the lights and the clothes and the hair and then the
catering and the music and scented candles. It's a daylong party
for those involved—or it's supposed to *look* like a daylong party—
but for publicists it's like jury duty. You have to sit there for hours
trying to look interested or at least awake. It's even worse if the
client's manager shows up and starts throwing their weight around.
Meanwhile you still have to work, return a million calls on your
staticky cell. It's just a pain.

"Unclear," Steven says, waving a message slip. "As far as I can
tell, the photo editor called either at midnight or six this morning."

"Typical," I say. Returning calls at god-awful hours is now a
standard way to deliver unwelcome news in Hollywood.

"At least Troy already knows," Steven says, dropping a second
message slip on my desk. "Or I should say Troy's manager knows.
Peg called this morning to say he—and she—would be there by
noon."

"Noon?" I look at my watch. It's ten-thirty. I have barely an
hour to rearrange my entire day.

"Yeah, I know," Steven says. "But if you hurry you can get there
before the caterers replace the muffins with the pasta salad."

For a second, I'm tempted to send Steven—officially you can
always send your assistant to cover a shoot unless the client is Tom
Cruise caliber—and get reception to pick up my calls. I have
a bunch of releases to edit, and I'm expecting a call from the
features editor of *Vogue*, which is the PR equivalent of getting
a call from the pope. Besides, I'm wearing new mules that have

already given me blisters just walking from the parking garage. The thought of standing around Smashbox is not appealing. But Troy is a new client and still a big enough star that I need to show the flag. For Val too, as long as I'm there. Besides, if Troy's manager is tense enough to go, I have to go.

"All right, but call me later with some emergency so I can leave."

"I'll tell you your house is burning down—in Spanish," Steven says. "That should do it."

Smashbox is the Fred Segal of photo studios, a chic sexy white space with the requisitely louche employees in cargo pants and T-shirts and bored-looking stars. *InStyle, Vanity Fair, People,* they all shoot here. It's publicists' Ground Zero. Smashbox is so hip it even has its own makeup line.

What it doesn't have is a big enough parking lot. By the time I pull up, the minuscule lot is already full and the valet waves me off. Great. Street parking. Not only do I have a fresh blister by the time I get to the door, but I'm sweating from walking three blocks in the blazing sun and my nice little blow-dry from the morning is shot to hell. By the time I hit the Black Box, Moby is blasting out the door. Inside it's the usual chaos, a million cables snaking across the floor, lights blazing as the crew guys in jeans and spike haircuts hump them around the room. The photographer, Blake Hashbein, a short, balding guy who shot a lot of those hip Gap commercials, is sitting on a lipstick-red sofa in the middle of the room ignoring it all, flipping through *US Weekly,* drinking coffee, and idly tossing a ball to two dogs wrestling in the corner.

Troy and the show's stars, of course, are nowhere to be seen. Probably still in makeup, one of the little rooms down the hall that will be lit like an airport runway and packed with its own personnel—the dewy-faced makeup artist, usually a gay guy wearing foundation, tight black jeans, and an air of fastidiousness; the hairdresser, another gay guy or an older (meaning thirty-plus) woman with great hair; and the stylist, who will already be getting an earful about the clothes. When forced to baby-sit a shoot, I usually wind up hanging with the stylist—not because stylists are always heterosexual women with great taste and good shopping tips, but because they also have little patience for actors' whims but have to satisfy them anyway.

"Better to get this over with," I say, taking a deep breath and picking my way across the cables toward the high-pitched chatter down the hall. As I round the corner, I pass the catering station with the requisite muffins, fruit, and coffee dispensers—regular, decaf, and latte. An ice chest holds bottles of water and sodas. That's the other thing about shoots. Unless it's with some nut case like Kirstie Alley who writes it into her contracts that the catering has to consist solely of unlimited trays of tuna sashimi, you just know you're going to eat a muffin—at least the top—or a cookie. Just to keep your spirits up.

"Hi-eee . . . . !"

I'm just reaching for a muffin—pumpkin, for the beta carotene—when I hear a squeal and the clatter of high heels behind me and brace myself for impact. "Alex, thanks for coming," Val says, flinging herself at me. "This means so much to me," she says, shaking her blond hair off her heart-shaped face. Like a lot of actors, Val has an unnaturally large head and just now, out of the makeup chair with her exaggerated Kewpie-doll eyes and pouty, cherry-red mouth, it looks even larger than usual. I have to rear back just to keep her face in focus.

"Hey, I wouldn't miss it."

"I know, but my first cover, I just really want it to go well."

I've been to enough shoots to know that *well* is a relative term. In fact, if there's any rule about shoots, it's that something will always go wrong, especially with a group shot. Although I've gone around and around with the photo editor over the choice of the photographer and the stylist and am praying it will all work out, I don't have to wait long for the bad news.

"Can I show you the clothes?" Val says, right on cue, tightening her grip on my arm and steering me toward the bulging racks. "I'm just not sure."

Not sure in this case means a knee-length flared red satin skirt Val is supposed to wear during one of the setups. There are to be three group shots of the three stars, each with its own color scheme—red, white, and blue, and the last two involving the red sofa. The white clothes are apparently fine with everyone, and Val especially likes her blue outfit, a tight, short sheath, but she hates the red skirt. It makes her look like a "fat cheerleader," she says, yanking it from the rack.

I close my eyes and take a breath. I've only been here what, five minutes, and already Val is on me to fix something? "Let me talk to the stylist," I chirp. "There must be another red thing you can wear. Don't worry. I'll take care of it."

I pry myself away from Val and head down the hall, keeping an eye out for Troy as I hunt down the stylist. The one thing I've learned: Never get between an actress and her wardrobe. So far Troy seems to be running late. As usual. I'm about to pull out my cell and call his manager, when I almost collide with the stylist wrestling with some sweaters on the floor. At least she seems even more exasperated than I do.

"Don't get me started about Val," she hisses. Not only is Val throwing a fit about the red skirt, which is meant to somehow evoke *Happy Days*, but the show's anorexic star—whom Steven dubbed "Leggo" during one of his more inspired moments—is freaking about the entire wardrobe. Too DKNY and not enough Dolce or something. She is now locked, suspiciously, in the bathroom after inhaling three muffins in a row. "I've got to get her out of there and into some different outfits," the stylist mutters with a shake of her head.

"Prada?" I say helpfully.

"*Sleeves*," she says, giving the sweaters a shove. "I mean, she's so fucking thin. Airbrushing isn't going to take care of it."

I make noises about one less cook in the kitchen, and head off to look for Troy. Val will just have to deal with the clothes on her own. I'm about to take another detour by the craft services table to bolster my flagging energy when I spot not Troy but Peg, his manager, coming through the door. She's dressed for battle, with her shades clamped on, something like three cashmere sweaters wrapped around her shoulders, and her headset wired for sound. *Fuck.* What is she doing here before Troy's even arrived?

"Davidson!"

Love being called by my last name. So needlessly butch. Like being back on the intramural field hockey team in college.

"Hi, Peg," I say, mustering a smile as I pick my way back over the lighting cables. Peg is one of the female leviathans Hollywood secretly breeds. You'd never know they exist unless you dig below the surface, but their numbers are legion among agents, managers, and publicists. Tough as nails, most of them could run a small country, and none of them are above just fucking with you because they can. Between their bulk and their need to control things, including whoever crosses their path, they are giant vortexes that just suck you in.

"What's the holdup?" Peg snaps, dispensing with any pleasantries as well as any acknowledgment that I've landed her client the damn shoot in the first place. "I thought Blake was one of the pros," she adds, glancing at her watch.

"Holdup?" She knows as well as I do no shoot ever starts on time. They're like the Caribbean, or Mexico: things start and stop with no relation to the clock. Besides, Troy isn't even here yet and he's supposed to go *after* the girls.

"Troy's been here an *hour*," Peg snorts, unhooking her earpiece. "I told him to get here early, because he's got an audition this afternoon. He called me when he arrived."

Troy's been here an *hour* and I haven't seen him? As far as I can tell, no one has seen him. For all I know Troy is out in his Porsche getting stoned.

I feel my pulse jump. Actually that scenario isn't that far-fetched. *Oh Jesus, let Troy have enough sense not to be getting stoned at his first photo shoot in more than two years.* "Uhm, where did Troy say he was when he called you?" I ask Peg. "Where, *exactly?*"

"*Here.* At the shoot." Peg gives me a look like I'm speaking in tongues. "I thought you'd be with him."

"Yeah, well, I'm actually headed in that direction now," I say briskly. The more I think about it, the more I fear Troy has to be in the parking lot.

"I'm going to check in with the stylist and see what she's got lined up for him," Peg says, moving off. "Grab me a water, will you?" she says, nodding at the craft services table. "And a muffin."

Like that's going to happen. Ignoring her directive, I head toward the bathroom. I don't want Peg on my trail and I need to clear my head. If I hadn't quit smoking under the misguided assumption that L.A. was obsessed with health, I would have two cigarettes in rapid succession. Now, a pee and fresh lip gloss will have to suffice.

I stare at myself in the mirror. It's not even one yet, but I already look exhausted, with mascara pooling under my eyes and my hair a mess. Wiping away the smudges, I root around in my bag until I find a pen to anchor my hair in a makeshift ponytail. I need to hunt down Troy and assess the damage. If he's halfway sober—or can fake being halfway sober—and Peg throws her weight around and manages to snap everyone in line, I might get away after the first setup and salvage something of the day.

Heading out of the bathroom, I pass one of the emergency exits propped open and catch a whiff. Oh God, I was right. I push open the door and scan the parking lot. It's a sea of cars gleaming in the midday sun. Across the lot, the red-vested valets are milling around the entrance like birds waiting for a handful of seeds. I can follow my nose, or I can cut to the chase and ask where Señor Troy's car is parked.

"Excuse me," I say, shielding my eyes from the glare as I pick my way toward the valets. "Excuse me, but do you know where Mr. Madden's car is parked? I need to leave him something in it."

"Maadaan?"

"Yes. *Troy* Madden. Tall, young guy. Blond. I think he drives a Porsche."

"Many Porsche today, lady. Many, many."

Yes, there would be many Porsches. Okay, let's try another tactic. "Troy Madden. The movie star?"

Blank stares. Yes, many, many movie stars today and bigger ones than Troy. Quick, which of Troy's movies would these guys have seen? God, even I'm blanking for a minute, it's been so long since he had a bona fide hit. "*'Blow Your Mind' Games?*" I say in desperation.

Bingo. Maybe I don't need to know Spanish after all.

"Sí, sí, sí. Señor Troy!" There is a flurry of laughter and a frantic hunting among the keys on the valet's board. Finally I am pointed in the direction of the far corner of the lot. I set off, the blister on my foot springing to life with each step. I've bailed my share of clients out of tight spots before, but it usually involved a phone call to an editor or a few choice words with a hotel concierge. I haven't had to physically intercede on anyone's behalf since I used to baby-sit for the neighbors' kids back in Upper Darby and for a time became very experienced at wiping up other people's shit.

Any hope I'm harboring that Troy is just—I don't know—*napping* in his car, dies when I hear the thudding sounds of some techno anthem penetrating the air. I sidle between a gleaming SUV and one of the old-model oversized BMW's and come up on Troy's Porsche from the rear. It's rocking slightly from the music and from what I can see is Troy's frantic drumming on the dashboard. He's in the passenger seat with a lit joint in his mouth, his eyes closed, fists pounding to the music. And he was supposed to be A-list at one time? I take a deep breath and knock on the window. Either Troy can't hear me or he's too out of it, but he keeps on pounding. Oh, fuck it. I yank open the door. A cloud of smoke, a crashing of drums, and Troy's entire right side hits me simultaneously.

"Hey, what the hell," Troy says, flailing for the door frame to pull himself upright. "Hey, man," he says, turning in my direction and squinting up at me. So far I'm not registering. "Oh hey, Alex, isn't it?" he says, a sleepy smile crossing his face. "Yeah, Alex. Hey, come on in, the party's just starting."

"Actually, Troy, the party's inside," I say, shouting over the music. "What do you say we go in and join the others? I'll go with you." Suddenly Val and her stupid skirt issues are looking like a cakewalk compared with getting Troy in photographable shape. His eyes are completely red and he seems even more unable to focus than he usually does. You'd think after all the dope he's done he wouldn't be so wasted.

"Party?" Troy says dumbly.

"Actually, it's the *photo shoot*," I yell again. "For the magazine." The music is starting to get on my nerves. Actually all of it's getting on my nerves, but the music is the easiest to fix.

"Listen," I say, ducking down and reaching into the Porsche and across Troy to turn down the volume. "Listen, they're waiting for you inside and it's my job to get you in there," I say, fumbling for the knob. At least one problem is solved. I'm just backing out of the car when I feel Troy's hand on my thigh. *Okay, just don't go there, guy. Just don't fucking go there.*

"Well, if they're waiting, let's give 'em a reason to wait," Troy says in his slow drawl. For some reason all I can think of is how many women would love, just *love* to be in my position right now—bent over Troy Madden with his hand on my naked thigh.

"Okay, Troy," I say, wriggling backward. "Troy, look—" But my wriggling only causes Troy's hand to crawl further up my thigh. "Troy!" I say, reaching back to dislodge his hand, a move that causes me to lose my balance. I feel myself start to career toward the dashboard, where the right side of my face lands with a thud, and I whack my head on the edge of the steering wheel.

"Ow. Okay, Troy—" I say, fumbling for my balance with my free left hand, which I realize has no other place to go than onto Troy's own thighs, which are thankfully fully clad in denim. I'm just righting myself when I hear my cell burble.

"Is that you or me?" Troy mumbles sleepily.

"It's me and actually I'm going to take it," I say, finally shaking myself free of him and up out of the car.

"Hello," I say a bit breathlessly.

"Alex?"

"Charles?" *Charles!*

"Alex, where are you? You sound out of breath."

"Oh, me? Uhm, at a photo shoot. With a client. I was, uhm, just lifting a few things," I say, turning away from Troy and rubbing my head, which is starting to ache where it hit the steering wheel. "Just helping the stylist carry a few clothes, you know. Where are you?"

"Who's Charles?" says Troy behind me.

"Actually, I'm at the airport."

It takes a minute for this to sink in. If Charles is at LAX it can only mean that his L.A. tour of duty is over and he's heading back to New York.

"The airport?" I say dumbly. "You're leaving? But we never had our lunch and I thought you were supposed—"

"I know, I know," he says. "And I feel bad about that."

Does he? Does he *really*? I can't tell from his tone of voice. All I know is I'm stuck here wrestling with a stoned, horny client, and the only glimmer of hope in my stupid little life is about to climb into a business-class seat and fly away.

I feel a tug on my skirt. "Who's Charles?" says Troy again.

I turn and glare at him and hear a click on my other line. Great. Probably Peg calling to ask where the fuck we are. "Uhm, Charles, hang on a second. Let me get rid of this other call."

"*Hola*," Steven says when I answer.

"Okay, you can really drop the Spanish," I say.

"What am I missing? It sounds exciting there," says Steven. "And I thought I had the exciting news."

"Not sure I can take much more excitement, but what is it?" I know better than to ignore Steven. When he says he has news, he has news.

"How's Val?"

"Uhm, Val's not really the problem right now," I say. "Unless you're trying to get her into a red skirt."

"With what underneath?"

"What do you mean, *underneath*?"

"I didn't want to tell you this before . . ." he says, letting his voice trail off.

"Tell me what?"

"Nothing, except G called the first all-agency staff meeting tomorrow. Their offices. Eleven and, ah, Val likes a fresh breeze where the sun don't shine. But that's only a rumor."

I can either start screaming or I can just fucking solve this, all of it right now. I turn back to the car and reach down and slam the door. Troy looks up at me through the glass with a hurt expression, like I've slapped him.

"Look, I didn't want to upset you," Steven hurtles on. "It may not even be true. I mean, what have you seen?"

"Nothing on that end, thank God. Look, I'll deal with Val, but right now Troy's stoned, Peg's already here, Charles is at LAX about to get on a flight back to New York, and I need you to tell me how to get Troy in shape for the photographers. You know more about drugs than I do."

"Eyedrops and food. How much did he smoke?" Steven says, immediately snapping to, but then he always knows exactly where the line is drawn.

"I think more than one joint. But I can't be sure. Guess rehab really worked."

"Where is he?"

"In his car. I'm thinking of locking him in there."

"Okay, get the drops from makeup—they always have them—and get him a water and tell everyone he's feeling queasy. Something he ate. Isn't he supposed to go at the end of the shoot? He's got hours to sleep it off. You'll be fine, but you might have to stay with him."

"Yeah, got it," I say, suddenly remembering Charles on the other line. "But stay by the phone."

"Charles," I say clicking over. "Sorry. Some office emergency—"

But he cuts me off.

"Listen, Alex, my flight's about to board and I just wanted to say I am leaving but I'm coming back next week. I just have to fly back for a few days. So I wanted to ask you, rather than lunch, can we do dinner? I want to make it up to you for all the cancellations."

I see Judy Garland skipping toward Oz with the chorus, "You're out of the woods, you're out of the dark, you're out of the night," playing in my head.

"Dinner? Well, dinner would probably be *easier*," I say.

"Great, well, I'll call you and we'll set it up for right when I get back."

I hear the Porsche door pop open behind me. Oh, God, he's getting free. "Okay, that sounds good," I say, hurrying now. "Have a good flight and call me. Call me."

The rest of the day is a blur, but I manage to keep Troy's delicate condition from everyone except the makeup stylist. I tell Peg that Troy's hungover and sleeping it off in his car. Amazingly she buys it. Or maybe that look in her eye just before she dials the casting director to reschedule his audition means more than I think it does.

"Sleeping it off? In his car?" she says, eyeing me sharply.

"Yeah," I say, nodding maniacally like some windup toy. "Yeah, well, you know Troy," I add with a shrug.

"Yes. I do know Troy," she says pointedly, and I realize if anyone has seen Troy at his worst, it's Peg. Suddenly all her massive bulk, her ability to mow down obstacles at will seems a source of strength, not terror. No wonder people hire her. "Call me if you need me," she says, giving me a rough pat on the arm before clamping on her shades and her headset and heading for the door. "But I know he's in good hands."

I swear on a stack of Bibles that I'll call, and then I fly into action. Water, eyedrops, and a turkey on whole wheat that I grab off the craft services table. I head back to the parking lot, where Troy is still in the Porsche, fumbling with the CDs.

"Okay," I say, slapping in some Bill Evans that he happens to have. "Take this and this and this in this order," I say, handing him the eyedrops, the water, and the sandwich. "I'll take this," I say, fishing the baggie of pot out of the glove compartment and slipping it into my purse. "And I'll be back in an hour." With any luck, Troy will just pass out. Now, I have to see to Val.

I'm just heading into the studio when I catch sight of her down the hall. She's dressed in the blue outfit, the skintight sheath, and singing to the catering guy, who's unloading trays of sliced vegetables and pita sandwiches. Grabbing a couple of carrot sticks, Val twirls off, humming the refrain from *Grand Hotel*.

By the time I catch up with her, Val's in the studio posing playfully for the crew. She's the only one of the actresses remotely ready, and given the woeful sounds coming from the dressing room, she will be for some time.

"Let's shoot some of Val since she's here," says Blake's assistant, looking at his watch. Blake shrugs and picks up the Polaroid. "Okay, Val, let's get sexy with the sofa."

Somebody throws some Frank Sinatra on, and the sounds of "I've Got the World on a String" fill the studio as Val preens and poses and Blake snaps away.

"Make it a *thong* string," I pray, as I watch Val move this way and that behind the sofa. She's in the middle of doing what looks like a vague imitation of Marilyn Monroe in *The Seven Year Itch*—vague in that Val's dress is so tight it wouldn't blow over her waist with a wind machine—when Blake suggests Val lie down.

"Try balancing on the back of the sofa," he says, standing up and positioning her so that Val's feet are suddenly at eye level. I feel the blood rise in my temples.

"I think she looks great right where she is," I venture, my voice all but drowned out by Frank. If Blake even heard me, he's choosing to ignore it.

"Yeah, good, lie down even more. That's it," he says, crouching and snapping away.

I stand for a minute just behind Blake, who's facing the sofa where Val lies horizontally across the back. Frank is deep into "You Brought a New Kind of Love to Me," when I notice most of the crew has moved to the far end of the sofa, where Val's feet are plying the air with little kicks. Oh God.

I start to move in the direction of Val's feet, dreading what I'm about to see. By now she's in full vamp mode, her head thrown back, mouth open, eyes blazing as she stares at the camera. The crew guys are rapt. I stand there watching for a few minutes before it hits me—Val is the star of this show in a way she'll never be on TV. For a minute, I almost feel bad for her. But then, with a little arch of her back so her knees part ever so slightly, Val flicks her legs in the air.

Sharon Stone never did it any better.

"How'd it go with Val?" Steven asks when I call him later. It's going on four and I've been sitting on the driver side of the Porsche for the last hour, watching Troy sleep it off. His head is angled back on the headrest, his mouth is open, and he's snoring softly.

"Like something from *Wild Discovery*. Grown men angling for a glimpse of fur," I say in a half whisper.

"So the rumors are true."

"Don't gloat too much."

"Oh, come on, it's not that bad."

"Not that bad? Val's an exhibitionist."

"Drew Barrymore flashed her breasts at David Letterman and everyone loved it."

"I don't think beaver shots count."

"Hey, just call her agent, tell them Val's a natural."

"For what?"

"*The Vagina Monologues.*"

"Very funny," I hiss.

"Why are you whispering?" Steven says. "Where are you? In a closet?"

"Troy's car. Watching him sleep it off."

"You know, in some countries that would be a stoneable offense."

"Yeah, well, luckily Hollywood's not one of them," I say. "I'm giving him another half hour and then it's into the makeup chair. I figure I'll be out of here by six."

"My money's on seven," Steven says. "But the big question is will he call you in the morning?"

"My money's on him not remembering anything."

Troy begins to stir next to me.

"I think Sleeping Beauty's coming to," I say. "I'll call you later."

I hang up and turn in the seat to face Troy. His hair is plastered damply to his forehead and a small spittle of drool is creeping down his chin. Suddenly, I'm embarrassed for him, even a little sad. Troy doesn't look any different from half the guys I dated in high school. College too, for that matter. Good-looking guys who got it all a little too easily and a little too early and didn't have a clue how to hang on to it, how to keep it from slipping through their fingers.

Troy stirs again, twisting now toward me, trying to get comfortable in his sleep. He moves his arms restlessly and suddenly drops his hand into my lap. I look down at his bitten nails and calloused fingers and then back up at him, but he's still out. I should wake him. Wake him and just get the day over with. Instead, I reach down and gently wrap my fingers around his. And I sit there. I sit there for many, many minutes, holding my client's hand while he sleeps.

4 | It's My Party and I'll Cry if I Want To

Driving back from Smashbox—actually, *driving* is a bit of a stretch given the parking-lot state of La Cienega—I impulsively decide to call Rachel for a drink. I'm so wiped from the shoot, I'd intended to head home and collapse. But suddenly the idea of a friendly drink seems a better exit strategy. Besides, I want to fly the whole day by Rachel. Get her take on Troy, Charles, and Val. Especially Val. Troy's hand on my thigh was one thing—as I predicted, he remembered none of it once he came to—but Val's little animal act is sure to light up the gossip mill. It's only a matter of time before it turns up in one of those nasty blind items "Page Six" loves to run. *"Just asking . . . what sitcom star flashed a beaver at her recent photo shoot—to the delight of the crew and the consternation of her publicist?"*

Or what if *US* got wind of it? Val's sitcom is hot, and that is the kind of juicy rumor they love to get their hands on. Exhausted as I am, I know I need a plan. But before I can speed-dial Rachel, the cell burbles. The *William Tell* Overture. Rachel's signature.

"So how was the lovely Val?"

"Funny you should ask," I say, stomping abruptly on the brake as the black Explorer in front of me comes to a sudden stop, a move that sends my bag hurtling to the floor, spewing the contents, including an apparently loosely opened bottle of water, onto the carpet. *"Fuck!"*

"You *are* in a bad mood."

"Photo shoots will do that to a girl."

"Photo shoots will do that to anybody."

"Actually, I wanted to talk to you," I say.

"You are talking to me."

"In person."

"Is it serious or gossip?"

"Both. What are you doing tonight?"

"Tonight? What am I always doing? A screening. I'm driving there now, but we can meet afterward."

I have almost twenty minutes to kill at Le Dome, nursing a white wine, sucking down olives, and leafing through the trades waiting for Rachel. Le Dome is Le Dead Zone—nobody comes here anymore—but Rachel's screening is in the building next door and it's technically on my way home from the office.

"So, how was the shoot?" Rachel says when she finally shows, flopping onto a chair, dropping her tote, heavy as a suitcase, and reaching for my glass. "God, I hate wine," she says, taking a slug and twisting around to look for the waiter. "You're the only one who's still into that eighties wine thing. Why don't you get on the fruit-of-the-month martini bandwagon like the rest of us? Makes life so much simpler. You're sober, you're drunk. You're working, you're partying. Wine's just a hazy, in-between thing where you're pretending to have a real conversation but you're really getting hammered. Frankly, it's too much fucking stress," she says, swiveling back around, tugging at her black leather jacket, which is still facing the direction of the waiters' station.

Rachel's body has that effect. She's always tugging things into place. Like the men in her life. Not that there are many of those.

At least not in L.A. Rachel sports a rack enviable even by Hollywood's silicone standards, but her New York persona is the price of admission—and outside the tristate area it's deemed a little high. Like so many transplanted New York women who haven't mastered the L.A. vibe, which, depending on the decade, consists of varying amounts of prescription drugs, plastic surgery, and a well-honed passive-aggressiveness, Rachel's place in Los Angeles is that of the lonely, workaholic expatriate.

"Why you didn't go to law school, I'll never know," I say, fishing an olive out of the bowl and sliding it into my mouth. "All that anger just going to waste."

"Hey, you didn't sit through the piece of shit I just did. Nor do you have to promote it to thirteen-year-old boys, which is even more demeaning," she says. "Besides, why do you think we're friends?"

"I don't think I'm as angry as you," I say, trying to sound ironic although I'm actually annoyed by Rachel's assumption. "I'm from Bucks County. I'm too repressed to be that angry."

"Actually, you're wrong about my job," Rachel says, half standing and waving both arms over her head to get the waiter's attention. "Being a publicist reinforces the cynicism I already have, and the fact it pays shit bolsters my self-loathing. Even my mother thinks I've found my calling."

Rachel may be what the guys in high school called a ball-breaker, but you have to admire her. She still has her fuck-it-all New York ways that I, despite my having spent a decade in Manhattan, have never really mastered. Other than Steven, Rachel is one of the only people I can be honest with. At least about Hollywood in Hollywood.

"So you called this meeting," Rachel says, after snaring the waiter and ordering a martini with her customary directive: *And supersize it.*

"Yes, I did and I appreciate your attendance, but first how was your day?" I say, trying to ease Rachel into a slightly lower gear. "Other than the screening?"

"Great if you don't count the hour and a half in the dentist's office this morning and three hours waiting for the Novocain to wear off," Rachel says, grabbing a fistful of olives. "I spent most of the afternoon looking like a stroke victim. I even had to sip my coffee through a straw. I figure it's practice for the nursing home."

It will take an elephant gun, or most of a martini, to slow Rachel down and that's nowhere in sight. "That's nice, honey," I say, skipping to the chase. "Troy got stoned and tried to feel me up and Val flashed a beaver at the photo shoot. Your thoughts?"

"That depends. Did you find it arousing or merely a gratuitous grab for attention?"

I'm about to ask if she means Troy or Val when the waiter suddenly appears, an icy pale green martini dripping on his tray. *"Pour la jeune femme sans cocktail?"* he says, arching his eyebrows. I wonder if that's his idea or an affectation Le Dome insists on.

"Put her down," Rachel says, leaning back to make room.

When the waiter skates off after an elaborate bow, Rachel takes a sip and smacks her lips. "Sugar and grain alcohol. My two favorite food groups. Okay, where were we? So Troy's a pig and Val's a flasher. Which one's the problem?"

"Is this a quiz?" I say, surprised at Rachel's lack of surprise. " 'Can you tell the problem client from the one who's merely an asshole?' "

"Something like that," Rachel says, eyeing me over the glass.

"Maybe I'm just being overly hyper because of G and the buyout, but I think they're both problems. Or could be," I say, slumping back in my chair. "I mean, a third of our clients are gay, in rehab, or seriously twisted. The rest are in denial. Those that have a pulse, anyway. But is that what we do? Protect the guilty?"

"Salud," Rachel says, taking another slug of the martini. "Look, no one's going to out Val in the media, at least not by name, and you knew Troy was obnoxious from the get-go. Sleep with him, don't sleep with him, but—"

"I'm *not* sleeping with him," I blurt out. "He just put his hand on my thigh when I tried to get him out of his car, where he was getting high."

"Yeah, that's classy," Rachel says, rolling her eyes. "Look, I'm just saying he has a reputation and there are probably a lot of publicists, especially those bimbos at BIG, who would fuck him in a heartbeat."

"He didn't even *remember* it after he sobered up," I say. "The whole rest of the shoot, it was like nothing had happened."

"Yeah, well, it's not like he's actually boyfriend material."

"Speaking of that," I say, reaching for my glass.

"Speaking of that, what?" Rachel says sharply.

Oh Christ, that was stupid. I should have just brought up Charles as a fellow publicist, nothing more. Now, I'd painted myself into this corner.

"Oh, nothing," I say, aiming for a breezy indifference. "There's just this cute guy in from the New York office and everyone's talking about him."

"Including you?" Rachel flashes me a grin. "Who is it?"

"Charles, the managing director. He's in for the transition. Supposed to take all the DWP agents to lunch or something."

"Hey, I know him," Rachel says, leaning forward. "I met him a few years ago at some industry thing in New York. He is cute. And smart, but I thought he was married."

"Divorced. Or at least that's the word."

"Who isn't divorced these days?"

"Well, you for one," I say.

Rachel gives me the finger. "So, what happened with him?"

"*Nothing* happened," I say. "We had to keep canceling our lunch date and now he's back in New York."

"Oh, this *is* promising," Rachel says. "I can see why you brought it up."

"Well, he's coming back next week and says he wants to take me to dinner instead."

"So, it *is* promising?"

"I don't know," I whine. "I don't know anything anymore. Every-thing used to be so clear. I hate my job. I hate Hollywood. I'm alone. Except for you and Steven. Now, there's Charles, *maybe*, and Troy's a pain but I kind of feel sorry for him and want to help him and now with G, I feel like I actually want to *keep* my job—which is really fucked up—just to beat him, you know? Just to prove I am a good publicist."

"I think that's an oxymoron, *good publicist*," says Rachel. "Maybe you could have been a *good publicist* years ago, when Hollywood had some integrity."

"Oh, please. Talk about oxymorons. You've never been able to use the words *Hollywood* and *integrity* in the same sentence with-out being ironic."

"Or satiric," Rachel counters with a wry smile.

"The studio system?" I say, unwilling to let this drop. "That's your bastion of integrity? You think we're paid to lie and cover up for clients now? It was even worse back then."

"I'm just saying I don't think Hollywood was always this cut-throat," Rachel says. "There was a time when the stakes were a lit-tle less high, the competition a little less nasty, and people seemed to make movies because they really liked the *movies*, not just the money."

"I think this town has always been about greed and narcissism and conjuring a fantasy by those who think the reality of their lives just isn't 'special' enough."

"Hey, you're the one who just said you wanted to keep your job."

"I also said it was fucked up."

"Speaking of that, how is G? Playing nicely with his new toy?"

"I guess we'll know more tomorrow," I say, raising my glass. "Our first all-agency meeting." Suddenly I'm anxious to put the day—and tomorrow—out of my mind. "Oh, fuck G. And all of Hollywood for that matter," I say, balling up my napkin. "Let's talk about something fun. Are you going to the Barneys sale?"

"Do I look like the kind of girl who enjoys trying on clothes in an airplane hangar?"

Which is how the conversation, several martinis and glasses of wine later, winds up on my late marriage. Actually, it's a cute story if you like that Jew-shiksa thing, except I wasn't quite sure where Rachel stood on that.

"Wait a minute. You married Josh because he was Jewish or in spite of it?"

"I married him because I thought I loved him."

"And because your mother didn't?"

"My mother wanted me to marry Tad."

"Who's Tad?"

"There is no *Tad*. He was just the ideal Bucks County– Rittenhouse Square–Ivy League blond I was meant to wind up with."

"Oh, *that* Tad. I was supposed to marry Isaac the Rabbi or, if that was too Talmudic, David the Park Avenue Doctor," Rachel says, downing the last of her martini and running her finger around the inside of the glass and licking it. "Now look at us. I'm bitter and you're confused."

"Yeah," I say, suddenly more sad than angry. "And the really sad thing is that if this was a script, no one would green-light it. Not special enough."

Dropping the mail on the kitchen counter and not even bothering to check the answering machine, I kick off my mules, grab a fresh bottle of water, and head into the den to fire up the Tivo. Christ, when did my life get so pathetic, so confusing? I sink into the arm-chair and spiral through the channels wondering, not for the first time, if I did the right thing divorcing Josh. It was hard enough making all those decisions the first time. Career. Mate. *Spouse.* Why tear it up and start all over again? God knows it's only harder figuring it out now.

Maybe I'd been too quick to bail. Too quick to unlash myself from another mooring. The way I'd bolted out of Upper Darby after high school and never looked back. Put as much psychic distance between me and the Main Line as I could find. As much literal distance between me and my parents' expectations and my precious, perfect sister, Amy, as I could find. It wasn't Josh's fault he'd been the handiest solution when I was looking to get my parents off my case about moving back to Philly after I quit *McCalls* and enrolled in NYU.

In fact, Josh had been one of my best friends. The differences between us were all part of the attraction—first as friends and later as a couple. Meeting his parents out in Brooklyn had been such a relief from my own family. Sitting in their kitchen eating cake and drinking coffee late at night was like stepping into a new world. Like high school sleep-overs: how safe, how exciting it was in the strange kitchen, with their different food smells. Like you could so easily become part of someone else's family. No history. No baggage. No expectations. Just included. Loved for who you were, not what you represented.

It was the same way with Josh's family: an easy fit because of the differences from my family. Even more so with the menorahs on the windowsills and the boxes of matzo on the kitchen counter. And Josh's dad, a big surgeon at Bellevue, had this really direct way of talking, just lobbing questions like I was some fascinating new patient and not this accessory, which was how I usually felt growing up. It was flattering and intimidating all at once to have the attentions of this intense, intelligent man who was so different from my own head-in-the-clouds-feet-on-the-golf-course Dad, and when I started talking about *The New York Times*—how I couldn't start my day without it, which wasn't a lie and not even a ploy— Josh's dad clapped me on the shoulder and let out a barky laugh, like I had passed or something. I looked over at Josh, who was pale and sort of damp but grinning wildly, and I decided, impulsively, to have another piece of cake. But then it's easy to get sugar and love mixed up. Almost as easy to get running away from something mixed up with running toward something.

We started as friends. Met at NYU when he was still dating

Beth, a milky-skinned education major from Rhode Island who was getting her master's so she could teach preschool at some private academy. At least that's what I gathered from all our late-night conversations at Coffee Shop in Union Square. All those anguished hours I sat there with Josh because he and Beth had had some stupid argument like whether Saturday or Sunday was the heart of the weekend and she'd flounced back to Little Compton or wherever she was from, until Josh called and apologized for being so culturally insensitive and would she please just come back to the city? It went on like this with me playing the interpreter of all things gentile until one night Josh reached across the table and put his hands on mine and said he'd broken up with Beth.

"You're kidding?" I said, thinking of all the hours I'd put in talking him through the fights because he seemed so desperately in love. Now, he had broken up with her just like that?

"I can't believe it," I said, more pissed just then than sympathetic.

"It's because I've met someone else."

It took me a minute to realize Josh was referring to me. I'd never been friends with a guy before where it had turned into a real relationship, and my first reaction was that it seemed totally wrong. Like trying to envision having sex with your brother. If I'd had a brother.

"I'm going to need something stronger than coffee if we're going to continue this conversation," I was saying when Josh somehow suddenly had his mouth on mine with such force that I had to grip the edge of the table to keep from falling backward in the booth. I was just on the verge of pulling out of the kiss, of putting everything back where it had been, when Josh dropped his forehead on mine in a way that was actually endearing and said, quite quietly given the roar of the restaurant, "I've been wanting to do that for a long time."

I can't say I loved him. Maybe I just loved the *idea* of being with Josh. At the very least, that kiss seemed like an answer to a question I'd given up asking myself. But like I said, it's easy to confuse running away from something with running toward something.

And being with Josh was *interesting,* and so different from the guys back at Brown, all those sun-streaked lacrosse players who were so big and taciturn and beer-filled that you never knew what they were thinking—at least off the lacrosse field—but it didn't matter, not for the two or three months those relationships lasted, because they were just so pretty.

Josh wasn't like that. He was talky and eager to tell me *exactly* what he was thinking and feeling and he wanted me to tell him everything I was thinking and feeling. Even when I really didn't feel like doing that, Josh always wanted to know, and after a while it was sort of flattering and even a little addictive to be the center of so much attention. Only later did being with Josh start to seem like a bad episode of *Mad About You.* When the differences between us became unmistakable no matter how hard we tried.

Even Josh's proposal was interesting—during our first and, as it turned out, only trip to Israel. The trip was ostensibly about introducing me to his old kibbutz buddies, guys like Josh who'd grown up in New York but who'd spent high school summers milking cows and picking grapes in Israel. But unlike Josh, his friends had moved back to Israel after graduation and were now teaching in Tel Aviv or studying in Jerusalem or shooting at Palestinians in the desert but mostly living off money their parents, comfortably back home in Westchester, sent them every month.

"Don't try to figure it out," Josh had said when I asked how American college graduates who could have been going to law school or med school or earning a bundle on Wall Street were living like refugees in a war zone. "Chalk it up to Zionism—or better yet, guilt," he added, as we'd headed out from the King David to the Old City. It was only our second day in Israel and I was still getting used to the heat and the blazing desert light. After several minutes of walking down one alleyway and then the next, I started to feel dizzy. At first, I thought it was the jet lag or just the strangeness of the Old City, all the twisty cobbled streets with their deep, slashing shadows and the smells of smoke and blood—like that kid pushing a freshly severed cow's head in a wheelbarrow—and the old men sucking on water pipes in the cafes. I thought I needed to sit down or maybe just head to the Christian quarter, when I turned to Josh and all but collapsed on his shoulder.

I was close to tears, when Josh steered me down an alley and leaned me against a wall and put his arms around me and whispered that we should get married. Maybe it was the shock or just too much Jerusalem but Josh took my sobbing as a yes. Only later, when we were having lunch at an outdoor cafe back in the new city, where thankfully U2 poured from the tinny little speakers and I downed about four glasses of iced tea and felt suddenly so much better, had I realized we'd mistaken dehydration for trembling passion. I was on the verge of telling Josh he could take it all back, that I felt like myself again and where was that cool shopping district he'd mentioned, when I looked over and saw him looking at me in a way that I had never seen and realized that however inadvertently, I was engaged. That what I had been playing at—what we both had been playing at—was for keeps.

Of course, my parents freaked. Or I should say Mom freaked—I'm not sure Dad even noticed except for the catering bill—but when she found out Josh's dad was a big-deal doctor, she at least had a bone to throw to her friends at the club. Besides, it wasn't like I had to convert or anything, even if the rabbi did perform part of the ceremony. Hardly anybody from my family came, which was fine by me, mostly just Josh's family and our friends at NYU. In the end, I think Mom told everyone I'd eloped.

So we were husband and wife. Or at least for the next three years that we stuck it out. Until finally, one rainy autumn day, the kind of day that makes you wonder what you ever really saw in any of it, what exactly was the point of it—the apartment, the job, the man coming through the front door who used to make you smile and feel full of plans, but now only makes you feel tired, restless, like a bad Noel Coward production that should have closed out of town months ago—that day, for whatever reason, I just told him it was over. And he didn't even act surprised. That was the worst of it. Or maybe it was actually for the best. I wasn't fooling myself anymore. And apparently, I had never fooled him. "I was never playing at this," he said, standing there in the darkened living room with his coat still on, still dripping with rain. "But I always knew you were. I just hoped you'd grow to love the role."

"So do you think I did the right thing?" I say when Steven picks up the phone. He may have been my assistant but in Hollywood that means 24/7 availability. Besides, other than Rachel, he's also my closest friend.

"About what?" he says mildly, or at least he's keeping the irritation out of his voice.

"Divorcing Josh."

"Divorcing Josh? The last time we talked you were worried about sleeping with Troy. And I thought *I* had guy problems."

"I'm not joking," I say with a sigh. "Maybe I should have stayed in New York with him. We'd have a really nice apartment by now. I wouldn't be wondering what to do on the weekends and I wouldn't be paid to take care of guys like Troy who can't even remember when they're being disgusting."

"Don't you have your old therapist on speed-dial for times like this?"

"That just shows you've *never* been to therapy."

"Well, first we know *that's* not true. And secondly, you haven't been here that long. I've known people who've been out here for *years* and never had a serious relationship."

"No, it's not just Josh," I say, and I can tell I'm starting to get worked up again. "I feel so much smaller here than in New York. So much less significant."

"You just need bigger clients," Steven says and I can tell he's trying to be helpful. "The whole G thing has got you rattled."

"No, it's more than that. In New York, I felt like I counted, even in my own small way. I had my life, my job, my friends, Josh. I felt plugged in, like I knew my place in the scheme of things. Like I belonged."

"Okay, but—"

"But out here, it's the opposite," I plow on, not caring if it's late and I sound drunk or like Peter Finch in *Network*. "Even if you're part of it, you still feel like you don't really count, that you couldn't possibly count, because the only people who count are on the covers of magazines and you helped put them there. Christ, even Clinton thought Hollywood was cooler than Washington and how twisted is that?"

I'm suddenly exhausted by my rant. "You work so hard to keep the celebrity flame burning, to make it the obsession of the world, and you wind up feeling worthless because you're not the object of the obsession. And nobody told me that," I say, and I realize my voice sounds very small and very, very whiny.

"Because you had to learn it for yourself."

"Don't quote *The Wizard of Oz* when I'm pissed off," I say, although I feel not unlike Dorothy when she finally spies the real Wizard. I landed at DWP on a whim, a lark, an answer to a failed marriage. A *fuck you* to my parents and all their buttoned-down expectations and Amy, who couldn't wait to fulfill them. Now, the whole thing has become much more than a temporary stop, an *entr'acte* in the larger drama of my life. "So how do I get back to Kansas? Call up Josh and beg him to take me back? Move to Maine and work with the indigent? Beg Charles to take me away from all this?"

"Look, most days it doesn't bother me. It makes me laugh. It makes *you* laugh."

"But you live your life with more irony than I do. Than I *want* to."

"That's only because I'm gay."

"All I'm saying is I want some authenticity that doesn't come saddled with celebrity. And I can't find it out here."

"If I was less ironic, I would say you've learned in three years what most people *never* learn in Hollywood. Or would never admit to learning. But since I'm not . . . ," he says, sighing, and I can tell his patience for my metaphysical breakdown is wearing thin.

"You know, it's fine," I say. If there's anything I can't stand more than pity, it's impatience with my fears. "It's fine and let's just forget it."

"No," he says, rallying now that the goal line is in sight. "We'll talk more tomorrow, but why don't you try and get some sleep now. You'll have enough to deal with, with Scooby and Scrappy."

I close my eyes and try to imagine who he's talking about. "Scooby and Scrappy? Am I meeting with someone from the Cartoon Network this week?"

"You wish. No, their human counterparts."

My eyes fly open. "No way!"

"Yes, Suzanne's handing them off to you. Actually G's handing them off to you. They're unhappy with Buffy or Muffy or one of his Biggies and the word is G's moving all his problem clients to DWP agents. Flush out the dead wood. I was going to tell you tomorrow but Suzanne said she's already set up your first meeting with them for tomorrow afternoon."

Suddenly I'm beyond exhausted. G has laid his cards on the table even before our first official staff meeting. He engineered the buyout of DWP and now he's trying to kill it off. It's kind of like the Time Warner–AOL merger, if you think about it. And my poison pill is to be Scooby and Scrappy, the gay couple of the moment. Actually, they *were* the gay couple of the moment, until they came out of the closet—so pious and so stupid—and now they're pariahs, out of work and scorned. A publicist's nightmare.

"I actually see this as a vote of confidence in your abilities," Steven says, and I can tell he's trying to soften the blow. "I mean, G's trying to thin the ranks but Suzanne obviously thinks you can handle it."

"Don't try and make me feel better. I may hate my job, but at least I wasn't in danger of losing it. Until now."

I close my eyes again. I have to bring this to a close and start all over again tomorrow. Tomorrow when I'll find the strength and clarity of mind to deal with G and Scooby and Troy and Val and sit in the office with my headset on and just make it all work.

But that's tomorrow.

Besides, I hear another call coming in. "Hang on," I say to Steven and warily click over.

"You're home? You're never home. I just thought I'd try and grab you before Mom does."

Amy. Or *Amee*, as she called herself now. Better her than Mom. "Hey, I just walked in," I say, starting out the way I usually do with Amy: with a lie. "Hang on, let me get off the other line.

"It's Amy," I say to Steven. "And we know she never calls unless it's important. Like she got a new horse. Or Barkley scored a hole in one. I'll talk to you tomorrow, and give me everything we have on Scooby first thing in the morning.

"I'm back," I say, clicking over to Amy.

"I meant to call you earlier but I figured I would miss you then and I wanted to give you a heads-up."

Amy and I hardly ever speak anymore. Not since e-mail. Such a chickenshit way of staying in touch. Not since she and Barkley moved out from Philly, bought a house twenty minutes from Mom and Dad, and she quit working full-time. Not that what she'd done at the design center or wherever she worked had been all that taxing. Still, she had to get up in the morning and look at fabric swatches or something. Now all Amy does is ride her horse, go to lunch, and help her friends decorate their houses. The only girl in captivity who wants to live like it's 1950, and she happens to be my sister.

Actually we've never been close. Too much like Jo and Amy in *Little Women* without Beth and Meg to balance us out. Once I left for college, that was pretty much it for us. Her marriage to Barkley the same year I left for L.A. was the capper. Officially we have nothing in common now except Mom and Dad, and as far as I can see they've always been on her side. Now calls between us are reserved for our birthdays or holidays but since we aren't anywhere near any of them, unless you count Rosh Hashanah, which we don't, this call from her now can't be good.

"Mom wants us all to spend Christmas together this year."

"We just did Christmas together. Like we do every year."

"She wants to do it in L.A. this year."

Instinctively, because every family trip has turned into a David O. Russell movie, I head for the refrigerator and the half-empty bottle of Pinot Grigio I pray is in there.

"Mom won't leave Bucks County," I say, pouring myself a glass and reaching for the box of crackers that I keep in the cupboard for emergency meals.

"She and Dad took you to France."

"Dad needed someone to help with the driving and neither one of them spoke French."

"You didn't either."

I pause and bite loudly into a cracker, which Amy interprets as anger. Not that she's wrong.

"Mom's serious about coming," she says, sounding wounded. "She's even got Dad talked into it and you know how much he likes to spend the holidays at home."

"Why?" I say, and I realize I'm starting to whine. "I mean, they could have asked me."

"She thinks it's going to be a nice surprise."

"Because I don't come see you? Thanksgiving and Christmas last year. What am I missing? Labor Day?"

"I just wanted to let you know before Mom called. She's already got some ideas mapped out."

I feel my chest tighten. That cramped, claustrophobic feeling I get when someone wants me to do something that I don't want to do. That trip to France. Joining the Girl Scouts. Buying jeans that don't fit because the saleswoman at Fred Segal likes them.

"And I've got a few requests. Like Barkley wants us all to go to Mr. Chow."

I see a Disneyland of bad rides in my future.

"Nobody goes to Mr. Chow here unless you're trying to be ironic."

"Well, Barkley read about it in *W* and he wants to go."

"Barkley's reading *W*?"

"*I* read *W.* Barkley looks through it sometimes. Anyway, we both want to go."

I hear my other line click. "I have another call."

"It's probably Mom," we both say at the same time.

"She was very hopped up about this."

"Hang on," I say, clicking over. "Hello?"

"Hi, honey, am I catching you at a bad time?"

"Mom. I've got Amy on the other line."

There's a moment of silence that I uncharacteristically let hang uninterrupted.

"Well, have you almost finished? Or has she totally ruined my surprise?"

"Mom, hang on a minute." I need to lose Amy rather than risk upsetting Mom anymore than she already is.

"It's Mom. I'm going to talk to her."

"Well, don't tell her I told you about L.A."

For the next thirty minutes, I sit on the kitchen counter, cradling the phone, drinking wine, and eating almost the entire box of crackers minute bit by minute bit so she won't hear me chewing, nodding and smiling as if my mother were right here in the kitchen with me. Of course I'm thrilled with her idea of Christmas in L.A. Don't be silly. It saves me a plane ticket, doesn't it? And the Four Seasons is lovely at the holidays. Almost as pretty as Rittenhouse Square, where Grandma and Grandpa used to have their annual Christmas party and where after all the guests had gone, leaving the living room smelling of pine and bourbon, Grandpa would put on his Louis Armstrong records and he'd dance with us, balancing me and Amy on his shoe tops, the glow of the tree lights reflected in his glasses.

I feel my eyes blur. I try to focus on the kitchen clock. Ten past ten. One in the morning in Bucks County.

"Mom. It's late."

"Well, honey, think of some things you want to do as well when we're there."

"I will, but right now I have to go," I say, my mind already drifting off, back to New York, to the little apartment near Gramercy Park where Josh and I moved after we came back from Israel and he bought a really great diamond, I had to admit, and then there was our engagement party at the Russian Tea Room. Afterward, I'd stood in the tiny kitchen looking down Twenty-second Street, gazing at all the people hurrying home in the dusk.

I'd looked at them for several minutes until they were just shadows. Then I'd turned and gone in to Josh, who was laying out our gifts in the other room, all the boxes and the bags, all of it proof of my new life, the person I was about to become.

5 | You're Not in Kansas Anymore

"You look awfully perky for someone not on medication," Steven says when I hit the office the next morning wearing my favorite Piazza Sempione suit and with my hair perfectly blown out. Outside it's pushing ninety at barely nine o'clock with a hot, searing wind out of the desert, but I'm dressed for my favorite season—fall. Actually, it *is* fall, September, in fact, but in L.A. it's indistinguishable from July.

"The mind is a powerful organ," I say, breezing by his desk. "Even when left to its own devices."

"And she comes complete with attitude," Steven says, following me into my office. "So how was Sis?"

"Threatening to come for Christmas. With Mom."

Steven gives a little shudder.

"Yes, well, in the even-worse-news department the word is Suzanne just lost Carla. I think G'll have bigger fish to fry at the meeting this morning than you and Scooby."

"No *shit*," I say. For weeks everyone at the agency has been following Carla's latest hissy fit—and Suzanne's increasingly ineffectual attempts to control her. Carla was the agency's prize client—one of our only hot clients and one of Hollywood's only bona fide Latin stars. If you don't count the Sheen clan, which nobody does. Carla came out of nowhere—well, Dallas, where she was a Cowboys cheerleader—but that's close enough. Now she is, amazingly, an A-list star. She's done it in something like three years and four movies—only one of which, a *Scream*-like horror film, did any business—and with one rapper boyfriend, who actually did some time on a weapons charge.

At first, handling Carla was like selling cocaine. There wasn't a magazine or talk show that wouldn't take her and on her terms. Rose petals need to be scattered down the hallway before Carla's arrival? No problem. No eye contact from any staff member shall be permitted? Consider it done. Will only travel accompanied by a massive entourage? We'll make it happen. Carla was one of DWP's great success stories, one of their only success stories, and they totally overshot their mark. They've created a monster.

But Carla understands what even Hollywood doesn't—that the movie industry is actually late to the Latin party—and she has no intention of limiting herself to its whims. As the new Latin queen, she is a one-woman industry ready to launch her franchises— recording an album, designing a line of sportswear, opening her restaurant. She is even in discussions with Nike about getting her own sneaker. And like Cher and Madonna, she's about to launch her brand name—"C.Se."

Unfortunately, the studio releasing her latest film, *Hack Attack*, a romantic comedy about a pair of computer hackers starring Carla and Charlie Sheen, hasn't caught up with this fact. The movie is scheduled to open in two weeks and Carla is insisting the studio pull its print advertising—all the posters and billboards, newspaper and magazine ads—and change "Carla Selena" to "C.Se." It is an absurd request, of course, impossible to pull off and costing something in the neighborhood of $1 million. Suzanne has tried to run interference, but Carla is insistent. The whole thing has dissolved into a series of increasingly abusive memos among the studio, Suzanne, and Carla's manager, Jerry "Paco" Gold that were already widely circulating around town on the Web.

"The latest salvo," says Steven, dropping a sheet on my desk. "For your reading enjoyment."

"You printed it out?"

"Suitable for framing."

To: Jerry Gold
From: Suzanne Davis
Re: Issues

Jerry, how can I put this? The studio's bottom line (and they've got backup on this): she signed onto the project as "Carla Selena." And she is going to be billed as "Carla Selena." The studio is adamant about this. As they conveyed their sentiments to me: "We can't help it if she's decided to get a diva transplant."

To: Suzanne Davis
From: Jerry Gold
Re: Nonissues

Maybe you and the studio can play these games with some of your other "stars." But Carla is not just another star. She is the world's preeminent female celebrity. She has more talent in her ass than most people have in their tiny finger. C.Se is not just an actress. She is not just a celebrity. She is a movement. (Why do I even have to say this?) She feels extra-determined that "Carla Selena" is not where her movement is at these days. She is C.Se. Unless this is acknowledged, Carla will not be available for studio publicity events.

"So, Suzanne finally got hit in the cross fire?"

"Jerry called her this morning," Steven says, dropping his voice to a mock whisper. "Since DWP can't protect 'C.Se' from these kinds of 'absurd demands,' they'll find someone who can."

"Like who, Benny Medina?"

"Well, God knows he's in the market since J. Lo fired him."

"Good point," I say.

"So, does G know?"

"Oh, I think we can assume he does. Someone from Richard Johnson's office already called."

"God, he's fast," I say, shaking my head.

"Like I said, I doubt your name will even come up this morning."

I'm about to suggest Steven laminate the e-mail and FedEx it to my mother as proof of the absurdity of my job, when my phone rings. "I'm only taking calls from Rachel, Suzanne, and, of course, Charles, and I need the Scooby file," I say, tossing the e-mail in the wastebasket, yanking my hair into a ponytail and anchoring it with a pencil, and heading for my desk.

I hear Steven on the phone and then *Peg* flashes on the Amtell. *No way!* I type back. It has to be about the shoot. Peg had seemed oddly human yesterday but I'm not about to push my luck. The one thing I don't need before my meeting with G is Peg's usual blistering harangue. Not when I also have to deal with Scooby in less than four hours.

Way! comes rocketing back.

Okay, I can dance with the devil if I have to. Besides, if there is any fallout from Troy's latest reefer incident, I better know it before G does.

"*Peg,*" I say expansively when I click on.

"Troy's ecstatic."

"Then I'm ecstatic. Remind me why we are ecstatic."

"He loved the shoot. And so did Blake. Forgotten how photogenic Troy was, et cetera, et cetera."

I have no idea where Peg is going with this, but knowing her, I could still get blamed for something. "*Great,*" I say, hoping to forestall any bad news with my continued exuberance. "*Glad* to hear it."

"Actually, Troy is very pumped up. Being back in the game, et cetera, et cetera."

By *pumped up*, I assume she means *sober*, but what's her deal with *et cetera*? "Well, I'm working on more where that came from," I say. "I should have a few more story commitments in a couple of days. *L.A. Times, USA Today.* Et cetera," I add as casually as I can.

Peg ignores me. "Actually, there's something you can do sooner than that."

Ah, the fucking shoe finally drops.

"You know the Harley-Davidson–Chanel event?"

Harley-Davidson and Chanel? Throw a rock any given night in L.A. and you'll hit half a dozen celebs posing for the paparazzi at some nonsense promotional event: *Join the editors of* Vogue *for a special event at Burberrys. Join the editors of* InStyle *for a special event at Barneys. Join the editors of* W *and fill-in-the-blank celebrities for a special event celebrating fill-in-the-blank fashion product at fill-in-the-blank boîte of the moment.* There are so many of these celeb-studded shucks to advertisers that no one bothers to keep track. Unless one of your clients is involved or the gift bag is rumored to be better than normal. But Harley-Davidson and Chanel? What PR genius cooked up that combo? And what is it promoting? Chanel's new line of biker chains? A new limited-edition Harley—"the Coco"—with a quilted seat and fourteen-karat-gold accents?

"You know Troy's a big Harley fan. He owns a couple and he's actually been involved in this from the beginning. He's friends with the local dealer."

I'm sure he's friends with a lot of dealers, but at least motorcycles are legal. "Okay . . ." I say, suddenly realizing where this is heading. "And you want me to cover it with him?"

"I meant to mention it before. Anyway, Troy reminded me this morning. And he specifically asked if you could go."

I know Peg is lying. If anything, she reminded Troy of the damn event and she probably had it down to go with him. Or more likely her assistant was to go. But now that I'm Troy's official press minion, I get to do the public hand-holding. Carry the hem of Troy's robe while he parades down the red carpet.

"How sweet," I say. "But when is it?"

"Well, that's the unfortunate part. It's tonight."

"Tonight?" Between our all-office meeting and my meet-and-greet with Scooby, my day is already stressful enough and, frankly, after bailing Troy out yesterday, I'm not all that keen to see him so soon. No telling what he'll do when liquor is available. I flip open my calendar, praying I've forgotten some can't-miss event. My own birthday. Someone's funeral. Nothing except a yoga class penciled in. It is either a big lie—*Aw, wish I could but I'm flying to Hawaii and never coming back!*—or bite the bullet.

"You know, it'll be fine," I say, dropping my head into my hand. "E-mail me the details and tell Troy I'll meet him there."

Peg barks a response that I take as "Thanks"—or as close to "Thanks" as I'm likely to get given that's one of the words everyone in Hollywood tries never to say, along with "Excuse me" and "Please"—and I hang up before her mood or medication wears off.

"Told you," Steven says, sticking his head around the door.

"Told me what?" I say grouchily, all too aware that my annoying day now stretches into the night.

"Told you it was good news."

"You call being made to go to a last-minute PR event good news? You know, I could technically make *you* go."

"Yes, you could but we both know you're not that kind of vindictive, small-minded boss," Steven says.

"I think I need to learn to be," I say, reaching for my headset. I still have a few million calls to make before the meeting at BIG's offices and I still have to prep for my drive-by with Scooby.

"Think happy thoughts. Think about the gift bag," he says, dropping a folder on my desk. Scooby's autopsy report. "By the way, Suzanne's scheduled your meeting at their house in Hancock Park and not their manager's office. She has the idea you could start there."

"Where?"

"At the house. They put like a million into it and Suzanne

thinks *InStyle* might be interested. Just a couple of gals at home. I mean, the magazine's done Melissa Etheridge like a million times."

"Meaning?"

"Meaning that although everybody knows it's so five minutes ago to be gay, you can still fool the public into thinking it's hip."

I stare at the folder and for a second my New York fantasy flashes in my head. A big expense account, my name high up a masthead and a job that consists of going to lunch. I would be cultivating vision. Girls got to have vision in Manhattan. Out here the best you can hope for is a good pair of tits. I would also be living in the same city as Charles. Speaking of Charles, why hasn't he called? He said he'd call today and it is already—I check my watch—coming up on 2 P.M. in New York.

"Any calls?" I say to Steven as casually as I can.

"No one you want to speak to."

If it's that kind of a day, it's that kind of a day. I sigh, redo my ponytail, and gamely attack the folder. It's a grim file of memos and e-mails, a litany of complaints and countercomplaints between Scooby and her various B.I. PR agents. There's also an old press kit on Scooby back when she was a rising young star. Back when she was in the closet. Those were the days, I think, flipping through the glossy cover stories—*Ladies' Home Journal, People, TV Guide, US*. All of them had embraced Scooby as a bracing new breed of woman in Hollywood. A woman who dared go where no man had gone: a woman who did not trade on her looks, her sex appeal, or even her acting chops to fuel her film career. Wit, intelligence, and sheer chutzpah were her calling cards. Scooby was Jodie Foster, only funny. Whoopi Goldberg, only white. Scooby was such a maverick, she even took roles that had been rejected by male stars like Martin Lawrence and Martin Short.

But Scooby was also restless. Her career was stalling—she was bored playing the plucky-single-gal secondary roles—and she was sick of showing up at premieres with some guy on her arm. At first, her agents suggested she do a series. TV was a lot kinder to women. Or at least less brutal. So many actresses come crawling to the networks when their film career tanks that prime time is like a battered women's shelter. "If you're in a studio film you're basically there to prove that star has sex," one of my clients told me in a moment of despair. "On TV, you'll never have sex but you can at least play a *character.*"

But Scooby was also in love. With Scrappy, another Hollywood starlet, who had a reputation for hitching on to older heretofore male stars. Now Scooby wanted to share her love with the world. "No," Scooby decided, "the answer is to come out."

God knows Hollywood has plenty of gay stars. Every agency has them. But most of them are safely in the closet, at least professionally, and for one very good reason: they continue to work. Very few actors are willing to put their careers on the line for a few moments of honesty about their sexuality. Especially when it is so effortless to stay in the closet. Half of DWP's gay client list live openly gay lives. They are seen around town, at screenings, at parties, at clubs, with their same-sex partners. And the media, with few exceptions, play along. Everyone might know you're gay, but you are still presented to the public as the rakish bachelor, the sexy single gal. Of course, the superstars, the $20 million celebrity club, go through a bit more cloak-and-dagger nonsense. Actual marriages. Children. Some of it by contract, some of it simply a handshake deal.

But Scooby was determined to come out. And at first it looked like a smart decision. Scooby was hip, Scooby was cool. Scooby was a *hero,* just like her cartoon counterpart. And in fact, she was the rare actor who had dared call Hollywood on its liberal pieties. For the first few months, she and Scrappy basked in their new glow as the priestesses of the moral high ground. They even got invited to the White House. Well, Clinton was president.

But then, Scooby's films began to open and die. The perception was they tanked because she was a "gay actor." Gradually and then suddenly, the big offers quit coming. Now, two years later, Scooby is all but dead. Worse than dead: she is a lesbian with a grudge. And now it's my job to fix it.

"Remember, nobody likes angry gays," Steven says as I'm packing up for my day of meetings, first at BIG and then Scooby's. "Not since the eighties, anyway. We're all happy gays these days."

"Just like *Will & Grace*."

"That's it," Steven says, straightening the shoulders of my jacket. "Think of yourself as Grace. I already do."

I'm feeling vaguely ready to face G and his minions when I glide into the garage on Wilshire, where I am waved to the farthest subterranean floor by the phalanx of excitable, red-vested valets. Great. Starting at the bottom although technically we're moving up in the world—or at least east on Wilshire. I angle the Audi into one of the remaining spaces under a RESERVED FOR BIG sign and sidle out the good four inches I'm left after wedging between a massive BMW and a vintage Cadillac the color of a Band-Aid. At least I've worn a black suit and my blow-dry is holding up. No grooming mistakes on our first day of school. I punch BIG's floor in the elevator and note, with a touch of envy, the cherry-and-brass paneling. We're moving here because BIG's digs are a better address than DWP's ratty haunt down in the Fairfax district, and according to the Hollywood rule: the weak always travel to the powerful.

Plus BIG has more room. Or they will have once the workmen finish renovating the law offices next door that are to be the DWP annex. I push past the brass-and-glass doors with B-I-G sandblasted on them, and am confronted by a Ken Russell movie—acres of plastic sheeting hanging from the ceiling, the sound of saws roaring, and a porn-ready, large-breasted blonde perched behind the massive reception desk.

"Yes?" she shouts over the racket. "You're here to see who?"

Whom, honey.

"I'm here for the staff meeting," I holler back just as the saws fall silent so my voice echoes way too loudly.

"Oh, you're with DWP?" she says, her little-girl voice a mix of surprise and condescension. "Right down the hall," she says, nodding at one of the larger plastic sheets. "Just push on through until you hit the conference room. Can't miss it."

My first reaction is that it's a lot like one of my old Girl Scout meetings only with better uniforms. The room is awash with women in black Armani suits and sweater sets in Easter-egg colors topped by shiny blonde heads—most of whom I barely recall from our drive-by visit a few weeks earlier. Forget remembering anyone's name. They're all variations on y, in any event. Muffy, Buffy, Duffy, with the odd "Amanda" thrown in. It's easier to tell the BIG agents from the DWPers by their odometers. A good ten, fifteen years separate the DWP agents from the BIG little sisters. Not one of them looks to be over thirty, and at thirty-three, I'm the ranking junior member on DWP's team, whose median age—given that Suzanne founded the agency back in the late seventies—is somewhere in the mid-to-late forties. God love us.

I take it as a good sign that no one even glances in my direction when I slip in. There are two large coffee dispensers and a tray of fruit and muffins on a table at one end of the room. But this is no time to get liquored up on sugar and caffeine. I spy an open chair next to Miranda, one of the veteran DWP agents, and slip in next to her.

"Any sign of Suzanne or the G-man yet?" I say.

She looks at me with a mixture of annoyance and suspicion. Miranda is old-school, with twenty years' experience and a respect for authority as impenetrable as aged hardwood that I can only marvel at. She's a card-carrying baby boomer, probably protested the war in college, and screwed her brains out with Canada-bound draft dodgers. Now she has the hips and the pinched, disapproving look of a soccer mom. Or a bank repo officer.

"They're in his office," she says stiffly. "I suspect they'll be in when they're ready." For more than half her life, this woman has been tending to some of Hollywood's creakiest stars. Protecting their eggshell egos from the slings and arrows of daily life, which these days mostly means maintaining the fiction that someone somewhere is dying to dish the dirt on them. I once heard her railing at some editor from *Smithsonian* over a photo spread on Ann-Margret's house. She is a mother to beat all mothers but her dedication has made her distrustful of almost everyone except her clients. As if the whole world lies in wait for her aging brood.

I give up on Miranda and scan the room. A clutch of Biggies is discussing the new Quentin Tarantino film in the kind of awed terms one would normally hear in the Prada store. Like anybody still thinks he's a genius. I glance past Miranda at the other DWPers lined up along the wall. They look like patients in a gynecologist's office: vaguely bored, nervous, and with the kind of flushed skittishness one has before being probed by a total stranger.

I'm about to head for the coffee when there's a commotion at the door. G, looking like a Beverly Hills Mercedes salesman: well oiled and predatory. He seems even shorter than a week ago. If that's possible. He gives the room a glance that makes me want to check my wallet, and steps to the head of the table.

"Folks, I think you've all heard the news about Carla Selena's unfortunate and unexpected departure this morning," G says, unbuttoning his jacket and flipping open a leather binder. He removes a pen from his jacket pocket and clicks it open like he's unsheathing a scalpel. "Needless to say, in light of this setback, we have work to do."

The meeting is more like a deposition than a flaying, a rapid-fire question-and-answer session that rolls on for more than two hours. The air is thick with contract quotas, clients' names and publicists' names colliding and then uncoiling into new, different patterns. It's impossible to keep track of who is sent where and with whom. When the dust settles it's not entirely clear who, other than G, is left with the spoils, and who is left with the dregs, although the DWP agents look, if possible, even more deflated than before. I've been publicly awarded Scooby and Scrappy—no surprise, right down to the patronizing smiles among the Biggies. Only once the meeting is winding down do I realize that in all the commotion, Suzanne is a glaring no-show.

I feel my pulse jump. That Suzanne is AWOL from the first official BIG-DWP staff meeting is at best surprising and at worst a very bad sign. Especially since no one, namely G, seems to be mentioning it. Or it could just be a scheduling thing due to Carla's abrupt departure this morning. Maybe she had to rush to the studio for damage control or something. That has to be it, but I make a mental note to get Steven on this. When the room erupts into the chaos of exiting, I instinctively reach for my cell to call him, when I feel a hand on my shoulder. I look up. Another one of G's Ken Russell extras. "Doug wants to see you before you leave. If you have a minute."

I check my watch. A minute is about all I have before my meeting with Scooby. "Sure," I say blandly. I've got time to go to the principal's office on my first day of school.

G's office is a symphony of leather. Eames chairs, black Moderne sofa. Right down to his white leather desk that looks like a Kelly bag on Viagra. I imagine whips in the closet. Of thick braided leather. That sting. I imagine this because I have at least ten minutes to cool my heels in Leatherworld before G rushes in, slightly out of breath and buttoning his jacket. I do not want to imagine where he's just been.

"Ah, Alex," he says, like he is surprised to find me here.

"I was told you wanted to see me."

"Yes, yes. I did," G says, moving behind his desk and nodding at me. "Have a seat."

I can imagine whips, but I can't imagine what G's about to say, although I suspect it will be less "Welcome to the team" than "We're thinking of making some changes." Any DWP agent would have to be an idiot to think G is on our side, buyout or no buyout.

As one of the newest hires, I am clearly one of the most vulnerable. Mercifully, I don't have to wait long.

"Obviously there's a lot of transitioning going on," G says by way of throat clearing. "And there will be more changes to come and I can't say that all of them will be to everyone's liking. Even my own."

He smiles a small, tight smile and plunges on in his droning-but-menacing way. Layoffs are coming and God knows it won't be among the precious BIG agents, but the long-in-the-tooth DWP team. Too few clients or too much duplication or the recession or whatever, but the ax is about to fall. "But with your, shall we say, younger and more desirable client list, you, Alex, are in a slightly different category," G adds, putting his elbows on his desk and pressing his fingertips together. From the light bouncing off his nails, I can see he's had a manicure. Probably a pedicure.

I have no idea why I'm being given the concierge treatment or even if that's what's happening, but I nod my head and make appropriately conciliatory noises. More likely it's G's way of head-fucking. Or maybe I'm being culled from the DWP herd to be more easily slaughtered. I may be the youngest DWP publicist and my client list slightly less anemic than those of my colleagues, but still, what's G's game? Presumably he knew what DWP was—and wasn't—when he bought it. So why does it feel like AOL just took over Time Warner? And why does it feel like Suzanne is being cut out of the loop already?

"So these next few months—and next few clients—will be crucial," G adds. "I want you to feel free to come to me if you have any questions or concerns. Any at all. Are we agreed?"

Agreed? It's not like you don't have all of us—even Suzanne—over a fucking barrel. You're the new owner and you call the shots and short of quitting, there's not much I—or any of us—can do.

"Absolutely," I say, nodding like an idiot. I make a few more amiable noises—I hear myself say "communication," even "trust," God help me—until I realize I'm starting to run dangerously late for my meeting with Scooby. I try to check my watch without G noticing.

"Yes, I know you have your meeting in"— G holds up his hand and checks his watch—"less than thirty minutes. So you better get running. But why don't you call me later and let me know how it went. We'll find some time to sit down and discuss it in greater detail after you've met them. Map out a plan."

I am out of there like a shot, down the hall, blow past the plastic sheeting, sending clouds of dust everywhere including my suit, give the porn star a nod, and head to the elevators. Plan. Must have a plan. Swaddled in cherry and brass, I push *Down.*

6 | Scooby and Scrappy

One down, two to go. One down, two to go. This is my mantra as I pull up in front of Scooby's house—a sprawling old Cape Cod right out of Cheever country. Or it would be except for its location in Hancock Park, one of L.A.'s oldest and most conservative Jewish neighborhoods, that's popular with two types of Hollywood celebs: Jews who want to carry the flag and live in a largely Orthodox or at least observant neighborhood, and non-Jews who could care less about the ethnic mix but who want an Ozzie-and-Harriet-type spread at below–Beverly Hills prices. Scooby falls into the latter category, and her house, with its sumptuous manicured lawn and acres of clapboard, just screams Old Money. Except for the concertina wire gleaming on top of the brick wall encasing the yard. That looks a little crack house. Or Dachau. Sure that was a hit with the neighbors.

I pull up to the massive wood gate with the same mix of dread and curiosity I always have when I'm about to meet a new client. Rolling down the window, I reach out to hit the buzzer. A voice squawks on the other end. Unintelligible. Or maybe Spanish. "Hi, it's Alex Davidson—" I manage to get out before the gate begins its tortured, stately opening. I roll up the drive and park next to the black Mercedes SUV (Scooby's), the black BMW 5 series (Scrappy's), the faded, dented Honda Civic (the housekeeper's) and the bright green VW Beetle (Amber, the personal assistant's). I'm just gathering up my bag when two drooling Rottweilers and a large German shepherd bound around the corner and head for my car.

Oh, fuck. I have no choice but to wait for help. Within a minute, a small dark-haired woman comes out a side door dressed in the generic children's clothing domestic help wear—T-shirt, baggy cotton pants, and cheap sneakers.

"I'm Maria," she says in heavily accented English, as she wrestles with the barking pack. "Come in, they won't hurt you. They're waiting for you inside."

I wonder if she's referring to the dogs or her employers as I pry myself from the safety of the Audi and follow Maria into the kitchen.

Kitchen isn't exactly it. The room is more like a set for the Food Channel. Carved paneling and copper pots everywhere. Like anybody would actually cook anything in here.

"Would you like something to drink?" Maria asks, heading for the Sub-Zero that looms against one wall.

"Uhm, sure. Water," I say automatically.

Maria hands me a dripping bottle of Evian and I take a minute to check out Scooby's abode. Not bad for a down-on-her-luck dyke. The room is huge, unbearably tasteful, and the view out the French doors is equally impressive—a rolling back lawn and a pool, a shimmering rectangle sheathed in sea-green tiles, with a spewing fountain at one end and what looks like a child climbing out of the other. Scrappy, naked except for the bright red bikini bottom she's wearing on her tiny, little-girl hips.

"Here comes mistress now," Maria says behind me. There's just enough edge to her voice that I turn to see if she's being ironic. But she's already fled.

"Oh, hey," Scrappy says, letting herself in through one of the doors. She stands there dripping all over the tile floor, rubbing her black, tufted hair with a towel. "Hey," she says again, extending a wet palm, ignoring the fact she's virtually naked and I'm dressed for a deposition. "Sorry, I was just in the pool," she says, nodding over her shoulder. "It's so great to be able to swim at home. When I was growing up in Oklahoma, we never had a pool, so this really is our heaven." Giving up on her hair she drops the towel on her shoulder and crosses her arms under her breasts.

"Yes, well, it's beautiful—" I start to blather, making a mental note to bone up on Scrappy's miserable, poolless childhood when she cuts me off.

"Is Maria around here?" she says, moving past me to look down a hallway. "Uhm, look," she says, turning back. "Amber will be in in a minute, but why don't you go into the living room and we'll be right in."

Right in is a relative term in Hollywood. Actually what Scrappy means is, "We'll be down when enough time has passed to remind you that we—and our time—are more important than you are." I'm guessing given Scooby's faded status but still contentious pride, I'll have a good thirty minutes before they deign to show.

I head into Scooby's equally sprawling living room, where I start to pull out my cell to see if Charles has called, when I catch sight of several oversized silver picture frames lining the fireplace mantel. I move in for a closer look. The family gallery. Scooby and Scrappy at the Oscars! At the White House! At an AIDS ride benefit! And a few artful black-and-white shots of Scrappy in various states of undress.

"Aren't they great?" a childish voice pipes up behind me.

I whirl around, startled by the intrusion. The voice belongs to a twenty-something sylph, long blond hair straight as a bedsheet, dressed in a pair of tight low-rise jeans, flip-flops, and a red cotton tank top. A pager is clipped to her waist and in one hand she carries a cell phone, keys, and a pen. Amber.

"I just love that one," she says, reaching past me to pick up one of the arty shots of Scrappy. "They took these themselves, which is just so cool." She studies the photograph before slowly replacing it. "Hi, I'm Amber," she says, finally turning and extending her hand. "Welcome."

Typical. Assistants. The mini-me's of Hollywood with their little-girl voices and assassin's eyes.

"Oh, hi," I say as frostily as I can. You misread assistants at your peril, but you can't give them an inch.

"Well, I see you're set with your water," she says in the kind of voice you would normally use on a child. "Can I get you anything else before I go?"

Of course, she wasn't staying. Assistants just act like they're important. "No, really, this is fine," I say, holding up my water like a victory wreath.

"Okay, well, I unfortunately have to be somewhere else this afternoon," she says, giving a luxurious shake of her hair.

"We'll miss you," I say, aiming for a chipper but unmistakably ironic tone and hitting it with deadly accuracy.

Amber shoots me a look. "I'm sure we'll be in touch," she says, firing off one last shot. "They've really been wounded enough."

Right. Wounded. I almost forgot.

After Amber flip-flops out of the living room, I flee to the safety of one of the sofas and punch up Steven on my cell.

"Yes, for God's sake he finally called," he blurts out before I can even ask.

"Did you tell him I'm out for the day and did you give him my cell number and did you get his?"

"Aye, Captain," Steven says, launching into his Scottie impersonation from *Star Trek*. "Aye, and now I'm working on securing the missile launch."

"Look, just because you're having regular sex doesn't mean you get to make fun of those of us who are, for all intents and purposes, celibate."

"Ach, define regular sex," he says, still in Scottie mode.

I'm just repeating the words *regular sex* when I hear footsteps behind me. I pray it's Amber again and whip around. Nope. Scooby. Barefoot, bright red jeans, white V-neck cashmere sweater. And she's not smiling. Why are the funny ones always so forbidding in person? Eddie Murphy was the same way. Took one meeting with him and he sat there for an hour, never removing his sunglasses, never once smiling. Like he was the head of the Crips or something.

I give Scooby a chipper little wave and vamp. "Okay," I say to Steven in my all-business voice. "So fax those figures to the studio and leave a copy on my desk and I'll go over them when I get back. Oh, and leave that number on my cell voice mail."

"Don't tell me," Steven says, laughing. "Scooby just showed."

"That's correct," I say, still in business mode.

"Hey, if there's anything Scooby gets it's the concept of regular sex."

"We'll see about that," I say and click off.

"So," I say, extending my hand to Scooby. Or rather I try to extend my hand but Scooby drops onto one of the other sofas and spreads one arm across the back. "Doug speaks quite highly of you," she says, still not smiling. "Alex, isn't it? Why don't you tell me a little about yourself. Why you're here."

Why am I here? *Why am I here?* I'm tempted to scream, Do you think I'd be here for one minute if I didn't have to be here? If my new, scary, unreadable boss hadn't made me take you as a client?

"You have such a beautiful home," I say, ignoring both my inner rantings and Scooby's directive. "I only bring that up because I'm thinking it's a great incentive for a piece in *InStyle*. Or *US*."

"Really? And why would that be our first move?"

I'm about to think of some bland but plausible response—*I don't know, because they're the only magazines vapid enough to write about you at this point*—when Scrappy bounds into the room.

"Hey," she says, all but throwing herself onto the sofa and curling up next to Scooby and pulling her hand into her lap. "What have you two been talking about?"

At least she is dressed. Sort of. She's wearing a thin white halter top in a wool so sheer, cashmere, I'm guessing, that her nipples show through. Her tiny, pubescent breasts are in no need of a bra, but rather, apparently, constant exposure. She also has on a pair of tiny black leather shorts. On her left hand flashes an enormous diamond. Just a girl in love.

Smiling, I launch into a reprise of your-house-is-so-beautiful BS, which Scrappy is all too happy to run with. For the next fifteen minutes, she goes through the play-by-play, how they found the house, where the furniture came from, and on and on until even Scooby looks bored. "I think Alex gets the picture," she says.

"Hey, I'm going to open a bottle of champagne," Scrappy says brightly. "Join me?"

"Are we celebrating?" Scooby says, smiling for the first time.

"When aren't we? I mean, I just think with Alex here, and her great ideas about the magazines and stuff, that we should drink a toast or something. To Alex. Or to us. Or to the beginnings of— what's that line Ingrid Bergman said? 'The start of a beautiful friendship.' "

I'm not keen to crawl into a glass of champagne. Nobody drinks in Hollywood. At least not while they are on duty. On the other hand, perhaps a few drops of the bubbly would loosen up Scooby. Scrappy looks pretty loose already.

"Sounds good!" I say, trying for amenable but essentially uninterested.

For the next two hours, I sit there going through my checklist of objectives and goals, never touching the crystal flute at my elbow, its merry stream of bubbles percolating like a tiny, golden lava lamp.

"Come on, Alex," Scrappy says, shaking the nearly empty Cristal bottle like a maraca. "You're not keeping up!"

I smile and check my watch. Almost five. Good enough for government work. I even have enough of a plan to snow G. A few articles in the mainstream press, nothing controversial. Some AIDS fund-raisers. The Matthew Shepard anniversary. Maybe even some testimony at congressional hearings or something. It could all just work. It'd better, otherwise all that's left for these two is cable movies and hosting *Hollywood Squares.* I reach for the glass and its gorgeous nectar gilds my throat. I look around the room, deep in shadow with the late-afternoon sun falling across the floor. I'm exhausted but I've done what I needed to do. Broken the ice, gotten them to trust me. At least it looks that way, since Scooby is all but prone on the sofa, her arms folded under her head, with Scrappy curled at her feet like a cat.

I take another sip of champagne. Maybe Scrappy will start licking her paws.

"It's all about perception, and the media creates that," Scooby suddenly blurts out, struggling to sit up, accidentally kicking Scrappy in the process. "If the media decided to say, 'Let's put them back on top because they're underdogs,' I guarantee you that studios would offer us jobs. But not one magazine has gotten behind us."

Okay, happy hour is over. "Well, I don't think that's true," I say, putting my glass down and wracking my memory for some recent article, *any* article on them that has been favorable.

"For some reason, collectively they all decided 'Let's not support them,'" Scooby goes on, her voice angry now. "I can't even look at magazines anymore."

I see my entire afternoon beginning to unravel. "Well, I don't think—" I start but Scrappy cuts me off. "Certainly this town could decide as quickly as they decided the other way that 'Hey, they're hot,'" she pipes.

"It *can* change," says Scooby gloomily. "But it's not up to *us.*"

I have to get out of here. Any moment, they'll turn on me and their whole fallen state of grace will be my fault. And my first assignment from G will just go south. "Yes, well, I think we've made some good progress this afternoon, although obviously there is a lot of work to do," I say, scrambling to my feet.

Who am I kidding? This is going to be an uphill slog all the way.

Actors are notoriously thin-skinned yet tone-deaf to the nuances of the public, but these two are in a league of their own. After making a hash of their own careers, they are still looking for someone to blame. And now I am the closest target. If G is trying to flush me from the herd, find a reason to fire me or whatever he has up his sleeve, he couldn't have picked a better weapon than these two.

"We're just trying to be truthful," Scooby says, sounding like she might burst into tears. "But we've learned this is a hard town to be truthful in."

Truthful? Truthful? It's a fucking tissue of lies out here in case you haven't noticed.

"Well, I recognize that," I say, knowing I have to say something more. Offer some balm, some salvation. After all, I'm the publicist. The one with answers. So I do what anyone does in Hollywood when her back is against the wall.

"I'll call you," I say, grabbing my bag and fleeing for the exit. "I'll call you and we'll do lunch."

7 | The Invasion of Troy

I have barely an hour at home between Scooby and meeting Troy to change out of my battle fatigues into something sexier but that still screams *I'm really working so don't get any ideas.* Which in my case means replacing my black suit with a pair of black pants, a black sweater, and my black leather jacket—leather jackets are now as ubiquitous in Hollywood as the baseball cap once was. What can I say, black makes me feel safe.

I grab the Pinot Grigio out of the fridge and pour a glass as I dial up my messages on my cell. The usual nonsense. A couple of editors. A studio publicist. Mom with more details about Christmas. Oh God. Deal with that later. Rachel saying she's bored, call her. Steven saying he's going home but call him later. Steven again, saying sorry but here's Charles's cell phone number. Finally. Charles. *Charles!*

"Hi, it's me. Sorry I missed you. Your assistant gave me your cell phone and told me you were doing your meet-and-greet with Scooby. Can't wait to hear about that. So listen, I'm coming back to L.A. on Saturday and was wondering if you can do dinner that night. I know it's kind of last-minute and you probably have plans but I thought I'd take a shot. I'm sick of work getting in the way of this. So leave me a message at the office. Or try me on my cell."

It takes a second for this to sink in. *I'm sick of work getting in the way of this? This?* Our dinner is a *this*, not work? I play the message again just to make sure. But yes, I heard right. Our dinner is a *this*. Jesus, that's almost a date. I think it's a date. If it's not work, it's a date, right? I mean, why would he suggest dinner instead of lunch if it's not really a date? I think it's a date. I'm going with date.

I punch up Steven's cell to fly all this by him but hang up before he can answer. Can't check in with nanny every five seconds. Besides, it's seven o'clock—ten in New York—and given that I have less than half an hour before I'm due to meet Troy, I'd rather talk to Charles than Steven. I start to dial Charles's cell but stop. Wait, what am I going to say if I get him? *Of course I have no plans on Saturday? I never have plans on Saturdays because I have no life and anything I was planning on doing on Saturday is just killing time before I die?* Fuck. I forgot there's a party Rachel was dragging me to. Oh, fuck it, there's always a party. I'm going to dinner. I take a breath and dial again.

Rats. *His* voice mail. Oh, well. "Hey, it's me. Got your message. Yeah, Saturday is actually good. I mean, there is a party. There *was* a party, but you know, there's *always* a party and I'm with you, let's do this."

Let's do this? What am I saying?

"Let's do this *dinner*," I say quickly. "And yes, I, ah, can fill you in on Scooby and also my meeting with Doug and Troy because my day is not over yet." I'm starting to ramble. Get out. Now. "So, yes, Saturday's good and call me. Call me and, uh, and I'll see you soon."

I hang up and realize I'm short of breath. An hour ago I was ready to open a vein and now I'm Dorothy waking up in a snowstorm sent by Glinda the Good Witch. Even the thought of spending the next three hours riding herd on Troy doesn't dampen my spirits. I drain the last of my glass, grab my jacket, and head out to the House of Chanel. To my evening, which is most definitely not a date.

Even before I make the turn off Santa Monica, I see the klieg lights raking the sky. This seems a little overkill for a retail event. Who's coming to this thing besides Troy? Should have checked. Oh, well, too late now. I turn left onto Rodeo and spot the clutch of valets and the crowd already forming in the glare of the video cameras down the block. I glide down the street past the glowing windows—Prada, Ralph Lauren, Armani, Hermès—and the side-walks empty of the usual Eurotrash tourists, slip into the valet line, and wait my turn.

Good evening, good evening. Yes, yes, I'm here for the event. Yes, thank you. Yes, yes, I will have a good time. I take the ticket from the chattering, smiling valets and head toward the crowd. My heels sink into the red carpet—that familiar cushiony walk of fame— when I feel one of the pangs I feel whenever I attend one of these things now. That feeling of what? Guilt? Fear? Or maybe it's just that gnawing sense that it's all a little too let-them-eat-cake. I mean, don't the valets ever get sick of telling perfumed, blow-dried, high-heeled chicas like me to have a good time at a party that they will never in a million years get closer to than where they are now? That there are limits to what even Carla Selena—the Latina queen—can do with a wave of her pop-cultural wand?

I move into the crowd, which is already packed with the usual pretty young things waving and smiling at the screaming photog-raphers, trying to shake off my unease—*think of Charles, think of our date.* Out of the corner of my eye, I see a cameraman heading in my direction and I duck quickly to get out of his way. Actually he's chasing some willowy blonde in a leather jacket up the carpet. Is that Charlize? Actually, it could be. Jesus. I look around, squint-ing in the glare of the lights, and realize there are a number of stars—Christian Slater, Daryl Hannah, Courteney Cox—on the carpet chatting with reporters. Why didn't I know this was a thing? Somebody else in the office had to know this was a thing. Why didn't I? For a brief second, I feel another stab of fear. That I'm being set up. I'm being set up by Peg, who is in cahoots with G.

Okay, I've already had enough paranoia for one day. I don't need to see ghosts everywhere.

"Hey, Alex!" I look over and recognize another publicist, from BOB, I think. Melinda, I think. Or Mindy. A million publicists in the big city. I can't know them all. Who would want to?

"Hey," I shout back and give her a wave like she's my best friend.

"Hey," Melinda or whatever-her-name-is says, wriggling through the crowd toward me. "Did you know this was going to be this big?" she says, shouting over the roar.

"I don't even know what it's for," I shout back. "I just got a call from my client's manager asking me to be here. A last-minute thing."

"Who's the client?"

"What?" I practically scream but my voice is all but drowned out by the crowd and some engine roar from the street. Some star's limo or maybe it's the Harleys arriving.

"*Who's the client?*" Melinda yells again.

"*Oh!*" I say. "Troy Madden."

"Troy Madden?" She sounds incredulous.

"Uh, yeah. Why?"

"Isn't that him?" she says, nodding over my shoulder toward the street.

I turn around in time to catch the crowd parting like the Red Sea and Troy, astride a gleaming Harley and with a lit cigar in his mouth, rocketing up the carpet, through the open front door, and into the Chanel boutique.

By the time I claw my way through the crowd and into the store, they're pretty much done sweeping up the glass. Apparently Troy managed to stick his Evel Knievel landing—his little stunt was actually planned, or as planned as Troy plans anything—but he did collide with one of the waiters, an accident that sent a tray of filled champagne flutes flying. Fortunately, none of the merchandise was hit by the spray; there are only a few slightly damp guests who are doing their best to laugh off the accident. At least it looks like they're laughing in the midst of all those towel-bearing Chanel minions. God knows Troy's feeling no pain. Blowing smoke rings while leaning against the Harley, which is parked now in the center of the store, Troy is all but holding court in his leather jacket and T-shirt. Like Steve McQueen in *The Great Escape*. A man who never looks better than when he's in some sort of trouble.

"I've ridden these for years," I hear Troy say in his unmistakable drawl. "And don't call 'em hogs. They resent that, you know," he says, giving the Harley a pat. "Best bikes money can buy. Shit, I rode one all the way from Des Moines to Tampa one spring break. Better than a car."

Well, at least he's not going anywhere for a minute. I take a second to glance around the store. What the hell is this event? More important, whose idea was Troy's rocket-from-the-crypt arrival? I hope the dealership's, although considering the Chanel gift bags lined up by the door, this is a Chanel event to promote its new "Harley" bag, which, judging by all the Plexiglas displays, is a slouchy shoulder bag in navy or black leather, with a rather nasty-looking chain available in stainless steel or vermeil.

"What do you say we fire it up?" I hear Troy say. My cue.

"Hey there, Troy." I dive into the crowd and surface next to his elbow. "Hey, how's it going? That was some arrival."

"Hey, Alex!" Troy says, looking at me in that lazy, unstartled way stars do. Like their every waking moment is just one endless tape loop of *This Is Your Life*—a parade of adoring faces so that the unexpected arrival of anyone from their long-dead mother to the president is greeted with cool indifference because, after all, who wouldn't want to be with them?

"Hey, did you see me ride up?" he says, tipping his head back and exhaling a series of smoke rings.

Very cute. At least it's tobacco. "Yeah, couldn't miss that," I say, shaking my head and smiling. Stay cool, stay loose, but stay on him. "Is this your bike?" I say, turning toward him and away from the crowd and dropping my voice. The last thing Troy needs is an audience. Here, anyway. "I think Peg said you had a couple of these."

"This? Nah, my bikes are home sleeping it off. This baby's brand-new. A loaner. In fact, I was just offering to give test drives," he says, slapping the Harley's gleaming belly.

"Well, maybe later," I say, grabbing Troy's elbow. "Actually, is the Harley dealer here yet? I think they probably want some pictures of the two of you."

I swirl into action, grateful to have a task, a toy to shove into the baby's hand. Find the dealer, find the photographer. Okay, everyone smile. Smile. One more? Sure, why not. Smile, Troy. Smile, Troy. Oh, here's the Chanel vice president. Oh, *executive* vice president. Sorry. Yes, a few more shots. Of course. Smile. The bags? Yes, let's get the bags in the shot. Now the Harley. Sure. The Harley. Okay, here's Courteney Cox. Sure, Troy and Courteney. Daryl. Where's Daryl? Here she is. Smile, everyone. Smile, Troy.

I look at my watch and realize more than an hour has gone by. My feet are screaming and I would kill for a glass of champagne, but baby-sitting Troy requires at least one of us to have a clear head and even if he were stone cold sober, that would never be true in his case.

I glance at Troy, who's locked in what looks like a serious discussion with Daryl Hannah and the Harley dealership owner. I decide to chance a run to the bar.

"Long night?" the bartender says, handing me a dripping bottle of Evian.

"Oh God, does it look like it?" I say, instinctively reaching to wipe mascara from under my eyes.

"No, I just saw you with that guy," he says, nodding in Troy's direction.

"Yeah," I say, rolling my eyes. "He's a handful."

"Is he your date?"

"Is he my date?" I blurt out. It would probably be a lot easier if he were my date. "No, he's my client. I'm his publicist."

"His *publicist?* That guy needs a publicist? Who is he?"

Who is he? Every photographer here and even the valets at Smashbox know who Troy is, but this guy, who is no doubt a wannabe actor just in from fly-over country, has no idea who Troy is? God, Troy was out of the picture in rehab for what, nine months? And this guy is acting like he's no more famous than a contestant on *American Idol.*

"Troy *Madden?*" I say, snapping into my best *and-you-are?* voice. Sometimes you just have to trot it out. Besides, even I'll admit Troy looks pretty damn good tonight in that jacket and cigar and the Harley between his legs. "He did a lot of movies. And then he took some time off." It's amazing how easily this stuff just falls from my lips.

"Oh, right," the bartender says, nodding again, and I can tell he's still clueless. "Well, it looked like you were his date."

"Okay, well, I'm not," I say, surprised at how annoyed I am. "This is my job. I'm being paid to be here."

Okay, that doesn't sound good. Even I can tell that, but before I can fix it, make it clear to this dimwit just how important Troy and I are at this party, I hear my name—"Alex, is it?"—being called in an accented voice over my shoulder.

"Yes," I say, whirling around to face one of the Chanel minions, a vision of blond hair and quilted leather. Must be nice, that corporate discount.

"Alex? You are with Troy, no?" she says.

"No. Well, yes. Yes, I am here with him. Is there some problem?" I say, looking past her to scan the crowd. No sight of Troy.

"Mr. Troy asked me to tell you that he was going for a ride."

"A *ride?*" I feel my pulse start to rise. "Where?" I say, scanning the crowd again, and I realize that the Harley is also AWOL. "What *kind* of a ride?"

"I don't know, but he asked me to tell you he would be back."

Oh God. What am I, away from his side for five, ten minutes and he just takes off?

"Okay, thanks," I say, flashing a steely smile and plunging into the crowd. Find the Harley dealer and find out what's the deal with the bike. If I can locate the bike, I'll find Troy. I roam the store a couple of times, but no luck. Where is everyone? I realize the crowd is starting to thin and already there is a steady stream of people heading for the door armed with their white Chanel gift bags. For a brief second I wonder what the gift is. Can't be the actual Harley bag? Not at fifteen hundred bucks a pop. Okay, forget the gift bag. Focus. Find Troy and the bike before something else gets busted up.

"Hey, Alex," I hear behind me. I turn and see Mindy, Melinda, whatever, coming toward me carrying three gift bags.

"Oh hey," I say distractedly. "You're leaving?"

"Yeah, they want to close pretty soon," she says, fumbling with the bags. "Are you walking out? Did Troy already leave?"

"Good question," I say, and instantly regret my candor.

"Yeah, I heard he took off on the bike with one of the Chanel people."

"Yeah, apparently it's a loaner," I say, backpedaling frantically. "Too bad we all didn't get them."

"Well, don't forget your gift bag," she says, shaking her stash at me. "It's a good one."

I could care less about the damn gift bag right now, but I play along. "Really?"

"Yeah, there's a key chain—it's cute, quilted and with the double C's—a copy of *Cycle World*, and a coupon toward the Harley bag. I'm hoping I can use three toward one bag."

I inhale sharply between my teeth. This is what it's come to? Hustling for a key chain and a coupon?

"Yeah, I know," Mindy-Melinda says, misreading my reaction. "It's a good deal."

It's nearly ten and I'm about to pack it in—just the caterers cleaning up and the valets standing around looking cold and bored, a few lingering photographers—when my cell phone rings. My plan—and I have one—is to give Troy until ten and then call it a night. God knows, Peg would have bailed hours ago. Unless it's an award show, the usual drill is show up, walk the carpet with the client, get them situated, and then split. So what am I doing here hanging around like a White House advance man?

"Hey," says the voice on my cell when I click on. Troy. Sounding like he's in a wind tunnel.

"Where are you?" I say casually.

"Well, turn around and you'll see."

I hear a roar like a 747 coming in for a landing.

I turn and see Troy coming up Rodeo looking like Steve McQueen trying to take that barbed-wire fence just before he got nailed by the Nazis.

"Hey," he says, pulling up and giving me a fat, lazy grin.

"Where's your date?" I holler over the Harley's throaty idle.

"My date?"

"The Chanel publicist?"

"Oh. I lost her."

"You *lost* her?"

"Yeah, back there somewhere," he says, nodding over his shoulder.

I don't really want to know.

"Okay, so you're good to go on that?" I say, nodding at the bike, trying to assess Troy's state of equilibrium. His chances of getting home without some Halle Berry hit-and-run.

"Yeah, let's go. Let's take a ride."

"No way," I say, shaking my head.

"Come on. Just down the block. Spago. One drink."

Normally this would be a no-brainer. Client and publicist getting to know each other. Kick around a few ideas. Form a bond. And frankly, a drink is overdue after the day I've had.

"Nah, got an early day tomorrow," I say. I start to add "Let's do it another time," when Troy reaches up and pushes a strand of hair off my cheek.

Okay, that's a little out there. But just ambiguous enough that I choose to ignore it.

"So let's do it another time," I say, shaking my hair off my face, when Troy runs his finger down the side of my cheek. Okay, *that's* a problem. I'm just deciding whether to say something or just let it go when I hear a commotion behind me. The valets.

"Okay, Troy," I say, fishing in my bag for my claim check when he slides his hand around the base of my neck and pulls me toward him.

Oh God! Troy Madden is kissing me on *Rodeo Drive.* Oh God! And in front of all the valets or whoever is making that racket behind us.

"So let me get this straight. He kisses you. The guy shoots the picture and then Troy hits him?" Steven says.

"Actually, he only tried to hit the camera. But he missed. Another guy got that picture."

I'm lying on my bed, a cold washcloth on my eyes, trying to get some early polling data on the night's events.

"So what do you think?" I say.

"That he's channeling Alec Baldwin."

"Thanks for that comparison," I say miserably. "Alec doesn't have a publicist anymore."

"Or a career."

"Oh, that cheers me right up." Five hours ago, I thought Scooby was going to be my big problem. Or Val. Now I'm costarring in an episode of *When Good Stars Go Bad.*

"Look, if the guy presses charges, it's a thing for Troy's lawyer. Not you," Steven adds.

"Except I'm in the shot and there's no way that's not going to wind up all over the tabs and *Access Hollywood.* I'm fucked."

Steven doesn't say anything for a minute. Which only depresses me further.

"You know, if it was still just Suzanne, I could explain it," I say. "But G. I swear he's just looking for a reason to cut me loose. Cut any of us loose."

"Okay, now you're definitely getting ahead of yourself. Look, get some sleep. Things will look brighter tomorrow. It's not like *you* hit the guy. Besides, you know what they say."

"If you can't afford a lawyer, one will be appointed for you?"

"All publicity is good publicity."

"Keep reminding me of that," I say. "Better yet, remind G."

I hang up and realize that in all the excitement, I forgot to tell him about Charles. My date with Charles. A call which already seems like a lifetime ago.

8 | Facing the Music

Morning arrives way too early, the way it always does in L.A. You're barely cogent at 7 A.M. but everyone in New York has already read the *Post* and is going at the world hammer and tongs. I pull the pillow over my head to stifle the noise. Upstairs in the kitchen, I hear the phone ring and decide to change tactics. Hide out in the shower, where I never hear anything except my own inner ravings. *Get a life, get a life.* Or its variant: *Get a haircut. Get a haircut.* I roll out of bed, late before I've even started.

By the time I pull into the DWP garage, I'm at least awake, although there is an unpleasant spasming somewhere in my nether regions that is proving to be not the chorus of choice to my inner closing arguments. There's no way the *Post* had my little *amuse-bouche* with Troy. And the attendant fisticuffs. Not yet. I don't know exactly when the *Post* closes, but it has to be before midnight, and given that Troy went off his rocker somewhere around 10 P.M. PST, well, Counselor, you do the math.

My theory lasts as far as the office.

"I have two words for you: *digital images,*" Steven says, dropping the *Post*—open to page ten, where "Page Six" for some reason inexplicably runs—onto my desk.

"Those *fuckers*."

As if last night weren't still vivid enough in my mind, now I'm confronted with wall-to-wall photos. "Boy Toy Troy" with his unnamed "Secret Gal Pal." And "Bad Boy Toy Troy" taking swings at everything in his path. The fact that I am unrecognizable but the Chanel sign is clearly visible does not improve my mood.

"And they say there are no more useful inventions in the twenty-first century."

Normally, I would whip out some snappy retort, some acidic Nora response to Steven's WASPy Nick commentary—all we needed was little Asta nipping at our heels—but this is a little too close to home and all I can get out is "Those *fuckers*," again.

"That much is clear, but I actually have to say, as Bad Boy Troy's Secret Gal Pal, your hair looks great."

Really? I lean over his shoulder to get a better look. He's right. My hair does look surprisingly good. Especially in the second shot, where my head is flying back as Troy takes a swing at the photographer.

"Wow," I say, before I can stop myself.

"But black-and-white is always kinder than color."

Okay, this is not the day for Nick and Nora. This is serious. This is bad. This could really be putting the bat in G's hands. As if he doesn't already have his own weapons cache.

"Oh, and before I forget," Steven adds, pulling out a stack of pink "While You Were Out" slips and dropping them onto my desk like confetti. "Your fans."

I look at the slips. *Access Hollywood. ET. Variety.* Peg. Oh *great.*

"How do they know it's me?" I mew, sinking into my chair. "I'm not ID'ed. Not even in the cutline."

Steven looks at me like I've taken leave of my senses.

"You're his *publicist*! Who else would they call? Actually," he pauses a little too theatrically, "a few of them did call Suzanne. And G. They both would like a word."

Like a word? I feel like I am skidding on ice. Yesterday, I was a girl in love, heading for the date of my dreams with only the speed bump of an annoying PR event in my path. Today, I'm all over the *Post*—or my hair is—and in a dog fight for my career. And Steven's little bitchier-than-bitchiness is not helping.

"Okay, can you just dial down the queeniness here? The guy I called last night seemed to at least understand the magnitude of the problem. Why are you acting like this is a huge joke?"

Steven hunches his shoulders, which I take to be contrition. "Sorry, we're genetically programmed to default to bitchiness in the face of stress. But you're right," he says. "And I haven't even mentioned the lawsuit yet."

Of course, there's a lawsuit. Why not turn the bad dream into a full-blown nightmare? Hell, let's go all the way and make it a segment on *Jerry Springer.*

"Peg called to give you the heads-up. The photographer filed suit against Troy in Beverly Hills court this morning. Assault. Or maybe battery. It's unclear if he actually struck him or they just collided."

The skidding gives way to the sound of squealing brakes. Before I can think of anything remotely cogent to say in response, there's a knock at the door. Leslie or Letty or whoever Suzanne's latest minion is, sent to fit me for the hangman's noose. "She wants to see you before you head over to G's," the minion says, her voice triumphant.

Even in my altered state, I know that's a mistake.

"She *knows,* Lexus," Steven says, whipping out his best fuck-off-and-die voice. I love it when he does that. On my behalf.

"It's A-*lexis,*" the minion snaps.

"Sorry," Steven says, not missing a beat. "I keep forgetting people actually named their children after *Dynasty* characters. Well, *Alexis,* I'll give you a heads-up when she's on her way."

The minion tosses her hair and huffs out.

"Thanks," I say to Steven and I mean it. I'll take my defenders where I can find them. "Is there anything else I should know? Has Troy called? Do we even know where he is?"

"No, but there is one thing in your favor. The rumor around here is that you're the gal pal, but so far no one from the media has made you. I'd go with a Chanel flack, but it's your call. But the bigger news is the Phoenix walked."

It takes me a minute to switch gears. "The Phoenix?" I repeat uncomprehendingly.

"As in Suzanne's legendary client. The one you handled off and on when you first arrived at DWP. The one who just signed her gazillion-dollar deal with MTV to star in her own reality series, which everyone says is just a rip-off of *The Osbournes*, but at least it's not Liza on prime time."

For some reason, Steven's chatter is the perfect white noise. I lose the squealing brakes and feel my mind begin to clear. Form actual patterns. I reach for a pencil and anchor my hair. The Phoenix walking—whatever the reasons—is a bigger blow to BIG-DWP than Troy's stupid antics. The Phoenix is a legend in Holly-wood. Half Swedish, half Latina—she is said to be distantly related to both Ann-Margret and Raquel Welch (née Tejada), as if that were even possible—the Phoenix is a class unto herself. Rock star, Oscar-winning actress, QVC queen, the Phoenix has had more careers than J. Lo has had husbands and she has always come up a winner with both the public and at the bank. Now at an age when most actresses shuffle off to the London stage and strip down to their breast-lifted, lipo-ed birthday suits to keep their ca-reer flame burning, the Phoenix is heading into her fourth or fifth incarnation with a $20 million TV deal.

Amazingly, the Phoenix has been a DWP client for years, our first and only trophy client until Suzanne signed Carla. Now with her abrupt departure so soon after Carla bolted, G is facing much bigger problems than me and Troy. Actually, *Suzanne* has much bigger problems than me and Troy. In fact, I'm a minor disturbance in this larger exodus of talent. Okay, talent is a stretch, but their checks clear every month. And in the case of the Phoenix's, they are considerable. Suzanne will have to answer for this, especially given how the rest of the DWP list is basically DOA.

As for Troy, it won't take much to turn this into a plus. Or at least not a negative. Russell Crowe is always taking swings at photographers. Shit, Sean Penn is always taking swings at photographers. And he went to Iraq and on *Charlie Rose* to talk about world peace. I just have to move Troy closer to Sean's righteous anger than Alec Baldwin's loutishness. Beside, isn't the whole paparazzi thing out of control? Ever since Princess Di died and Disney bailed out Jann Wenner's annoying *US Weekly* so it could go neck and neck—and dollar for dollar—with *People,* the bar has been unduly raised on the Hollywood celebrity photo. And clearly digital cameras are *not* helping.

"So has Suzanne met with G yet?" I say so suddenly that Steven looks startled.

"Uhm, no. I think words were just exchanged over the phone. He's supposed to meet with her later today."

"So she'll be much more focused on trying to finesse the Phoenix's bolting than Troy's contretemps, although she'll try and act like I'm the one whose neck's on the line."

"A minute ago you were Bambi in the headlights, now you're Donald Rumsfeld?" Steven says, arching his eyebrows.

I ignore him. "So we're not talking to the media until I meet with Suzanne and G. Meanwhile, call everyone back—except Peg, I'll deal with her—and give them some bullshit statement to tide them over. 'It's all a misunderstanding and Troy Madden looks forward to setting the record straight.'

"No, wait," I say, raising my hands. " 'Ever since Troy Madden returned home from rehab, he's been trying to lead a normal private life, but the constant hounding of the media—and photographers in particular—has made this all but impossible. While Mr.

Madden regrets any confusion that occurred last night and he looks forward to setting the record straight, he would like to plead, on behalf of himself and his family as well as his fans, to be given a chance to continue his recovery without the constant and disruptive presence of the media.' "

"I'd hire you," Steven says, grabbing a pen and starting to scribble, "and I know you're making it up as you go along."

"Look, this all goes away. It *always* goes away. Jack Nicholson? Halle Berry? It's just a question of how much money has to change hands and when. Unless someone actually gets murdered."

"Or gets caught shoplifting at Saks."

"Yeah, but this is the media and everyone hates the media. Especially photographers. I'm telling you, the public buys the magazines, but they identify with the star. How else do you explain the success of *InStyle*? I'm betting one court appearance and the judge dismisses or Troy writes a check."

"So there's just one question, Counselor," Steven says, smiling. "Who's the 'Gal Pal'?"

Right. The Gal Pal.

"Let me see the pictures again," I say, reaching for the *Post*. My face is a blur but my hair does look good. A Clairol ad.

"It's not like you actually see him *kissing* me," I say, thinking out loud. "I'm just *there*. Why wouldn't I be out with my client? Can I help it if I look like his date and not his mother?"

"Gal Pal," Steven says, extending his hand. "I've always wanted to meet you."

I send Steven out for coffee, tell reception to pick up my calls while I hit the wires. Judge the damage for myself.

Other than the *Post* and an AP and Reuters item on the entertainment sites, there's not too much. Not yet. *ET* and *Access Hollywood* will have it tonight. Probably their lead item. The lawsuit will make the legit papers tomorrow, so there's definitely work to do.

I decide my counterattack of the-media's-relentless-hounding-of-the-just-out-of-rehab-trying-to-get-his-life-back-in-order-so-leave-my-client-alone tactic is the right one. I just have to make sure Troy doesn't surface and fuck it up. I try his various numbers and get only his machines. Probably still sleeping it off. I leave messages on them all telling him to stay put and whatever he does, do not—do *not*—talk to anyone. I put in a call to Peg to cover my ass. Thank God you can never reach her even when all hell is breaking loose. I tell Steven to fax her office with our statement—our *provisional* statement—and alert Ms. Lexus I'm on my way.

My plan is to test the waters with Suzanne—find out where on the Richter scale Troy actually registers vis-à-vis the Phoenix—and then face G and spend the rest of the day on the phones doing damage control. Already the word in the hive is that the Phoenix walking is big, but not *that* big. She is making the inevitable "changes" now that her career is taking off again. On the advice of her lawyer. Or her agent. Or whoever has put the bee in her bonnet that DWP, even BIG-DWP, isn't big enough for her. Normally such musical chairs among clients and publicists isn't even newsworthy, barely makes *Variety*. Only when *agents* lose clients can heads roll. But given BIG-DWP's fragile state and G's take-no-prisoners attitude, any blood loss is cause for concern.

By the time I get to Suzanne's office, I'm far more anxious to see how she'll spin the Phoenix debacle than I'm worried about any attempted wrist-slapping of me.

"Let me see if she's ready for you," Suzanne's minion says frostily, waving me toward the sofa. "She just got a call."

I shoot her a blissful smile—*hey babe, knock yourself out*—and stay standing, not even bothering to pretend to study the ancient Georgia O'Keeffe lithographs Suzanne keeps on her walls. So seventies. So oddly endearing.

"It might be a minute," the minion says, trying again. I shoot her another *fuck-you* smile. *Like I said babe, I got all day.*

When I am finally, grumpily waved in, Suzanne is predictably tight-lipped, dressed like Ashley Wilkes in another one of her white suits and going in a million directions at once in her South Carolina drawl.

"Alex, we ah not off to a good start," she says, not looking up from her desk, but focusing, a little too intently, it seems, on the piles of papers she's sorting through.

What does she mean, *good start*? To the day? To the merger? To my signing Troy? But then, obfuscation, not precision, is the name of our game.

"Tell me whut exactly happened," she says, glancing up and waving me to her office sofa—white Haitian cotton, another seventies affectation. This time, I obey and sink gingerly onto its spongy, stained surface.

"Look, I won't pretend this is a plus, but we can spin this in a way that works for everyone," I say, bypassing a recitation of last night's events and moving directly to The Solution. If I'm supposed to fake out the public, why not my boss?

"Really?" Suzanne says, eyeing me sharply. "How's that?"

Okay, maybe this won't be a slam dunk. There's a reason why she's lasted as long as she has: that before she became officially over the hill, Suzanne was once considered good at her job. Brilliant, even. Still, these are dangerous times and I'm reluctant to be totally honest.

"Look, I'll be honest," I say. "Troy is proving to be more of a handful than I—than *we*—were led to believe. It's one reason why I'm having to baby-sit him at so many routine events. I'm meeting with Peg to go over exactly where we are in his rehab schedule. I mean, it could be that we're in some recidivistic situation here, although I don't want to use the words *Robert Downey, Jr.* At least outside this office."

It's a bit much but I'm betting that among the BIG-DWPers, she and I are the only ones who can use *recidivistic* in a sentence. And that she knows it.

"Go ahn," she says, mustering a sterner tone than her expression conveys.

"Well, until we get a clearer bead on Troy's, ah, behavioral limits, I'm recommending that we take him, temporarily of course, out of circulation. Forget the events. The meet-and-greets. Let Peg do the heavy lifting. Get him an actual job and then we'll go back to work."

Suzanne nods, which I take to be a green, or at least a yellow, light and plunge ahead.

"In the meantime, I'll be dealing with the media today. I've already prepared our statement," I say, rising and handing her a printout. "And I'll be getting on the phone this afternoon. Then, depending on what happens to the court case—although I'm banking on a dismissal—I'll handle that."

She doesn't say anything for a minute as she reads my statement. And then rereads it.

Okay, I can wait for my final grade. I slide my hands underneath my thighs and hunch up my shoulders, leaning forward on the sofa. If my feet didn't reach the floor, I would wag them. Just a kid in the principal's office.

She picks up a pen and makes a few editing marks. And a few more.

Oh, come *on*. It sounds like a plan and you know it.

"So, Gal Pal," Suzanne says, looking up finally. "Sounds like ah plan."

It's a good parting shot, but we both know I'm home free with the requisite slap on the wrist. Time for my *mea culpa*'s and I'm outta there.

"Look, I was there. *Of course* I was there," I say, dropping my eyes to my lap—*okay, you got me*—where I realize bits of Haitian cotton have shed onto my black pants. No wonder it went out of fashion. "But if you're asking me did I see Troy's inclination to fisticuffs and could I have stopped it?" I say, raising my face, eyes wide. "No."

"So the photo was just—"

"Routine," I say quickly, cutting her off.

You got me. I'm the Gal Pal. Now, let's move *on.*

"Troy had left and then he suddenly showed back up on the bike, looking a little the worse for wear, I might add."

Let's not forget who's really the asshole here.

"They snapped. Literally. Who wouldn't shoot him?"

"And yew wuh just—"

"Waiting for my car," I say, shrugging. "I assumed Troy was long gone."

Spinning always goes best when you wind up at the truth. Even if you have to lie to get there.

"Speaking of long gone," I add, eager to move to new business. "I hear we actually did lose a client."

Suzanne's smile evaporates. I may be off the hook, but don't fuck with her.

"Don't believe everything you hear, Alex," she says evenly and I wonder, for just a second, if I don't hear more sadness than anger in her voice.

"So I'll let Doug know you and I have spoken," she says, standing, handing me my edited statement. My trip to the woodshed is officially over. "But he'll want to meet with you in any event. And I want you to keep us both apprised of what happens today and with the court case."

I make the appropriately conciliatory noises and head for the door. But when I glance back over my shoulder to make my goodbyes and catch her standing there in her suit that I realize is a little rumpled, I feel a similar stab of, what—guilt? fear? sorrow?— that I felt for the valets last night. At one time, she was a legend. Or as much of a legend as a woman who is not an A-list star is likely to be in Hollywood. *Suzanne Davis. The publicist who pioneered the post-studio-era Hollywood PR machinery.* She'd even won a Producers Guild Award and had a whole section in *Variety* devoted to her. Now, at fifty-three, she looks battle-weary, and the same town that once lauded her is ready to consign her to the discard pile. And they've sent G to do the actual garroting.

"You know, I meant to say this earlier," I say suddenly, and I feel my face flush. "I've really learned a lot from you. I mean *you*. Not just DWP," I add, stammering slightly. "So I'm just glad. Glad I got to work here. When it was just your agency. Yours. And not Doug's."

I stop and I realize I'm not spinning her. That I actually mean what I'm saying. *Whoa*. Isn't this what I was wailing to Steven about the other night. *Authenticity?* Well, be careful what you wish for. Because authenticity or sincerity or whatever this is feels odd. Like a "very special episode" of *Frasier*, or *Friends*, or something.

"Okay," I say, rushing to restore the world to rights and my tone of self-mockery. "Alex, thanks for sharing—"

But Suzanne cuts me off. "If Peg gives you any shit," she says, matching me olive branch for olive branch, "tell her to talk to me."

My warm and runny feminist bonhomie lasts as far as BIG's outer offices—still Christo-ed in all that plastic sheeting—where I am instantly waved on in. I should take this as a good sign. *A member of the team*. But I have only the look of the guilty. A sheep to the abattoir.

I take a minute to hide out in the bathroom, gather my thoughts. But it's amazing how even here, with the tasteful white phalaenopsis and the flickering red currant bougie perfuming the air, I feel G's bullying presence.

I make a note never to buy overpriced French red currant candles—and certainly never date any man who does—and head out, hoping some fresh burst of courage will hit me. But the distance from the bathroom to G's office is short. Much too short. Not even the second minion—again I am waved on in—slows me down.

And then I am here, swaying slightly on G's spongy carpet,

breathing in his leather-scented air, ready to meet my maker. The glowering Toby jug behind the leather desk, the *Post* spread out before him. Even before he speaks, I can tell this will be much worse than I anticipated. That I'm about to get up-close-and-personal with G's legendary short fuse.

"I know you've been through this already, but if you could, ah, indulge me with an explanation of last night's events, that would be so helpful."

Sarcasm. Right off the bat. Whatever playbook I had driving over here is clearly out the window. I take a second to stall for time. Look around, like I'm not sure whether I should sit or stand. Which I'm not. But G is not into any routine pleasantries.

"I don't care if you stand on your head," he snaps, spittle flying. "Just tell me what happened. Or should I say your *version* of what happened."

I feel my face instantly flush. Like I've been slapped. Which, I realize, I have. In all my time as a publicist, I've had my share of spoiled clients, bossy managers, and patronizing assistants. Seen plenty of petulant, rude behavior. Head-fucking, even. But I've never had any real contact with the pros—the screamers, the producers who throw phones at their assistants, the studio bosses who physically threaten their lessers, the agents who—well, agents are in a class by themselves. I do not realize, until this meeting with G, how incomplete my Hollywood education has been.

"I'm waiting."

G drums his nails on the desk, the light glinting from their polished surface.

I take a good breath. The old Hail Mary.

"So you actually broke down crying?" Steven says when I reach him on my cell as I'm heading out of the BIG garage. Burning rubber, actually. Can't put enough distance between me and G.

"No, it was more like *tremulousness*. The quivering damsel in distress."

"But the effect was what? 'If you hit me, I'll fall apart'?"

"Are you kidding? With all that leather in there? I was going for 'If you hit me, I'll come.' "

"Oh, *fuck* you," Steven says, sputtering with laughter. "You were not. Besides, you don't even live in West Hollywood."

"Hey, I've been to the Pleasure Chest," I say. "No, I just beat G to the punch. 'You can't punish me worse than I'm punishing myself.' It always worked great on my parents."

"But I thought he blamed you for letting the evening get out of hand."

"No, I blamed *Troy* for letting the evening get out of hand and I asked G for his advice and counsel, blah, blah, blah. By the end, he was practically showing me tae kwan do moves. That whole Mike Ovitz thing. 'I'm a killer, but I'm Zen about it.' He said it was a great way to fend off 'overly aggressive' photographers. And clients, I guess. He never got that specific and I sure didn't. Besides," I say, anxious to move the conversation along, "G has bigger fish to fry with Suzanne and the Phoenix."

"Speaking of which. Suzanne put out a memo."

"I heard that. What does it say?"

" 'A loss but not unexpected. Redouble our efforts. A time of consolidation and change.' The basic."

The basic. If there is anything about this day, this week, it's definitely not basic. What was it, a month ago, I was bored out of my mind? Now every breath requires a game plan. Just to get through the day.

"So you're coming back?" Steven says. "Because there are tons of calls."

Where else would I go? I glance at my watch: just about three. Just twenty-four hours since Charles asked me out. Since daylight pierced the shroud. Now, I'm back in the smoke and ash. Hours of phoning ahead of me, hours of stamping out Troy's fire. Suddenly I'm exhausted, wrung out from my meeting with G.

"No, I'm coming back to put out the fires," I say, a tad too heartily.

"To put out the fires," Steven repeats.

"And then I'm getting ready for my date with Charles."

"Your date with Charles," Steven says, and I can't tell if he's teasing me or mocking me or is just as spaced out as I feel.

"Yes, my date with Charles," I say, clicking off. My date with Charles. My date with Charles. My date with Charles.

9 | No, but I Can Hum a Few Bars

Saturday dawns, not with salvation but terror. My date with Charles.

Oh God. I haven't been on a date since . . . I can't even remember when.

There was a producer, I think, when I first moved to L.A. Or maybe he was just a DWP client I was baby-sitting. Anyway, he spent more time talking on his cell phone than talking to me. And then there was drinks with that stuntman. That was more like Margaret Mead out with the natives than a date, although Steven thinks I cut the research unduly short when I decided not to sleep with him. "Five percent body fat, but you couldn't get past the lack of a BA," Steven had said, sounding genuinely shocked. "You'll never get laid in this town."

And then Rachel tried to fix me up with some cousin. A dentist or a chiropractor from Scarsdale who was in town shopping a screenplay.

Oh, fuck it. I haven't had a real date since I left New York. I don't even know what a real date is anymore. But then, I'm not supposed to know what a date is anymore. I'm supposed to have moved *on* to a real relationship.

I roll over and stare at the magazine pile moldering by my bedside. Isn't this what *Vogue* is for? Or the *Psychoanalytic Review* I'd mistakenly subscribed to back in my therapy days when I was trying to be my own best friend? I root around the pile and find amid the *Food & Wines* and the Brown alumni news a *Vogue* with Charlize on the cover. Jesus, how old is this? And why have I kept it? I flip through the issue. Nothing but the usual fashion screed, which was out of date two minutes after the issue went to press, a feature on brow lifts—have I been thinking of this? *should* I be thinking of this?—and, oh yeah, that director client I had that I managed to get into "People Are Talking About" when in fact no one had talked about him for years.

I toss the *Vogue* aside and roll back in bed, checking my watch: 8 A.M. I've been awake since five and have pretty much memorized all the cracks in the ceiling, not to mention the bags under my eyes when I mistakenly looked in the mirror earlier this morning.

I knew going out drinking last night was a mistake. But it was almost impossible not to. Not after the day I had. Not after we finished rolling the last calls on Troy, and Steven all but dragged me down to Tom Bergin's on Fairfax, our usual hangout when we're on "*E!* Watch"—monitoring news about clients on the Hollywood shows—because they have a TV and a bartender Steven once dated when he was in his Irish phase and we can get him to switch channels at will. Especially when Steven is doing shots.

"You're not watching for Troy on *Access Hollywood* and *ET* in this office," Steven said, handing me my bag. "Not with everyone here waiting to see blood in the water."

In hindsight, we should have stayed, since my spinning of the whole thing—poor, harassed, recovering Troy—played like gangbusters. *I* almost felt sorry for him. They even flashed my official publicist statement on the screen. Word for word.

"I think this means you're a published author," Steven said, raising his glass.

After that we hit Ago. And then Falcon, where even in my lubricated state I realized the crowd was about a generation and several IQ points below where I tend to hover in the food chain. After that, things got hazy. I just remember feeling incredibly happy when I finally got home and found another message from Charles on my machine. "Just checking in." *Checking in? Checking in?* How cool is that? We hadn't even been on our date and already he was "checking in." I was so happy, I crawled into bed with a box of crackers and my cell phone and caught almost all the *Law & Order* rerun I'd Tivo-ed before I fell blissfully asleep.

Now, all I feel is crumbs and the lump of the cell phone and the remote underneath me. And my head. Movement is clearly in order. The tidal pool that's collected under my eyes is not going to recede by itself.

I make my way to the bathroom, where I fumble around for the Advil and squintingly assess the damage. In the early morning light . . . well, never mind. If I can spend the rest of the morning in the tub, tea bags on my eyes, downing about a gallon of Arrowhead, I should rejoin the land of the living. Or at least pass under Orso's lighting. One of the best in town. All shimmery pinks and golds, like a Caravaggio painting. Or a Barbra Streisand special. Everyone in the restaurant looks rested. Serene. Ready for their close-up.

By the time I land at Orso, I feel about as ready for my close-up as I'm going to feel after hours in the tub, a quick trip to Fred Segal, and a professional blow-dry, although at the moment, the only one eyeing me is my sulky-looking waiter. Because Charles's plane is late—he called while they were still over Albuquerque and I was still in the stylist's chair—and because I live way up in the hills and not anywhere near the Peninsula Hotel, where he's staying, he suggested we just meet at the restaurant.

Oh, *great.* Two cars, which will screw up any chance of a long and lingering good-bye at my house or his hotel. No chance of that now. Not in the Orso parking lot buzzing with valets.

"No problem," I lie, yelling over the dryer. "I'll meet you there."

"Look, I know the car thing is a bummer," Steven said when I reached him right before I was leaving for the restaurant. "But let's remember what's really important."

"That we're *both* designated drivers?"

"That no matter what happens, you still have to work with this guy. *For* this guy."

That is unfortunately true. The latest rumor going around is that Charles is the heir apparent to head the New York office. That Stan Woolfe—the W of DWP—is definitely retiring and Charles is to take his place. That he and Suzanne and G will be the jolly triptych heading BIG-DWP although G, technically, is the head cheerleader. Or owner. Or the ranking partner. Or whatever he is.

"So think twice before you fuck your boss," Steven said. "Since you're already fucking with G."

"Thank you, Dr. Phil," I said, clicking off. "I'll be sure to keep my knees closed and my résumé open."

I check my watch. I've been here for ten minutes and still no sign of Charles. First the car thing and now he's late and the waiter has already been by twice—"No, I'm *still* waiting for my guest, thanks"— and I'm starting to get paranoid. Maybe I got the night wrong. Or the place. Maybe I got the whole thing wrong. Why didn't I bring something to read? Right. Marion the Librarian. Just the look we're going for.

I think about calling him. See if he's stuck in traffic. Or lost. It happens. No. Too anal. Too something my mother would do. The waiter drifts by again and I wave him off with another shrug and pained smile. The universal sign for No-I-still-don't-know-where-the-hell-my-date-is-but-I-swear-he's-coming-so-don't-pity-me-yet.

I'm in the midst of feeling officially pathetic when a new fear hits me. I haven't seen Charles since before the photo shoot with Troy, which was almost two weeks ago, and what if I'm remembering him wrong? What if he's not Mr.-Nantucket-sailing-trip-taxi-ride-through-snowy-Central-Park-perfect but really an asshole? Just an East Coast asshole and I don't recognize the breed anymore? I'm starting to work myself up into a genuine panic, when I see a blurred figure at the door.

Okay, forget Fear Number One. He didn't stand me up. As for Fear Number Two, there's no way this guy's an asshole. Not in that button-down shirt, suede baseball jacket, and with his wavy gray-streaked hair, although I admit I'm a pushover for preppy-looking guys. A holdover from college that even my three years with Josh couldn't erase. Like bisexual women who go back to men because they just miss fucking.

"Hey," Charles says, putting a hand to my shoulder. "Sorry I'm late."

"Hey, no problem," I say, half-rising and giving him a brilliant "no-problem" smile. That's me. Miss No Problem.

He sinks into the chair, gives me one of the crinkly-eyed smiles I remember, and I feel Miss No Problem begin to weaken. "So," I say brightly, fumbling for the menu.

We do the "God, flying these days" speech, which ends in the usual "What can you do?" eye rolling, and then head into the "Should we order a drink?" portion of the evening, and I'm thinking we are off to a good if not exactly great start when Charles says something behind the wine list that I can't quite catch.

"Sorry," I say, lowering my menu.

"I said, I'm so glad you were able to move our meeting to dinner. Made it so much easier for us to get together, given my time here."

Your *time* here? *Your time here?*

I must look stricken. Or pissed. Because he starts to backtrack. "And I mean your time, your time as well," he says, stammering slightly. "I know you've been busy. With Troy. And actually I want to hear about that. I've heard versions from Suzanne. And G, of course. But I need to hear about it from you. Get up to speed."

I am falling down a rabbit hole of my own stupid hopes. This isn't a date. This isn't Kevin Costner and Susan Sarandon getting together at the end of *Bull Durham* after two hours of sexual tension. This is a *business* dinner. With my new boss. How could I have been so blind? Didn't I go over this and over it? Fly it all by Steven? And didn't I play and replay his message a million times? *"I'm sick of work getting in the way of this." This!* This! How the hell did I mistake that?

I feel my face flush and my shoulders sag under my new black cashmere sweater. The one I bought just a few hours ago. The one with the boat neck. The one that makes me look like Audrey Hepburn.

In my dreams.

I am losing my will to live. Or the energy to get through the rest of the evening. The rest of this business dinner.

Before I can say anything, the waiter flies up and in the flurry of drink ordering—yes, a bottle will do *nicely*—I try to rally what dignity I have left. What forces I have left. Like Henry V before the St. Crispin's Day battle. If it had been waged at the intersection of Wilshire and Santa Monica boulevards. I mean, I finessed Troy. And G. And without the advantage of Orso's lighting and a good bottle of Pinot Grigio. I can certainly finesse Charles. If this is a business dinner, then I'm working it. And *you*. I *am* Miss No Problem.

"Ah, Troy, well that *is* a story," I say, shaking my head and putting on my best you-don't-know-the-half-of-it smile. "But first," I say, raising my water glass in mock salute, "thanks for taking the time to meet with me."

We're on the last of the bottle and the remains of the *osso bucco* is crusting on our plates. We've tagged all the bases. Work. His promotion. G. Troy. I take it as a good sign that I got him to laugh during my recitation of Troy's shoot-out at the Chanel boutique. But then I did leave out the part about Troy kissing me. Not going to push my luck. Not when G doesn't know about it. Not when it's the only kiss I'm ever going to have for the rest of my life.

We've also talked about the Yankees, real estate, our junior years abroad (I went to Scotland, he went to Madrid), our intended careers (mine in publishing, his in international law), our detours into publicity (both accidental, and in my case criminally so).

"It doesn't sound like it's the kind of job you ever envisioned for yourself," he says, looking in the candlelight less like a boss than a friend.

"Well," I say, fiddling with my wineglass. "I try not to think about it, Counselor."

We talk more. About our childhoods (mine in Philly, his in D.C.), my divorce, his divorce (I *knew* it), how it seems like you can never live up to your parents' expectations no matter what you do (well, with my parents that was true; his father was a lawyer, so technically no one except his clients lived up to his expectations), whether the electoral college should be abolished (Gore would be president!), and how we both love, love, love the bar at the Ritz Carlton in Boston. A table overlooking the Garden on a crisp fall day, a nice Sauvignon Blanc, and a lobster sandwich. "Sometimes I think I could live in a Cheever short story," I say before I remember my own upbringing on the Main Line was supposedly pretty Cheeveresque.

"I think you should get back to that bar one day," Charles says, and for a second I can't read his expression—wistful, mocking, sincere, patronizing?—and I wonder if I was wrong about this being a business dinner. You go out for dinner with girls, even girls you don't know, and of course you wind up talking about your divorce and your parents and how you can't stand your own sister most of the time. But not with guys. Not straight guys. And certainly not with your boss. Not unless it's a date.

Before I can parse this further, I hear a burbling sound. And another.

"I think that's you," Charles says.

"Excuse me?"

"Your phone?"

"Oh," I say, fumbling for my bag. Why didn't I turn it off? "Actually this could be a Troy thing," I say, suddenly fearing the worst. "Hello?"

"Where the fuck are you? And don't say in bed."

Rachel, and from the roaring sounds in the background at a party. Oh, the *party*. The one I said I'd meet her at and then forgot to cancel when I made dinner plans with Charles.

"Actually, just finishing dinner," I say casually. "With Charles. You remember I said he was coming back to L.A."

" 'Charles.' That's cute. At least you stood me up for a good reason," Rachel says, and I can tell she's only slightly pissed. Or on her second martini.

"So how's it going there?" I say.

"How's it going *there*?"

"Oh, you know," I say blandly, giving Charles a what-can-you-do? shrug.

Rachel gives me the rundown—the party's at the house of some kid director of one of her studio's upcoming releases—and tells me that if I'm, if *we're* not there in thirty minutes, she's leaving. I know the party will be the usual cutthroat jockeying of egos disguised as fun. Like a Jim Carrey movie. I make noncommittal noises and hang up.

"There's a party?" Charles says. He sounds surprised but not unpleasantly so.

"You know Hollywood. There's always a party."

He asks me if I'm planning on going. I'm about to say, are you crazy, I'm planning on going home and crying myself to sleep, when I realize it's the perfect face-saving coda to the evening.

"Actually, I did tell her I'd stop by."

"Well," he says, leaning forward and smiling in his warm, crinkly-eyed way. "Then let me go with you."

Really?

Not so fast. "Oh no. You must be exhausted," I say, waving him off. "Besides, it will just be a work thing. They're all work things."

But no. He's keen to go. *Eager* to go. To get out and experience the Hollywood scene although, thank God, he doesn't use those exact words. Nothing worse than some out-of-towner dying to find The Hollywood Scene.

"Get the address and I'll order the espressos," he says, signaling for the waiter. "I'll even drive us." He turns back and gives me another crinkly smile. "Let's keep this going."

The party is north of Sunset off Doheny. A good neighborhood although technically not Beverly Hills. Still, the house itself is impressive in that bullying L.A. way. New England Colonial on steroids. So Greenwich manqué. Or *Home Alone*. We dropped my Audi at my house, so Charles is driving us in his rental. A black BMW. The 5 series. Nice. And he can actually drive in L.A., which hardly any New Yorkers can.

By the time we hit the valet stand at the end of the drive, the party is going full bore. Probably the third quarter. The front door is open and light pours onto the flagstones. Voices and laughter float in the night air. Over in the shadows on the front lawn, I see a group smoking and laughing.

"Very West Egg. Or is it East Egg, I can never keep those straight," Charles says as he hands the keys to the valet and we begin our trek up the drive. Up is right. It's one of those houses sited at about a twenty-degree angle up from the street, and in my mules, I feel myself starting to slip. *Fuck.*

"Here," he says, reaching out for my arm. "Hang on to me."

Oh, honey.

Outside might be faux Greenwich, but inside we step into a corner of Britain's Home Counties. Black and white slate and limestone tiles cover the hallway floor. On the wall, an equally dizzying series of hunting prints. Some dogs, some horses, some horses *and* dogs. Against the other wall, an antique bench and a coatrack holding a riding coat, a checked driving cap, and several riding crops. On the floor are several pairs of well-worn riding boots. As if.

I know for a fact that the director is the latest thirty-year-old whiz kid. Grew up in Jersey. One low-budget indie comes in a gusher. Now he's got a studio deal and this stage set. Usually these overnight wonders head to Malibu. Rent a beach house. Or Trousdale. Pick up some mid-century white box, toss down a shag carpet, some Eames chairs, a little Noguchi, and call it home.

But this is off the charts. Almost Old Hollywood in its clueless ostentation. Like Tony Curtis. Or Nancy Reagan. The house is steps from the Strip, with the clubs and tattoo parlors and Larry Flynt's house of sex, where the dazed-looking tourists and weasel-chested rockers kill time fingering the crotchless panties and the rainbow-hued dildos. But up here, up here this is Disneyland.

"Well," I say, rolling my eyes at Charles. "Tallyho."

We head into the living room. More Hollywood English manor. Beamed ceiling. Leather sofas. A DJ scratching out Kid Rock. And the usual Hollywood demimonde. Guys in baggy jeans, T-shirts, and V-neck sweaters. The women: low-riders, tight, midriff-baring sweaters, and three-inch heels. Britney may be over but like Farrah's hairdo, her navel-baring style lives on. Over the pounding sound system, snatches of conversation drift our way. *Turnaround. Development deal. Option clause. Yeah, I'll have another hit.*

"I told you it was a work thing," I say to Charles, hollering over the crowd.

"No problem," he hollers back, and I wonder if he's making a joke. "Let's find the bar."

I know by now the bar will be a figment of imagination. Judging by the hour and the energy in the room, everyone has moved on to other mood enhancers. The bar, or what's left of it, will be dead soldiers in a kitchen manned by the usual bored-looking, non-English-speaking help.

"Sure," I say, heading for the kitchen. Or where I think the kitchen might be. But we've barely moved when Charles is waylaid. Some actress. The usual Amazon with surgical enhancements and special needs. They met in New York a few months ago when she was looking for new representation. Or that's as much as I gather before she hauls Charles off for further consultation—"Hey, I'll catch up with you," he says—and I'm left to make my own way to the kitchen. Nothing like taking someone to a party where they know more people than you do.

In the kitchen, the bar is clearly finito. Empties and tired-looking Latinos. I give an embarrassed smile and am about to back out, when I spy a half-empty bottle of warm Chardonnay and pour myself a glass. Probably not the best idea after last night, but then so far, not much of this evening has been the best idea.

I head back out and scan the crowd. Some mid-level actors. Studio people. Agents; no party is complete without agents circling the waters. A few producers. A few ersatz producers. No one I feel like talking to. Or even pretending to talk to. I know I should work the crowd. Get the lowdown on the movie. The actors. Meet them. Woo them. Bag them. Mount their heads on BIG-DWP's walls. But you need one of three things to get through a Hollywood party—energy, celebrity, or the right drugs—and at the moment I'm lacking all three.

"Hey, you made it."

I whip around. Rachel. A little glassy-eyed. But then she's better a little glassy-eyed.

"I didn't think you guys would show. Given your date, I mean."

"What date?" I say glumly. "It was just a business lunch that got moved to dinner. And now he's out doing some more business," I say, waving vaguely toward the crowd, "with a potential client."

"At least you got dinner," she says, and I can tell she's trying to be helpful.

"And if you came in the same car there's still some chance for nooky on the way home."

I look at her. "Nooky?"

"I think it's the decor," she says with an airy wave. "It's getting to me. I just told someone 'Cheerio.'"

"Yeah," I say, eager to talk about anything besides my nondate.

"What's with this guy? Couldn't just head to Trousdale like the rest of the anointed?"

"I don't know. I think one of his relatives was English or something," she says. "Or maybe he bought it like this. Who cares? All the studio knows is that his movie tested through the roof."

"What is it again? Some Martin Lawrence comedy?"

"Which I used to think was an oxymoron, but the cards came back off the charts."

I take another slug of wine and gaze around the room. No sign of Charles. My *ride*. I feel like a Macy's parade balloon with a fatal leak. All bloated expectations slowly expiring. In public.

"Did I ever tell you I actually hate talking about the movie business?" I say.

"Several times."

"Hey, Rachel. Alex." Some studio exec floats by, his arm around some actress on the WB channel. "How's it going?"

"Great, great," we say in unison, although I have no idea who the guy is or why he knows my name. The actress smiles coyly.

"Love your series," Rachel says.

"Yeah," I say automatically.

"What's her show again?" I say when they drift out of earshot.

"Like it matters," Rachel says. "So do you think you'd hate the movie business if you actually had a date with Charles tonight? I think it's just a defensive reaction."

I am in no mood for the analyst's couch. "I mean it," I say. "Unless you're an A-list whatever—actor, producer, exec—coming to these things is just a Sisyphean exercise. You have to be at the top to make it all work. I'm just not powerful or famous enough."

"Actually, I wouldn't be too sure of that," Rachel says, grabbing my arm and pulling me away from the crowd. "I wasn't going to bring this up, given your frame of mind and yesterday's *Post*, but there's a rumor that you and Troy are, ah, an item."

I laugh so hard wine spurts out of my nose.

"Come on, you're not that hard to ID in the pictures," she says, rooting around in her jeans pocket and handing me a balled-up cocktail napkin. "What'd you think? No one would figure it out?"

"So *what* if they know it's me?" I say, dabbing at my face. I realize I'm using on Rachel the exact line I tried out on Steven. "I was at the event with my client. I'm guilty of what? Being a dutiful publicist?"

"Look," she says with a shrug. "You don't have to convince me. All I'm saying is what I'm hearing. That you and Troy are an item. Or—"

"Or what?"

"Well, there's a second opinion that you're just trying to make it *look* like you guys are an item. That you planted the story in the *Post*. To goose your profile. In light of the merger."

I am Barney collapsing all over Broadway. "Troy fucks anybody! You said so yourself. But *I* don't make the cut?"

"See, I knew you'd like the first rumor better," she says but I've stopped listening. I am not Barney. I am a dead woman. Not only am I *not* on a date, but I have managed to drag my new boss to a party where people either think I'm sleeping with my client, which is totally unethical, or I am such a loser that I *want* them to think I'm sleeping with my client, who would *never* sleep with me. Whatever shred of dignity I had when I started this evening is now shot to hell. I have to get out of here. I have to get *Charles* out of here. And preferably out of town.

I dive into the crowd. Cinderella on uppers. Racing to find the prince before I turn into more of a pumpkin than I already am. But faces leer up out of the crowd.

"Hey, Alex, how's it going?"

"Hey, Alex."

"Hey, Alex, I hear you're handling Troy Madden now."

"Hey, Alex."

"Hey."

I feel like I'm caught in that dream when you're naked in a roomful of people. Then I spy him. Out on the patio. With the

same actress. The one who seems to have her tongue planted in
his ear.

"So you told him what, that you were sick?"

We're in Rachel's Jeep Cherokee heading up Laurel Canyon
toward my house.

"It's not like I was lying," I say, leaning back in the passenger
seat with my eyes closed. Or as closed as I can keep them without
feeling carsick on the twisty road.

"I thought the plan was to get *him* out of the party."

"Well, it didn't look like that was possible. Not with Miss Thes-
pian going in for the kill."

"But he did offer to drive you home."

"He *said* he would. Look, I'm sorry if I made you leave earlier
than you wanted." I twist in the seat so I can see her. "It just
seemed like the least humiliating option."

"Don't be retarded," she says, downshifting so abruptly that the
gears grind and I can't tell if she's pissed at me or Charles or just
the evening in general.

I close my eyes again and then, suddenly, we are at my front
gate.

"Do you want me to walk you to the door?" she says, her voice
softer now. "It's late and your stairs are pretty steep."

I feel tears spring to my eyes. This *town* is pretty steep and for
the first time I think I might not make it. Navigate the highs and
lows of Hollywood. The highs so out of reach and the lows all too
easy.

"No, I think I can make it," I say, glad Rachel can't see me too
closely in the dark. "But thanks."

I get out of the car and head for the stairs.

Down.

10 | Girls, Interrupted

It's all *so* high school. "Hollywood is high school with money." Just like the saying goes. I just hadn't realized how true it is. Until now. Until my nondate with Charles. My nondate with Charles and our *Carrie*-like homecoming party. And of course my paranoia about running into him at the office on Monday.

To his credit, he did call. Early the next morning after the party. Actually he left a message, since I was in no shape to answer the phone, let alone lie at 9 A.M. on a Sunday morning. Apologies all around. For being late, for the car mix-up, for getting roped into a business conversation at the party, for not taking me home. For all of it. He's sorry and hopes I feel better and call him. And he sounds sincere—even contrite—and for a moment I'm tempted to try and put the genie back in the bottle.

"Are you out of your *mind?*" Steven says, when he calls later in the morning looking for a full accounting of the evening. "You think only gays are into self-abusive relationships? Honey, I'm about to make you an honorary member."

"Yeah, well, hold that thought because I'm *not* calling him." I'm sitting up in bed, sun pooling on the sheets, a mug of coffee strong enough to dance on, the Sunday papers, and Steven in my ear. The world has turned again on its axis. Miraculous, and I am in no position to question it.

"Look, whether it was a business thing or a date that went south, I'm treating it like business. It's the only way out." I add, "Charles is my colleague. My boss. End of story."

"Still, he told you about his parents," Steven says, and I can tell he wants to analyze the data again.

"Forget it." And I mean it. It's Sunday. In L.A. I'm going to read the papers. Maybe garden. Or hike a canyon. I hear it's what people do in L.A. on Sundays. Besides, I'm more concerned about the rumors about me and Troy. Or I am until Steven comes apart with laughter when I mention it.

"Rachel *wishes* people were talking about her and Troy. About her and anyone," he says. "That girl is so deluded. Besides, who'd she hear that from? Other studio people? They never know anything."

"Look, I know you don't like her, but try to keep your well-honed animosity toward all females except me in check. She *is* one of my closest friends."

Steven snorts. "It has nothing to do with her being a woman, which if you ask me is debatable. I just think her tough-girl act is a little old."

"My tough-girl act is a little old."

"You guys are not remotely similar," he says. "You're confused. She's just mean."

"She isn't mean," I say. "You just don't get what it's like to be a short brunette woman with a brain and a mouth in a town that values none of those attributes."

"Why do you think I live here?"

"Okay, we're getting off the track," I say, starting to feel flickerings of last night's despair. "About me and Troy. You don't think I need to mount a counteroffensive?"

"I'm more worried you're using military metaphors, but nooooo," he says, ticking off our usual list of reasons why nothing bad ever really happens in Hollywood unless it involves money: all publicity is good publicity, no one reads anything, and J. Lo. "It will only be a matter of time before she gets married again. Or divorced—or wherever she is in her social calendar—and everyone will have something else to talk about. You know attention levels in this town."

"I do and it's why we're hanging up now," I say, feeling better than I thought was possible twelve hours ago. "I have to go hike a canyon."

Of course, our paths do cross. On Monday to be exact. When Charles comes by my office. To apologize. In person. The evening might have been fucked up, but the guy's got manners. I give him that.

"So at the very least, I owe you a ride," he says, running his hand through his hair with the kind of gesture that if I hadn't just spent the world's most embarrassing evening with him, I would describe as bashful.

"No, no, no. No problem," I say, busying myself with some papers on my desk. Miss No Problem again. "Really, Rachel was just leaving and it worked out great."

I look up with a steely smile and realize Charles looks—what? Crestfallen? Surprised? Well, too late now. This is-he-or-isn't-he road only leads to heartbreak. Or a bad country-and-western lyric.

"So did you manage to sign—what did you say her name was? Stella?"

"Oh please," he says, shaking his head. "She has no idea what she wants."

I'm about to say she seemed to have a pretty good idea Saturday night, but think better of it. I may not know if Charles was or wasn't my date two nights ago, but I do know, in this office, he's my superior. "Well, at least you tried," I say. Another steely smile.

"So?" I add briskly. Old business? New business? Move to adjourn before I lose my cool here?

"So?" He looks at me like he's trying to read Proust in the original and can't quite make it out. "So, I'll see you around the office?"

Could not sound more like Chinese water torture. Or reading Proust in the original.

"Absolutely."

"Unless you have time for lunch before I leave. To make up for the ride—the nonride—home."

Just when I'm out, they pull me back in. I feel Miss No Problem beginning to crumble, when there's a knock at the door. Steven. With news from the front, apparently, judging by the look on his face.

"Yes?" I say, bracing for some new emergency with Troy.

"You have that lunch meeting today?"

"Lunch meeting?" I look at him blankly. Then at my calendar. I have nothing down for today. "Oh, you mean the *thing?*" I'm guessing Steven is trying to pry me away from Charles by doing that scene from *Annie Hall* where Woody Allen tries to keep Diane Keaton away from Paul Simon by reminding her that "we have that *thing.*"

"No," Steven says archly. "Kelly *Cohen.* At her house," he adds, looking at his watch. "At one."

"Oh, Kelly. Jesus. That's today?"

It's true. I do have a meeting with Kelly Cohen, but why I don't have this down in my book, I have no idea. Probably too distracted by my dating Troy and not dating Charles. An actress-turned-screenwriter, Kelly also happens to be my favorite client. Actually, now that she's got her medication adjusted, she's the only client I can stand to spend any time with, and given that I still need an exit strategy from the *Days of Our Lives* scene playing out in my office, I'm not about to reschedule.

"Hey, you're busy," Charles says, raising his hands and heading toward the door. "I'll let you go."

I feel like Kate Winslet drowning in the North Atlantic, watching the lifeboat row off into the fog. "Well, let's see if we can work out lunch," I say. If I had a whistle, I would blow it. "I'm sure I can move something around."

But he's gone. An enigmatic smile and out the door. Out of my life.

"Well, that was close," Steven says like he's saved me from a burning building. Or from buying a pair of acid-washed jeans.

"I don't know," I say, shaking my head. "I cannot read that guy."

"So read this instead." He hands me a copy of the press release I have to approve for Kelly's new movie, some family comedy she wrote called *Butterfly Girls*. "If you want my advice," he adds, "talk to Kelly. If anyone has seen it all, she has."

This was true. Although I'm not sure if a woman with two ex-husbands, including one who'd turned out to be gay, is really the fount of relationship knowledge. What Kelly does know is Holly-wood. All too well. Her mother, Lily, was an MGM stock star, and her father, Dave Cohen, a fifties game show host. Until his embez-zlement scandal. Kelly did some acting as a kid. Guest-starring stuff on *Lassie* and *Donna Reed*. But after her parents divorced, she got shipped off to boarding school and when she resurfaced, Kelly had given up acting to become a screenwriter. She'd also acquired a husband, a drummer in a seventies heavy-metal band. Or he was her husband until his drug habit got the better of him. Kelly refers to her first marriage as "my Black Panther phase." Or if she is feel-ing more cynical, her "Heather Locklear phase." Then there was her brief marriage to a hot young producer, a close friend of David Geffen's like *that's* not a clue, who wound up coming out of the closet and out of Kelly's life.

Now, Kelly is mostly famous for being famous. In addition to her famous parents and famous ex-husbands, she has a famous house, a rambling Spanish-style hacienda off Coldwater that once be-longed to Fay Wray and later, George Hamilton. Under Kelly's aegis, it is the site of lots of famous parties where there are so many famous guests that Kelly uses a velvet rope to cordon off the less famous from the really famous. It is about knowing the difference between Liz Taylor and Matt LeBlanc. Or it would be if Kelly bothered knowing Matt LeBlanc.

As Kelly's publicist, I don't have to worry about the velvet rope. I don't have to worry about much with Kelly, unless she is changing medication. There was a bipolar thing, but that's pretty much under control now. Most of the time, Kelly's on autopilot because there's nothing to publicize. She writes her scripts. Actually, she mostly rewrites scripts. She sees the doctor.

But then she wrote *Butterfly Girls,* a cable movie about some high school honor students who go to South America to study Monarch deaths but stumble on some ancient ruins. Normally this was the kind of thing Kelly would run from, even if it was based on an article from *The New Yorker* and supposed to star Britney Spears, who wanted to shoot a companion video at an Inca temple if they could get the Peruvian government to sign off on it. But when Kelly got an estimate from her roof contractor that took all of her summer-in-the-Hamptons budget and then some, she allowed her agent to talk her into writing a draft. She also extracted a stipulation—or as much of one as a writer can extract—that her mother would be considered for the role of a teacher. Or Britney's grandmother. Or something.

Amid her own career ups and downs, Kelly was worried about her mother. Like many a star who came of age during the studio system, Lily never earned big money. She also weathered one too many bad marriages. Or one too many bad managers. Anyway, given Hollywood's brutal sell-by dates, Lily was not exactly living the *InStyle* lifestyle. If Kelly didn't want to see her wind up in the SAG retirement home or in some cramped, one-bedroom condo down on Doheny like Evelyn Keyes, who played Scarlett O'Hara's sister in *Gone with the Wind,* something, even if it was as loathsome as *Butterfly Girls,* had to be done.

In Kelly's mind the script deal was a twofer and she gave it six weeks and her usual professional approach, which meant sitting cross-legged on her bed with its six-hundred-thread-count sheets, smoking about eighteen cigarettes an hour, surrounded by a pile of coffee-table books about Machu Picchu and some old Hayley Mills videos, before she could bring herself to type lines like "Girls, I think we should stick to the map," and "Hey, I didn't know you could sing!"

Of course, Britney wound up passing, they always do, and when *Butterfly Girls* finally got a green light more than a year later it had morphed into a cable movie shot in Veracruz starring a bunch of Britney wannabes. Still, Lily had a part—she played a tourist who befriended the girls in Lima—which at least meant a paycheck even if it was cable. And now there's talk of a possible series commitment.

"I know it's cable but Lily's terrific in it," Kelly is saying when I finally arrive. After letting myself in the kitchen—*hi, hi, hi* to Marta, Kelly's housekeeper busy frying bacon, Chris her assistant, busy waiting for the bacon, and all the dogs yapping away—I follow the sound of Kelly's voice, its whiskeyish resonances, through the cool barrel-vaulted living room that could stand a paint job, and into her bedroom. The one with the gold stars on the robin's-egg-blue ceiling.

"And if it goes to series, she can do it," Kelly says. A tiny red cell phone adorned with Swarovski crystals is jammed against her ear while she wiggles enough of her upper arm out of the neck of her black cashmere sweater to slap on a nicotine patch. I reach out to help her adjust her sweater sleeve.

"Well, if it shoots a season in three months, she could do it," Kelly says, nodding at me and rolling her eyes. "Look, I have to go." She wiggles her arm back into the sleeve. "I'll talk to her when I see her this weekend."

"Hi, honey," Kelly says, putting the phone down and giving me a hug. "Did you eat? You look great. But then my standards aren't much these days. Visible features qualify."

Kelly quit smoking a month ago and gained something like ten pounds. Or maybe twenty. Now she's on the patch and the Atkins diet. Or her version of it, which, by the looks of things, is not a match made in heaven. Atkins is *the* Hollywood diet: broiled fish, bottled water, and belligerence. Naturally, everyone is on it. Even Chris, her hyper assistant with the build and attention span of a schnauzer, is on it. But for an orally fixated, sugar-addicted woman like Kelly, eating bacon to lose weight makes about as much sense as eating dog food. Still, as Kelly's publicist, her diet is my diet.

"No, I ate," I say, straightening Kelly's sweater again. "In your kitchen, a second ago. The bacon's on its way."

"I hate this diet, but what can I do?" Kelly says, moving on from the sweater adjustments to fishing a Diet Coke from the cooler built into her bedside table. "I feel so fat I'm only wearing black. Or mumus. But they don't come in black."

Kelly snaps open the can and flops onto the bed, where a plate of peanut butter cookies—the store-bought kind with filling—lies next to her Apple laptop. With most clients, I would have brought the meeting to order by now. But Kelly is one of those celebrities who takes a while to notice that others are in the room—and that they have a reason for being there—so I tend to let her run on a bit.

There's a knock at the bedroom door: Marta with the plate of bacon. "Time for my afternoon feeding," Kelly says, ignoring the bacon and reaching for a cookie. Expertly, she twists the halves apart and begins licking the peanut butter filling between slurps of Coke.

"I'm eating the insides of cookies."

"Well, who doesn't?" I say, reaching for a cookie. I've noticed Kelly likes to comment on what she is doing as she is doing it. Maybe it makes everything seem more significant. Or maybe it's just the way her brain works. The bipolar thing. Or the drugs. Or maybe it's her genius as a comedy writer. Everything is fodder. Her conversations are just rough drafts.

The first meeting I had with her—at home because she actually doesn't like to leave her house all that much—Kelly spent the entire time in bed, fully dressed under the hand-worked Pratesi sheets, smoking and fingering chocolate chip cookie dough from a bowl on the nightstand.

"People say this house is so Catholic," she said, blowing smoke at an antique-looking statue of some saint perched on a ledge up near the star-painted ceiling. "But that's original. It belonged to Fay. Or maybe George. But I have thought about converting," she said, stubbing out the cigarette and immediately lighting another. "Catholics seem to get over things so quickly. They go to church. Sing. Confess. Or they become Madonna and go on TV and say *fuck* a million times and everyone puts their picture on T-shirts."

It was that kind of thing. And if I hadn't had a filing drawer full of undereducated, overpaid, overgroomed narcissists as the rest of my clients, I would have run screaming from the room. But Kelly was worth knowing. Plus, she had great parties.

"I'm eating the insides of cookies," Kelly says again, reaching for another. "But this day is doing that to me." She suddenly changes course and leaps up to snap off the gas fireplace that is blazing away on what is a cloudy if not actually cold day. "God, I'm hot and now I've got to get packed to get the flight to Vegas."

From what I gathered from Chris in the kitchen, Lily is getting some lifetime achievement award at the MGM Grand and Kelly is to present it along with the expected witheringly-funny-but-affectionate speech. "And I don't have that," she says, running a hand through her fine, expensively streaked hair. "It's all so very exciting."

"Your hair looks great," I say, realizing I actually mean it.

"It's the *only* thing that looks good now. But we're working toward something . . . ," Kelly pauses with the kind of timing that gets her upward of $150,000 a week for rewrites. "Magical."

I would be happy to spend the rest of the afternoon hanging out, eating cookies, and listening to Kelly riff on whatever catches her attention. Besides, I want to see if I can get her advice—or at least commentary—on Charles. But I have to get her to sign off on publicity for *Butterfly Girls*, and given that her normally fluky attention span seems even flukier today, I decide to just jump in with the requests: a *People* magazine story and photo shoot with Lily, a Q-and-A with Lily for *TV Guide*, an NPR interview with Lily, and—this was the long shot—pose for a photo with Lily and a local troupe of honor students for the *L.A. Times* "Calendar" section.

"Ugh," she says, when I mention the two photo shoots. "I forgot there's always this end of things. Okay to the interviews but forget the photos. I look like shit." She brushes cookie crumbs from her pant leg. "Even in black."

"Well, what if we did something creative?" I say, trying to think of something to save the *People* shoot at least. "We can put you guys in a car. Like Thelma and Louise. Or behind some giant South American statuary or something. Or," I say, scanning the room, looking for something, anything big enough to hide two actresses, when I catch sight of the hot tub burbling out the bedroom window. "Or what if we went for some vintage seventies shot? Black-and-white. You and Lily in your hot tub. Like just your head and hands on the edge."

Kelly pauses just long enough so I think she's seriously considering the idea. "Why don't I just put my boobs up there if we're trying to distract people? I mean, it's the only part of my body that isn't fat."

Okay, moving on. But before I can bring up Plan B, Marta appears back in the doorway, this time draped with what looks like a dozen pairs of black trousers. "Kelly, do you want me to pack the cashmere pants or do you want to wear them?" she says.

"Pack. No, wear," Kelly says, jumping up to fetch another Diet Coke.

I forge ahead. I need to get this nailed down before Kelly's attention fully sails away. "All right, forget the *L.A. Times*, but think about *People* because I know they can shoot around you," I say. "You could just stand behind Lily or something. How is she, by the way?"

"I think she doesn't notice how much better she is since that last husband left. That's the thing about our family," Kelly says, bored now with the publicity requests, flopping back on the bed. "We're survivors, but the bad thing is that you keep creating things to survive. To show off your gift."

"I don't know. Do you think that's you or Hollywood?" This is the good thing about Kelly: you can actually ask her stuff like this. "It seems like there's a lot of things to survive here."

"For me and Lily? Yes. But I think that's pretty much true for women here in general. You have to survive Hollywood."

"Yes, but some women do well here," I say, suddenly trying to think of one even as I say it.

"Well, *Liz* lives well," she says, and I know she means Liz Taylor because Kelly always says things like that.

"No, I mean some women continue to work into their sixties."

"Name one who isn't just doing cable films."

"Shirley Maclaine. Meryl. Susan Sarandon. Goldie."

"Except for Shirley, they're in their *fifties*. You don't get culled from the herd and killed until you're sixty. Look, the point is, it's hard for women in this town, and it's almost impossible for older women."

"I read somewhere that Joan Collins tries to make a million a year."

"Jesus," Kelly says, sounding genuinely nonplussed. "How does she do that?"

"I read it in *TV Guide*," I say. "When she was doing that guest-starring role on *Will & Grace*. But look at you, you do great as a script doctor."

"I *don't* do all that great," she says with such vehemence that I'm startled. "I do *some* of that, but it's such an inflated notion that I do that a lot. It would be great if I could do more—financially, I mean, but there's a lot of people who do that sort of thing—a lot of *guys*. I'm just one of the few who happens to be a celebrity."

Before I took her on as a client, I knew Kelly had had some hard times. That she'd put her house on the market for a while. And then there was a jewelry line she and Lily had talked about doing—the Cohen Collection or something—and trying to sell it on QVC. But that's a lot of actresses' dirty little secret. Hawking something—a diet plan, a skin-care line, jewelry, clothing—on the home-shopping channels when your acting career goes south. Which it almost always does. And usually sooner rather than later. Unless they get lucky and make a lot of money, like a studio exec or like Julia Roberts or the actresses on *Friends*, and have the brains to save it or build a real business with it, like Connie Stevens did with her day spa down in West Hollywood, women never really stop looking over their shoulder.

"Yeah, and the industry has changed," Kelly goes on, shaking her head. "It used to be a lot of people could earn a good living. Now it seems like there are the phenomenally rich and then the rest of us in this weird no-man's-land."

"That's not what the rest of the country thinks. They think everyone working in Hollywood is phenomenally rich."

Kelly snorts. "That's because it's in their interest to think that. And the media only encourages it. Hollywood is still our collective fantasy. Our big wet dream. We could all be rich and famous if only we had the right nose job. But the reality is, Lily can't get a job. And it's harder and harder for me to get jobs. It's like being an athlete and having to retire at age thirty-five. Not because you can't do it anymore, but because that's just the way the business works."

I decide to take a flyer and interject men into the equation. "Well, you could just meet the right guy and live happily ever after."

Kelly looks at me. "Okay, stop right there, because we're not talking about me. Not with my track record. Did you meet someone?"

Just when you think she's totally on her own planet, she comes back to Earth. "Uhm, well, yeah. I don't know." I sound like I'm in third grade. "He's a publicist. In our agency."

"He's a *publicist?*" she says. "Well, *that's* your problem. Women are not only screwed professionally in Hollywood, but you can't date any men here. Look at Lily. Look at me."

Frankly I'd rather not, but she isn't giving me much choice. "Well, why not?" I mew.

"It's all food-chain rules. In a one-industry town, your social standing is always relative to others'. Someone's up. Someone's down. If he's higher on the food chain than you, it's all about him. But if he's lower, then it's all about him sucking up to you. Or you *think* it's all about him sucking up to you. Either way, you can't trust it. Because it's never about being equals."

"So, I should just forget it?" I say. "I should have just stayed unhappily married back in New York?"

"No, there are men you can date in L.A. You just have to know where to look."

"Like where?"

"Plastic surgeons. They have great incomes, you get free work done, and they love hanging out with an industry crowd but aren't competitive with it because they know eventually everyone comes crawling to them."

"Oh great," I say miserably. I realize I'm starting to feel worse—about Charles, about Hollywood, about all of it—not better.

"But it will get easier," she says, smiling at me like I'm her kid although she's not even ten years older than me. "I mean, it's not like sex stops. Unless you're like Joan Collins, who's maintained a very active sex life, and you have to admire that. Sex just diminishes. It's diminished for Lily. It's diminished for me."

Oh *God.* I do not want to know this. I seriously do not want to know this. Or see the world through Kelly Cohen's eyes. Parsing out life in dollars and orgasms. Then you die. I have a sudden panicky urge to call up Charles, beg him to date me—marry me—and let's figure it all out later, from some farm in New Hampshire, when my cell phone rings.

"Are you into the sugar or the drugs?" Steven says when I pick up.

"Yes and *no*. Actually, we're just wrapping up. What's up?"

"Suzanne moved that staff meeting up by an hour."

I can't tell if this is actual news or if Steven is just trying to provide me with an exit strategy. Whatever. "I'm on my way," I say, giving Kelly a what-can-you-do? shrug.

"Have a cookie. For the road," she says, offering the plate. "Or take all the bacon. It will only go to the dogs."

I make some final noises about the publicity requests and start gathering up my stuff, when I notice a large signed photograph of Richard Nixon on Kelly's dresser: *To Kelly Cohen, from one of her biggest fans, Richard M. Nixon.*

"I never saw this before," I say, reaching for the photo. With Kelly's fabulously famous life, it seems strange that she should have a photo of Nixon.

"That gets a lot of attention because I'm not much of a Republican," she says, heading into the bathroom. For a second I fear she's not planning on shutting the door. She did that once, but that was back when she was still drinking.

"It's a long story that started when I was a kid," she says, her voice muffled by the door. "I didn't want to go to the White House but my mother made me and got me a picture of him then that said, 'To Kelly Cohen, may all your dreams come true.' So I wanted to write him back and say, 'I dreamt you were impeached,' " she says, her voice drowned out by the flushing toilet.

"But I lost that picture somehow." Kelly opens the door and turns to the sink and begins brushing her teeth. "And I told that story to someone who happened to be doing Nixon's book on tape and so she got me that photograph."

Kelly wipes her mouth and examines her teeth in the mirror. "It just goes to show you."

"What?"

"Well, he died two weeks later."

"So?"

"So, I hated him while he was alive, but once he died, I realized I missed the bastard," she says, giving me a tired smile. "But then, that's what fame is all about."

"What?" I say, suddenly anxious for one piece of workable advice. "What's fame all about?"

"That it's no respecter of persons."

11 | How Old Did You Say You Were?

"Don't say I didn't warn you."

Steven tosses a square red envelope onto my desk. "I'd say open it at your peril, except I already know what it is."

I stare at the envelope, in no mood for surprises since it's taken weeks to get everything tamped back down to workable chaos. Troy is under wraps until his court date, whenever that is. Carla Selena is a distant—bad—memory at the agency. I've gotten Kelly to agree to the *People* shoot. And most important, my stay in the doghouse is over after Suzanne took me to lunch at the Grill last week and asked me to help with the Phoenix. The Phoenix, who might or might not be quitting BIG-DWP. Depending on what her astrologer says. Or maybe it's her psychic.

We've even moved our offices. Finally. The one good thing about our merger with BIG. I now have a real office with a window—a view of a dying palm tree and a parking lot, but still—sisal carpeting, a new computer system, an Aeron chair, and my own orchid. With someone who comes in and waters it. Or mists it. Or maybe just talks to it. There's even a masseuse who comes in on Fridays to give head and neck massages for those who feel the need. So far, I've felt the need every fucking Friday.

"Well, I know it's not from Charles," I say, poking the envelope suspiciously.

Charles. He's the only unresolved issue. Ever since our disastrous date, or nondate, depending on your view, and his aborted *mea culpas—culpas interruptus*, as Steven said—I've taken to just avoiding him. Which isn't hard given the chaos of the office move and the fact that there are at least twenty-five other DWP publicists he's to meet with before heading back to New York. Most days we never cross paths.

"Oh, come on," Steven says impatiently. "It's the invitation to G's birthday party. All the DWP publicists got them. It's a goodwill gesture from the Biggies. 'Our first joint social event.' "

Oh God. *The* birthday party. Rachel warned me about this. "Oh, great," I say, gingerly slipping open the envelope. No telling what might be inside given that twenty-year-olds are planning the thing. But then twenty-year-olds plan a lot of stuff in Hollywood. Sparkly glitter rains down on my desk. Oh God. I hear a choking sound that I realize is Steven. Trying not to laugh.

"Hey, he's your boss too," I say, shooting him a look.

"Don't look at me. I didn't get an invitation."

"Well, you're my date to this thing no matter what."

I shake out the rest of the glitter and pull out the invitation. Engraved. Red ink. At least it's not shaped like a heart. Or a pair of tits. I'd heard that happened one year. I scan the details.

What: *Our own Doug Graydon's Birthday!* **When:** *Friday!*
Who: *All of us!* **Where:** *The office conference room.*

"Oh, *that's* special," I say. "They send out an engraved invitation to a party in the conference room?"

"I think it's about the spirit of the thing," Steven says, making another choking sound.

"You're not helping."

"I'm sorry," he says, wiping his eyes. "I've just never seen a sorority rush before and it's actually kind of moving."

"Since you're so into it, you can RSVP for both of us." I toss the invitation aside and reach for my headset. "And find out what the deal with the gifts is. We don't want to be left out of that."

I hear my cell phone burble inside my bag. Against my better judgment I fish it out and answer. Probably Mom with more details about their trip out here, which I'm already regretting.

"So I hear the party is Friday."

Rachel.

"What is this? G's birthday is a local holiday?"

"I told you, it's a huge deal. At Sony it was like sorority rush. You either made the cut or you didn't. Believe me, G's keeping score."

"Okay, so I'll get a big gift. A custom-made bullwhip. Or some chaps. One size too small. I'll go to Henry Duarte, king of custom leather wear. That should make his day."

"I'm serious. Has he laid off anybody yet?"

"You know he hasn't," I say with more irritation than I intend. It has taken me weeks to get the whole merger and G's arrival, not to mention my trip to the woodshed after Troy's little dust-up, into some kind of workable perspective where I'm not looking over my shoulder every second. Now I'm starting to get riled up again.

"Look, all I know is that at Sony, he usually found a way to dump a few people every year and he tended to do it right after his birthday," Rachel says. "Read into that what you will."

"I choose to read nothing into it. Not since Suzanne took me to lunch and I'm no longer officially on the agency shit list. Besides, I just don't have the energy."

"Well, it's your party," Rachel says.

"Actually, it's G's," I say, anxious to bring this to a close. When Rachel is in her apocalyptic mood, it's best to just get out of the way. "But I'll give you a full postmortem."

"Thanks," she says, brightening. "You know I love hearing about other people's misery."

By the time Friday rolls around, I have a packed schedule. Overly packed. A conference call with the New York office at 7 A.M., followed by a breakfast meeting over in the Valley with some Warner publicists to go over an upcoming campaign. Then I have to spend the rest of the day baby-sitting the *People* shoot at Kelly's that I just know, given Kelly, will become the Bermuda Triangle—the black hole from which I will never escape in time to make it back to G's party by five.

Plus, it's roasting and humid as all fucking get-out—the wind is off the ocean, straight up from Mexico—so I have no chance with my hair this morning. I couldn't get it together to book a blow-dry the day of G's party? Now, heading back from Warner's with the car's AC roaring, I'm already melting in my gray suit and white cashmere tank top, my hair all but exploding out of my ponytail.

"So if you're not out of Kelly's by four, I'm coming over to relieve you," Steven says, when I reach him on my cell.

"Funny, that's exactly what I was going to say," I say, scrunching the phone up to my ear as I wiggle out of my jacket.

"By the way, what are you planning on wearing to the party?"

"What I'm wearing now. A sheen of sweat and a bad mood. Why? What are you wearing?"

"A gray suit. And a red satin bow tie."

"You're going for what there? Pee-wee Herman?"

"Before the arrest."

"Oh, nice call," I say, throwing my jacket into the backseat. I can only imagine what G will think about my Boy Wonder in full West Hollywood mode. "Look, I'll call you later. But promise me you'll rethink the tie."

All in all the shoot goes about as well as these things go. Which is to say five hours of fucking around with the lights and the clothes and the hair and the setups—the endless setups—for two workable three-by-fives that Kelly and the magazine can live with.

There's a little trouble when the hammock—in which the stylist has carefully arranged Lily and Kelly over Kelly's objections that it makes her thighs look "even fatter to be pressed together with knotted rope like two smoked hams"—gives way, dumping them to the ground. Lily thinks she might have sprained something and Kelly disappears into the house to change, or rest, or make a call, or take something.

And then there is the minor accident with a pitcher of pomegranate juice Marta brings out after Kelly announces she's moving on from Atkins to antioxidants. "I couldn't get rid of any fat cells, so I thought I'd try eliminating free radicals," she says, hoisting a glass. "Plus, it sounds so seventies."

I would be more appreciative in my laughter if half the juice hadn't wound up all over my white tank top when Kelly's dogs chose that same moment to make their appearance. Since Kelly owns nothing that remotely fits me, she has to go into "the archives," as she puts it, "when I still resembled normal human form," and emerges triumphant with an old T-shirt silk-screened with a caricature of Richard Nixon and FUCK THE BIG DICK scrawled below. At least it's white. If I can bear to put my jacket back on in this heat, you won't really be able tell it's Nixon. Besides, none of the Biggies are old enough to know who he was.

"Hey, do I still have that old cashmere cardigan in the office that I kept there for emergencies?" I'm on my cell to Steven, speeding down Coldwater toward the office. It's four-thirty and I have no time to swing by my house to grab something else to wear. Not if I'm going to make the party in time, and according to the tart-tongued follow-up e-mail from the Biggies, late arrivals are strictly forbidden.

"Negative. You took that to the cleaners when we moved the office," Steven says. "Why? What happened to that uptight Kate Spade outfit you had on this morning?"

"Yeah, well, Kate had a little run-in with a glass of pomegranate juice. Now my chest is covered in a protest poster from the seventies."

"I'm sure there are some who would find that a turn-on."

"Well, only if you're a Democrat and old enough to have voted in 1972."

"No one in this office will admit to even being alive in 1972; better just keep your jacket on," Steven says. "Besides, everyone will be looking at G, not you. He's gone hedgehog finally."

Maybe it's the heat or the chaos of the day, but I have no idea what Steven's talking about. "Hedgehog?"

"Hair transplants. You know, the Jack Nicholson–Harrison Ford overgrown brush cut where their hair stands straight up. Like new sod or the white guys' version of Don King's 'do. Actually, I think it's a sign for 'I can no longer get it up, but at least my hair can.' "

A car swerves to a stop right in front of me—must have finally picked up their cell connection in the canyon—and I slam on my brakes. "Well, God knows you and not I are the expert on men getting it up," I snap.

"And she's already feeling sorry for herself. Good thing there's a shitload of sugar in your future," he says, and I can tell he's trying to be nice. "Better hurry. I already hear singing down the hall."

By the time I pull into the garage and take a second to check the damage in the rearview mirror, I realize I am beyond repair. The T-shirt is the least of it. After a day sweating through a photo shoot on Kelly's sun-baked back patio, my suit is wrinkled, my face is shiny, mascara pools under my eyes, and my hair is a mess after I managed to break the only hair clip I had with me. I fumble in my bag looking for a pen or a pencil, anything to make an emergency ponytail. Nothing. I try the glove compartment. Maps of Marin County and New Orleans, a stained *Entertainment Weekly* baseball cap, Burger King napkins slightly used, and red lacquer chopsticks from some Jackie Chan press junket. Oh well, no time to quibble.

I yank my hair into a knot and anchor it with one of the chop-sticks, wipe the mascara from under my eyes, and blot my face with the Burger King napkins. Fresh lip gloss and a spritz of Creed to cover the smell of ketchup. It's as good as she's gonna get.

I don't even bother to hit the ladies' room when I get to the of-fice. I looked scary enough in my rearview mirror. Hardly need a bigger view. I drop my bag in my office—Steven must already be at the party—finish buttoning my jacket so only the top of Nixon's head is exposed, and head down the hall. Toward the high-pitched squealing.

No wonder. The conference room looks like a bridal shower. Masses of white flowers from Mark's Garden, silver balloons, and hyper-looking blondes. Instinctively, I head for a corner. As I pass by the conference table, I see the cake. Cakes, actually. One large white one from Sweet Lady Jane with the frosting done up in black and green like a *Variety* front-page headline: GRAYDON DOES IT AN-OTHER YEAR! with a squiggly head shot of G in black icing, al-though it's unclear if that's his new hairdo. At each end of the table are more cakes—cupcakes, actually, dozens of them deco-rated with tiny Gs in silver icing and stacked on tree-shaped cake stands. At least there are what looks to be half a dozen bottles of nicely chilled albeit nonvintage Dom on the table.

"Isn't it adorable?" I hear one of the Biggies say. "We're going for a silver anniversary theme although we don't actually know how old Doug is."

Surely old enough to know better.

I scan the room. Where the hell is Steven? I hate coming stag to office events. Leaves me open to conversations with my fellow publicists, which is something I try to avoid.

"It looks like a Hostess truck exploded in here," he suddenly hisses in my ear.

"Oh, forget the room. How do I look?" I say, trying to smooth the worst of the wrinkles from my skirt.

He gives me the once-over. "Is that a chopstick in your hair?"

"Oh, that really hurts," I say, glancing at Steven's skintight gray suit and red bow tie, "coming from you, Pee-wee."

"No, I like it, it's kind of Kate Spade–goes–Suzie Kwan," he says, reaching over to pull open the top part of my jacket. "Tricky Dick," he says admiringly. "You *are* a mass of messages in that outfit."

Before I can think of a snappy fashion-worthy comeback, I catch sight of a pile of bags—Barneys, Tiffany's, Fred Segal, the usual Hollywood sacrificial offerings—on one of the conference table chairs, and I freeze.

"What's with the gifts? I thought we all gave toward the one big gift."

"Apparently the Biggies went the extra mile."

"Those *fuckers.*" I should have known they'd do something like this to embarrass the DWP publicists. "We all chipped in for the stupid Steuben eagle and they get him the good stuff?"

"Relax. See that Fred Segal bag? It's from you."

"*What?*" Visions of silver-plated condom holders or roach clips dance in my head. No telling what Steven would think is a suitable gift for G.

"Oh, you would have picked it out yourself if you had time." But before he can elaborate, there's a commotion at the door. Suzanne, Charles, and G. In his new spiky hair, G looks like Badger in *The Wind in the Willows.* An impenetrable pelt and temperament to match. But to the Biggies, it's like Mick Jagger has arrived. The room erupts into screams.

"So what exactly did I get G?" I shout over the noise as the Biggies surge toward the door. I glance over at Steven, but he is busy waving a red silk handkerchief. Oh well, at least it matches my chopstick.

One hour, two cupcakes, and three glasses of champagne later, I've had as much of G's birthday as my blood sugar can handle. The eagle has been opened, which means G has tried to kiss all the

DWP publicists, which means between dodging him and Charles, who is diligently working the room in a coat and tie as the agency's newest senior partner, I've spent most of the party hiding out in the ladies' room. It's during my last visit that I overhear two Biggies talking about another party for G. At some club, tomorrow night. A party to which neither I—nor any of the DWP agents—are invited. Apparently, Rachel was right. G is culling the herd and using his birthday party to do it.

"Hey, Alex," the Biggies say in unison when I emerge from the stall. They shoot one another nervous looks. "Nice eagle you guys got Doug."

I head to the sink and turn on the water with such force that it splashes the nearest Biggie. "You think so? Because there was some debate about whether it should be a seagull."

"That would have been pretty too," the other Biggie says in the kind of *oh-really* voice you would use on a child.

"Yeah, that's what I thought," I say, wiping my hands and turning for the door. "Garbage eater. I thought it would have been perfect."

I head back into the conference room. I need more info on this after-party party. If Steven knew about the Biggies' extra gifts, he must know about their little suck-up soiree. I find him foraging among the empty champagne bottles.

"Did you know there's another staff party for G—a private one, tomorrow night?"

"No, but I'm not surprised," he says, pouring the dregs into his glass and downing it. "G just screams velvet rope."

"Okay, Pee-wee," I say, reaching for his glass. "I'm heading back to the clubhouse now, but I need you to find out more about this party. I don't mind not being invited, but I need to know what I'm not being invited to."

I'm just heading for the door when I feel a tap on my shoulder. One of G's minions.

"Doug wants to see you in his office."

"Now?"

She draws back like I've slapped her. "*Yesss.*"

"Uh, sure," I say, glancing over at Steven. What's another visit to the principal's office?

"Okay, Suzie, watch what you say in there," Steven says when the minion moves off.

"I think it's going to be more about what G has to say."

"Look, we've all had way too much sugar. Things could get ugly. Just nod politely and get out. If you're not back in fifteen minutes, I'm coming in after you."

"Pee-wee, you do care."

"Make it ten minutes," he says, checking his watch. "I'm going to the movies later."

When I hit his office, G is already sitting at his desk. The crystal eagle, a red ribbon tied around its neck, and an untouched piece of birthday cake, the one with his own head shot, are in front of him.

"Alex," he says, waving me in, "thanks for coming by. And thanks for coming to the party. It's great when we can all get together like that, don't you think? Since the company is still all so new?"

I may have had three glasses of champagne, but I can bark on command.

"Absolutely," I say, glancing first at the eagle and then over at the sofa where the pile of gift bags, including my Fred Segal bag, are stacked. *Shit.* In all the commotion, I totally forgot to ask Steven what he bought.

"Please, have a seat." G gets up from behind his desk and moves toward me. His new hair comes along too. Up close, it looks even more dense. Like a thatched roof. Or the rough at Augusta. Small animals could live in it and never be seen.

"Oh, no, I can't stay," I say, instinctively backing away. Last time I was here, I thought he was going to throw something at me.

Well, it's been known to happen. "It's been a long day and as always," I say, nodding at the door, "there's more to do."

I have no idea what this meeting is about. Maybe G wants info on Troy. Updates on his court date. Or news about the Phoenix. Her on-again, off-again departure. Or maybe he's just fucking with my head. Trying a different tactic than fear and intimidation. Between the cake and champagne, I'm too wired to run the options. I shoot him a steely smile. All business. Sir, yes, *sir!*

He meets my gaze for a second and then gives me a chilly smile. "Actually, I wanted to let you know that a few of the publicists are getting together at another, ah, smaller party, and I was hoping you could join us. It's tomorrow night. At the Viper Room. I know it's kind of last minute, but I'm hoping you can stop by."

Stop by? *Stop by?* There is no place I would rather *not* be than at this stupid party. But there is no place I need to be more than at this stupid party. Even on my sugar-and-champagne high, I know somehow and for some reason I've made the cut. Made it past G's velvet rope. It's just not clear what's on the other side.

"Oh, that sounds fun."

The Viper Room is a black hole under the best of circumstances. Literally. You need a coal miner's helmet and at least three drinks to make it through an evening there. I can only imagine what it will be like when G is running the room. Probably need to get my shots.

"I'm sure I can move some things around and stop by."

"Great," he says, stepping closer. So close I catch a whiff of his cologne. Or maybe it's the new-car smell of his hair. "By the way, we're not inviting all the publicists so if you could just keep this to yourself. You know." He gives me another tight smile. "So, I'll see you there."

He steps toward me again and I realize G is about to put his arm around my shoulder. Maybe it's the champagne or his new hair, but I step back again, this time stumbling a bit in my mules.

"Great," I say, catching myself on the door handle. "Great. So, I'll, I'll see you all there."

G leaves his hand in midair for a second—so I can't miss his thwarted gesture—and then smiles and looks down. "I look forward to it. And feel free to wear your Nixon T-shirt," he says, looking up and nodding at my chest with the kind of expression John Huston wore through much of *Chinatown*. "Dick looks especially good there."

"He actually *said*, 'Dick looks especially good there'?"

I am back in the relative safety of my office, pacing and being debriefed by Steven.

"Even I think that's gross."

"That's because you always think in double entendres," I say, yanking off my jacket and tossing it onto my chair.

"Oh, come on. How else do you think he meant that? As a fashion compliment?"

"Look, I'm trying to give him the benefit of the doubt," I say, pausing to look down at my T-shirt. Actually, Nixon does look pretty good swelling out over my breasts.

"Why? Because he invited you to his supersecret party?"

"Of course not. I just don't want to start seeing plots behind every damn thing he does. It's depressing. And exhausting. And it makes me feel even more cynical than I normally do. Besides, I have enough to deal with keeping up with my clients."

"Oh God. You're falling for his tactics. You're doing exactly what you swore you *wouldn't* do. You're believing what he says. You don't believe what *anybody* says in Hollywood. Hello? 'I'll call you!' 'The lawyer's drawing up the papers now.' 'Of course you're on the list!' 'We *love* it!' "

Steven is starting to get agitated. Or maybe the circulation in his legs is starting to go, given his Pee-wee suit.

"I could take you a lot more seriously if you would just lose the tie," I say, suddenly heading for my desk and rooting around in the drawers. "It's hard to have a conversation with someone who looks like a pedophile."

Steven scowls but loosens his tie. "It was indecent exposure, actually, and what are you looking for? A Gideon Bible in your time of need?"

"Since we're out of champagne, I thought a cigarette might do."

"You haven't smoked in three years and now you want a cigarette?"

"I want a cigarette every day of my life," I say, slamming the drawer shut. I realize I'm shaking. Between being up since five, heatstroke from Kelly's damn photo shoot, all the champagne and cake, and now G's creepy invitation to his private party, my nerves are screaming for the steadying influence of nicotine.

"Well, I don't smoke."

I shoot him a look.

"Well, not at the office."

"Fine. But can you go downstairs to the bodega and get me a pack of Camel Lights? Please."

Steven shakes his head. "Then will you play nicely with the other children? And realize they are all lying sacks of shit? You have to play by the rules or you really will get hurt."

"You're a godsend," I say, reaching for my wallet and handing him a five. "And buy yourself something. Like a lawyer."

"Just for that . . . " he says, slipping off his tie. He drapes it around my neck and starts to retie it. I'm so happy he's going for cigarettes I just stand there and let him knot it.

"There," he says, pulling the ends tight. "Now you look like a waitress at Hooters. At least they know when some guy's trying to bullshit them."

"Like you would know," I say, waving him off. "And remember, Camel Lights."

After Steven leaves, I reach in my bag for the bottle of Arrowhead I have left over from the photo shoot. I take a slug, make a halfhearted attempt to untie the tie—I never got these stupid bow-tie knots—and give up. I'm still hot from the afternoon in the sun at Kelly's and all the sugar is only making it worse. I pull out my desk chair and drag it over to the corner of my office that is directly under the air-conditioning vent. I sit down, put my feet on the wall, lean back, and close my eyes. I am waiting for cigarettes. For sweat to dry. For salvation. God knows how long I'm sitting there, semiconscious, when I hear a knock and my office door opening.

"Just hand them to me," I say without opening my eyes. "I don't think I can get up."

"Actually, I just came to say good-bye."

I leap to my feet so fast, I spill the rest of the water on my skirt. Charles. In his neatly pressed shirt and tie. Oh, *great*. I've managed to dodge him for two weeks and now he corners me when I look like a dropout from clown college.

"Oh, sorry, I was just waiting for Steven," I say, rubbing at my skirt. "He went on an errand."

Charles smiles. "No, *I'm* sorry. I didn't mean to startle you." His tone is polite, but I can only imagine the impression I'm making. Or not making in my stained skirt, Nixon T-shirt, and bow tie. Whatever chance I had with this guy has clearly sailed. And taken my dignity along with it.

"Oh, this," I say, pulling at the tie. "It was just a little joke."

I pull on the tie some more but can*not* get it to untie. Actually, I manage to only make it tighter.

"A very little joke, apparently," I say, giving up on the tie and giving him an embarrassed if slightly strangled smile.

"Here, that looks very uncomfortable," Charles says, moving toward me. "Even if it does match your chopstick."

I squeeze my eyes shut just for a second. Oh God, could this day get any worse? Could I be any more of a train wreck? But he reaches out and begins to gently pull the tie apart.

"I think you have to have gone to a million ballroom dance classes to learn to do this," he says, working at my neck.

"Well, there you go," I say. "I only took piano lessons and there wasn't any dress code."

He works at the tie some more and I can't tell if he's becoming annoyed or not. "Here," he says, tilting my head back slightly. "That's easier."

I close my eyes again as he works at my neck for a minute. And for another minute. I feel the tie begin to loosen and I open my eyes. He's so close I can see the flecks of gold mixed in the green of his eyes. He looks at me looking at him and smiles.

"So wait," I say, pulling back, suddenly self-conscious again. "Why are you saying good-bye? I thought you weren't leaving for another—"

"Shhhh," he says softly, putting his fingers on the sides of my neck and pulling me toward him. "You're making this harder than it needs to be. Don't move. Don't even talk."

I breathe out slowly. "Okay," I whisper. "But why are you leaving? I mean so soon."

It's something back in the New York office. Some legal thing. Or insurance or Stan's departure. Or something that means he has to take the red-eye. Tonight. "But it doesn't matter," he says, leaning in closer, his mouth brushing my ear, "because I plan on being back and forth." He leaves his mouth there. Just for a second, and I feel his breath on my neck. I want to stay here forever. No cigarettes. No clients. No G's party. Just Charles and his warm, soothing voice.

"There," he says, sliding the tie free and stepping back. "You're free to go." He hands me the tie and smiles.

Maybe it's his smile. Or the gold in his eyes. Or the fact that he's leaving. Or that he just had his hands on me for the first time. Or maybe it's because I have nothing more to lose. "But what if I don't want to go?"

I smile, embarrassed.

He smiles back. Not embarrassed, like he's deciding something. "Well," he says, putting his hands in his pockets and shrugging. "That would be an entirely different story."

I've lost him. I've overplayed my hand and fucking lost him.

"Okay, well, uhm, have a good trip and I guess we'll see—" I sputter when suddenly Charles's mouth is on mine. Oh dear God. I didn't lose him. I did not fucking lose him.

We stay that way for several seconds or years and then he pulls back and smiles again. I could get used to that smile.

"Uhm, given that you're technically my boss, I'd say that was sexual harassment. If it wasn't so nice."

Oh God, do I have a complete death wish?

"Hey," Charles says, smiling at me. "Can you please shut up? Just for a minute."

"Okay, that definitely sounds like harassment," I say, but Charles's mouth is on mine again.

And there's more. Oh God, there's more. My chopstick is knocked loose and my hair falls to my shoulders. I feel his hand on the back of my neck and now lower and now he's pushing me where? Against the wall. I am up against the wall with Charles leaning into me and I am suddenly very, very aware that I am wearing a skirt. And that my legs are bare. And that they are starting to be lifted off the floor. I reach out and fumble for the light switch that I swear is right here. Where, *where* is it? Here? Yes, here. No, the lamp. Oh, wait.

There's a crash.

Oh God, the lamp. Oh fuck, the lamp.

"Hey, so they didn't have any Camel Lights."

Steven. With a pack of Marlboros. In the doorway.

Everything stops. Oh, don't *stop. Please* don't stop. But we do stop. We stop and I slide back down the wall until my feet touch the floor. For a second we all look at one another. Frozen. We are a Mexican standoff in a Tarantino movie. No one can shoot without being fatally wounded.

"Hey," Charles says finally.

"Hey," I say for no real reason.

"*Hey,*" Steven says, smiling. "I was just going to say . . . but I'll try a different store," he says, reaching out and flicking off the light switch. "On my way home."

It's dark now except for the light from the parking lot coming in the window and my back is still pressed against the wall. "So, hey," I say softly in the dark.

"Hey," Charles breathes, his mouth on my ear again. "Hey."

12 | Party Animals

I am not the kind of girl who goes to a place like this. Not of my own free will. Not even if it is owned by Johnny Depp. I'm not a clubgoer. Never have been, and at this age, never will be. I just can't do that many drugs to transform standing around a dark, howling loud room at 2 A.M., jostled by people who are drunker and prettier than I am, into something other than the torture that it is.

But then up until yesterday, I wasn't the kind of girl who would think of having sex in her office. Let alone actually have it. Actually, I didn't. Have it. Not that I didn't want to. Not that *we* didn't want to. But after Steven's little coitus interruptus, followed by a troupe of Biggies trooping noisily down the hall with the last of the cake, followed by the realization that Charles's limo was arriving at his hotel in less than an hour, we didn't. Have it. But we wanted to. And that's the important thing.

"Absolutely," Steven said, when I called him the next morning to thank him for his swift and perceptive exit and, God, I owed him one. "Intention is nine-tenths of the law."

"Actually, I think possession is nine-tenths of the law and we didn't get quite that far."

"All I know from watching *Law & Order* is that if you intend to commit a crime, it's much more serious. So if you and Charles intended to commit sex, even if you didn't actually commit it, it's serious."

Serious. Boy, that's a word that will get you in a serious amount of trouble. I thought I was serious with Josh and looked what happened there. I just became seriously depressed. There's no way I'm going there with Charles. Not yet.

"You know, you should just break down and go to law school," I say to Steven, dodging the whole "serious" thing. "I mean, one of us should know something useful in life. Besides how to get a client in *Vogue*. Or how to sneak them out of a hotel. Or that even publicists need to get their hair blown out before red-carpet events."

"I'm serious—he's serious," Steven counters, unwilling to let this drop.

"Well, I'm not doing the 'serious' thing. Not yet. Although he did call me from the airport. Twice."

"Seriously?"

"Look, I still don't even know how we wound up where we did. Besides, he lives in New York and technically he's my boss."

"So?"

"So where do we go from here?"

Now, that all seems like hours ago. Actually, it is hours ago. It's going on 11 P.M. in the VIP lounge of the Viper Room, which truth to tell is indistinguishable from the non-VIP part of the club. Just another black box up a cramped, code-violating staircase from the ground-floor black box. You just need a Day-Glo-colored wristband to get in. I've been here, at G's so-called party, for more than an hour. Of course as a non-clubgoer I was one of the first to arrive, and even my 10 P.M. arrival required a stop for espresso at the Coffee Bean and Leaf back in Sunset Plaza. So far all I have seen are bartenders, a crew setting up sound equipment on the room's miniature stage, and a few fellow early birds who look like G's old Sony cronies, given their jeans-and-sports-jackets outfits and the restless way they keep checking their Cartier watches.

I scan the room again. Nobody I remotely know. And it will take more than espresso to make me talk to studio execs. Besides, I've had about as much as I can take of Lil' Kim or whoever is wailing over the sound system. I can either hit the ladies' room and check my messages again or wander downstairs and try to kill half an hour mingling with the vox populi.

Actually, it's ladies' room and messages followed by Diet Coke—part penance for yesterday, part the need to pace myself for the evening to come—downstairs in the main club followed by another trip to the ladies' room. When I emerge it's 12 A.M. Sunday morning, which in clubland means the planet has turned on its axis. The stairway to the VIP room is now packed with Biggies in black leather jackets, tight jeans, and big, lush ponytails that take an entire afternoon to craft. They all seem to have brought along five dates each. Guys in jeans and buzz cuts and a few in porkpie hats. The newest in geek cool. Why is it that women have to kill themselves to look beautiful in the most casual surroundings while guys can get by on dorkiness? Adam Sandler has a lot to answer for.

But at the moment, he is nowhere in sight. Just this teeming river of Hollywood pilot fish fighting their way upstream. "Hey, Alex," "Hey, Alex," the Biggies chant as they thunder by, sweeping me into their wake, a dark sea of black leather jackets, and on up the stairs into the VIP room, the white-hot center of it all.

I lose all track of time. And space, for that matter, given that it's dark enough in here to develop dailies. I have no idea how long I've been here, or how many drinks I've had—Diet Cokes alternating with white wines—or how many times I'm wedged in a knot of people, shouting and peering and nodding in the near pitch-black—shouts and nods and peering are what pass for conversation in a club—until I am ready to pass out from the sheer effort it takes to have a good time. I have made the rounds of the Biggies, the inner circle, and their geeky, arrogant dates—screenwriters, agents, lesser studio execs—with whom I barely register. To them I am just another publicist. Not blond. Not twenty-something. Except for my clients, I do not exist.

I try to check the time but can't see my watch, it's so dark. I scan the room. G is nowhere to be seen and no one seems to have any idea where he is or exactly when he is arriving. Or even that it matters. I am hot in my leather jacket and sick of carrying my purse, tiny and useless as it is, and my feet are killing me in my new kitten heel boots. I scan the room again. Still no G. He's my boss and I don't trust him, but even my paranoia has its limits. I reach through a knot of people, slide my empty glass to the bar, and turn toward the stairs.

I hear the drawl before I make out its owner.

"Hey, Alex, don't tell me you're bailing already?"

Troy. Heading up the stairs with the kind of wide-awake-at-midnight eagerness possessed only by the young and well-fueled and with the kind of coltish, vacant-looking arm candy possessed by almost every male in Hollywood.

"Hey, what are you doing here?" I blurt out before I realize my mistake. I have been here for hours spinning my wheels, but the real party, the heart of the matter, is only just beginning. And I nearly missed it.

"Hey, it's the G-man's big night. Can't miss that, darlin'," he says, sweeping by my question as he sweeps by me, hauling the leggy blonde after him. "Sorry," she breathes as I lean back to let them pass in a cloud of perfume. The King of Good Times and his Queen for a Day.

"Hey, Alex," floats back down the stairwell. Troy again. "Let's try and hook up later. I need to talk to you."

I know we will never hook up later. Never mind that we do, actually, need to have a conversation, more than one, in fact, before we make our way to the Beverly Hills courthouse for his pretrial hearing or whatever it is. And never mind that he has never once apologized or even acknowledged that his little display of star pique on the steps of the Chanel boutique has cost me some serious capital at work. That I narrowly avoided being put on probation. And it's why I am standing here at God knows what hour, exhausted and bored, trying to suck up to my boss. Never mind any of that. Because it is just the way it works. And I know it.

I also know that I have to put all that out of my mind, my whining and my pounding eardrums and my screaming feet, turn around and work this sucker like the grown-up that I am. If Troy is here, then other clients are sure to follow. And frankly, what the hell is Troy doing here? If he didn't hear about this party from me, who invited him? Suddenly the idea of getting a look at G up close and partying among the faithful is much more intriguing, even imperative, than it was a few minutes ago.

"Hey," I say, charging up the stairs after Troy. "Let's definitely hook up."

I am all too correct in my assessment. A stream of celebs, some BIG clients, a few DWP clients, and a few others not signed to the agency, flow up the stairs into the room. They are minor and mostly TV—Rose McGowan, Selma Blair types—but still. I know this because I have positioned myself at the top of the stairs, leaning casually against the wall, armed with another Diet Coke and my suspicions. This party is getting better, which is to say weirder, by the minute. Not only am I the only DWP agent here—even Suzanne is glaringly absent—but the celebs, such as they are, keep coming. Claire Danes. Eddie Furlong. Tracy Ellis Ross. One of the Hilton sisters. I can never keep them straight.

Not that it matters. As a rule, celebs do not turn out for anything that doesn't have something in it for them. A movie premiere. A charity event. A fashion show. But not a publicist's party. Stars guard their presence like currency. Unless they don't mind becoming a banana republic like Jennifer Tilly, who turns out for any event, no matter how small and insignificant, they don't risk devaluation by showing up at just any party. Especially one thrown by publicists for a publicist.

Just then, a beefy-looking guy in a goatee, black sport jacket, draped in a trio of babes, and with a cell phone pressed to his ear plows up the stairs. Nikki Gans. Hollywood's official, off-the-books party planner. Well, that explains a lot. The Iranian-born Londoner, or London-born Iranian, or maybe he's just Israeli, no one seems to know, has become Hollywood's go-to guy for papering a party. His Rolodex is better than half the agents' at CAA. The fact that he looks like one of Tony Soprano's gang doesn't hurt his chances for rounding up the usual glittery suspects. For the right fee. Of course G would have hired him if he wanted to make a statement with his party.

I press against the wall to let the party-meister and his entourage pass in a veil of cologne. "We just got here," Nikki is saying into his phone. In his unplaceable foreign accent, he sounds like an arms trader. "No, New Line is *next* week. We're going to the Standard after this. What? No, we still have to hook up with the MTV people at Opaline and arrange all that."

"Nikki," says one of the babes, plucking at his sleeve. In her skintight satin sheath, hair extensions, and three-inch heels, she looks like an exotic dancer. She probably is an exotic dancer. "Nikki, when are we going to meet Carla Selena?" she says. "Is that tonight?"

Nikki holds up a hand in the air as he keeps walking and talking into his cell. Carla? Nikki might have gotten the Rose McGowan crowd to turn out for G, but there's no way Carla would show. Not here. Not after she fired Suzanne. Not when there's not another celeb of her stature in residence. Still, I'm curious. But before I can catch Nikki's answer, they disappear into the crowd.

I'm just deciding whether I have the energy to follow them, when one of the Biggies comes to rest by my perch.

"Hey, Alex, pretty amazing turnout, don't you think?"

I slide over to make room. She takes a sip of her martini and scans the crowd. "I mean, I knew my clients were coming but I didn't know so many others would."

I make convivial noises—Nikki notwithstanding, at this point she knows more about the inner workings of this party than I do—and let her prattle on.

"I know Nikki helped out, but it must have to do with G having been at Sony," she says, scoping out the crowd. "I mean, a lot of our clients worked with him at Sony before they joined our agency. And others. Like Carla."

"Carla? Carla Selena?" I say. This is too much of a coincidence. Paths cross in Hollywood, but I'm stunned at this news. I didn't know Carla and G had had any dealings. When Carla flounced out of DWP, leaving Suzanne in the lurch just after the merger with BIG, G never said a word. Never tried to step in and mend fences. Acted like it was just Suzanne's fuck-up.

"Oh yeah," she says, turning to look at me. "He was the marketing guy on one of her first films. Her first *hit* film. I think they go way back."

Going "way back" in Hollywood usually means one of two things. You just met and you need to suck up to the person bigtime. Or you met a while ago and you still need to suck up. It's all part of the Food Chain Rules. Of course, G would want everyone to think he was tight with celebs. It's why he hired Nikki to stock his birthday party. *All* publicists want everyone to think they are tight with celebs. But with few exceptions, no one believes it. Clients come and go. Publicists come and go. Shit, careers come and go. If G marketed one of Carla's films, it didn't necessarily mean anything. Except that G never mentioned knowing her when she fired the agency. Just let Suzanne twist in the wind.

"Oh, well, I guess that explains it," I say as casually as I can. But the well has run dry.

"Yeah," she says, pushing off from the wall. "Well, I'm gonna mingle."

I decide to hunt down Troy. If he's not too stoned, I should be able to get something coherent out of him. Normally, on a Saturday night Troy would be home, smoking dope in his unfurnished rental house high above the Strip—his possessions consist largely of what one would use on a camping trip: sleeping bag, dog, SUV, and plenty of weed—followed by a tour of the Strip with the boys until he's killed enough brain cells and heads back home with the night's arm candy. Come to think of it, Troy is one of the few celebs who *would* be at the Viper Room on a Saturday night. Still, he's the only star I know well in this room and even if he is high, he's at least got to know who invited him here.

I push off from the wall and move into the crowd. Given the hour and the fact that some band is now holding court on the room's diminutive stage, much of the crowd is dancing. Or at least moving rhythmically. I start to sway and edge into the throbbing sea. But pushing through them is like swimming upstream in a fast-flowing river. It's useless to fight against it. I flail about for several minutes. Eventually I catch a current and ride it back out, coming to rest at the far end of the bar.

"You want another?" the bartender shouts. I shake my head and shove my empty glass across the counter. I turn and scan the crowd. No sign of Troy. Why didn't I bring Steven along? He's so much better at working a crowd than I am and we could have covered much more ground than I'm plowing, or rather not plowing, here by myself. But he had a date. Or dinner with the boys. Or some other West Hollywood thing. Oh, screw it, these are desperate times. I reach in my bag for my phone and turn toward the stairs to find some place where I can make a call to my special teams unit, when I collide with another body being jettisoned from the dancing crowd.

"Sorry," I say, looking up. G and his hair and with the kind of blurry smile that suggests the birthday boy has been celebrating for a while now.

"Hey, Alex," he says, his eyes and his smile widening.

"Hey, Doug," I say, reaching out my hand automatically. And instantly regret it. G grabs it like he's grasping a rudder. What is it about seeing people socially that you see all the time that you have to reach out and touch them—or worse, kiss them—like they're long-lost friends?

"Alex," he says again, giving my arm a tug like he's trying to reel me in.

"Hey," I say, pulling my arm back. "I didn't see you arrive."

G gives up on my arm but hangs disconcertingly on to my hand. "Not surprising," he says, nodding at the surging crowd. "It's impossible to see anything in here."

"Actually, I've seen quite a few people. Your birthday must be more special than I thought."

"Well, it's not every day you turn forty."

And I'm twenty-two. "Still," I say, finally extricating my hand from his. "I didn't know you knew so many people so well." I'm tempted to add "and Nikki," but think better of it. Only just got out of his doghouse. No reason to go rushing back in.

"Well, you know." G gives a vague wave. "By the way," he says abruptly, "I wanted to thank you for your gift."

"Oh, that was actually everyone's idea. Someone said you collected Steuben."

"I meant your personal gift."

Fuck. How did I manage in the space of twenty-four hours to forget to ask Steven what he got for G? Charles. Of course. But if anything was on a need-to-know basis, it was this.

"Oh, no thanks necessary," I say, giving him my own vague wave. Let's move on, let's please move on.

"Well, it fits perfectly."

I smile and nod.

"I'm actually wearing it now."

"Really?" I swallow hard and smile, picturing the worst. Animal-print satin briefs. An ankle-strap pistol holster. A tiny silver ring for his penis, *which just happens to be pierced.*

G smiles back. "See." He turns his head and pushes his left ear-lobe forward, where a tiny diamond stud sparkles.

Oh, Jesus Christ. Thatched hair and a pierced ear? Is this guy channeling Harrison Ford or what?

"Great," I blurt out, relieved, "because some people think diamonds on a man are so five minutes ago."

G looks confused. "So *what?*"

"So eighties, so yesterday, you know," I say, recovering fast. "But on you it works."

I realize I'm sweating. I haven't gotten anywhere near figuring out this evening. Like why I'm the only DWP agent here and what's the connection between G and Carla. But given the hour, and G's well-lubricated party mode, not to mention the three white wines with Coke back that I've had, this is about as much of him as I can handle in one stretch. Without a whip and a chair.

"So listen," I say, nodding toward the stairs. "Don't let me keep you because I was actually just on my way out."

"Really?" G says, reaching for my shoulder and turning me back toward the bar. "Because I was hoping we could have a little chat."

The chat is more like a shakedown. Or it would be if I could hear anything G says. As it is, between the band and the crowd, I'm catching about every third word. "You know, I really can't hear you, Doug," I say, waving my hands next to my ears and shrugging. It's true, but I'm hoping he just lets me go. Lets me get the hell out of here.

No such luck. Maybe he's too drunk, or maybe he really is not to be denied. "Let's go outside and grab a cigarette," he says, or rather screams in my ear.

"I don't smoke, but okay," I say, as he grabs my arm and drags me through the crowd toward the stairs.

Outside there's the usual madness at the rope line with bounc-ers and wannabes stacked ten deep and the photographers trolling for their nightly catch. "Here," G says, propelling me past the crowd to an emptier stretch of the sidewalk. He plucks a pack of Marlboros from his jacket and offers them to me.

"No thanks, I quit," I say, shaking my head. I can't believe G smokes. Or is willing to smoke in front of me. Smoking in Hollywood is like masturbation. Everyone might do it, but you would never let anyone see you do it.

"Good for you," he says, pulling a cigarette from the pack. "I did too. Or I tried to. But hey, if you can't smoke on your birthday, when can you smoke?"

I don't say anything. This is G's party—literally. He can do the talking.

"So," he says, taking a heavy drag and blowing smoke over my head. "How are you getting on? I mean since the merger."

How am I getting on? You *know* how I'm getting on. You practically reamed me a new one until I did some fast talking in your office just a few weeks ago. "Uhm, fine. Well. I mean, good. I think we have a few bumps to get past but—"

"So you know, there's going to be changes," he says abruptly. "But I'm sure you guessed that. I mean every merger brings additional changes. Some good," he says, pausing to exhale another plume of smoke. "Some, well, let's just say some require getting used to."

I nod silently at my boss, the fire-breathing dragon.

"It's one of the reasons I wanted to see you here, tonight. To clarify those changes. In person. Away from the office." He exhales again and smiles.

"Sure," I say, nodding, instinctively clutching my jacket tighter against the cold, against G.

"Because what I'm about to tell you, not many at the agency know. Or are meant to know."

"But you're willing to tell me?" I say, trying to keep my teeth from chattering.

"I am, Alex," he says dropping the cigarette and stubbing it out with his Gucci loafer. "I am, indeed."

"Can I ask why?" I say, pulling my jacket even tighter.

"You're cold," he says, looping his arm around my shoulders and pulling me back toward the club. "Let's talk inside."

It is later. How much later, I have no idea. All I know is that I've been to the mountaintop with the devil, who has showed me the vast lands that I can occupy if I bow down and worship him. The details are hazy but the intent couldn't be clearer. The merger was just the beginning. Restructuring is coming. Cost-cutting. Layoffs. Times are tough. No one will be immune. Certainly not a publicist who allowed her client to become the butt of "Page Six." Not even Suzanne.

"Suzanne? She's a partner," I say, incredulous, pushing away the glass of wine I've barely touched but G insisted I order when we worked our way back inside and found a relatively quiet corner at the bar during a break by the band.

"If you say so."

But there are ways to avoid the pogrom, he says.

"Such as?"

Loyalty. Proofs of commitment. Dedication.

"Such as?"

G smiles. Bad Cop morphs into Good Cop. "Let's just say that as consolidation occurs, your loyalty to BIG-DWP, whatever its incarnation, will be appreciated. That those who stay the course, who do not, shall we say, question the changes, will find a different financial arrangement at the back end. There will be incentives for those who prove themselves invaluable to the agency."

"Really," I say, shoving my hands in my pockets. Of all the things G has said tonight, this is the strangest. Layoffs and buyouts are to be expected. At least in this economic climate. But that he's willing to dangle actual cash incentives, or even says he is, suggests a whole different ball game. Still, I don't expect a level playing field and I don't have to wait long to have my expectations confirmed.

"I mean, this offer is not being made to everyone," he says, running his finger down the side of my arm. "So I'm glad you made it tonight. It shows aptness of thought. Exactly what I was hoping to see."

I practically run for the stairs. At the top, I pause and look back. But G has melted into the crowd. The band has retaken the stage and lashes into another number. The crowd surges forward. I turn and head down.

"Hey, Alex."

Troy. An hour ago, I was desperate to find him. Now, he's just an impediment to my exit. My escape.

"Hey," I say. "I'm actually heading out. Let me call you tomorrow."

"Listen," he says, ignoring me and pulling me aside. "Do you have a twenty I can borrow?"

I must look like I haven't heard him because Troy repeats his request. "I thought I had more cash, but I need to get my car out of the valet."

I've done many things as a publicist. Lied, paid bills, wiped up vomit, and just two minutes ago, I listened politely to Sherman describe his coming march through Georgia. But I have never been hit up for cash. Troy makes, what, eight million times what I make but I'm the one with cash. I check my purse. I have exactly $20. "I have a twenty," I say, fishing the bill from my bag. "Why don't I get change at the bar and—"

"You're the best," he says, grabbing the twenty and planting a kiss on my cheek. "Put it on my tab. And let's definitely talk this week."

Yeah. Definitely.

I turn and head on down out of the club and into the street, squinting as I emerge in the light. It's very late. Even the strip clubs and tattoo parlors are closed, the coffee shops not yet open. There's just a few desolate souls still waiting by the rope line. Even the photographers have melted away. I look east. The sun will be up soon.

"ATM?" I say to one of the valets. He holds up two fingers and nods up the street.

"Thanks," I say. "I'll be back."

I turn and head out toward Doheny and the far end of the Strip and beyond that, the vast green lawns of Beverly Hills. Beyond that, the ocean. If I walked as far as I could walk, I would walk into the gray-green sea.

I keep walking. The noise from the club fades. The street is deserted as a Hopper painting. A dry riverbed. The cold wind off the desert is blowing harder now. Trash scuttles against the curb. I pull my jacket tighter and keep walking, west toward the ocean and the still-black sky.

13 | All Rise

Like all important real estate, the thing about the Beverly Hills courthouse is location, location, location. The otherwise unremarkable three-story building is on a leafy block of Burton Way, which puts it within hailing distance of the L'Ermitage and Four Seasons hotels so you can escape to a decent place for lunch. Or if you're not into eating, like most of Hollywood, you can buzz over to Barneys or Burberrys, valet to save time, and spend your court-appointed break shopping. Or have your eyebrows waxed at Anastasia, the Martha Stewart of Hollywood's eyebrow industry.

That's if you're on jury duty. Which hardly anybody ever is out here, civic duty not being high on the list of desirable activities. If you're appearing in court, well, that's a whole other ball game, with its own set of issues. Like limo or private car? Marc Jacobs or Earl Jeans? Guilty or not guilty?

By the day of his pretrial hearing, Troy has made his choices. Or rather Peg has made them. In consultation with his lawyer and a psychic. Troy would drive himself, dress like a cowboy in his Sunday best—nobody would buy him Marc Jacobs anyway—and plead not guilty. Which everyone knows really means *"I'm only stalling until the judge dismisses or you cave because your pockets aren't as deep as mine or I just write a check and you go away."*

The morning of his hearing, I'm still not sure which of the not-guilty scenarios Troy is banking on. It's been more than a week since I've seen him at G's party and for one reason and another—it doesn't take many with Troy—I wound up confirming all our arrangements, including my riding shotgun with him to the court-house, for the hearing via Peg.

"So what's your plan here?" I say as we pull up to the courthouse parking garage. I glance over at the defendant. At least he looks choirboy innocent in his jeans, boots, blazer, and tie. I'd have to remember to get the name of that psychic from Peg. Get a few wardrobe tips and the outlook for my own future.

Ever since I went to the mountaintop with Beelzebub at the Viper Club, I've tried to put the whole conversation with G out of my mind and not mention it. Not to anyone. I mean, half of Hollywood operates like that, on threats and sexual favors. Shit, more than half. And life somehow goes on. Besides, it was proba-bly mostly bluff on G's part anyway. I mean, how can Suzanne just leave? She owns half the agency. And now Charles is becoming a senior partner or whatever he'll be and I'm in good with him. Or I was the last time I saw him. Besides, it's not as if I don't have enough to worry about. Like exactly what my relationship with Charles is. I mean, besides our million phone calls—all good but still just phone calls—since he left more than a week ago. And then there's the clients to deal with. An endless chain of worry beads. Especially Troy. The cowboy defendant.

"My plan?" Troy says, lowering the smoked-glass window of his SUV and reaching down to take the ticket from the bored-looking attendant.

"Yeah, I mean are you prepared to go to trial with this guy? If it comes to that? I would ask if your lawyer's prepared to go to trial, but I take it as a given that lawyers are always prepared to go to trial."

Troy shoots me a lazy, teasing smile, barely avoiding colliding with a black Mercedes rocketing out of the garage. "You know I'm not supposed to discuss my case."

I know I should find this amusing. But after all he's put me through in what, less than a month, the amusement factor of Troy's good-ole-boy antics has dwindled to a dangerously low level. Dangerous for a publicist who is paid to tolerate those antics.

"Troy, I'm your publicist," I say, trying to keep my voice ironic and failing miserably. "You're *supposed* to discuss things with me, then I make sure no one else discusses them. That's how it works."

"Hey, easy. I was just kidding," he says, raising his hands. "Look, you were there. You know I didn't hit the guy on purpose, that I was going for the camera. How do you think I should plead?"

He's right on that account. Even high, Troy had the sense to lunge for the camera, not the photographer who apparently hadn't the sense to get out of the way of a 210-pound former college baseball star who was stoned and very, very pissed off. Still, in my book, no good ever comes from logging time in a courtroom. Not as a defendant. Not as a plaintiff.

"Look, I know you're not guilty, but I vote for doing whatever it takes to make this go away. Make *him* go away. Pay him, bribe him, have him killed. Just get rid of him. Let's get back to promoting your career, not your innocence."

Troy eases into a space, turns off the engine, and turns toward me. "Look, I know you think I'm an asshole—"

Whoa. It's okay to think your clients are assholes, but it is *not* okay to have them think that you think that. "Hey, I don't, and I don't think I've ever said anything to give you that impression," I say, cutting him off.

Troy shoots me a cut-the-crap look. "My point is, whatever you think of me, I am not a bad guy. Not really."

He sighs and turns and looks out his window. "I mean, you try being me for a week. Last time I checked I was trying for division play-offs, hoping for a shot with the minors. Next thing I know, I'm on the cover of magazines. Now look where I am," he says, turning back toward me. "In the bottom of the Beverly Hills court-house."

It's touching and largely true, but I'm not buying this sob story from Troy. Stardom is never that simple. If there's anything I've learned, it's that most stars think things just happen to them—because they are talented or beautiful or just *special*. It's a childlike—and childish—view of the world and it keeps them from developing any sense of responsibility about their own lives. It's why publicists were invented. And why I'm sitting here riding shotgun with a guy who actually feels sorry for himself.

"Well," I say, gazing out my own window. "Then we better go in and set the record straight."

It's worse than the red carpet inside. Mostly because there *is* no carpet, no rope line. Just a sea of photographers, cameramen, and reporters, who quickly surround us.

"Troy!"

"Troy, over here!"

"Troy, how are you going to plead?"

"Troy, is this just a nonsense suit?"

I can only imagine what Winona went through here during her trial. I take a deep breath, throw a bunch of "no comment"s in the air, loop my arm through Troy's—the effect is about as intimidating as a kid sister running to keep up with her older brother—and hurry past the guards toward the elevators.

"Troy!"

Tom, Troy's lawyer, and a second guy in an expensive suit and haircut who I assume is the trial lawyer, are holding an elevator. We dive in, the door slides shut. Safe at first.

The courtroom is less of a zoo; packed, but at least a modicum of decorum exists in here with all the guys with guns standing around. The press pretty much fills the gallery, talking among themselves and craning to get a better look at Troy. At least they can't shout questions in here. Or, more important, take pictures.

We slide into the defendant's table according to pay scale: the trial lawyer, Troy, Tom, and then me. While the three of them huddle, I look across the aisle at the opposing team. There's just two of them: the photographer and his lawyer. Judging by the cut of their suits, I'm guessing the photographer folds sooner rather than later.

I glance back at the gallery and recognize a few faces. *L.A. Times. US. AP.* Ah, the *Star. Access Hollywood.* The usual opinion makers. I turn back. Our team is still huddling, but I already know how this will go. The photographer's lawyer will stand and speak. Then Tom and Troy will stand and Troy will plead. There'll be some Q-and-A with the lawyers, the judge will toss out a court date, and we'll head for the exits, where I'll spring back into action. I've already decided, no matter what happens today, I'm not letting Troy make a statement. No fucking way. Not after all he's pulled.

Tom breaks from the huddle, leans toward me, and starts writing in his notebook. On TV these conversations look so important, but over his arm, I can see he's just doodling. "Alex, once we get started, the whole thing will only take about fifteen, twenty minutes tops," he says, sotto voce. I'm about to ask him, sotto voce, exactly when it's all going to start when there's a commotion at the front of the room. The bailiff snaps to attention.

The judge enters. She actually looks pretty good in the robe.

"All rise."

We rise. And then we sit. And we listen. First to the judge. Then to the photographer's lawyer. And then to the judge. Then it's our turn to speak. First the trial lawyer and then Troy, who stands and pleads not guilty.

The judge is leafing through her calendar looking for a trial date, when Troy interrupts her. "Your Honor, may I say something?" Oh God. This isn't in the game plan. Or is it? I glance over at Tom. I have no idea what Troy's about to say, and judging by the look on Tom's face, neither does he. I look at the photographer's table, where he and his lawyer are talking furiously. Normally, a defendant, even a famous one, doesn't speak at a preliminary hearing. But the judge lowers her glasses, peers at Troy for a minute, and waves him on. "Proceed, Mr. Madden. But keep it short."

"Thank you, ma'am. I mean, Your Honor," Troy plunges in, in his best Midwest twang. "I just wanted to say that in my life, I mean as I have known it—lived it—that I consider myself a smiler."

Oh God. I squeeze my eyes shut for second. Even when he's not stoned, Troy can just sound so out there.

The judge continues to peer over her glasses at him. "Mr. Madden, I suggest you get to your point."

"Yes, ma'am. I mean, Your Honor. Where I come from, we used to say people were either smilers or they weren't. You know, did they have a good attitude about life and their fellow human beings? And in our family, we were known, famous, even, as smilers. You could ask anybody and they'd tell you Brad Madden and his kids were some of the best folks around."

"Mr. Madden, that you were a model citizen back in Iowa is immaterial to this court. What's at issue is your behavior of late."

"Your Honor, I'm getting to that. But I just wanted to make clear to you, to all of you," he says, turning to the photographer's table, "that if there is any place that will wipe the smile off your face, it's Hollywood. I know because it's happened to me. And I've paid the price for not understanding that. I screwed up. I admit it."

Troy pauses and sighs and looks down at the table.

"Are you finished, Mr. Madden?" the judge asks.

Troy shakes his head and then looks up. I see something glint on his cheek. I lean forward to get a better look. That son of a bitch. He actually got himself to cry.

"I just want to apologize to everyone here," Troy goes on, his voice husky now. "I'm sorry if I've hurt anyone. But all I'm saying is I'm still learning. Hell, I'm still technically in recovery, so I'm still making amends. But personal pride is all any of us have. In the end. That's one thing my daddy taught me. So I would just like to say," he says, turning again to the photographer, "that maybe the world would be a little better place if we all respected each other more. As people. As people who make mistakes. And who need time and space to undo those mistakes."

Troy sits down and abruptly stands back up. "And thank you. Thank you, Your Honor, for letting me speak. To say my piece."

Troy sits back down and stares into his lap. That speech is bull-shit, but you have to give him credit. He might not be a great actor, but Troy *is* an actor. And he knows how to pull focus. I look back at the photographer. He's glaring at Troy. He knows he doesn't stand a chance. Not here. Not in front of an audience. Not in front of a jury. Not in the tabs. There's another flurry of standing and speaking by the lawyers. Finally it ends. Our team breaks into smiles. In exchange for dropping the charges against him, Troy agrees to attend an anger-management course—shit, they hold them at his rehab center—and make a donation to the charity of the plaintiff's choice. Safe at home. With barely a scratch.

We have about three minutes to make the elevators before they let the press go. The four of us stride down the hall. Like the credit sequence on *Law & Order* except I have to dogtrot to keep up. I sidle in next to Troy and remind him that he is not talking to the press. Even if he is the day's winner. I tell him to head for his car, that I'll catch a cab back to the office and issue the statement from there. That we're gratified at the outcome, now putting it behind us, looking forward to getting back to work. The usual.

"You're the best," Troy says, loping on ahead, still flanked by his lawyers. Behind me I hear the clatter of footsteps and shouts. The hounds have been loosed.

"Go on," I say, as Troy dives into the elevator. "I'll deal with them."

"By the way," he says, turning back, holding the doors open. "It was never anything personal."

"Right," I say, nodding. "Go on now."

"I just wanted to make sure you knew that."

"Got it," I say, giving him a wave. "Seriously. Go."

Troy releases the doors, they glide shut, and I brace myself for the onslaught to come. Of course it's not personal. It never is.

"So what do you think he meant by that? 'It wasn't personal'?" Steven leans in the doorway of my office, nursing a latte.

"I don't know," I say, staring distractedly at my computer screen. I'm back in the office trying to craft the release in time for the afternoon's deadlines. "Maybe he was apologizing for being such a dick."

"About what, exactly? Embarrassing you in public? Acting like it never happened? Or hitting you up for cash?"

"How about all of it?"

"Oh, you don't believe that."

"I don't know," I say, looking up irritably.

"*Okay,*" Steven says, raising his hands. "I was just trying to help. You're usually the suspicious one."

"Well, let's give him the benefit of the doubt this time."

"*Okay,*" Steven says again, turning to leave. "I'll give you both the benefit of the doubt. Let me know when you're ready to send that out and I'll get the carrier pigeons saddled up."

When Steven leaves, I lean back in my chair and reknot my hair with a pencil. He's not wrong about my irritation levels. Ever since my conversation with G at the Viper Room, I've been avoiding Steven. Or avoiding talking to him. I called him on my cell when I was leaving the club that night but only got his machine. When he reached me the next afternoon, I had already decided to try and forget the whole thing. I told Steven I saw G. That he loved my gift—*our* gift—and that he's no less creepy off-duty than he is at the office. But I didn't mention his doomsday scenario for the agency and Suzanne leaving, nor his suggestions on how I could avoid the coming conflagration with special displays of loyalty.

Now, every time I see Steven I feel guilty. I've never not told him anything. Well, not anything to do with the agency. But denial can be a good thing. Preserves your energies. Keeps you from getting worked up about stuff that will probably never happen. Or at least happen later. But it tends to make you a little bitchy with certain people. People who can read you better than you can read yourself. People you respect. Luckily, other than Steven and Rachel, there aren't too many of them around. Besides, I still think I could have misunderstood G. I mean, it was very dark and very loud and he was pretty drunk. I know there's a recession, but it is technically possible that no one will get laid off, that Suzanne will stay on, and that I will never be called on to display any further proof of my loyalty than showing up here every day, which, depending on the day, can seem like punishment enough.

I re-anchor my ponytail and check the time. Less than a hour to get this out. I turn back to the computer and reread what I've written. Like I don't have enough lies to tell as it is.

I spend the rest of the day getting out the release, answering e-mails and calls. Normally, Steven and I would head down to Tom Bergin's and catch the returns over a beer. But Steven has a racquetball game—"It's so retro it's even hipper than bowling now," he says—and although he offers to cancel, I beg off.

"You know, I'm wiped from the courtroom," I say. "I'll just catch the news here and then head home."

"Well, if you want it, the Dewar's is in my desk. Third drawer on the right."

"First you're channeling Ryan O'Neal in *Love Story,* and now you're Hildy Johnson?"

"Oh, thank God," Steven says, coming over and giving me a hug. "For a minute there, we thought the little girl was a goner."

"Hey," I say, giving him a halfhearted hug back. "You know how much I love it when you quote from *The Wizard of Oz.*"

When Steven leaves, I head down the hall to the kitchen and

grab a fresh water out of the refrigerator. Frankly, scotch and water doesn't sound all that bad. I root around and find some leftover cookies, sent from someone somewhere for something. Okay, drink and dinner. I'm just heading down the hall back to my office, to catch up on the trades until the nightly Hollywood shows come on at seven, when I hear a door open behind me.

"Alex, do you have a minute?"

Suzanne.

I turn around slowly. At least it's not G.

"Of course," I say. "I'm just waiting for the news. To see how Troy's trial goes down."

I've only been in Suzanne's new office once and it's even bigger than I remember. A spacious corner suite with a sofa and armchairs in plush sage green chenille, two windows, and a fabulous view up Wilshire. There's one orchid on her desk and another on the coffee table. A girl could get used to this.

"You know, I still can't get over how much nicer our offices are here," I say, staring out the window to see how far east I can see. If I can actually see Barneys.

Suzanne looks startled. Or maybe she's just distracted. "Oh yes," she says, looking around like it's the first time she's seen her office. "It is much bigger here."

She shuts the door and asks me to sit—God, a sofa in your office is so great—and then tells me that what she's about to tell me is confidential. Just between us and can she count on that confidentiality? Oh God. First G and now her?

"Uhm, sure, but I can't imagine what you have to tell me really requires confid—"

She cuts me off with a wave and plunges in.

So much for denial. It's exactly like G's speech, with a few more details. Times are tough. Recession in the industry. Foreign financing is drying up. Production deals are not being renewed. Clients have less work. Publicists have less work. "I've already spoken to Doug about this and he feels—we both feel—that the fairest thing will be to offer small buyouts, compensatory packages, to those agents who choose to take them," she says.

So it is true. There will be layoffs. I brace myself. "So you're suggesting I resign? Take the buyout?"

Suzanne looks startled. "Oh, no, you're misreading me."

"Then what are you saying?"

She holds up a hand and continues. Once the buyouts are accepted, the remaining staff will be assessed. If there are still too many publicists to support the client base, then actual layoffs will begin.

"So you *are* telling me to take the buyout?"

"No," she says, shaking her head. "I'm only telling you what will happen agency-wide. I am also telling you that I hope you do not take the buyout because you will probably not be one of the ones laid off. Not at your age and salary level."

Okay, this is officially strange. First G tells me I will definitely be let go unless I demonstrate my loyalty. Now Suzanne is telling me exactly the opposite. Frankly, G's scenario makes the most sense. I'm not one of his handpicked Biggies, I'm the most recent DWP hire, and I nearly landed on probation for mishandling Troy. There's no way they would keep me on before the others. Something is definitely up. I need to tread carefully.

"Okay," I say slowly. "That's good to hear although I'm not sure I understand why."

But Suzanne moves on. "Yes, but there's a whole other part to this," she says, dropping her voice. "And this is where I really need you to keep this to yourself." She looks at me expectantly.

Cross my heart and hope to die.

"The fact is that I may not stay on."

Shit. So G is right. The agency is heading for a complete overhaul. I mean, she's pretentious in her white suits and Southern accent that comes and goes depending on her audience, but Suzanne is old school, which means she's not totally without principles. More important, she's the heart of DWP. Without her and

Stan in New York, we'll be left without any of the agency's original partners. Even with Charles heading up New York, BIG-DWP will essentially belong to G.

"Why would *you* leave? Are you retiring?" I say, trying to keep my voice level. Stay calm. Stay cool. Maybe she's just selling her third of the agency to G and getting the hell out of Dodge.

Suzanne shakes her head and leans back. "It's complicated and it might not even happen. I mean, I will retire one day, but it's probably not a surprise to you that I had hoped this merger with BIG would bolster the agency. That we could grow faster together and that we could, within a year or two, be acquired by another larger company, and then I would retire. I mean, I'd like to think that DWP didn't completely miss the big PR wave, when the rest of the world discovered that celebrity can sell more than just movies and that Hollywood publicists have the keys to the kingdom."

I'm stunned by this conversation, this level of intimacy. As long as I've been at DWP, the agency has been run largely by the same rules my parents kept when I was growing up: When in doubt, don't talk about it. Especially if it's unpleasant. Now, I'm sitting here with Dr. Phil. "I'm sure you're right," I say, still choosing my words carefully. "This recession can't last forever. The agency will grow and someone will want to buy us."

Suzanne shakes her head. "I don't know. Sometimes I think Stan and I had our heads in the sand. That we underestimated the whole 'youthquake' and we didn't make the changes we needed to make when we should have. I mean, we should have hired you— and half a dozen more like you—ten years ago. We should have gone after younger clients—all those kids on the WB and MTV that you can never keep straight or even care to. But I really thought we could remain a white-shoe firm. Handling Old Hollywood. Now, I think I was wrong. I mean, we should have been signing people like Courtney Love."

"Oh, forget Courtney Love. Besides, you're making the right

changes," I say, jumping into full cheerleader mode. Or maybe it's just denial in a uniform. "I'm here and Charles is coming on and we're getting younger clients and BIG is certainly a youthful agency and it should still work out like you planned."

She looks at me like I have the brains of a cheerleader. "Look, whatever pressure you feel to keep your clients, to add to your client base, is not dissimilar to what I feel," she says. "What we all feel. And we've had some high-profile defections, as you know. The agency has suffered and I take responsibility because most of those who have left were my clients."

"Clients always come and go," I say, still in cheerleader mode.

"Well, let's just say it's awkward at this juncture. With the merger. And in this economy. First Carla and now the Phoenix. Technically she's fired us, but it's not finalized and with her new MTV show coming up, it's potentially a huge, embarrassing loss."

I'm beginning to catch on. "How huge?"

"Let's just say, if we can't retain her, then there is a very good chance that I will leave the agency as well."

"But why? You *own* half this agency."

She sighs. It's too complicated to explain, as most things with lawyers are, but it's how the merger was done. How it was written. "G and I each have contractual obligations to the agency, to the maintenance of the agency, to its *value,* and if either one of us does not fulfill those obligations, then—"

"Then what?"

"Then bad things happen."

"You might leave."

"I would have to leave."

This is crazy. She either has the stupidest lawyer in town or she was so desperate to get in bed with BIG that she agreed to those terms. It's always been difficult if not impossible to put a value on a PR agency. It's why no one bothered with them until recently. What were you actually buying? The publicists or their clients? And everyone knows clients come and go. It's why publicists are essentially independent contractors. It's all too fluid. But that's how it works. Or has until now.

"You're right," I say, holding up my hands. "I don't get it, but I get what you're saying. But why are you telling me?"

It's fairly simple, as she spells it out. Nothing I don't do every day of the week. She's asking me because she trusts me. Because the client trusts me. And because I'm young.

"Do you know what it's like to feel old?" she says, getting up and moving to the window, where she stares down at Wilshire in the dusk. "Do you know what it's like to feel like you no longer matter? That you don't count?"

Every day of the week.

I almost get away clean. Key in the ignition, car in reverse, eyes on the rearview mirror so I don't run over any Biggies no matter how much I'd like to, when I'm startled by a knock on my driver's-side window. I turn, expecting to see one of the valets with instructions not to use the west exit or something. *Fuck*. G. Smiling and waving his finger at me to roll down my window.

"Heading home?" he says when I get the window down.

"Uhm, yeah, actually," I say, looking up at him. Except for Steven, I've never spoken to anyone from the agency down here. Bad enough dealing with everyone in the office.

"Well, don't let me stop you."

"Okay, I won't," I say, eyeing him because this is more than a little strange and maybe even scary running into him like this, right after my meeting with Suzanne.

"I just wanted to say one thing."

"You followed me into the garage to tell me something?"

"I wouldn't say 'followed,'" he says. "I would say our paths crossed. Fortuitously."

I don't say anything. This is way too much of a coincidence to be remotely fortuitous. Creepy, yes; fortuitous, no way.

G smiles, puts his hands on the car door, and leans toward me.

"It occurred to me after our conversation at the club last week that I left out a crucial piece of information."

"Oh?" I say blandly.

"Yes, some additional information that should help you come to your decision."

"My decision?" As I recall, G basically laid out the coming pogrom—the slaughter of DWP agents with the implication that those who manage to survive will be compensated. Like the finalists on *American Idol*. If there was something to decide, I missed it.

"Well, see," he says, nodding. "There actually is a decision to be made. So I'm glad I can clarify that now."

The Audi isn't all that roomy to begin with and it's getting more crowded in here by the minute. I shift in my seat, pulling back a bit from the window.

"I promise to make this as painless as possible," he says, smiling again.

I don't smile back, which G takes to be a green or at least a yellow light. In the next few weeks, there will be more fallout from the merger—maybe even a further exodus of clients. "Although I don't know that, I am braced for it," he says. "So we'll all just deal with these events as they arise. But BIG-DWP will survive, I can assure you of that."

"What are you saying?" I say, not following him.

"I'm saying that whatever happens, I don't want you to be concerned about the short term. I mean, there is more than enough to do, for everyone to do, servicing their own clients without worrying about others."

"Others?"

"Other publicists. And their clients."

He says this casually. Too casually. In fact, if I was the suspicious sort, I would say that G was 1.) onto my meeting with Suzanne and 2.) telling me expressly *not* to do what she asked me to do not thirty minutes ago.

"I'm sorry, I'm still not following you." If you want me to side with you and let Suzanne twist in the wind, you're going to have to spell it out.

But G just shakes his head. "I've kept you long enough." He drops his hands from the window and steps back. "Is this a BMW?" he says, glancing at my car.

"Audi."

"Oh, right," he says, smiling broadly. "Right. Volkswagen." And he keeps right on smiling as I roll up the window, put the car in reverse, and rocket out of his lair.

14 | Dr. Faustus, Line One

I'm home staring into the refrigerator trying to decide if I want a Diet Coke to perk myself up or wine to calm me down. After the day I've had, it could go either way. I'm just deciding on hedging my bets and making a cup of tea—*tea, there's an idea*—if I actually have any, when I hear my phone ring for what seems like the millionth time since I walked in. I don't own a thing. The house is rented, the car is leased. I don't even have a magazine subscription, but telemarketers still hunt me down.

"Land Shark" comes floating over the machine.

Steven. I pick up.

"Where are you, still in your Ryan O'Neal phase playing racquetball?"

"Actually, he played squash and rather well. At least better than me. So how'd it go with Suzanne?"

"News sure travels fast in the big city."

"Yes, it does. Now open up."

"Open up?"

"*Land Shark?* Don't tell me you don't remember that episode of *Saturday Night Live?*"

"Wait a minute, you're here?"

Steven and I are close, but we have our limits. Our one unspoken rule is that we don't go to each other's houses. The office. Drinks after work. Parties. Constant cell phone contact. But not home visits. That's a little *trop intime* even for us. Other than the time I had the flu and he dropped off a week's worth of chicken soup from Greenblatt's, Steven has never been here.

"Yes, now open your gate. I have food."

"You have food? That changes everything."

I buzz him in through the front gate and flick on the porch light. It's always amusing to watch people navigate my stairs at night. Not exactly user-friendly. Stone, pitched at roughly thirty-five degrees, which is probably not even code, and with half the path lights out.

"God, you need a funicular to get up and down your stairs," Steven says when he finally reaches the bottom. "Or a guide dog."

"Bitch, bitch, bitch," I say, opening the door.

"Here," he says, handing me a large white bag. "I may be uninvited, but I don't come empty-handed."

I peer into the bag. A white take-out container of salad, another smaller bag, and a bottle of Viognier. Good Viognier. "You brought me Viognier and salad?"

"I brought us the Viognier and you the salad. But not just any salad. It's that salad from that restaurant in Laurel Canyon."

"We're *in* Laurel Canyon."

"I live in Coldwater and I can never keep all the canyons straight. They're like all those former Soviet republics that became countries. Like where is Chechnya and who really cares?"

"The salad?"

"It's the one that's supposed to make women go into labor."

"Okay, first that's a myth and second, you thought I needed it why?"

"Because I thought it might make you let it all out. Like what the fuck is going on with you lately?"

"You're right and I'm sorry," I say, taking the bag and heading into the kitchen. I was wrong not to tell him about G's little come-on at the Viper Room. And I was seriously wrong in thinking Steven wouldn't notice. "But first, I have to have a glass of wine."

I open the wine and tell him everything. Hop onto the kitchen counter and go through it all. G at the Viper Room. His threats about layoffs and his creepy implications about how I can keep my job, right down to his running his hand down my arm.

"Ew," Steven says, leaning against the counter and giving a little shudder. "I still can't believe you never told me."

"I was too busy telling myself I imagined the whole thing."

"I suppose," he says, nodding like this could be true. On Mars. "But didn't he tell you what venal acts you could commit to keep your job?"

"I'll get to that."

Then I do Suzanne. Our little come-to-Jesus meeting this afternoon. When I finish, Steven stares morosely into his wineglass. "She really asked you to beg the Phoenix to stay on, on her behalf? That's so sad."

"No kidding. I mean, I worked with her for what, maybe a month when I first got out here? I didn't think I made any kind of impression. Now, out of the blue Suzanne thinks I'm the one with keys to her castle?"

"Look, you got me," he says with a shrug. "I still don't get why it's so important she stays on. I mean, clients come and go all the time."

"I don't totally get it either," I say, hopping down and reaching for the salad. "But Suzanne made it sound like it was the way her contract with G was written. That they each had to maintain a certain number of clients. For all I know, specific clients were listed by name."

"So what are you going to do? Go out to Malibu and get Rapunzel to let down her hair?"

"I haven't gotten that far yet," I say, dishing out the salad onto two plates. Steven peers at it suspiciously.

"It's lettuce," I say, holding out the plate. "I don't think it's going to cause you to give birth."

He tastes a leaf, shrugs, and takes the plate. "Okay, where were we?"

"That I don't know if I'm going to go out to Malibu to plead on Suzanne's behalf."

"Right. So why not? I mean, what's to lose besides your self-respect which apparently neither of your bosses thinks you have anyway?"

"Because G asked me not to."

"*What?* When?"

"You asked me if he spelled out the venal acts I could commit to keep my job? Well, he did. Tonight, in the parking garage after I finished up with Suzanne. We just happened to be leaving at the same time. As if."

"Normally, I would say some wiseass thing about Deep Throat—"

"Yeah, I know, so just save it because this is really freaking me out a little," I say, cutting him off. "G basically said if I wanted to ensure my future with the agency, I needed to cast my lot with him. Become part of his team."

"How? By fucking him?"

"I think he has other employees for that," I say, rattling off G's little speech in the garage. "All of which comes down to letting Suzanne twist in the wind—whichever way it blows."

Steven looks incredulous. "Come on. Two weeks ago G was practically putting you on probation. Now he's recruiting you for his special ops team?"

"No, he's saying that when Suzanne leaves—not if, but when—her equity position in the agency will be divvied up among a handful of key employees who have apparently proven themselves worthy."

"Which is worth what, a few grand a year maybe?"

"Now. But if they sell the agency, it could be worth millions."

"Okay, and don't take this wrong, but why you? Why is G offering this to you? You're hardly the most devoted employee now."

"I think that's part of it. That I'm the newest DWP hire and presumably have the least amount of loyalty to Suzanne. I also think that he needs at least one DWP publicist and her clients on his handpicked team. I mean, BIG-DWP can't just be BIG with a different name."

"So what are you going to do?"

I look at him. "I guess what everyone does in Hollywood. Betray someone."

An hour later, the salad is gone, no one has given birth, and we are no closer to figuring out what I should do. But after half a bottle of Viognier, I'm starting to get sick of the whole thing.

"I'm just going to quit," I say, all but prone on the sofa with Steven sitting facing me at the far end. "I mean, I'm sick of publicity anyway. Why should I help either one of them? They're both just using me."

"Is that patio furniture?" Steven says, ignoring me to study my dining table that is, yes, wrought-iron patio furniture dragged in from the back deck.

"Yeah, it came with the house. I only got the sofa and chairs when Josh and I split up. So I brought that inside for the winter."

"Oh, good thinking," he says. "I mean, it goes so well with the rest of your stuff."

"Hey, have you priced furniture lately? Every time I go shopping for a new table, I just get depressed and wind up buying a new handbag instead."

"Okay, why shouldn't you quit?" Steven says, off the furniture issue now. "Because if G is serious, you could be looking at some potentially serious money, as you say. Or the potential for some serious money. Which is the only reason anybody comes to Hollywood. To quote the late, great Sam Kinison, the assholes would show up for yard work if it paid as well as Hollywood does."

I'm just wondering if that's actually true, when Steven suddenly jumps up. "Wait," he says, heading into the kitchen. "I totally forgot. The coup de foudre."

"'Clap of thunder'? Don't you mean coup de grâce?"

"Wait till you see what it is."

He emerges a minute later carrying the second, smaller bag. "Here," he says, handing it to me. "Open it."

"What is it? OxyContin?"

"That would be nice. But no."

I sigh, sit up, and unfold the bag. Inside is a white ceramic soufflé dish covered with tinfoil.

I look up at him. "Open it," he says again. "You'll be happy."

I pull back the foil. Rice pudding. With a crinkly wrinkled top, like the top layer of paint that has congealed in a can. "Oh my God, where did you get this?"

"Did you notice it's baked, not stirred? Just the way you like it. And no raisins."

"I'm not kidding. Where did you get this? You can only get stirred at Greenblatt's."

"Where do you think? I made it."

"You *made* me a rice pudding?" Either I am to be completely pitied or Steven has unknown talents.

"It was on the Food Channel. That crazy English guy. He was doing a menu of nursery food, whatever that is. Anyway, I thought of you and your stories about the rice pudding at your grandmother's club back in Philadelphia."

"I told you about the Union League?"

"Several times," he says. "Now, should I get spoons or do you want me to just put the bowl on the floor and the puppy can go nuts?"

"No, the puppy can share," I say, flopping back on the sofa and cradling the pudding. Suddenly the day looks to have a much better finish than I thought possible even an hour ago.

Steven disappears into the kitchen and begins opening what sounds like all my cupboards looking for bowls. "I don't think I've eaten rice pudding as an adult. At least not willingly," he says, shouting a bit over the noise. "Are these Waterford?" He appears in the doorway a second later holding up two cut-crystal bowls.

"Wedding present."

"Nice," he says, holding one up to the light. "Should we use them?"

"Use them? They've never been used," I say. "Just like everything else from my life. Still waiting for the starting gun to go off."

"I thought we were over the my-marriage-failed-my-life-is-a-mess phase," Steven says, heading toward the sofa armed with bowls and spoons. "I mean, there's Charles now."

"Maybe," I say, more sulkily than I intend. "Can you have a relationship that's just on the phone?"

"Honey, there's an entire toll-call industry devoted to just that," he says, sitting down beside me and patting my hand. "Look, you guys are just getting started. He's called you what, every day since he left? You're golden."

"Well, it feels like vermeil. Looks good, but who really knows?" I flop back on the sofa again and watch Steven spoon out the rice pudding. One scoop for him. Four for me. Four should do it. Plus a little left over for the morning.

He hands me my bowl and then takes a bite from his own. "Okay, that was fun," he says, putting the bowl down.

"Don't worry, it won't go to waste," I say, licking the back of my spoon.

Steven watches me eat for a second and then gazes around the living room again.

"So other than your patio furniture, this all looks pretty cool. Is this antique?" he says, nodding at the Oriental rug.

"Yeah," I murmur between bites. "Grandma's. As was that and that and that," I say, nodding at the burled walnut coffee table, the Spanish leather folding screen in the corner, and the sideboard against the wall holding my stereo system and TV.

"Is that a Frank Lloyd Wright?" he says, getting up to examine the sideboard.

"I think so," I say. "*Grandmère* was a tad eccentric in her tastes. I have two red leather chairs downstairs in the bedroom that she had made from the seats in their old Mercedes. They sit about five inches off the floor, but they are striking. Are we surprised that Amy took the family silver and the Limoges and left me the dregs?"

Steven turns and looks at me. "The dregs? You have all this fabulous stuff and you're so busy feeling sorry for yourself that you can't get it together to buy a fucking dining room table?"

I stop in midbite. "Hey, I never said I felt sorry for myself because of my furniture. I love this stuff. It makes me feel more at home than anything Josh and I ever bought together. I feel sorry for myself because the rest of my life is a mess."

Steven shakes his head. "I'm beginning to think it's not so much of a mess as you want to *believe* it's a mess. You bitch about your clients not taking responsibility for their lives, but I don't know if it isn't exactly what you're doing as well."

I drop my spoon into the bowl with a clatter, gather up the rest of the pudding, and stalk into the kitchen. "Hey, don't be mad," Steven calls out.

"Too late for that," I holler back. I bang the tea kettle around for a few minutes until my anger passes. Or I start to feel ridiculous. "Do you want some tea?" I say finally.

"No."

"It's as much of a white flag as I'm going to wave."

"Okay, then yes."

I find some ancient Lapsang in the freezer and make two cups. I take a sip. Like drinking liquid smoke. Oh well, it's a gesture. "Here," I say, heading back into the living room with the tea. "Although this probably would have been better if we smoked it."

We sit next to each other on the sofa sipping the awful tea. "I feel like I should read some Emily Dickinson. Aloud," Steven says.

I elbow him in the ribs. Our fight is officially over.

"Does that work?" he says, nodding at the fireplace.

"Yeah. It's gas."

"Shall we have a fire, dear?"

I put down my cup, reach for the matches on the coffee table. I crouch down, fiddle with the gas lever and the matches for a minute. Finally, a blue flame leaps across the empty, soot-stained bricks.

"That looks real," he says, squinting at the flame. "Sort of."

"I was thinking of getting some fake logs to go with it."

"And ruin the Bunsen burner effect? Don't you think there's something about the purity of a naked flame?"

"If you're a chemist. Or cook PCP in your basement."

"If only we had some crack. Or marshmallows."

"Okay, and this is scary—we do," I say, leaping up and heading into the kitchen. Once you're into the sugar, you might as well go all the way. Besides, we need a chaser for that tea. I root around the cupboard and find the half-empty bag of marshmallows. A girl doesn't need much. Just wine, crackers, good coffee, Scharfenberger cocoa, and marshmallows. That combination has gotten me through many a night. And the next morning. I open a drawer and pull out two metal skewers—did I know I had these?—and head back into the living room.

"Burnt sugar coming up," I say, handing him a skewer. We load them up and go at it for a while. "Smells like Girl Scouts in here," I say, wiping the corners of my mouth with my fingers.

"Wouldn't know," he says, reaching for more marshmallows. "If only we had more wine, we could be like Sunny von Bulow and lapse into a coma. So what are you doing for Christmas?"

"Haven't gotten that far. I have to get through Thanksgiving first. My parents are coming, remember?"

"I thought they were coming for Christmas?"

"The anticipation was killing me. I convinced them to come for Thanksgiving instead. Get it out of the way. I already got them a room at the Chateau."

"You got Jack and Helen a room at the Chateau?"

"Jack and Helen and Amy and Barkley."

"The dog's coming?"

"Amy's husband. Such as he is."

"I'll say it again, the Chateau? Nobody's parents stay at the Chateau. Not unless they're English."

"They said they wanted to be near my house. They said they wanted something with 'atmosphere.' I was thinking of sticking them in the Standard, but I thought that was pushing it."

"I think the Chateau's pushing it."

"I booked them a bungalow suite."

"The John Belushi memorial?"

"Look, it'll be fine," I say. "Mom'll love the lobby. Dad can read the paper in the courtyard and pretend he's at the club or wherever he likes to pretend he is. And Amy can lie around the pool and think she's at the apogee of Hollywood cool."

"It is the apogee of Hollywood cool."

"Well, I know that, but I'm not going to tell her."

We roast a few more skewers. I'm starting to feel slightly jumpy from all the sugar, when the phone rings.

"Don't answer it," Steven says, licking his fingers. "We don't have enough even for us and I'm not comatose yet."

"It's my phone, not the front door."

"Oh, then answer it if you want."

I check my watch—going on ten—and decide to let the machine pick up.

"Hey, you, I thought I'd check and see if you were home before I tried your cell—" is as much as Charles gets out before I grab it.

"Hey," I say, vaulting across Steven to grab the portable off the coffee table. "How's it going? It's pretty late there." I look back over at Steven. He is mouthing "He calls you *you*?" and gives me a thumbs-up.

Later, much later into our conversation, after Steven has gone and the fire is out, I feel the ground slip. Just slightly. But enough. Enough to change things. To change everything.

"Look, the point is that you and I appear to be the only DWP agents not in Doug's crosshairs," Charles says. We've been at this for over an hour. G. Suzanne. The Phoenix. He knows as much—no, more—than I do. Like the fact that G has already had a few meetings with ad agencies in New York. "It's just wrong, Alex. Doug came to us, convinced the DWP partners to get into bed with him, and now he's trying to screw them, particularly Suzanne, out of what is rightfully theirs."

I do what I've been doing for the past hour: lying on the sofa, murmuring my assent. It's comforting listening to Charles's voice. Plus the fact that he seems to have a plan and that he's confiding in me. "Well, I think you've got it all figured out," I say.

"Look, I don't have it all figured out. I don't know, given the intricacies of Suzanne's contract, that it's possible to even stop him at this point. We're talking to her lawyer now, but it's crucial to maintain all of Suzanne's remaining clients."

"Oh, I thought you knew how. How to stop him."

There's a pause. "Look, I'm not getting reams of anger coming off you," he says suddenly. "Where are you on all this?"

I sit up on the sofa. "*Reams?* Well, of course I'm upset. I don't like Doug any more than you do and I really don't like being dragged into the middle of this feud—"

"Feud? This is more than a feud. This is the future of DWP here."

"You mean the DWP where you're already a senior partner?"

"What's that supposed to mean?"

Now it's my turn to pause. What *did* I mean? "Look, I'm just saying yes, it's wrong that Suzanne looks like she's going to get screwed out of what is rightfully hers. But she signed that deal. She chose to merge with BIG. I feel bad that she might lose everything, but it's not my fault that she and the agency are in this situation."

"I didn't say it's your fault, but you are in a position to do something. To help us try and stop him."

"Am I? Am I really?" I stand up and start to pace. Maybe it's the late hour. Or the sugar that I can feel fleeing my bloodstream like scaffolding collapsing. Or maybe I'm just tired of the whole thing. Ever since G showed up, it's just been one thing after another and it was pretty damn sucky before. "Look, I know Suzanne thinks I can do something to help and apparently you do too, but I really doubt that. I mean, if the two of you and your lawyers can't stop Doug, you think I can? That's almost funny."

"What's he offered you?" Charles asks coldly. "This doesn't sound like you. Or what I thought was you."

"What's that supposed to mean?" I say, knowing perfectly well what he means. "Yes, Doug's approached me. You're the one who just said you and I are about the only two DWP agents not in his sights. Now you're blaming me because Doug has talked to me about my future at the agency? Look, you said it yourself. People are going to get laid off no matter what. People *should* get laid off. We don't have the client base to support everyone. But I'm supposed to fall on my sword for the good of old DWP?"

"Well, I think you've answered my question," he says stiffly. "It sounds like you've made up your mind. Thanks for letting me know where you stand."

"I *haven't* made up my mind," I say, angry now. "But it's very easy for you to be righteous about this. You're a partner. I'm not. We're in totally different positions and from where I sit, I don't have a dog in this fight. Not really. Not the way things stand now."

"Well, apparently that's about to change."

"Look, I just told you, I haven't decided anything. I'm not *with* Doug. I'm not against him. But, frankly, he's given me more reasons to side with him than you and Suzanne have."

"Oh," Charles says very, very quietly. "And I thought I had. And I thought you were happy about that. But apparently I was wrong."

"Look," I say, scrambling now for something, anything that will put this conversation back on track. Put *us* back on track. "Look, I didn't mean what—"

"Look. Let's forget it. Let's forget all of it. I'll just talk to you later."

He hangs up. Oh, *fuck*. Two fights in one night and this one isn't going to be fixed with a cup of tea. I throw the phone onto the sofa. Now what? I check my watch. Nearly midnight. I'm exhausted but there's no chance I'll get to sleep anytime soon. Not after that conversation. God, how did I manage in the space of a single phone call to blow both my relationship, such as it was, and my job? Unless I totally throw my lot in with G now, I'm screwed. Alone and screwed.

I check my watch again. Still midnight. Fuck it. I head into the kitchen, grab my bag, fish out my keys, and slam out the front door. If I can't sleep, I might as well drive. Besides, it's a cold, clear night. A good wind off the desert. If I take Mulholland, I should be able to see the city spread out below me, the lights spiraling out like lit circuitry.

I pull the Audi out of the garage. I've heard you can take it all the way, Mulholland. All the way to the ocean. If you know how to go. I slide open the sunroof. The icy night pours in. I speed across Laurel Canyon, drop the car in third, and head out. I have a long drive ahead of me.

15 | We Gather Together

 "Honey, this rain. I mean, we could've just stayed at home."

It's pouring and I'm in the lobby of the Chateau with my parents staring at the rain-soaked courtyard, reassessing this whole family-in-L.A.-for-Thanksgiving idea. Actually, Helen and I are staring at the rain. Jack is deep in an armchair with *The Wall Street Journal.*

"Well, I thought the point was to actually visit *me,*" I say, trying to keep my voice out of the whiner's circle.

"It's El Niño," says Jack distractedly, as he flips through the paper. "Although it's pretty early for that. Usually it doesn't get going until late January. Even February."

I look over at him. "How do you know more about L.A.'s weather than I do?"

"Honey, you know your father," Helen says, staring at the rain sluicing off the hotel roof. From the look on her face, I can tell she's taking this as personally as she possibly can, that someone, probably me, has already ruined her trip to California.

"Look," I say, jumping into my salvage campaign. "There's usually a heat wave in L.A. in November. I thought it would be a good time to be here. Amy could enjoy the pool and you and I could have lunch outside at the Ivy. So I'm sorry we have to change our plans. But at least it's *green*," I say, nodding at the palm trees blowing in the stiff breeze.

"Oh honey, there's no need to go on about it," Helen says, turning back to the lobby. "We'll be fine. We'll just go to lunch somewhere else."

I'd forgotten how quickly my mother can turn on a dime, leaving you in the lurch, the ditch you had frantically dug on her behalf just a second earlier. It's why I'm not breathing a word to her, or frankly anyone in my family, about my job and Charles and whatever our relationship is. Was. Is. If I can't figure out the reasons and wherefores of my being a Hollywood publicist three years after I made the decision to move here, I certainly know enough not to drag Helen into the discussion. She and Jack are on a need-to-know basis only. And they don't need to know much. Two years ago, on their first—and only—trip to L.A., they saw my old DWP office. This time, they get my new business card—*Alex Davidson, Senior Publicist BIG-DWP*—and an endless stream of "It's great!" when questions about my job—hell, my life—come up.

"So, Dad, you're interested in lunch, right?" I say, changing strategies. If my mother is a fucking quarter horse with her moods and tactics, Jack is a Budweiser Clydesdale. This won't be the first time I've taken refuge in his plodding obliviousness.

"Sure," he says, not looking up. "Wherever you gals want to go is fine with me."

"All right, let me think a second," I say, running through my options. It's Wednesday, the day before Thanksgiving. My parents arrived last night, the same night I had planned for us to go to dinner on Orso's patio, where I envisioned balmy breezes and a few celebs my parents might actually recognize. Like Suzanne Pleshette or Steve Martin. Of course their delayed flight torpedoed that plan. By the time they got to the Chateau, after nine, they were so wiped they just collapsed with room service.

Now, after getting an earful from Helen about their Spartan suite—"Honey, there's not even a rug on that wood floor"—I'm now being called to account for the weather. I'd planned that Mom and I would eat lunch at the Ivy (it's the ideal Mom place, with chintz pillows, overpriced salads, and ancient celebs), followed by a little shopping along Robertson while Amy and Barkley hung out at the pool and went off on their own; typically they had rented their own car, a massive SUV. But this storm, which does not look to be adjourning any time soon, is now forcing me to reschedule Day II and God knows it has been hard enough to come up with an original set of Hollywood activities suitable for the Bucks County crowd. Like trying to program the Food Channel for anorexics.

At least Friday looks foolproof—a day at the spa with Amy and me and Helen, if she feels up to being touched by strangers. And there's no changing Thursday's plan for Thanksgiving dinner at the Getty. I had to reserve more than a month in advance and frankly, even if it's pouring, the place will still be impressive in that over-the-top L.A. way. "A modern Acropolis," as I described it to Helen, who, of course, thought I meant they served only Greek food—a misunderstanding that required several minutes of further discussion before she agreed to let me book our Thanksgiving there.

But first I have to deal with lunch. I check my watch. It's getting late enough that we can probably just eat somewhere and then Helen and Jack can head back here for a nap before the evening's festivities, such as they are, begin at Mr. Chow. Booking dinner at that tourist trap is my only nod to Amy and Barkley, who turned out to be a dog with a bone about the whole We-have-to-eat-at-Mr.-Chow-because-I-read-about-it-in-W thing. I mean, what heterosexual guy reads W, even if his wife does subscribe?

Given that overpriced MSG will be dinner, what to do about

lunch? I run through the likely suspects. The Grill. The Palm. Barney Greengrass. Agents, managers, lawyers. Hollywood's equivalent of lions, tigers, and bears. My parents would never know what hit them. Sushi in a valley mini-mall? No way. A.O.C. doesn't serve lunch and besides, the idea of a wine bar and "small plates" would be lost on Jack and Helen. Four Seasons? Campanile? For one reason or another all the usual suspects seem wrong for a rainy, slow afternoon when most of L.A. has had the foresight to be in Hawaii. Oh, screw it, I'll take them to Kate Mantilini. It's a classic and has enough of an industry vibe that even Jack might notice it.

"You know, how about a great burger and a nice glass of wine at this really cool diner? They even shot a scene in *Heat* there," I say brightly. If you smile at the baby, the baby will smile back.

"Oh honey, a burger the day before Thanksgiving?"

"Mom, they have salads and other—"

"And what's *Heat*?" she adds, looking bewildered.

"Sounds great," Jack says, tossing aside the paper. "Tell you what, I'll even buy."

"So what's your goal with them this weekend?" Steven says, when I call him after dropping Helen and Jack at the hotel and have collapsed at home. My half-time respite in the locker room before suiting up for tonight's game. Lunch turned out okay. Actually, better than okay. Like stealing home after two outs in the third. We got a booth overlooking Wilshire, Helen had her salad and iced tea—at least she's on Hollywood's wavelength with her beverage choices—and Jack, who loved the whole businessman-in-a-baseball-cap vibe, had a burger and two Anchor Steams. I can't remember what I had, but just as we were leaving Al Pacino walked in, which, given that he's probably one of the few celebrities my parents would recognize, allowed Helen to trot out another of her backhanded, inside-out compliment-and-reproaches all in one:

"Oh, he's so much shorter than I thought."

"Mom, they're all shorter than you think. Except Nicole Kidman, who takes steroids or something so her height actually matches her self-regard."

"Alex, I'm sure you're used to seeing these people all the time and can afford to be blasé, but your dad and I aren't."

Game, Mom.

"What's my goal?" I say to Steven. "To get through their visit in one piece."

"I'm serious," he says over the sound of chopping. Steven is already deep into preparations for his annual Thanksgiving-for-the-boys feast he does every year. "Do you want them to have fun? To realize Hollywood is the sham you know it to be? Or do you want them to think you have the most fabulous and difficult job and that you and not Amy are the brilliant, talented daughter they didn't know they had?"

"You know, I'm sure you're right. If I had a goal, this might all be clearer, but I am just honestly trying to get through this weekend pleasantly and with minimal explosions. Especially since Amy is here. If it was just my parents, I might be able to get in some of that. Like what I'm doing in Hollywood. But not with Amy around being her usual spoiled, superior self. She's even better than Mom at peeing on everyone's parade. So no, I do not have a goal except to get them in and out of town in one piece."

"Denial, denial, denial," he says, rhythmically whacking some poor vegetable. "You sound just like your mother when you talk like that."

"How would you know? You haven't even met her."

"We've talked on the phone. Besides, it's not for lack of trying," he says, whacking away. "I invited you guys for Thanksgiving."

"We went over that."

"And I told you I would go out with you for a meal or a drink. Or come here on your way to dinner tonight. I'm just cooking for tomorrow. Just me and the twenty-pound tom. *Home Alone with the Bird.*"

"I told you, my parents are from Philly. They wouldn't understand the concept of my having a gay male friend."

"They've seen *Will & Grace.*"

"That's set in New York. Not Philadelphia. And they wouldn't get it with their daughter. Not when she can't manage to find herself a nice heterosexual male to be her friend."

"So Charles is on the need-to-know basis as well?"

"Uh, *yeah,* when I don't even know where we stand. Look, there's only so much I can deal with over a holiday weekend, and right now my parents are it."

"Then just tell your parents I'm your assistant."

"Who happens to live in a house bigger than the White House? No, they wouldn't get that either."

"Okay," he says, sighing, and I can tell he's getting bored with me and my parents. God knows I am. "Well, I'm here if you need me."

We hang up and I check the time. Going on five-thirty. I'm not due back at the Chateau until seven, when we'll all pile into the Lincoln Navigator Barkley insisted on renting and head to Beverly Hills for humiliation and dim sum. Time enough for a soak in the tub and maybe a little predinner drink. Just to keep my game face on.

Heading downstairs to the bath, I try to remember where I was last Thanksgiving. Home? Here? I'm drawing a blank. What about Christmas? Home, I think. As if it mattered. It seems like ages since a holiday meant anything. Maybe that's what happens when you get older. It all runs together. Maybe if I had kids, it would be different. Home to Grandma and Grandpa's for Christmas. God knows Jack and Helen's Colonial on their 2.2 acres of prime Main Line real estate fits the bill, especially when it's snowing, which is fairly frequently, according to Jack. But I can't remember the last time I felt any joy being back there.

I must have at one time. I do remember that. It's there at the back of my mind, like a name just out of reach. Or a taste you vaguely recall. Like the cones at the Dairy Queen, where Jack used to take me and our old boxer, Bull, on Saturday nights when I was still a kid. Or the smell of the cedar closet in the guest bedroom, where Helen keeps her mink jacket wrapped in tissue and where I used to hide out during those long summers home from college.

I know it's there because I remember one Thanksgiving, one of the last ones when Grandma was there. I took a nap upstairs in the guest room after dinner, with our white cat, Blue, and with the ticking clock on the bedside table. I'd fallen asleep with the watery winter sun bathing the room. But when I awoke, the room was muffled in dusk and my heart was pounding. How long had I been asleep? Hours? It felt like days. I lay there without any sense of time or place, just the metronome of the clock ticking.

And then I heard them. Downstairs. My mother talking to her mother in the kitchen. No words. Just their voices. The music of their voices rising through the house. I looked over at Blue, who was cleaning herself, oblivious to my little resurrection.

That's what I miss. Feeling safe. Not trapped. Safe.

"Alex, I think Barkley can find it on his own," Helen says.

I'm in the passenger seat next to my brother-in-law, who's punching at the satellite navigation button on the Navigator's roof. A boy with his toys. "Mr. Chow's," he repeats in his robotically slow voice. "In Beverly Hills on Canon."

"Camden," I say.

"That's what I said," Barkley says without looking at me.

"It's *Cam-den*, not *Can-on*," I say again.

"Alex, let Barkley do it. He wants to test out the system."

"Okay, I won't say another word." I flop back in the seat and turn my attention to the rain-sloshed Chateau driveway.

"You know, the one we have in the Volvo at home works great. Your mother can even find her way into the city with it," says Jack, who is wedged in the backseat between Helen and Amy. Amy, who's in full I'm-just-a-devoted-suburban-wife-and-daughter mode. Talk about denial. She doesn't remotely understand her life any more than I understand mine—how we wound up on opposite ends of the parental-expectations gauge—but unlike me, she refuses to question it, even when I can tell her patience for her doltish Ken-Doll-of-an-attorney husband is wearing thin. I know that about her, just like I know that even if I stay out of her way, keep our conversations banal and upbeat this weekend, the dam will eventually give way. It's just a question of when and where.

"Jack, I've been finding my way into the city since before we got the Volvo," Helen says, slightly miffed. "I don't know why you say things like that."

"They're fine once you get used to them," Amy says, retying the sweater around her neck. "I finally got used to ours and it's great."

"I was just commenting on the system," Jack says, raising his hands. "Frankly, I consider it a safety feature. Like a cell phone."

Barkley punches the button again. "Mr. Chow's," he repeats.

"It's *Chow*, not *Chow's*," I say, without thinking.

"*Ciao?*" says Helen. "I thought we were eating Chinese."

"We are eating Chinese," says Amy, still fiddling with her sweater.

We've been at this for at least five minutes, parked on or rather blocking the hotel's slip of a driveway. Out the window, I see two cars behind us in the garage, three in front of us trying to get up the drive, and the valet heading our way. I'm about to suggest that Barkley just fucking chill with the high-tech directions and drive, at least off the hotel property, when the navigation system springs to life: "Mr. Harbinger, your directions." A glowing list flashes onto the tiny screen. I don't even bother to look. If it sends us to Pasadena, I could care less as long as we get off this driveway.

"Okay, here we go," says Barkley, peering at the screen. He studies it for a second and then puts the Navigator in gear. "Next stop, Mr. Chow's," he says, heading down the rain-slicked drive, honking wildly at the cars we've blocked.

"No, no. This table good. Good one. Banquet. You sit here."

We are in the back at Mr. Chow. Five of us wedged around a four-top in a banquette, squeezed between two couples, one of which looks to be two male models on their first date, given the number of aqua-colored martinis going down, and the other a couple of stunned-looking tourists with *Zagat* guides and un-colored hair. Across from us is a party of some British band, or wannabe band, and their groupies, who are already whooping it up in that annoyingly loud *Oy, mate* way Cockneys love to do in America. So far, it's exactly what I predicted. Siberia. And all its lovely denizens.

"I don't know why we couldn't sit in the front room where Tony Curtis was," Helen says, looking mournfully over her shoulder. "I thought I saw an empty table there."

"Mom, there were three empty tables, but that's how it works here," I say, fishing out a menu from the pile the waiter dropped on the table. "If you're not a star or a regular, they dump you back here."

"I'll talk to them," says Jack, pushing back his chair.

I have visions of a ten changing hands. Like that would do any-thing.

"Dad, don't even bother. They'll just tell you they're reserved. Let's just stay here."

"I'll never understand this town," Helen says with a shake of her head, reaching across me for a menu. "You'd think they'd want people to sit next to Tony Curtis, for goodness's sake. So you'd know he was there."

"So how was the visit to the animation studio?" I say, as I stare, or pretend to stare, at the menu. Eating is the least of my con-cerns.

"Fine. If you're into animation," says Amy, behind her menu. She and Barkley spent the afternoon taking a private tour of Dis-ney's animation building because an old college buddy of Barkley's worked in marketing or something and arranged it.

"Fantastic. You should see the way they do computer graphics up close," says Barkley. "It's so amazing. Nothing like you'd expect. You know, they actually have to get the actor to perform the role first, film it, and then do the animating. That's why it takes so long."

"Yeah, I heard that," I say, trying to keep the sarcasm out of my voice. Christ, every kid with a PlayStation knows that. "Dad, what are you going to have?" I say, changing tactics. The sooner we get started, the sooner we can get out of here.

"Well, what's good here?"

"You know, I don't eat here that often—"

"No, no," Barkley interrupts. "We have to let them order for us. For the table. That's the way to do it."

"Was that in the article too?" I get out before Amy elbows me sharply in the ribs.

"Honey, then you do it," Amy says, laying aside her menu with a flicker of impatience, the first cracks in the dam. "We'll let you take care of it."

"Okay, but make sure there's some fish dish. And a chicken," Helen says, eyeing Jack over her menu. "We're trying to eat less red meat these days."

Jack tosses down his menu. "I don't know about the rest of you, but I could use a drink. And I can order that for myself."

I look up. Nailing a waiter in here is about as difficult as getting an agent to return your call. Chinese guys and the occasional whippet-thin Caucasian are rushing around, beads of sweat gleaming on their brows. It's so humid with the crowd and the rain that steam is gathering on the glass divider atop the banquette. The noise is deafening, the Cockneys are shrieking with laughter, and I'm starting to get a crick in my back from sitting jammed in between Amy and Helen.

"You know, our firm just opened a branch in L.A.," Barkley says over the din. "It looks like we'll be starting to do some entertainment business. I'm probably going to be coming back out."

I suddenly have a horrifying vision of Barkley and Amy moving to L.A. Pasadena. No, the Palisades is more their style, especially given what Barkley could earn as an entertainment lawyer. I look over at Amy, but she has the hatches battened down. What am I worried about? It would take a nuclear explosion, or some serious therapy, to get Amy out of Philly permanently. Barkley may come out, but he will go back. Still, of all my family, the guy who is least equipped to leave Bucks County is the one who loves L.A. Go figure.

"Really," I say, trying to sound enthusiastic. "Well, that would be great."

"Yeah, so I might even be able to help you the next time one of your clients has to go to court."

I can't tell if this is a dig about Troy and my job or if Barkley is just being his eager, clueless self. Before I can parse it, a waiter miraculously stumbles to a stop at our table.

"Drink. You want drinks?"

We practically fall over one another to get our orders out. Scotch for Jack. Barkley wants a Tsingtao. Helen and I go for white wine.

"Amy?" I say, turning to her.

"I'll have a mineral water with a lime," she says, smiling up at the waiter.

"You're having water?" My sister isn't much of a drinker, but she always has a glass of red wine. For the antioxidants.

"Didn't Mom tell you? I'm pregnant."

"Honey, do you want to say grace?"

"No, Mom, not here I don't," I say, looking around the Getty's dining room. I'm not inclined to indulge my mother's holiday traditions under her own roof, let alone in public, and at 3 P.M., Thanksgiving afternoon, this place is packed.

"We could have said it in the car in the garage," says Barkley. I look over at him. He's either serious or doing some major sucking up. You'd think he'd be beyond that, having fathered what will be the family's first grandchild.

"Oh well, I just thought it being Thanksgiving and all . . ." says Helen, letting her voice trail off. Normally her *poor-me* strategies don't guilt-trip me anymore, but she looks so disappointed—I know the trip has largely been a letdown with the rain and the hotel, or maybe I'm just still so obviously a letdown, still divorced, and now not with child—that I relent.

"But I will propose a toast," I say, picking up my glass of the Veuve Clicquot Jack has ordered. "To us," I say, as we all clink glasses. "To the first Bradford family—sorry, Bradford-Harbinger family—gathering in Los Angeles. Thank you all for coming. And for the meal we are about to share," I say, dropping my voice on the last part. "May it be the first of many."

"Thank you, Alex," Helen says, smiling at me over her glass. "That was lovely, although I don't know about the first of many."

"Really?" I say, sticking my toe in that frigid water. "You wouldn't come back? I mean, I know the rain has cramped our plans, but I think L.A. has its charms."

"Well, yes, of course," says Helen. "And we haven't even seen your new office yet. Or met your friends." She lets the last part hang in the air.

"Well, everyone is away for the holiday," I say, foolishly taking the bait. The unspoken accusation that my life, however tricked up with celebrities and movies and limos and court trials, is just compensatory Plan B. Plan B because I willfully fucked up Plan A, which was pretty fucked up to begin with.

"It's been fine," says Jack. "Next time, might even get in a little golf. I think a couple of the guys at the club back home know somebody at Riviera. Get in a round that way."

"I'm sure our firm will be having some sort of local club membership," Barkley pipes up. "I'm sure I could work something out there."

"No, I just meant that with Amy expecting the baby in June, we won't be traveling much in the immediate future," Helen says, unfolding her napkin like she's opening a hymnal.

"Mother, I've already said that you and Daddy do not need to turn your lives upside down just because I'm having a baby," Amy says, taking a sip of her water. Evian with lime and no ice.

Of course not. Not when they can turn their lives inside out for *you*. Against golf and this baby, I don't stand a chance. Forget my job, my office, my clients. Even if I had thrown a party at Skybar and the entire DWP-BIG client list had shown, it would have been wasted on them. Except for Barkley. L.A. is just another oddity in my odd little life. Steven was right. I had wanted something from their visit. Not praise. Not awe. I wanted them to understand why I had come to Hollywood. Even if I don't fully understand it myself.

But I've failed. Tripped up by rain, an unborn fetus, but mostly by that disconnect, that gap that exists between the movies, the TV shows, the racks of magazines at grocery store checkout lines—the endless fat issues with their beaming celebrity covers—and the reality that is Hollywood. The country is besotted with celebrity, obsessed with it, but somehow the place that creates it, churns it out by the bucketful, is still a little unseemly up close. Still leaves a bad taste in the rest of the country's mouth. And now I'm part of it.

"Right," I say, nodding. "The baby. Well, it was a thought. Maybe another year."

A waiter cruises by and we bury ourselves in the menus, heads bowed as if in prayer. Festive offerings are listed: pheasant, foie gras, strawberries with blackberry coulis, and pumpkin tart with a walnut crust. The room is blazing with light. The first sun we've seen in days and the views are astonishing. The hills, green from the rain, and the gray-green ocean are visible with the slightest turn of the head. The crowd too is good. Well-dressed foreigners. Japanese. Italian. Families with quiet, gleaming, ebony-haired children. And locals who look like they work for foundations. Or the museum. Not studios. Who are faithful contributors to NPR. Women in long skirts and with their long gray hair wrapped in chignons. Men in blazers and ties. Anonymity at its most perfect. Its most acceptable.

"Oh, this is lovely," my mother says, turning excitedly in her chair. "Alex, I'm so glad you chose this place."

The pace of our conversations, so halting and awkward over the past two days, quickens, loosens. We talk about the baby, the hideous inappropriateness of the Chateau, and how next time, yes, next time, the Bel-Air Hotel with the swans and the stream. And golf. And no rain. And a drive. Yes, a day trip up the coast to Santa Barbara. And lunch at the Biltmore, yes, where the press used to stay when Reagan was at his ranch. Yes, all of it sounds lovely. Yes, California is lovely, lovely, after all. And we are lovely, lovely, after all.

"So, I'm sorry I didn't tell you about the baby."

"It doesn't matter."

Amy and I are in the upstairs lounge of the spa at the Century Plaza Hotel watching the cracks in the dam grow ever larger. Actually, we're dressed in identical butter-colored microfiber robes lying on lounges gazing out at the rain lashing the giant floor-to-ceiling window. Or I'm gazing. Amy has a lavender satin eye pillow over her eyes.

I take a sip of my raspberry tea in the little sea-green ceramic cup and take a poke at the largest crack. "But why didn't you tell me?"

Amy sighs. "Because we only just found out and when I told Mom she said, 'Don't tell Alex yet. Let's let it be a surprise.'"

"Yeah, well, it was."

Amy rips the eye pouch from her eyes as the water bursts through the dam. "Well, I'm sorry I didn't clear it with you first. I hoped you might be happy for us. For *me*. But I knew you'd be mad. You always have to see everything in terms of you."

"I do not see everything in terms of me," I say, struggling to sit up and managing to spill the tea on my robe, so it looks like a pale bloodstain. "That is such BS."

"Really? Then why have you been such a bitch the whole time

we've been here?" she hisses. "Even Mom thinks you've been acting weird."

"Mom always thinks I'm acting weird. She thinks it's weird that
I moved to L.A. You *all* think it's weird. Except for your husband,
who's so whipped up about Hollywood. At least he has the grace
to talk about my work. The rest of you could give a shit."

"Leave Barkley out of this. I just want to know when you're
going to stop being jealous of me. I was so stupid to think that my
having a baby might make things easier between us."

"*Jealous?*" I can't believe Amy is going this far back. Here in my
own city, on my own turf, she is managing to yank me back twenty
years, to the fights we used to have in our old bedroom in Upper
Darby. The little house we lived in before Jack and Helen moved
up in the world and out to Bryn Mawr. "You think I'm jealous of
you?" I shake my head, disbelieving. "You are so far from the truth.
So far."

"Oh really? Well, believe what you want," she says, replacing
the eye pillow and sinking back on the chaise. "We all know what
it looks like."

"Oh gee," I say, flopping back on my lounge. "Next, you're
going to tell me Mom always liked you best."

An attendant cruises by wearing a kimono and an alarmed
expression. "Ladies, is there, ah, anything we can get you?" she
says in her whispery Asian accent. "Some ice water? Or more
tea?"

"No thanks. We're fine," I say, forcing myself to smile. "We're
just waiting for our massage appointments."

The attendant checks her watch, gives us another worried
glance, and shuffles off. Silence radiates off Amy. I stare out at the
rain. We never could travel as a family. Even when we were kids.
Stupid to think we could get along now. I look over at her. So
pious in her stillness. Her marriage. Her pregnancy. In the *rightness*
of her life and the *wrongness* of mine. I close my eyes and try and
force myself into stillness. I take a few deep breaths. Shit. All I

want to do is knock that pillow off her eyes and tell her to stop being such a jerk. That I am not jealous of her, have *never* been jealous of her, that I actually feel sorry for her, stuck back in Philly with Barkley and seeing Mom and Dad every other weekend. That I moved to L.A. precisely to *avoid* that life.

"Oh, honey, this is such a lovely place."

I open my eyes a crack. Helen. At the foot of our lounges, wearing her own buttery robe and a blissful expression. "I'm so glad you suggested it. It's so, I don't know, *calming*," she says, sinking onto the end of my lounge.

"Yeah, Mom, it's calming all right," I say, sitting up. "How was your facial?"

"Oh, it was wonderful," she says, rubbing her cheek. "Not that I'm any expert. But the girl was so nice. Hmm . . . Where'd you get that tea?"

"Oh, it's over there," I say, nodding toward a sideboard at the back of the room. "I can get you some if you want."

"No, I'll get it. In a minute." She turns to the window. "I have to say, even with all this rain, this trip has really turned out surprisingly well."

I look at her looking out the window. I know I should just let it go. But I can't. If the dam is broken, the dam is broken. "Why? What were you expecting?"

She turns back to me, looking slightly startled. "Well, I didn't mean surprising. You know, it's just what you hear about Los Angeles. What you expect."

"Like what exactly?" I say. "You mean the riots and O.J. or the Oscars?"

"Oh, Alex," she says, sighing. "You're always so defensive. I only meant that whatever I was expecting from this trip, it's been different. That's all. In a good way."

"So you were expecting it to be bad?"

Amy snatches the eye pillow from her eyes. "This is what I was talking about," she snaps. "This kind of hostility."

"Oh, girls," Helen says, shaking her head. "Don't spoil this, this way."

"You know, I'll just get you that tea," I say, clambering up off the lounge and nearly colliding with a therapist.

"Mrs. Harbinger? We're ready for your pregnancy massage now."

Amy gives her a blazing smile—the beaming Madonna—and the two of them float off. Since I'm up, I decide to get the tea anyway. Give myself a minute to calm down, get out of the raging torrent. When I come back, Helen has taken Amy's place on the lounge.

"Thank you, honey," she says, taking the cup. We lie there for a minute, sipping our tea and staring out at the rain.

"What are you having done?" she asks after a minute.

"Shiatsu."

"Doesn't that hurt?"

"Not if you're used to it."

We fall silent again.

"What was Dad doing this afternoon?"

"He and Barkley went to the automotive museum."

"Oh, right," I say.

We sit there silently again, sipping our tea.

"Honey, we really have had a wonderful time. Whatever you may think. Whatever Amy may have said."

I stare straight ahead. I know she is looking at me. That she wants me to take the olive branch she's holding out. And I should take it. For all our sakes, I should just take it.

But I can't.

"Well, I'm glad," I say evenly, my eyes never leaving the rain-lashed window. "I'm really glad."

We sit silently again. After a minute, I hear the rustle of her robe.

"Well. I'm going to go down and change," she says, getting to her feet. "We have a long trip home tomorrow."

She stands next to me and suddenly I feel the weight of her hand on my head. "You always had the most beautiful hair," she says, stroking my head. "Of all of us, you were the lucky one."

I don't say anything. Luck is not something I've ever, ever had. Even if she doesn't know it, I do. So I just nod and keep staring out the window. Staring until it all blurs together and I can't see the rain anymore.

16 | Running as Fast as I Can

The deal with the Phoenix, like all celebs, is you don't just show up. Not without an invitation. And FBI clearance. For one thing, the fortresses are not equipped to just let people in. For another, the fortress owners usually need twenty-four-hour notice. Just to get ready. Unless you're like Cybill Shepherd, who likes to run out the clock while her visitors cool their heels in her living room watching the fish guy clean out the saltwater tank.

My pilgrimage along PCH to the Phoenix's latest nest has required dozens of calls. Suzanne and the Phoenix's manager. Suzanne and the Phoenix's assistant. The assistant's assistant. Me and the second assistant. Finally, I am in. I have no idea what the pretext for my meeting is—no doubt something Suzanne cooked up having to do with the Phoenix's new reality series—but I am clear on my mission: Save Suzanne's Ass.

Or at least Suzanne thinks that's my mission. I have yet to decide, despite G's Deep Throat efforts in the parking garage. As far as I'm concerned, I have an audience with the Phoenix, but no idea what I will actually say once I am there. Maybe this is my way of backtracking from the line that I apparently drew in the sand during my phone call with Charles. A call that was, predictably, the last time we've spoken, but that's a whole other issue. Or maybe it's some proactive reaction to my parents' visit over Thanksgiving, a visit that has left me, ironically, determined to make a go of my demeaning but still-so-glam job. Nothing like a visit from Mom to focus the mind.

Or maybe it's my way of hedging my bets in the shifting inter-office wars between Team Suzanne and Team G. According to the latest intelligence, Suzanne's lawyer is threatening counter suit—that classic Hollywood ploy—so now G's attempts to thin the ranks have been put on the back burner. Temporarily.

Besides, the week after Thanksgiving, Hollywood is neck-deep into its annual year-end madness, the flurry of big-budget holiday releases and pious Oscar hopefuls, and with the chaos of award season yet to come. Given the all-hands-on-deck mode now oper-ating at every studio and publicity agency, even G knows it's no time for head rolling. Still, the feeling is that it's not a question of *if* Suzanne and most of the DWPers hit the road, but when and how. Already the smart money is on an exit strategy during the post-Oscar doldrums. But as we all know, a lot can happen in Hollywood in those few short weeks.

"Here you go," Steven says, dropping the directions to the house on my desk. "But before you leave, can we go over your call sheet?" I glance at the directions. One of the far corners of Malibu near Point Dume, with no doubt the requisite fabulous ocean view.

"Wait, which house is this?" I say, staring at the address. Last time I had seen the Phoenix, she was holed up in some monster rental off Doheny. But that had been between tours or boyfriends or surgeries or something.

"The one she bought last year. The one that's already for sale. Because it's been in *Architectural Digest.* Because she's bored with it and because she already bought a new house that she's reno-

vating," he says, distractedly flipping through my massive call
sheet.

"Oh, right," I say vaguely, recalling pictures of a bunkerlike
beach estate with morbid, Addams Family interiors. Or maybe
that had been her furniture catalog when the Phoenix had been
in her retail phase. "You know, why is it that female stars buy and
discard houses like they're Manolo Blahniks? I mean, just take
the Phoenix, Scooby, and Courteney Cox. Between them, they've
probably owned more than two dozen houses in the past five years.
But all the guys, like Jack and Warren, Johnny Carson and Michael Douglas, buy houses and hang on to them."

"That's because they just trade up the women they put in them.
Or down, if you're looking at it chronologically," he says, without
glancing up from the call sheet.

I ponder this a second. "Like baseball managers and the free
agency system."

"Or plastic surgery," Steven says, looking up impatiently. "I
mean for the women. Redo your face. Redo your house. You know,
moving on. Like we need to be doing now, given all these calls."

"I don't know," I say, ignoring his impatience. One of the ironies
in my making a more concerted effort at my job is that I am slower
at returning calls. Like any publicist worth her Palm Pilot. "I think
it's because women have more of their self-esteem wrapped up in
their home. And it's not just celebrities."

"I guess that explains your penchant for patio furniture in-
doors," he says, giving up and heading for the door.

"Hey, I cooked you marshmallows," I say, flinging a pencil after
him.

"Women and sugar," he says, dodging. "More sacred than sex."

I always forget that, even without traffic, getting out to the far
reaches of Malibu is a haul. No wonder nobody lives out here full
time. Except for surfers, has-beens, and retirees like Johnny Carson and Barbra. I pass the old Getty museum. And the nursery

that was almost wiped out in the floods two winters ago. The Colony. Geoffrey's restaurant. The road where I used to go horse-back riding when I first moved to L.A. and, like every new female transplant, felt it my duty to leap aboard some dusty steed every weekend. Just so you could say casually on Monday mornings, "How was my weekend? Great. Went riding. In Malibu." After I got hives from plowing through one too many thickets of fennel, and especially after the time I nearly got thrown when we encountered a rattlesnake on the trail, I started spending my Sunday mornings at the car wash, reading the papers at the Starbucks down the block. There were snakes of a different sort, but at least I didn't get hives.

I check the address again. Cliffside Drive. God, did I pass the turnoff? I reach over to the passenger seat and fish out the *Thomas Guide*, heavy as the Yellow Pages, and flip to the Malibu section. Or try to. You think driving while talking on a cell phone is dangerous, try reading the *Thomas Guide*. I fumble with the book for a minute—where is page 667? torn out, of course—nearly driving off the road before I give up and dial Steven. My personal satellite navigation system.

"Where the fuck is this place?"

"Where are you?"

"Just passed Geoffrey's. And Coral Canyon," I say as I whiz by.

"You know, I've got three other calls going," he says.

"Well, I'm missing the right *Thomas Guide* page and who am I supposed to ask for directions out here, Nick Nolte?"

"Oh, hang on," he says, putting me on hold. He clicks back on in a minute. "Okay, two more miles. Take a left at Dume Drive."

"Thanks, Hansel. Next time, I'll definitely drop bread crumbs."

In about three minutes I see the turnoff and hang a left. It's a narrow road snaking down toward the beach with the water on one side and sprawling estates on the other. Like every upscale L.A. neighborhood, it's also stone empty. Not a soul or a FedEx truck in sight. As if nuclear winter has fallen. You only know money lives here because the carapaces remain. I try to count down the address, but hardly any are posted; the houses just get bigger as I get closer to the water. Finally I see it. Just like I remember from the magazine, only more massive. And more bunkerlike. A genuine fortress.

It's the usual drill getting in: roll up to the gate, punch in, recite password *BIG-DWP*, drawbridge comes down. I expect the usual pack of animals. Mastiffs. Or Irish wolfhounds, given our surroundings. Instead, I see only a lone gardener in a straw hat stooped over the far end of the lawn. For a second, I feel like I'm in that scene in *Chinatown* where Jack Nicholson shows up at Faye Dunaway's estate, where only the gardener is working. Except for the faint roar of the ocean, it's utterly silent. And a little eerie. Most stars thrive in the midst of chaos. Kids, dogs, assistants, nannies, ringing phones, a million cars in the driveway, overbooked schedules. Too many commitments and not enough time. It's their way of stilling the demons that stalk them: *What if they forget about me?*

But apparently the Phoenix's self-esteem needs no such shoring up. At least not here. No one would ever accuse her of being a minimalist, not with that showgirl wardrobe and all those wigs made out of Christmas tinsel, but her house has the bunkered, deserted feel of a secret government lab.

I am admitted by the side door. The servant's entrance. Amazingly there are still no dogs. And even more amazingly, no Latinos. Just a slim, thirty-something brunette in tight jeans and a T-shirt. Tracy. Or Stacy. The Phoenix's personal chef. Or her trainer. Or a post-op nurse. It's not clear and I don't bother asking. Tracy/Stacy leads me through the kitchen. Acres of black granite and chrome with not a pot, pan, or piece of food in sight. Just a plate on a tray wrapped in something like six layers of plastic wrap and holding a wan-looking chicken breast, broccoli, a few cherry tomatoes. It looks like punishment. Or a public school lunch. Not a meal for someone who once hawked $2 million worth of cosmetics in an hour on QVC.

We leave the kitchen—and the twenty-first century—and push through a door into, yes, I was right, the Addams Family abode. Or Harry Potter's dungeon. It's so dark, I can't make out much except for the crucifixes and swords hanging on the walls, and the mirrors with their frames in the shape of snakes. The few pieces of furniture I can make out in the gloaming look edged in gilt and covered in leopard-print velvet. What Henry VIII might have owned if he'd lived in Vegas.

"She's upstairs," Tracy/Stacy says, as she leads me to a curving marble staircase. We climb up, passing a giant tapestry hanging in the stairwell. I gaze up at it, trying to make out the looming female figure. Joan of Arc? Hillary Clinton? Or maybe the Phoenix herself? It's hard to tell, it's so dark, smoky, even.

We climb on and I start to feel dizzy. Maybe it's the elevation. Or maybe I just have to sneeze. Finally, we hit a landing, a hallway with what looks to be a cat scuttling down the far end. If Maggie Smith suddenly leapt out at us, I wouldn't be surprised. "Here we are," Tracy/Stacy says, stopping in front of a large carved-wood door. She knocks, waits, then pushes it open. A blast of sandalwood and patchouli hits me.

Given all the smoke, my first reaction is that the room is on fire. But as my eyes adjust, I make out half a dozen smudge pots of incense and scented candles smoldering away. Probably a séance with the Phoenix's dead husband. Actually ex-husband, her former-manager-turned-Christian-radio-talk-show-host who died in a freak recording accident two months ago—something to do with his microphone shorting out when he bowed his head in prayer—and who was, according to the tabs, now communicating with her from beyond the grave. Presumably telling her to have her wiring checked.

I turn back to Tracy/Stacy, but I've been abandoned by Charon on the banks of the Styx. Oh well. I brace myself and take a step into the perfumed murk. "Hello?" I say, feeling my way into what appears to be a huge bedroom. At least she's consistent. Last time

I met with her, she held court in her darkened bedroom from atop her leopard-print-covered bed.

"Hello," I say again. Nothing but the guttering candles. Suddenly, I see a flash of light and, like a vision out of the mists, the Phoenix is here—the corn-silk-white hair, barefoot, gray sweats, and baggy pale blue cardigan sweater. And cradling a cat. Venus on her day off. "Hi," she says, in her familiar foggy-brassy voice. "This is Botox. She just had her bath."

"Really," I say, springing into action. At least this part is familiar. Whatever they trot out, just go with it. "Oh, she's so clean," I say, rubbing the cat's still-damp head.

"And that's Lipo, her brother," she says, nodding at a second cat who's crept out of the shadows and is winding himself damply around my ankles. "She just loves him," she says, bending down to put Botox on the floor. "And that's pretty much it."

"Okay," I say brightly, as I try to disengage my feet from the cats.

"So Alex, right?" she says, eyeing me now.

I'm tempted to remind her that we've actually met and spoken on the phone several times, but think better of it. "Yes. I'm Alex. Davidson. From Suzanne's office?" I say, trying to address her without staring at her face, its waxy perfection, astonishing on camera but even more compelling in real life.

"Right," she says, nodding and turning toward a second door. I stand there, not sure if I should follow her. "They're in here," she says, turning back to me. "You need to see them, right?"

"Uhm, sure. That would be great." I have no idea what she's talking about, but I follow her through the doorway into a small closet. A closet of jewelry. Rows upon rows of beaded necklaces, bracelets, and earrings, like a booth at a mall.

She reaches out to finger some of the strands. "These are just a few of the ones that I've made over the years. Like this is an early one," she says, handing me a necklace of tiny glass beads strung on a cord. It looks like something I made as a kid in camp.

"Stunning," I say, taking the necklace. "Really beautiful."

"And these are some of the more recent ones." She reaches for larger, chunkier strands with beads of turquoise, citrine, and aquamarine. A couple have crosses dangling off them.

"Yes." I nod. "I can see the difference. Wow."

She hands me a few more strands. "Wow," I say again. "I had no idea you did this."

She looks at me quizzically. "It's why you're here. That's what they told me. The magazine wants them. Which one is it, *InStyle?*"

Oh Christ, how could Suzanne not have warned me? Probably her bitchy little assistant who forgot, her way of fucking with me. So this is the excuse for my visit—that *InStyle* is doing a feature on the Phoenix's jewelry making. Actually, it's not a half-bad idea, given how many unemployed actresses in Hollywood string their own worry beads as a way to calm themselves down and remind themselves that they really are *artists*. Still, it would take Spider-Man to leap from this to "Hey-do-you-think-you-could-consider-not-firing-the-agency?" And I only have an hour.

"You know, these are great. Why don't I take as many of them as you're comfortable letting me have and we can get some preliminary shots out to New York and go from there?"

She shrugs. "Take your pick. I'm kind of over the whole beading thing. You know how you go through phases? Sometimes I like being a blonde. Other times not. Besides, I'm so busy with the show now, I was actually thinking of selling them on QVC or eBay—for charity, of course—and keeping the cat toys in here."

Great, the show. At least we're moving in the right direction, where I can bring up her agency contract without sounding like a total idiot. "Yeah, how's that going?" I say, gathering up a few more of the necklaces. "Are you going to let them film here?"

"Oh God, no," she says, heading for the door, bored with jewelry now. "Sharon and Ozzie might have no pride, but I would never let a TV crew in here. I bought a house down the road that we're going to shoot in."

She disappears back into the bedroom. By the time I put away

most of the necklaces, tucking a few token strands into my bag—
hey, if this is my ruse, I better make it plausible—and follow her,
she's already climbed onto the giant bed and curled up against the
pillows. I look around for a place to sit, but unless I'm to crawl
onto the bed as well, I have no choice but to take a seat on one of
the two leopard-print chairs flanking the fireplace on the far side
of the room. With all the incense smoke and the shades drawn
tight against the blazing beach sun, I can barely make her out.

"So," I say, deciding to just plunge in. "As long as I'm here,
maybe we can talk a bit about your publicity campaign for the
show."

"Let's not," she says with a wave. "I'm still getting the house set
up and dealing with the network. The rest of it will come when it
comes. The earliest we'll air is March and maybe not even until
June. Meanwhile, I'm just letting my manager deal with all that."

"Okay," I say, trying to remember exactly who her manager is.
Funny, Suzanne didn't bring it up in our discussions. "You know,
I'm sorry, who is your manager these days? I have a hard time
keeping track."

"Well, that's probably because I just changed managers after
something like twenty years. Jerry Gold."

I'm stunned. "*Jerry Gold*'s your manager? As in Carla Selena's
Jerry Gold?"

"Or as in Carla Selena has *my* Jerry Gold. I've known Jerry for
years, but it was just never the right time for us to work together.
Until now."

So all roads lead to Jerry Fucking Gold. The same Jerry Gold
who abruptly fired Suzanne over Carla is now trying to walk off
with the Phoenix? This has to be more than a coincidence. A coincidence that just happens to bolster G's case against Suzanne. I
decide to go for innocent. "So Jerry came to you with the idea for
the series?"

"*I* had the idea for the series. MTV came to me. I hired Jerry to
work out the details."

"And has he talked about what he wants to do about the publicity yet?"

"Not really. I mean, he mentioned we should try some new things, some new approaches, but nothing specific. But like I said, I'm not there yet."

"So you haven't talked to Suzanne about any of it?"

I hear her sigh. "No. Until your office called about this necklace thing, I hadn't talked to anybody in a while. I mean, what was there to promote?"

She has a point. After her retail phase— her skin-care infomercial and QVC sales—the Phoenix kind of disappeared. Took her Oscar and her platinum albums and just faded into the woodwork. That she is back in the public eye in her fifties now armed with a $20 million TV deal is remarkable even by her standards of self-reinvention.

"You know, they used to call me The Cat when I played Vegas because I've done more than most people have in nine lifetimes," she says. "I don't go into anything with a lot of confidence, but I do have my fuck-it-all attitude. But also, money has never been my primary reason for working."

"Well, that makes you different from about 99.9 percent of the people in this town," I blurt out before I think better of it. My job as a publicist is to stroke the clients, reassure them, manipulate them, even lie when necessary, but never challenge them.

A laugh explodes out of the gloaming. "Well, we *know* that. One time I was making a fortune on the road and I quit to do a play off-Broadway. I went from making $500,000 a night to five hundred a week."

"You're lucky you don't have to worry about money."

"Don't kid yourself. *Everyone* worries about money in Hollywood. Even David Geffen. I just happened to come into the business with a chip on my shoulder. It's one reason why I've done what I've wanted to do and not what anybody else wanted me to do. I have a talent for making money, but I'm not a smart businessperson. I mean, after that infomercial, I didn't work for years. I made a shitload off it, but it annihilated everything—the Oscar, the albums—that came before it."

"But a lot of celebrities do businesses on the side. Quarterbacks buy car dealerships. Magic Johnson bought a movie theater chain. Look at J. Lo and Britney Spears. They opened restaurants that *failed,* but nobody writes them off."

"Right. And Arnold and Bruce ran around and promoted Planet Hollywood and at the time, everyone thought that was cool too. But that's the thing. What I did with the infomercial didn't look cool and that was the difference. But you know, failure is very underrated. That whole experience was a good lesson for me. It taught me that it's not how things *are* in our business that counts, it's how things *seem* that matters."

Maybe it's the dark, that we can't see each other that makes this feel so confessional. "So what do you think about your reality series? That's cool."

She sighs again. "It's a shot like anything, but you never know. Look, most of the time it's all shit. Scripts are shitty, albums are shitty, people are shitty. But every once in a while, something comes along that's really right for you. The trick is to know your-self well enough to know that when you see it. And to take yourself not so seriously when it doesn't work. There's always another gig."

"I don't know. I think you're one of the exceptions. I think the clock is ticking for most women in Hollywood. And when it's over, it's over. I don't think there are a lot of second acts. Or even second chances."

"Hey, I never said it was easy. I hate getting older. I hated it when I was in my forties and let me tell you, that's a day at the beach compared to being in your fifties, when nature basically says, 'Fuck you.' The clock is ticking. For all of us. And there is nothing positive about it. Not in this business. You don't get better because you get older. You get older and you get forgotten. I know that. But because I plan on being able to do all the things physically that I want to do before I die, I'm going to be out there killing myself."

There's a knock at the door. Tracy/Stacy with the two-minute warning. "Yeah," I say, reaching down and fiddling with my bag, enough of a feint that she backs out. Still, better wrap this up. In the glow of the candles, I make out the Phoenix sliding off the bed.

"So you seem a little, I don't know, out there," she says, heading toward me. "I mean for a publicist. Usually the ones I've met have clipboards and agendas. You know, lists and you're on it."

"Oh, that's more like studio and network people," I say, getting to my feet. "We're not that organized. Mostly we just say no a lot."

"I don't know," she says, shaking her head, the corn silk wagging. "Do you like being a publicist? I mean, do you like coming out here for *necklaces?*"

I'm tempted to come clean. Tell her, of course, I hate being a publicist. Even she gets it that hiking out to Malibu for necklaces is about as demeaning as it gets—for all of us. After our confessional little conversation, she just might understand.

There's another knock at the door. Tracy/Stacy again. Might as well be wearing a jack-in-the-box's hat with bells.

"You know, that's a good question," I say, rushing now. "It's a question I've been, or should be, asking myself, but actually, I really need to ask you one thing before I go."

There it is. My line in the sand. Whatever I had intended to do or not do when I set out here this afternoon has changed. God knows, it would be easier to do what G asked. Nothing. Just say my good-byes and get the hell out of this dungeon. Let the chips, and the Phoenix, fall where they may. But the Jerry Gold thing is just too much of a coincidence. Besides, the Phoenix seems too much her own woman to just let Jerry make all her decisions. I have to take my shot.

"So here's the deal," I say, plunging in. "Jerry has talked to Suzanne about dropping the agency from handling you." I pause and look up.

"What? What are you talking about?" she says. "Jerry and I

haven't even talked yet. Not about publicity. He couldn't have talked to her."

"Well, I'm pretty sure that's the case, and frankly," I pause and take a breath, "that's the real reason for my visit here today." I close my eyes for a second and brace for impact. "Not the necklaces."

There's another long pause. "What are you saying? That you lied about needing to see me?"

"No, I did need to see you. I just didn't need to see the necklaces."

"*Tracy!*"

"Okay, wait," I say, rushing now to plug this hole in the dike. "It's not her fault. The office told her I needed to see you for the story."

Tracy sticks her head in the door. "Yep?"

"Will you find out what the fuck is going on?"

"Yep," she says, nodding and backing out and then back in. "About what?"

"About why she—what did you say your name was again?—is here today. And why you let her in."

Okay, so this is going well. At this rate, even if the Phoenix wasn't inclined to fire DWP when I walked in here, she will surely do so now. Probably before I can even get out of here. Maybe G was right. I do have hidden talents.

"Okay, look, blame me, not her," I say, nodding at Tracy. "But I think you owe it to yourself to know the full story."

"I don't need to know the full story. I *am* the full story," she snaps. "And what I know is that I have wasted, what, an hour with you? Do you have any idea how many people would kill to have an hour of my time?"

Tracy looks at us like she's watching a tennis match—a match that could go either way. "So should I—" she says, unsure whether to throw me out or just keep watching.

"I'm sure that's true," I say, cutting Tracy off. "What I'm trying to tell you is that it's in your best interest to hear me out."

The Phoenix doesn't say anything, which I take as an opening. "Look, I'm here to ask you not to fire DWP. You've been well served by us in the past, and given our history, you have no reason to drop us as your publicists now."

"You're giving me a pretty good one."

"Fair enough," I say, raising my hands. "Look, Jerry Gold just fired DWP from handling Carla. Now it looks like he's planning on doing the same thing with you."

"First of all, Jerry doesn't decide these things. I do. And even if that were true—if I approved Jerry's decision to fire you—why should I care?"

Ah, the moment of truth. Why should she—why should any of them—care about something other than her own self-interest? "Because it's wrong," I say. "And it will hurt people."

"Are you serious?" she says. "This is what we do. We take our business to the highest bidder and tough luck to the losers. I say no all the time. Appearances, charities, film offers. It's what *I* get to do. *I* get to say no."

I look at her. Is there anybody is this town not watching their own back? "So all your proto-feminist talk about taking chances and self-empowerment, that was just, what, talk?"

I am way over the line here, but at this point I have nothing else to lose. Besides, Tracy's hardly bouncer material.

"I think we're done here," she says icily.

"Fine, I'm going," I say, reaching for my bag. "But you ought to know that if you let Jerry Gold take you out of DWP like a piece of baggage, Suzanne, your publicist and a woman your own age, will take the fall for it. I just thought you should know that. That your actions have consequences."

I stand up and head for the door. I may have lost a client, but my integrity is intact. Which will get me exactly nowhere.

"Okay," Tracy says, leaping to lead me out, relieved that I'm leaving of my own volition.

"First of all, Jerry Gold is a terrific manager," the Phoenix says suddenly. "Secondly, if he has any agenda, I can only assume it's in your favor, since Jerry and, who is it—Doug Graydon?— apparently go way back. I don't see why Jerry would take me out of his friend's agency. But even if that's the case, I still approve any and all decisions, as I said. No matter what Jerry thinks, it's my decision. Besides, Alex," she adds, eyeing me closely, "it's only publicity. It's not like it really matters."

It's only later, when I'm in the car heading back down PCH, squinting in the oncoming headlights, trying to find a radio station playing Christmas carols, anything to calm me down, that I realize I still have the necklaces.

17 | And the Nominees Are . . .

I'm so wiped from going ten rounds with the Phoenix, I can hardly dial Steven on my cell as I'm driving back into town.

"Yes, I'm still here rolling all the calls you should have been rolling if you'd gotten back in time to help," he says.

"Forget the calls," I say, not bothering to decipher Steven's tone, if he's really annoyed or just being hissy for the hell of it. "I have much bigger news."

"Like the Phoenix was wearing a brown wig? Or her actual hair?"

"Very funny," I say, reaching to turn down the stream of carols pouring from KCTK. "Seriously, guess who her manager is?"

Steven sighs. "And we should care because?"

"Because it's Jerry Fucking Gold."

"Paco?" he says, laughing. "No kidding. That guy gets around."

"Yeah, but there's more."

"Wait, there's more," Steven says, mocking me. "If you call now, you'll also get the steak knives—"

"Look, I know you've had a long day, but I can guarantee you, I've had a longer one."

"Okay, what?" he says sulkily.

"The point is that Jerry and G apparently go way back."

"So? Everyone in this town goes way back. Even if they can't stand each other. We've talked about this. It's how Hollywood works."

"No, they really *do* go way back," I say. "I don't know how and we need to find that out, but the Phoenix told me they did. She also told me a bunch of other stuff which I'll tell you about, but when I brought up the whole thing about Jerry pulling Carla out of DWP and how he was threatening to do the same with her, she said they go way back. Actually, she told me to fuck off and die, then she told me they go way back."

"She used those exact words?"

"She said whatever Jerry was up to with DWP couldn't be bad because, and I quote, 'Jerry and what's his name, Doug Graydon, go way back.' She also said who cares because it's just publicity, but that's a whole other issue."

"Words to live by after the day I've had."

"Okay, am I missing something here? I nearly got my head handed to me a minute ago and you're acting like I'm giving you the weather report. Why don't you think this is the smoking gun that we've been looking for? That G and Jerry are somehow in cahoots?"

"To do what? Siphon clients *away* from the agency G just bought? That would be a first."

I don't say anything. Just wait to see if Steven gets it. He should or I've seriously misjudged him. I mean, any guy who's smart enough to cheer up his boss with a rice pudding should be able to read this landscape.

"Oh, I get it," he says slowly. "Those clever fuckers."

"Meet me at Le Dome. No wait, Tom Bergin's in—" I check my watch. It's six-thirty and I'm just passing the old Getty. "Give me thirty minutes to get across town in this traffic. And call Rachel and tell her to meet us there as well. We're going to need her."

"Roger," he says, snapping back to life. "By the way, what's that you're listening to, 'God Rest Ye Merry Gentlemen'? I love that carol."

"You love that carol? You're Jewish."

"That's right, I'm a gay Jew and I love Christmas carols. I don't work on Broadway and I'm not in Hollywood's gay mafia but I—"

"Wait. You're not in the gay mafia? That's why I hired you."

"Honey, you've gotten a lot of mileage out of your little shiksa image, but don't push your luck."

"See, it's so much more fun when we're not fighting."

"I still did all your work today."

"I know and I love you for it," I say. "See you in thirty."

The beauty of Tom Bergin's is it's just so fucking dark. Besides, it's always full of serious drinkers who, given Hollywood's mineral-water pieties, need to hide out to nurse a pops or two while catching a Lakers game. Between the boozers and the lack of light, you can while away the hours in a back booth and no one is the wiser. Plus, it's one of the only places, other than Barneys, that reminds me of being back in New York. For some reason, I just think so much more clearly when I can forget I'm actually in Los Angeles.

By the time I exit the 10 and slog my way up Fairfax, it's already way past seven. I tear into the lot, toss my keys to the valet, and head for the door. The yeasty smell of hops and the roar of the crowd two deep at the bar watching the Kings game hits me like the blast of an oven. It takes a second for my eyes to adjust, but I finally spot Steven in a booth around the side.

"Hey," I say, sliding in across from him. "The traffic was its usual cooperative self. There was a truckload of bananas overturned at Robertson that closed a whole lane."

He leans in my direction and sniffs. "I can tell."

I ignore him. "Did you reach Rachel?" I say, reaching for his glass and taking a sip. Heineken, I think.

"Yeah, but she can't get here until after seven-thirty," he says, taking back his glass. "So I took the liberty of starting without you guys."

"Did you tell her what it was about?"

"Not really. She asked me if it was gossip or serious, but I just said it had to do with G and his time at Sony and Jerry Gold, and you thought she could help."

"Good," I say, glancing around for the waiter. God knows, I need a drink.

Steven raises his hand. "So before you call this meeting to order, can I just ask what's the plan here?"

"What's the plan?" I say, turning back. "We're here to make one. I mean, the Phoenix nearly threw me out when I asked her not to quit the agency."

"Wait a minute, wait a minute," Steven says, suddenly focused now. "You came right out and asked her to stay? What brought that on? You didn't know what you were going to do when you left the office this afternoon."

"I kind of stumbled into it. When she told me Jerry was her manager, I just put two and two together."

"Objection."

"Okay, don't play *Law & Order* now," I say, shaking my head.

"I'm not. I'm just trying to make sure that we really know what we think we know."

"Okay," I say, sighing. "What do we know?"

Steven nods. "Okay. We know that Jerry manages at least two of Suzanne's biggest clients. And we know the Phoenix apparently doesn't like being told what to do. What did she actually say to you when you asked her to stay?"

"I'll get to that," I say, waving him off. "We also know Jerry's fired Suzanne from handling those two."

"Only one. Carla."

I sigh. "Well, after today, I'm betting the Phoenix is also history."

"Okay, two, then."

"Right, two," I say. "So now we have to figure out Jerry's con-nection to G. Which is why we need Rachel. I assume they met when G was head of marketing at Sony. I mean, that's where G met Carla, when Sony released her first hit film."

"So what are you having?"

I look up. A waiter, blond, in jeans, T-shirt, and with the kind of silky forelock that usually makes me go weak. Or it would if I wasn't so hopped tonight. Or if I didn't still cherish memories about Charles's silky forelock, which I will probably never see again. "I'll have a Heineken. And a menu."

"Oh God, do you want to eat here? Nobody eats here." Steven says.

"No, but I'm starving and I refuse to eat one more night of Greenblatt's take-out."

"So a Heineken, a menu, and you want a refill?" the waiter says, nodding at Steven's glass.

"No, I'm stepping up to high-octane," he says. "Bring me a Corona and a shot."

"What kind?"

"Cuervo Gold."

"Got it," the waiter says, skating off.

"Cuervo Gold?" I say.

"Don't worry, I'm paying, not the agency."

"No, it's just that it's a school night."

"When did that ever stop us?"

"Oh God, that's so sad if that's true," I say, trying to recall all the nights we've spent here watching *Access Hollywood* and com-plaining about work.

"It's not," Steven says with a wave. "I've just had a long day. So what's step three?"

"Okay," I say, looping my hair behind my ears and leaning for-ward. "So first we should double-check the agency records to see if Jerry's suddenly handling any more of Suzanne's clients. To see how far this could go. And then we find out how far back Jerry and

G go. But what we really need—and this is what's going to be hard even with Rachel's help—is to figure out exactly what they've got cooked up. I mean it's easy to surmise—"

"Objection."

"What?" I say, exasperated. "I said *surmise.*"

"How are you ever going to prove it?"

"Prove what? You're not letting me finish."

"I know what you're going to say. 'Kickbacks,' and I'm telling you, you'll never be able to prove it. Unless one of them admits it."

I flop back in the booth. "Kickbacks? That's where you think this goes?"

"Well, where else?" he says, leaning forward and dropping his voice. "Think about it. What's in it for Jerry Gold? Nothing, now. He moves his clients around. So what? There's got to be a payoff down the road. A payoff from G."

"Or maybe they're just fucking Suzanne over because they can," I say crankily, annoyed that somehow I've gone from being Sherlock Holmes to Watson. "I mean, it's not like it would be the first time the boys didn't want to play nicely with the girls. Besides, you're assuming G has something to pay Jerry off with. Enough to make it worthwhile. Which means that he's planning on selling the agency and I think there's a few steps to make before that."

"Like?"

"Like restocking the agency with good clients and finding a buyer, and in this economic climate I don't know that anyone is going to pony up the millions for a Hollywood PR agency like they did back in the nineties."

"Well, what else would it be?" Rachel glides into the booth. "God, could you guys be talking any louder? You might as well call up Peter Bart and ask him to check it out."

"Hey," I say, sliding over to make room. "So you think it's kick-backs too?"

She shrugs. "I've been thinking about it ever since you called and what else can it be? I mean, Hollywood is all about guys scratching each other's backs. G acquires DWP. He arranges for Jerry to bolt with the biggest clients. Suzanne gets the ax and G is left as the agency's sole partner. Jerry brings the clients back. G puts the revived agency on the block. Pockets millions for himself and pays out whatever percentage he's promised Jerry."

"Right," Steven says, leaning back victoriously. "And we'll never be able to prove it."

I shake my head. In a single afternoon, we've gone from "Hey, Jerry Gold also manages the Phoenix" to "Book 'em"? "I still think we're getting ahead of ourselves. All we're trying to do is give Suzanne, actually Suzanne's lawyer, some leverage to keep her job. I don't think sending G and Jerry to Parker Center is really our goal."

"They'll never wind up there," Steven snorts. "There are no state laws governing publicists—just agents."

"Actually, I don't know why I didn't think of it sooner," Rachel says. "Of course they knew each other at Sony. Jerry briefly worked in the marketing department when G was the head of it. He left to go work for Brad Grey briefly, before going out on his own."

"We didn't *think* of it," I say, "because I only just found out Jerry was the link. None of us suspected any of this until the Phoenix told me Jerry was her manager. Now you guys are ready to string them up as white-collar criminals?"

"They're all criminals as far as I'm concerned," Rachel says, looking around for the waiter. "Although, I could always call up my Deep Throat friend at the *L.A. Times* and see what he thinks."

"Wouldn't *you* technically be the Deep Throat?" Steven says.

"Look, I think we need to keep our eye on the ball here," I say. "Move forward with what's doable. And so far that seems to be the coincidence of Jerry Gold handling Suzanne's clients."

"No, you're right, Nancy Drew," Steven says, raising his glass. "Let's take a minute to remind ourselves that you've done the real spadework. Trekked out to Malibu and got the Phoenix to spill the beans."

"Thank you," I say. "Now there's only one question. What are we going to do to stop them?"

An hour later, an hour in which I've delivered a blow-by-blow description of my WWF encounter with the Phoenix, all that's left on our plates are a few fries and smears of ketchup. Actually Steven and I had steaks. Rachel's had two martinis and half our fries.

"I have to remember you can actually eat here," Steven says, wiping his plate with a last fry. "I mean, eat here and live to tell about it."

Rachel eyes him over her glass. "Let's talk again tomorrow."

"You know the center of a steak is actually sterile," Steven says, wagging the fry at her. "It's not like a burger, where the surface and the interior of the meat is all ground together."

"Okay, I'm not even a vegan and that's disgusting," she says, spearing her olive.

Steven purses his lips and makes kissing sounds.

"Okay, kids, we've all had a long day," I say, waving for the check. "Are we all set? Do we all know our tasks?"

They both nod.

"By the way, what's our name?" Steven says.

I give him a look. "You mean like the Hardy Boys?"

"Actually, I was thinking more the Powerpuff Girls. Or something like the Pentagon. 'Operation Free DWP.' Or 'Operation Screw G to the Wall.' "

"How about 'Operation Do the Right Thing'?" I suggest.

Steven shakes his head. "I won't be a party to anything named after a Spike Lee movie."

"What have you got against Spike?" Rachel says in the tone of voice that sounds like she's only half kidding. Or that she's had a long day, two martinis, and basically no food.

"Kids, don't make me send you to your rooms," I say, trying to calm the waters. Steven and Rachel may be my best friends, but like a lot of Hollywood relationships, they are my friends, not each other's.

"First of all, I was kidding," Steven says evenly. "But since you asked, I think he's an overrated director who plays the race card when it's to his advantage. The rest of the time he's just like any filmmaker. Out to make a buck. Including directing commercials for Nike, which is one of the most exploitative companies around."

"Sorry, for a second my Jewish liberal pieties got the best of me," Rachel says, reaching for her bag. She pulls out her wallet and tosses down a twenty. "Okay, I'm out of here. We've got a marketing meeting in the morning. About our Christmas movies, which I can tell you will suck no matter how many meetings we have, but we're still going through the motions. But I'll find out about Jerry and G and call you."

Rachel slides out, gives me a fast hug, and threads her way through the crowd. "God, she's *so* great," Steven says after she's out of earshot.

I know that tone a mile away. "Oh, stop it," I say, thrusting my credit card at the waiter as he sails by. "Do you know how hard it is to find an intelligent woman in this town you can stand, let alone trust?"

"I wouldn't know," Steven says, reaching for his jacket. "But if she makes you happy, then I'm happy."

"You sound like my mother."

"Except I actually mean it."

"At least someone does," I say. "Okay, let's review the plan. You're going to check the agency records for managers' names. See if Jerry's turns up again."

"Yeah, but that's easy. You have the harder job. Calling Peg and the Phoenix, shaking them down for more info on G and Jerry. Are you sure you're up for that? I mean, after what you went through today?"

"No, but someone has to," I say, when I suddenly have a thought. "But first I'm going to call Troy. There's something I need to ask him."

The next morning, I get to the office early to hit the phones. But Suzanne is already ahead of me. When I log on, I have an e-mail from her asking for a recap of my meeting with the Phoenix. I was expecting this, but before I debrief her, I want to try and reach Peg and the Phoenix again if I can. Get a few more ducks in a row. I'm in the middle of answering her e-mail, subtly stalling for time and not so subtly ratting out her assistant for not giving me a heads-up about the bogus *InStyle* piece, when my phone rings. Steven's out getting coffee, so I impulsively pick up.

"Hello, Alex. Nice to see you're in so early."

Fuck. G.

"Well, it is that time of year," I say as blandly as I can, still typing the e-mail.

"I also see you visited one of our clients yesterday."

I stop typing. "Well, it's been that kind of a week," I say carefully. There's a few ways G could know about my visit to the Phoenix. None of them good.

"Well, I'd like to hear about it. Can you stop by my office for a second?"

"Uhm, sure," I say, vamping frantically. "I was just in the middle of rolling a few calls."

"Say, in five minutes?"

I close my eyes. "Sure. I'll be right there."

G is standing in the middle of his office leafing through *Variety* when I am ushered in.

"So," he says, not looking up. "Tell me about your visit to our client yesterday. Our very big client with the very big TV deal and the new manager."

There's a couple of ways I can play this. Depending on exactly what G knows. Or thinks he knows. But since I have no idea what he knows, or how he knows it, I opt for the bluff.

"Oh, it was nothing. Routine," I say, shrugging. "Just going over some publicity coming up."

"Routine?" he says, looking up.

"There's an *InStyle* piece that I needed to talk to her about and I also wanted to touch base with her about the show. Get a feeling for how much she was willing to do."

"Really?" he says, eyeing me.

Come on, asshole, show your cards. "Really," I say, meeting his gaze.

He drops the magazine to the coffee table. "You know, Alex, I thought I made myself fairly clear about the future of this agency and specifically your place in it. Or what could be your place in it. I'm sorry that you don't seem to understand that."

Maybe it's the residual effect of my confrontation with the Phoenix. Or maybe I'm feeling emboldened after meeting with Steven and Rachel last night. Or maybe I'm just sick of nothing being what it should be in this town. That nothing is ever taken at face value. That movies are products, stars are commodities, and what we do is a job. Not a calling.

"Well, then I guess I'm confused," I say. "Because I assumed doing everything one could to retain the agency's clients would only be considered supportive of this agency. And of you."

G looks at me like I've struck him. "How very enterprising of you, Alex. In fact, you surprise me. You really do." He smiles a tight smile and turns toward his desk. "But I suggest you think again about what we talked about the other night. I suggest you rethink your decision. Your decision about exactly how and where to channel your energies. Do I make myself clear?"

I'm tempted to tell him that ship has sailed. That he's closing the barn door after the horse has escaped. And any other clichés I can think of to describe how pointless his threats are now. That if I was ever inclined to side with him, do his bidding, that I'm certainly not now. "Perfectly," I say, flashing my own tight smile. "Perfectly."

"So that was close," I hiss, as I glide by Steven's desk and head into my office.

"Right behind you," he says, leaping up with my latte.

"I think I was just marked for death." I reach for the coffee, pry off the lid, and take a hit.

"Where were you? Suzanne's office?"

"G's."

"G's?"

"I think he heard about my visit to the Phoenix from Jerry Gold this morning," I say, taking another sip of coffee. "Wanted to know what I was doing out there. I played it dumb."

"Thatta girl."

"But then, I don't know. I just got mad."

"How mad?"

"Well, I didn't quit or anything. I just said if it wasn't in the agency's best interest to try and retain our clients, then I was in the wrong business."

"You *are* in the wrong business."

"I know," I say, flopping into my chair. "I just don't know what business I should be in. But until I figure that out, I might as well do something useful around here. I mean, if G's going to fire me along with Suzanne and the rest of us, then let's give him a reason to fire me."

"Thatta girl."

"Will you stop that?" I pull on my headset. "And get back out there. We have a lot to do today."

By the end of the day, we're two for two. Rachel's called with the news that Jerry and G were tight during their time at Sony. More than tight. Used to play golf and hit the Strip together. And Steven's found Jerry's name listed in the agency records as the new manager of two more of Suzanne's clients. Clearly the plan to in-fect and kill off Suzanne's client list is spreading with SARS-like speed. In addition to Carla and the Phoenix, Jerry now handles Lily Tattinger and Cybill Shepherd. Lily could be a problem, given that she's a big new client—twenty-two, blond, bubbly, and the star of the WB's new hit series *Makin' It*—but nobody cares if Cybill walks. Actually, everyone would be happier if she did.

But my calls to Peg and the Phoenix have turned up nothing. At least so far. When I tried to reach the Phoenix, I got as far as Tracy. "Okay, can you give her a message? Tell her I have more information about what we spoke about yesterday."

"Oh, like that'll get a call back," Steven says, handing me my fourth latte of the day.

"Well, I'll just keep calling. I don't know what else to do," I say, prying off the lid and taking a sip. "Unless you can find out her cell phone number. You know, from the gay mafia, of which you're not a member."

"I'll see what I can do. Remind me what good you think it will do talking to her again?"

"Like it would be the first time a star changed their mind for no good reason," I say, shrugging. "Besides, we know more than what I knew yesterday, and I want her to know as well. That it looks like something really is going on with Jerry and G."

"Okay, I'll see what I can do. So what did Peg say when you reached her?"

"Basically reamed me a new one."

"God, you are a glutton for punishment. Tell me what she said. Exactly. It's so much more fun that way."

"Maybe for you. Peg likes me and she still scares the hell out of me."

"Oh, come on."

"Okay, but only if you promise to get the Phoenix's cell number," I say, sighing and launching into my pathetic imitation of Peg. " 'Davidson, I don't know jack about Jerry Gold. Or Doug Graydon, for that matter. But if you or anyone there thinks I place my clients at DWP out of personal loyalty, think again. I put my clients where they can afford it and DWP just happens to be one of the cheapest agencies around.' "

"God, I love her," Steven says.

"No, you don't. She just confirms your worst fears about women. Frankly, she confirms *my* worst fears about women."

"Well, at least we can cross her off our list of sources."

"Yeah," I say, sinking into my chair. "Which leaves us not much farther along than we were yesterday. Jerry and G are in cahoots to sabotage Suzanne and we haven't a clue how to stop them."

"What did you tell Suzanne, by the way, when she asked you about your meeting with the Phoenix?"

"I told her it was inconclusive. Which isn't, technically, a lie."

"Good thinking."

"I figure she'll know soon enough how it shakes out. We'll all know. It's just a question of what we do in the meantime."

"We could still call the *L.A. Times*. That friend of Rachel's."

"And say what? Jerry Gold fired DWP from handling Carla? They already did that story."

"Well, it was a thought. I was watching *Three Days of the Condor* again last night and that's how Redford screws his old boss."

"Honey, it's a movie," I say, shaking my head. "Don't get your expectations up."

"So what're we going to do? Nothing?"

"No," I say, nodding at my phone. "I have one last hope."

As I pull into the Chateau garage, I try to remember when I first met Troy here. Seems like a lifetime ago, but it must have been, what, September? The start of the fall season when he got that guest-starring gig on Val's show. That had actually worked out pretty well—a one-off that turned into a recurring role. Now there's even talk of a Golden Globe nomination.

Still, Troy isn't any more punctual now than he was then. When I hit the lobby, he's nowhere to be seen. Actually, given that it's a Thursday night in the middle of the holiday movie season, the room is packed and it takes me a minute to figure out that Troy is not one of the chic young things holding court here. I scan the room again and spot an empty love seat by the door to the courtyard. I sink into it and pull out the trades. I've already read them, but I can't just sit here staring into space. God forbid you not look frantically busy in Hollywood. Frantically in demand.

I'm actually deep into the real estate ads, just pondering, ordering a drink to help me come down from my four lattes of the day, when I feel a cold, damp muzzle hit my thigh.

"Hey, darlin'."

I look up. Little Troy Madden and his trusty dog, Miss Sue.

"Hey, you," I say, reaching for Miss Sue's ears and rubbing them the way she likes. "Hey," I say, as Troy sinks down next to me and I catch his familiar smell of leather and cigarette smoke. "Thanks for meeting me."

Troy gives me one of his good-ole-boy grins. "Well, you know what they say."

"I probably do, but tell me anyway."

"If you can't help out those on your payroll, who can you help?"

"Don't tell me. Another one of Daddy Madden's pearls of wisdom?"

"Hey, don't knock Daddy Madden," Troy says, his smile widening. "Daddy Madden knows a thing or two. Besides, he likes you."

"Your dad likes me? Your dad doesn't even know me."

"He knows your work. I tell 'em. All those stories about me being on TV and in the magazines. It's 'cause of you."

For a second, I'm tempted to let fly with my usual smart-aleck response. To back Troy into his corner and keep my distance. Maybe it's the end of a long day, or maybe I know I need his help. Or maybe it's just easier not to think of one more cynical remark to prove how tough and clever I am. Whatever the reason, I let it go. "Well, thanks," I say, looking down at Miss Sue and rubbing her ears again. "Thanks."

"So," he says, smacking his thighs. "What do you say we get ourselves a drink and you tell me what you need?"

We flag down a waiter and order a beer for me, a Diet Coke "in the can" for him, and a burger, what the hell, between us. A few minutes later, a corner table opens up and we take it.

"You know, I don't think I've been here since that time I first met you," Troy says, emptying his Coke into a glass.

"Really," I say, slicing the burger and handing him his half. "I thought you came here all the time."

"Nah, this place is too much of a scene for me. You know, I meant what I said in court," he says, gazing around the room. "At least part of it."

"What part?" I say, my mouth full of burger.

"That Hollywood can wipe the smile off your face."

"That's for sure." I reach for a napkin.

"But I guess you gotta be here to really understand that," he says, looking back at me.

"You got that right. Although you seem to be doing okay now."

"Yeah, it's okay," he says, nodding. "But I also meant the part about making amends."

"Well, you've done that." I wipe my fingers on the napkin. "Haven't you?"

"Not all of 'em. I mean, I actually owe you an apology."

"Wow," I say, leaning back in the sofa. "An actor who apologizes."

"Hey, don't give me any shit about this. I'm supposed to do this."

"Are you kidding? I love this," I say, laughing. "I wish I had this on film. 'How to Be a Successful Star. Lesson number one: Don't be afraid to admit when you're wrong. Especially to the little people.' "

"Are you gonna let me apologize or are you gonna just give me endless shit?"

I hold up my hands. "Please, proceed."

"Okay, I apologize for my inappropriate behavior at that Chanel-Harley thing we went to. Getting drunk and riding my bike into the store."

I nod at him. "Well, thank you."

Troy reaches into his back pocket and pulls out his wallet. "And I believe I owe you this," he says, handing me two tens.

"Really, that's okay," I say, shaking my head. "Let's just consider it an agency expense."

"No, take 'em." He thrusts the bills at me. "Please. And there's one more thing."

"There's more?"

Troy sighs and scans the room. "And I'm sorry I kissed you," he says, dropping his voice to a whisper. "And I'm sorry if it caused you any problems. I mean, when I took a swing at that photographer and we had to go to court."

"I thought you were just trying to grab the camera," I say, reaching for my beer.

"Whatever. It got out of hand and it was my fault." He shakes his head again. "I knew I never should have agreed to do it."

I practically choke on my beer. "Wait a minute. What did you say?" I say, wiping my mouth with the back of my hand.

"I said it was my fault."

"After that."

"That I never should have agreed to do it."

"Agreed to what?"

"To make a play for you. It was his idea."

"*Whose idea?*"

"Doug's."

I practically leap off the sofa. At best I've been hoping Troy would cough up some info about G's party. Like why he was there and how he knew G. But this was a fucking home run. "And why would he ask you to do that?" I say, trying to keep my voice calm.

Troy shrugs. "I don't know. He said it was hazing. A way for him to find out who he could trust at the agency. What can I say, I was still using at the time so it sorta made sense. Besides, I probably would have made a play for you anyway. I usually do. Or I did. And I owed Doug a favor."

"You owed him a favor?"

"He kind of covered my ass on a movie I did at Sony a few years ago. It was a piece of shit—I don't think I shot a single scene sober—and he got the studio to throw some extra money at the marketing. Not that it made any difference. But still, it was a gesture."

"Yeah, Doug's a prince." I say, my mind going in a million directions. So G deliberately tried to set me up by having Troy make a play for me in public. But why? It seems a long shot, but what else could it be but the stick of G's carrot-and-stick plan to line up supporters? If I wasn't won over by his dangling of financial incentives, I would presumably go along with him if I feared my job was in jeopardy after being caught in a compromising situation with a client. God, G is even sleazier than I thought. Knowing this won't get me any closer to being able to prove he was engaged in illegal kickbacks with Jerry, but it might be just enough to get the ball rolling, to keep Suzanne's job.

"You know what, apology accepted," I say, leaping up. "But I actually have to make a call." I reach for my bag and start for the door, but impulsively turn back. "Thank you," I say, bending down and giving him a quick kiss on the cheek. "I'll be right back."

I practically fly out to the courtyard, fishing my cell from my bag. I punch up Rachel's cell. Come on, come on. Pick up, pick up, pick up.

"What now?" she says when she answers.

"I have to meet you," I say. "Tonight."

"Is it serious or gossip?"

"Oh, both," I say, staring up at the giant billboard, the one where the Marlboro Man once towered, blazing in the night sky. "Very much both."

18 | And the Winner Is . . .

Christmas is a bit of a bust. Actually, more of a blur. Between the parties and the premieres and the jacked-around awards calendar, what with the Oscars moving up a month and dragging all the rest of the wannabes—Golden Globes, SAG, People's Choice, Independent Spirit—up as well, it's amazing anybody gets away at all. Rachel flies back to New York, Steven flees to the Big Island with some of the lads, while I grit my teeth and head home to Philly for all of four days, one of which is spent stuck in O'Hare waiting for the runways to be cleared. Or spring. Whichever comes first. Turns out, spending twelve hours at Gate 21C is twelve hours I don't have to spend with Amy, who is barely showing but in full I'm-about-to-become-a-mother mode, which means she is even more of a princess than usual.

"All she did was sit around rubbing her stomach with this pious, blissful look on her face," I tell Steven when I reach him on my cell the second I get back to L.A.

"What kind of a look? I can't hear you over the blender," he says.

"Where are you?"

"At the beach bar. It's still happy hour out here."

"I hate you," I say, staring out the limo window as we snake up traffic-clogged La Cienega. "It's already dark here and supposed to rain tomorrow."

"Why don't you fly out for New Year's," he says over the roar of the blender. "You can sleep on the sofa bed in my suite."

"Don't tempt me," I say, sighing. Between Troy and the Phoenix and Val, God help us, all going to the Globes, I have way too much work to do. *We* have way too much work to do. "I'm actually going into the office tomorrow."

"What?" he yells.

"I said," I say, raising my voice so loudly the driver eyeballs me in the rearview mirror, "I'm going to the office tomorrow."

There's a blur of static that I take to be Steven's response.

"What did you say?"

"I said, what are you doing for New Year's?"

"What I do every year," I say, practically shouting. "Ignoring it."

The days leading up to the Globes are an even bigger blur. But then they always are, given that they're basically the kickoff to Hollywood's Super Bowl. The endless meetings and phoning and arranging of limos, dresses, shoes, hair, jewelry—all for three hours of televised self-congratulation. If you think Hollywood secretly winks at awards handed out by a bunch of photographers and part-time "reporters" from Israel, Germany, Spain, and South Africa, think again. Actors will take anything for free. Especially if they can be photographed receiving it. Just when you can't take one more call from a stylist or an assistant or an *E!* producer, you remind yourself that it's only going to get worse before it gets better. If that doesn't work, you comfort yourself with the fact that at least the Globes serve booze, so there's always the hope someone famous will do something outrageous, like Harvey Weinstein publicly flaying his publicists in the hotel lobby, and make the whole endeavor worth attending after all.

"Okay, so let's review our plan of attack," I say to Steven. It's Friday afternoon, two days before the award show on Sunday when, blow-dried, Botoxed, and even more high-strung than usual, two-thirds of Hollywood will converge on the Beverly Hilton dressed in black ties in the middle of the afternoon. All week there have been endless meetings during the day and cocktail parties and events at night, and I still have to confirm two limos, sit through a conference call with the Fox publicists, and have a final confab with the Phoenix's stylist. A confab because the Phoenix is, for the moment, still our client, this year's Lifetime Achievement winner or whatever they call it, and, as of two days before the show, undecided about what to wear. As far as I can tell, the Phoenix is either dressing as a statuette in a Versace gold-lamé number and her white wig, or she's going for Vegas showgirl in a black satin-and-lace number she's designing herself. Not that it matters. She'll stop traffic just by showing up.

I also have to get myself in gear. Such as it is. Publicists fall into two groups when it comes to award shows: those who think of themselves as perpetual bridesmaids who accompany their clients dressed in floor-length gowns and looks of blissful beatitude; and those of us who take the White House security detail approach, who come in black pantsuits and a don't-fuck-with-me look. Buying a new black suit and having my hair blown out Sunday morning—because you never know when even a publicist might wind up on camera—are as far as I'm willing to go.

"Okay, but I still don't get how we're going to ride herd on three clients at once," Steven says, staring at the itinerary—actually the third revised itinerary—the Foreign Press Association has e-mailed over. Other than photo shoots and junkets, award shows are the one time assistants can come out from behind their headsets and work with the clients.

"I told you, the Fox publicists are taking care of Val because the series has been nominated for Best Comedy," I say. "We have to do Troy because he's nominated as a guest star. So you and I will double-team Troy and the Phoenix. If all else fails, think of it as the running of the bulls at Pamplona. Just try and stay ahead of it and not get trampled."

"You know, I did that once," he says.

"The bulls?"

"Well, close. The White Party out in Palm Springs."

"Look, are you sure you're up to this?" I say. "We've never had this many clients at an award show before."

"Are you kidding? And miss the chance to see the Phoenix in person? I want to see if she shows up in that ballerina outfit she wore to the Oscars a few years ago."

"You're getting her mixed up with Lara Flynn Boyle."

"Oh, please," Steven says, rolling his eyes. "I can tell the divas from the wannabes. Besides, I'm really rooting for the Hindu princess getup she wore during her farewell concert last year."

"What are you talking about? You know stars never wear the same outfit twice."

"Well, a girl can dream, can't she?" he says. "So what do you want to do—flip for who handles who?"

"No, we're not flipping," I say, trying not to sound as exasperated as I feel. Steven is a genius behind the scenes, but he's less reliable in the field. "Suzanne wants me to help her with the Phoenix on the red carpet, so you get Troy. But we can trade off on the parties because Suzanne said she didn't care which of us helped her then and God knows I'll have had my fill of the Phoenix by then."

"Okay, so I'll, what, ride with Troy in the limo at . . ." He pauses to scan the itinerary again. "Three?"

"God, yes, you're going in the limo. I know Troy's sober now, but I still don't trust him to show up anywhere on time. Besides, you can get him to wear a tie."

Steven scans the list again. "Okay, so I guess we're good. By the way, do we know yet if Charles is flying out?"

"No, we do not," I say crisply. Ever since our disastrous phone call before Thanksgiving, my relationship with Charles, however vague it had been, has become even vaguer. Vague and existing solely in cyberspace—a series of totally businesslike e-mails. As far as I'm concerned the whole thing is dead. Or on hiatus, which in Hollywood everyone knows means "dead but we don't want to take the heat for its death just yet."

"What's his problem, anyway?" Steven says.

"You know, I wouldn't know."

"Well, he knows you went and groveled to the Phoenix. And that she's at least delayed her departure from DWP. What else does the man want?"

"Like I said, I wouldn't *know*." I may have no idea where things stand with Charles, but I do know that between the chaos of award season and the coming showdown with G and Suzanne, my nervous system is about topping out at "Manolo or Jimmy Choo?"

"Well, maybe the stiff will come around when the last piece of the puzzle falls into place on, what, Monday?"

"I don't know, and really," I say, dropping my voice and eyeing my door, which is only partially closed, "we can't talk about it. Not here. It's done and when it comes out, I don't know. Rachel doesn't even know."

"Okay," he says, raising his hands and heading for the door. "Fine, but if I see that guy Sunday night and he does not have you locked in his arms, I'm going to throw a drink in his face."

"Oh, that's okay," I say. "God knows in this town that counts as chivalry."

The day of the Globes dawns gray, damp, and cold. Might as well be Seattle except for the helicopters already buzzing over Beverly Hills. The capper is that rain is predicted, which means the clear plastic awning will go up at the Hilton and my hairdresser has to use the flattening iron to give my hair a fighting chance. By the time I head out in the Audi, a light drizzle is falling and I feel like Cinderella. Not because I'm going to meet my prince, but because the clock is ticking on when my ironed hair turns back into the unruly pumpkin.

I'm driving because the Phoenix has insisted on coming in a Toyota Prius limo—the first limo made from a hybrid car, or so I've been instructed to tell the press—which means there's only room for the driver, the Phoenix, and her outfit. Instead, I'm to meet her and Suzanne at the entrance to the red carpet. Which is like saying you'll meet somebody in Times Square on New Year's Eve.

By the time I hit the parking garage in Century City, wedge myself into the hotel shuttle bus that's packed with the other non-celeb funeral guests—grim-faced, dressed in black, and reeking of perfume and Altoids—it's just past three and a steady rain is falling. Nearly two hours until the show begins, but it's already chaos, between the rain, the screaming fans, the limos, and the helicopters. Just getting *on* the carpet requires pushing through the crowd to the layer of cops ringing the hotel driveway, flashing my credentials, having my bag searched, and being waved through a metal detector.

Finally, I am squirted out onto the plush red runway and under the clear plastic tent. I shake the rain from my hair and scan the crowd. Everyone's pretty much in place except the A-listers—aka this year's Oscar hopefuls and the HBO stars—who will not arrive for at least an hour. But everyone else is here. The press and photographers are jammed into their booths, cordoned off to the sides. Media outlets are assigned their own minute square footage that they zealously guard and from which they scream like carnival barkers at a county fair. *"Step right up and try your luck with Joan Rivers!"* *"Right here, folks,* Access Hollywood!"

Later, they'll be herded into the press room, one of the hotel's ballrooms that has not been rented out to a studio or a network for its after-party, where they'll scream out their questions to the winners. So much for the glamour of the Hollywood press corps.

As for the river of celebs, it's still early. Mostly careers-on-the-wane-or-rise presenters like Julia Louis-Dreyfus and Hilary Duff anxious to milk the moment, a few long-in-the-tooth TV stars like David Caruso and Kelsey Grammer and their wives. Wives are their own special category, falling into one of two camps: sylvan or porcine, both of which merit close study and raised eyebrows.

But mostly the carpet is populated by the folks you can't tell without a scorecard—dour-looking agents, executives, and producers. There are also fleets of my colleagues already looking panicky, expressionless security people in headsets and sunglasses—even in a downpour, sunglasses are de rigueur—and the requisite eye candy, the portfolio-free pretty young things in pastel evening dresses and expressions of great self-possession. Well, they're still young.

I check my watch. Just past three-thirty. The Phoenix won't arrive for at least half an hour—other than the Best Actress nominees, she's the queen of this ball—so I decide to hunt down Steven and Troy, who for all I know are stuck in the limo line out front. I reach in my bag for my cell and try dialing, but can't get a signal. Figures. I fish out my new BlackBerry. It's our latest gizmo from the office, but I still can't get the hang of typing on a keyboard the size of a credit card. I scrunch up my thumbs and type, *Qgwew r U?*

Shit. I try again. *Where r U?*

BH 90210 comes flying back.

Fk U, I type back. *WHERE?*

"Actually, we're right behind you," Steven says so suddenly that I drop the damn thing as I whip around.

"God, these things are great," he says, waving his BlackBerry. "How'd we ever get by without them?"

"Yeah, they're great," I say, diving to retrieve mine from under a security guard's feet. "So, you look nice," I say when I resurface, shaking my hair from my eyes. Actually, he looks better than nice. New Armani tux, slicked-backed hair, and the remnants of his Hawaii tan. "God, if I didn't know you were gay, I'd assume you were an agent."

"I'll take that as a compliment," Steven says, straightening his tie. "Although I wouldn't try that line at CAA."

"Right," I say, glancing around. "So where's Troy?"

Steven nods over his shoulder. "Back there somewhere. He got snagged. By Merle, I think."

"He got *snagged?*" I can't believe Steven is being this casual. "Then we're going back there and unsnag him."

I press through the crowd, scanning the little pas de deux's going on at the press booths. No sign of Troy. I catch sight of Merle Ginsberg, the indefatigable entertainment writer and fixture at these events, deep in conversation with Shalom Harlow about the lineage of her skintight flame-red gown.

"Great," I say to Steven. "You've been here, what, ten minutes and already you've lost him?"

"Wait, there he is," Steven says, nodding down the carpet. "Talking to *People,* or is that *The Today Show?*"

I turn and see Steven Cojocaru, aka Cojo, the legendary wispy-headed, acid-tongued style writer, talking animatedly with Troy. "Oh, fuck!" I say, turning and sprinting down the carpet. G will have my head here and now if he sees Troy talking unescorted to a TV outlet.

"Hey, guys," I say, pulling up breathlessly, clamping my hand on Troy's arm. "How's it going?"

"Hey, girl," Troy says, flashing me a blazing smile.

"Alex, you look fabulous," Cojo says, bending down to give me a kiss.

"Not as fabulous as you."

"No, but then no one does," he says, shaking his highlighted and flat-ironed locks from his eyes. "Although this lad comes close."

"Well, Troy *is* hard to beat," I say, smiling up at them. "Especially in Armani."

Troy looks confused. "Wait, isn't this Gucci? Steven?" He looks at Steven hovering behind me. "Gucci, right?"

"Right," Steven says, giving him a thumbs-up.

"Honey, it's Gucci," Cojo says, running his hand down Troy's lapel. "And with what, Tony Lama?" He glances down at Troy's snakeskin cowboy boots.

"Good eye," Troy says, sticking out his foot. "With a walking heel."

"A classic," Cojo says in a tone of voice that is a little too sarcastic for comfort.

"So Gucci, then. My mistake," I say brightly. But this is what I do here. Prattle, prattle, prattle. Fashion, fashion, fashion. Flatter, flatter, flatter. Keep things moving. Everyone smiling. Everyone talking about bullshit.

The prattle continues while I take a second to gaze around the crowd. It's almost doubled in the past few minutes. The carpet is a river of black shot with color—red, fuchsia, azure—and with more famous faces swimming into view. Tobey Maguire. Vin Diesel. Reese Witherspoon. Debra Messing. God, is that Kevin Costner? But what's with the hair? I make out the cast of *The West Wing* strolling in the way they always do, like the class valedictorians. Just wait until they get canceled. I stand on my toes to get a look at the entrance. Still no sign of the Phoenix—better call Suzanne and find out their ETA—but I make out Val and Melba and the rest of the show's cast streaming in flanked by Fox publicists. Val's got a tiara or something glittery clamped to her head, but what else is she wearing? I stand on my toes again. Her dress looks flesh-colored but floor-length, thank God. Still, I better do a drive-by.

"So I've been hearing good things about DWP, Alex."

"What a minute, what?" I say, turning back to Troy and Cojo.

"Troy was just saying the agency is really doing great," Cojo says. "After the merger. That you guys are really clicking."

"Really?" I say, giving Troy a what-gives? look.

"Ah, come on, Alex," he says, grabbing me by the shoulders. "I told him I wouldn't be here except for you."

"Oh, don't believe a word he says, except when he's talking about me," I say, laughing and leaning into him. Happy Client and Happy Publicist.

"Oh my God," Cojo says suddenly, catching sight of Kevin Costner. "Can you say 'thatch roof'? Kevin," he says, waving wildly. "Kevin, over here."

"Okay, we're done here," I say, pushing Troy back into the crowd and looking around for Steven. Already, I can hear Troy's name being called farther down the press line.

"I'll take it from here," Steven says, surfacing next to me.

"Are you *sure?*" I hiss. "You can't let him out of your sight."

"Yes, I'm sure. Go find Suzanne and the Phoenix. I'll see you inside."

I push off, dive into the crowd, and head upstream. But paddling against the current is difficult. I am jostled around, thrust up against Sharon Stone, the unofficial queen of the Globes who will show up at this thing when she's in a walker, and nearly trip over Brad Pitt, who looks even cuter and more stoned up close. I finally surface next to Melba, Val's costar. Actually, I surface next to her breasts. Melba herself is still a few inches away. "Hey, Melba," I say, trying to wedge past her. Val is just behind her, holding forth to KNBC, her tiara glittering in the light of the video camera.

"I don't know, I mean the Globes is just, it's just the start of something big," Val says, breaking into the song and flinging her arms over her head. The reporter laughs delightedly. Bingo. My little flasher just made the evening news.

I catch sight of the Fox publicist flanking Val. She rolls her eyes at me and I roll mine back. No point in waking the baby. I give the publicist a little wave and disappear back into the crowd.

I head farther upstream, trying to fish out my BlackBerry to check Suzanne's whereabouts. Suddenly, there's an eddy in the crowd, like water's parting. I stand on my toes again. Down at the entrance, surrounded by security guys, the Phoenix emerges from the Toyota like Venus on the half-shell—a blaze of sequins with a black feather boa wrapped around her shoulders and a plume of ostrich feathers exploding from her head. She is flanked on one side by Suzanne, who is grinning wildly and—who's that on the other? Oh God, it's G. G, who looks about ready to kill someone.

I try to push my way through the crowd, but get stalled behind some slab of a security guy. I have to stand on my toes and crane halfway around him to keep the Phoenix in sight. God, I still can't quite see her. I twist further past the security guy. Wait, there she is. A small moat has formed around her as she stops to pose for the photographers. *"Over here!" "Over here!"* The Phoenix smiles, hugging the feather boa to her chest. Suddenly, she turns and flings it aside. The crowd screams its approval. On the sequined black lace stretched tight across her very visible buttocks, *B-I-G* is spelled out in black satin. She turns again. I almost choke. Three more letters are spelled out across her equally visible breasts: *D-W-P.*

It takes me several minutes to swim upriver. It's the first time I've seen the Phoenix since my disastrous visit to Malibu before Christmas. In fact, I haven't spoken to her since she predictably did not return any of my calls. But something has definitely happened. I mean, why would she be wearing a billboard for DWP if she planned to let Jerry fire us? "So what's with the outfit?" I say, sliding in next to Suzanne when I finally reach them, stuck now at *E!* where Joan Rivers has the Phoenix under house arrest. "Oh my God, who's that you're wearing?" I hear Joan say. But then she says that a lot.

"Got me," Suzanne says, as she keeps her eye on the Phoenix, who is still flanked by G. "All I know is that right about now, five million people are getting a good look at the best advertising we ever had."

"Which seems weird if she was planning on firing us."

"She still might," Suzanne says, turning to me. "The last I heard from Jerry was that we had her through the rest of award season. After that, 'we will talk.' "

We stand there and watch them for several minutes. "So you

designed it, but why promote your publicity agency?" I hear Joan say. The Phoenix says something I can't make out, but G turns and glares in our direction so it must be good.

"Yeah, Doug looks happy," I say to Suzanne, as I smile and wave at G.

"You think so?" Suzanne says. "Well, fuck him."

"Go, Suzanne," I say admiringly. I have no idea how much she knows of G's plan to sabotage her clients—or what I suspect is G's plan to sabotage her clients—but it's out of my hands now.

We stand there for a few more minutes when I feel the crowd start to ebb toward the hotel, like a tide receding. "Ladies and gentlemen, please take your seats, the show's about to start," comes blaring over our heads.

"Shit," I say to Suzanne. "We still have to hit *ET,* the *L.A. Times,* and probably *W* so the New York fashionistas can hear about her dress firsthand."

"Then they'll just have to seat her at the first commercial," Suzanne says. "Go in and give them the heads-up."

I dive back into the crowd and ride the current down to the hotel's front entrance, where the lemmings are streaming in. Except for the gowns and tuxes, it feels like trooping back into high school after a fire drill. I make my way into the main ballroom with its ghastly glittery black ceiling and corner the first person in a headset I see.

"Well, she's seated at a table in front so it won't be the easiest thing," the gofer huffs at me after conferring into his headset.

"Well, what can I tell you?" I say, raising my hands. "She's going to be late." Sometimes celebrity perk actually works in my favor.

The crowd pours in around us, landing according to their caste: nominees and a select handful of A-list producers and studio execs flow to the tables on the ballroom floor; agents, managers, assistants, and other guests scatter to the various parties to drink champagne and watch the ceremony on closed-circuit TV; publicists herd into the SRO ghetto at the back of the room, just off camera.

I turn and start for the door again, but am caught in a whirlpool of stars rushing for their tables. Courteney Cox. Tom Cruise. Tom and Rita. Michelle Pfeiffer. Katie Holmes. Ed Norton. James Gandolfini. Brad and Jennifer. It's like the pages of a magazine fluttering by. Troy floats by talking animatedly to Kate Hudson. Somebody ought to cast them in a movie together. The lights dim and the crowd settles into their seats. Finally, my chance to escape back outside to Suzanne and the Phoenix. I start again for the door, when I feel a hand on my shoulder.

"I need to see you."

G. Looking about as incendiary as he did when he arrived.

I don't even pause. "Hey there," I say, pulling free of his grasp. "Having a good time?"

But G is quick. Quicker than I am. "Not yet," he says, clasping my arm again and turning me toward the door. We push through the crowd of publicists gathering at the back of the room and burst into the blazing hallway, squinting in the light.

"I assume this is your doing?" he says, still gripping my arm and propelling me past the latecomers sprinting down the hall. We come to rest against the wall, hemmed in by a large planter just opposite the doors to the auditorium.

"What's my doing?" I say, shaking free of him. "She's late because she's late."

"I don't mean that. I mean her dress."

I look at G. So it is true. He really is trying to get control of the agency by eliminating Suzanne's clients. Otherwise, why would he care that the Phoenix is wearing a dress promoting the agency?

"Her dress?" I say, stalling him, my mind going in a thousand directions. So I was right about his plan. Still, why blow his cover here and with me? The Phoenix could still end up walking. G could still end up the victor. Why, unless he thought it was all in the bag? Until tonight.

"Her little publicity stunt," he hisses.

"Oh, if you think I knew about that, I can assure you I did not,"

I say, holding up my hands. "But it's cool, don't you think? Great promotion for us."

G ignores me. "You lied to me. I told you to stay out of it."

"Out of what?" I say, still playing dumb.

"I told you to stay away from other publicists' clients. I asked you and you deliberately disobeyed me."

Okay, you want to play it that way, we'll play it that way. "Well, then I'm confused," I say, smiling and shaking my head. "If I had anything to do with one of our biggest clients staying on—and I'm not saying I did—how would that be wrong? How would that merit this—"

"I don't care about the clients," he snaps, so loudly that a few heads swivel in our direction.

"You don't care about the *clients?*" I say, all but batting my eyes.

"I *care*," he says, drawing out the word, "that employees do what they're asked. I care about loyalty. And you've just proved that I can't trust you."

"I think you're making a few leaps of logic here," I say, dropping my voice. If G's going to have my head, I'd still prefer it didn't make the morning's gossip columns.

"We both know what's going on," he says, leaning in close, so I catch a whiff of his cologne. "I thought I could count on you. And I don't like being wrong. I don't like—"

Just then the gofer with the headset bursts out the door and catches sight of me. "It's the break, it's the break, where is she?" he all but screams. "If she's coming in, it's got to be *now!*"

I see my opening and I take it. "Okay, okay, I'm going," I say, wriggling out from between the planter and G. "Hang on and I'll get her." I turn and all but sprint down the hall toward the hotel's front entrance and the haven of the red carpet.

We're heading into the second hour of the Globes—the second hour that I've been standing at the back of the room with the rest of the publicists cursing Manolo Blahnik's name—when I decide to take a break and hit the bar for a Coke. Actually, I need something stronger, like a chair, but I'll settle for sugar and caffeine.

Steven was here with me for about thirty minutes, until Troy miraculously won his category—and even more miraculously managed to thank Daddy Madden, the Fates, his AA group, me, Suzanne, "and the whole DWP gang," without mentioning G or Peg. Although I intended to walk him through the press room, I decide to let Steven do it. Given G's glowering presence—for some reason he and Suzanne are seated at the Phoenix's table looking like Churchill, Stalin, and Roosevelt at Yalta—I want to stay close at hand when the Phoenix takes the stage. Besides, if I leave now, I'll never make it back. Even sober, Troy still has his unerring party instincts. In fact, I bet Steven fifty bucks Troy heads straight from the press room to the Fox party.

U right, U win! flashes on my BlackBerry as I'm standing in line at the bar.

Told u, I type back, *btw, cash only.*

I take my Coke, down it, and head for the ladies' room pondering the odds that if I collapse into one of the chairs in the lobby I'll ever get up again. The Phoenix isn't on for another half hour and there's still a ton of awards to get through, most of which are the who-cares-except-for-their-mom-and-their-agent Best Supporting Whatever kind.

I slip into the ladies' room with the awful pink tile, the conga line of women, stalky and bulky by turns in satin and perfume, and the Latina attendant not speaking, not meeting anyone's eyes. I wedge in front of the mirror next to two agents with pencil-thin arms and eyes like cobras. I stand there assessing the rain damage to my hair, to my psyche, trying to remember how many of these things I've been to. How many more I am likely to attend. The thought is just too depressing. Growing old at black-tie events for others. I stand there for several more minutes. Until the agents move off. Until I realize if G doesn't fire me, I'm going to quit.

When I get back to the ballroom, Rob Lowe has just won for something and is choking up onstage. I check my watch. Just past seven. I bend down to fish a program off the carpet and flip to the list of awards. I can't make it out in the dark, but we must be getting close. Sharon Stone takes the stage to present something to someone. Or maybe just to show off her dress. Robin Williams, the show's host or one of them, comes out and tells some more jokes. At least he's funny, even if all that sweating is gross. Then two young blond actors I don't recognize come out and talk about the need for diversity in Hollywood. Must be referring to brunettes. But then Danny Glover, Whoopi Goldberg, Wesley Snipes, Cuba Gooding, Jr., and Halle Berry join them on the stage and the whole room lumbers awkwardly to its feet and applauds. In the dark I hear someone say, "God almighty, alls we's missin' is Uncle Tom."

"And DMX," says another voice.

There are a few TV awards involving Vanessa Redgrave and another ancient English actor I can't recall. Finally, it's the Phoenix's moment. It's so big, it comes in three parts. A lullaby of a speech by David Geffen, who looks positively spectral out of his cave. A film highlighting the Phoenix's career that also vividly recaps her plastic surgery. Finally, the Phoenix takes the stage minus the headdress, but with the feather boa wound strategically around her body. The applause is deafening. "She's fucking great," I hear a voice say in the dark.

The room falls silent. The Phoenix shades her eyes with her hand and gazes out at us. "Lifetime Achievement?" she says, looking down at the statuette. "That's a little scary. I mean, it's kind of like saying, 'Thanks, don't let the door hit you on the ass on the way out.' "

The audience roars.

"Plus, I have to talk *you* through it—and there's a high bar. Remember the year Barbra won?"

The audience titters.

"I didn't think she'd ever shut up."

The audience explodes.

"So shit," she says, shaking her head. "I could stand up here and talk about all my movies. My albums. My furniture line . . ." She pauses expertly and the crowd laughs again. "My 'work,' " she says, making quote marks with her fingers. "But I figure, why? I'm bored to tears by it. Besides, you just saw the compilation reel, which," she pauses again and shakes her head, "proves once again that real change in Hollywood is only skin deep."

The audience laughs again. They're in love.

"So instead of talking about myself and my career, as weird and great and crappy as it's been, I thought I would take a minute to talk about this strange business we're all in."

The audience shifts in their chairs. Settling in for the long haul.

"People always say we're artists. Actually, they don't always say it. *We* say it, because we have this need to believe it. But I'm here to tell you that after all the highs and lows I've been through, I don't believe we are artists. And I don't believe Hollywood is about making art. It may have been at one time. But it's not now."

The audience shifts awkwardly, uncertain now.

"I would suggest to you that we're actually athletes playing a very strange game. Sometimes you're lucky enough to be on the winning team. Most of the time you're not. But the thing to remember is that it *is* a game. And we're paid—usually overpaid—to play it. A lot of people think acting is a calling, and maybe there are a few of you lucky ones out there for whom that is true. I mean Vanessa," she says, shading her eyes again and staring out at the room. "I think we can safely say you're probably an actor first and a celebrity second."

"Only because I'm English," Vanessa shouts back, and the crowd laughs, grateful for this interruption.

The Phoenix laughs too and goes on. "Right. But I would suggest that for most of us working in Hollywood, making movies and television shows is no more or less significant than playing for the

Yankees. Or the Mets. And requires a hell of a lot less talent. Not less determination. But less native talent."

She pauses and looks down. The room is dead still. I can't tell if they're ready to lynch her or carry her out on their shoulders.

"It took me a long time to learn that," she says, looking up. "And frankly, the times I've failed were more important to my understanding than the times I've succeeded. This is a good time," she says, staring down at the statuette again. "And I have many people to thank for my being here. And I'm sure you'll be relieved when I tell you that they all know who they are and don't need to be reminded of that."

The audience chuckles, relieved to be back on familiar territory.

"So I'll leave you with two thoughts. Don't take yourself too seriously, because God knows in the end, nobody else will."

The crowd laughs, bolder now, sensing the finish line.

"And loyalty. You're less important than you think you are, but others are more important than you think they are."

Loyalty? She's talking about loyalty after that speech she gave me? Either this is the biggest bunch of BS, like Troy tearing up in court, or somehow, somewhere, the Phoenix has changed her mind.

"This is a real 'me first' town," she says, plunging on. "Actually, it's a 'Where's mine?' town, but let's give it the benefit of the doubt. Maybe that will never change. I mean, why should Hollywood be any different than the rest of the country? But if I've learned anything on my way here, it's the fallacy of that attitude. So for what it's worth," she says, raising the statuette over her head, "thank you all."

The room explodes, grateful that it's over. From where I stand, I can't judge any more of their reaction to this wrist-slapping from one of their own. I hardly know what I think of it. For all I know, they think she's an infidel or Moses come down with the tablets.

"Well, that was interesting," I hear someone next to me say.

"Please, she knows exactly what she's doing," comes another voice. "That just proves you can say anything and they'll love you, if you've got a twenty-million-dollar TV deal in your back pocket."

The crowd is on its feet now, hands pumping wildly. The Phoenix starts to exit and then turns back. "In case you're wondering about my next career move," she says, leaning into the microphone and speaking over the applause, "I'll just tell you that my dress, customized with any six letters of your choosing, will be available on my website in the morning."

The after-parties, like all award show after-parties, start early—it's not even 8:30 P.M. PST when the lights come up—and go late. At least with the Globes, they're all under one roof. Besides, with no Governors Ball to attend—everyone ostensibly eats during the award show, which is bullshit, because no one wants to be caught chewing on camera—everyone scatters to their home-team soiree the second it's over.

This year, Miramax is down the hall in the Grand Ballroom, right next to NBC in Trader Vic's. Paramount is up on the roof, as is Fox. HBO has taken over Griff's downstairs next to the pool. *In-Style* has claimed the largest conference room off the lobby. Depending on who has won what during the show, the cachet of each party varies from year to year. Except for Miramax, which always acts like it's the coolest girl in school no matter what pretentious nonsense it's released.

As the evening's big winner, the Phoenix has free reign to roam. Despite all the guys with headsets and clipboards guarding the door to each party, she will not be turned away from any of them. So far she's hit *InStyle*, where she spent many minutes posing for pix in front of the magazine's giant letterhead, and Paramount, because Viacom owns MTV and she needs to show the flag for her upcoming series.

Now she's come to rest at HBO because everyone does, and here the Phoenix is holding court in a corner booth behind an invisible velvet rope. Actually, she's picking at a plate of shrimp while greeting those few supplicants the bouncer admits to this party-within-a-party. Suzanne and G are somewhere around working the crowd, but it's my job to stand next to the bouncer and give him the thumbs-up or -down on those seeking an audience. Mostly this is a no-brainer. Yes to Brad Grey. No to the woman in the see-through lace dress and top hat. Yes to Chris Albrecht. Okay, he doesn't even stop, but then it *is* his party. Yes to Sarah Jessica Parker. A baby could do it. A baby should do it.

I've been standing here playing traffic cop for about thirty minutes wondering how many more shrimp the Phoenix can eat and whether she will actually speak to me this evening—so far I've been invisible—when Suzanne rolls up. "You must be starving," she says, handing me one of the two glasses of champagne she's carrying. "Why don't you take this, get some food and sit down for a second, and I'll deal with this."

She doesn't have to ask me twice. I'd share a table with the scary chick in the top hat if I can just sit the fuck down. I do a drive-by of the nearest food table. The usual beef-salmon-roasted vegetables that all looks even more tired than I am. There's also a sushi table, where I scoop up about three California rolls, and a pasta table, which I give a pass to. I swing by the dessert table, grab a mini crème brûlée tart, and turn to scan the room for a chair. Any chair.

I'm about to throw caution to the wind and squeeze into a table of Biggies sitting with some *Sopranos* cast members, when I spy an empty chair adjacent to one of the several television monitors set up around the room. Great. A chair, and I don't have to talk to anybody to get it. I all but collapse into it, take a slug of champagne, and start in on my California rolls when the TV suddenly springs to life.

"Ladies and gentlemen, please welcome your host, Robin Williams."

Oh God, they're replaying the entire show now? The sound

from the set is deafening. Several people are staring in my direction at the screen. Didn't you guys see it the first time? I look around for a place to move, but there's not a chair in sight. Fuck it, my ears will just have to suffer to give my feet a break.

I sit there, trying to tune out the show while eating as fast as I can without choking. I'm just finishing the California rolls, heading for the crème brûlée, when I feel someone jostle my leg. I slide my legs out of the way and pop the tart in my mouth. But my leg is jostled again. Oh God, what? I turn. G, squatting by my side, smiling the most lethal smile since Jack Nicholson leered at Shelley Duvall in *The Shining.*

"So, Alex, here you are," he says.

Or at least I think he does. It's impossible to hear over the music and waves of laughter screaming from the TV. I smile and nod. Fuck you, very much. G says something else I can't hear, but it must be serious since his smile disappears. I swallow the last of the brûlée, shake my head, and raise both my hands. Only dogs can hear you now, G.

"Ladies and gentlemen, please welcome Sandra Bullock!"

G smiles, closes his eyes for a second, and then half stands and leans into my ear. "I said, you have thirty days."

19 | Girls Rule

The thing about getting fired is, no matter how much you prepare for it, are primed for it, for hearing those very words, it's still a kick in the head.

And it is. Or it would have been, if it had ended there with my mouth full of crème brûlée and G literally screaming my epitaph in my ear. It doesn't matter that he has no grounds to fire me. No grounds except what he was reading into the Phoenix's dress and the fact that he couldn't dispose of Suzanne. Or at least, not yet. And of course, the fact that he is my boss, or one of them, and can technically fire me at any time.

I don't know. Maybe there is a God. Or maybe we all have our *Wizard of Oz*–like moments of clarity and salvation. But, like Billie Burke materializing out of a bubble, my own glittery Glinda the Good Witch chooses that exact moment to wander by.

Actually, the Phoenix is heading for the ladies' room and needs me as her guard dog, but never mind. The result is the same. "Alex, where've you been?" she says, the HBO partygoers parting like Munchkins before their queen. "We're leaving."

"Where've I been?" I say, leaping up, nearly kicking G over in the process. You mean besides being ignored by you all evening? "Why, just here," I say blandly. "Getting fired."

I don't know what I am hoping for exactly. Maybe nothing. Or maybe just the exhilaration that comes from speaking the truth. Finally. Of no longer being afraid. Of saying what needs to be said, and not what's expected. Certainly, I'm not anticipating a house landing on G, although with the Phoenix, God knows you could never be too sure.

"Oh, please," she says, looking at me and then down at G. "Do I know you?"

G stands up and sputters something about Jerry Gold and the agency. And having been next to her for most of the evening. Like that mattered.

"He's the G in BIG-DWP," I say.

"Oh, I have you right here on my ass," she says, nodding over her shoulder. "So as the G, you're in a position to tell my publicist she's not doing her job?"

G smiles, clears his throat. "You know, this is really not the time or place for office matters," he says, coming toward us. "I think this is something that—"

"*Office matters?*" the Phoenix says, shaking her head so the crystal and jet beads hanging from her wig clack together. "Look, I may have just given a speech about the bullshit nature of celebrity. But let's not kid ourselves. We both know how it works here. So I suggest you rethink your decision, because if you fire her, I'll fire you and hire her to be my personal publicist."

"Now, why would you want do that?" G says, taking a step closer.

Even I know the answer to that one.

The Phoenix looks at him and then the crowd. "Because I *can*."

"Ladies and gentlemen, please welcome David Geffen," blares from the television.

"And while you're at it, G, turn that shit down," she says. "I can't stand to see myself on camera."

If this had been a movie, my own personal movie of which

I was, finally, the star, this is where the audience would cheer, someone would toss G into the pool, and the sound track—maybe Gloria Gaynor, although she's so eighties, or maybe Dorothy's anthem, "You're out of the woods, you're out of the dark, you're out of the night"—would swell. But given that it's just a Globe after-party, and late at that, with everyone looking a little the worse for wear, it's a lot less cinematic.

Having dispatched G, the Phoenix turns for the exit. "Are you coming?" she says, in the tone of voice that reminds me that if her scenario comes to pass, I have just exchanged one boss for another. Still, I follow her and hold her feather boa and her purse in the ladies' room, where the conga line of women is nonplussed to find the Phoenix coming in to pee just like the rest of them.

And then the evening is pretty much finished. The other parties are deemed unworthy, thank God, and it's just a cell-phone call to the driver and a short hop to the Toyota. And, like Cinderella back in her coach, or actually I'm so tired I can't keep my metaphors straight, it's over.

"Did you mean what you said?" I say, bending down by the passenger door.

"When?" she says.

"Back there. When you said you'd hire me if he fires me."

"Yeah, I meant it."

"But I thought I was history after our last meeting."

"Yeah, well, I thought better of it," she says with a shrug. "After what you said. Besides, there's going to be a ton of stuff with the show coming up and somebody's got to deal with it. Might as well be you."

"Thanks," I say.

"Don't thank me yet," she says. "But I think you should get a new job one way or another. That guy looks like a jerk."

And then she is gone. A tiny black limo creeping down the hotel's rain-slicked driveway. Like Glinda floating away, leaving me almost, but not quite, where I started.

"So you go, then I'll go," Steven says, when I reach him on my cell as I'm driving home.

"Actually, the only place I'm going is home," I say, turning onto Wilshire. "Where are you?"

"Still on the roof at the Fox party," he says, and I make out the roar of laughter in the background.

"Is Troy still there?"

"No, he split hours ago. I think he left with Sandra Bullock. Weren't they an item at one time?"

"No, that was Matthew McConaughey," I say, turning off onto Santa Monica. "Look, I'll tell you all about it in the morning, but the short version is that G fired me."

"He fired you?"

"Well, he tried to."

"Wait, does that mean I'm fired too?"

I guess the Phoenix was right. This really is a "Where's mine?" town. "No. Or I don't know," I say. "I don't think I'm even really fired because he gave me thirty days and—"

"Just until the Oscars. Nice, G."

"But the point is, the Phoenix intervened."

"And hit him with her feather boa?"

"Offered me a job."

"Oh, man, can I come too?"

"Look, I don't even know how this is going to shake out. If I'm fired or hired or if I even want to do this anymore. I just know that I'm too tired to think about it now."

We make noises about talking tomorrow. In the office. Figure it all out then.

"By the way, I bumped into Rachel," he says. "She said she had one word for us: *tomorrow.*"

"No kidding," I say. So the other shoe's about to drop. Perfect fucking timing. "Look, I'm making a detour," I say, heading up Beverly toward Sunset, toward Laurel Canyon and the twenty-four-hour newsstand in the Valley. Unless I miss my guess, Monday's L.A. *Times* should be hitting the sidewalks just about now.

The day after an award show is like a snow day in Hollywood. Everyone is so wiped they either stay home or straggle in bleary-eyed sometime after noon. Unless your clients won, then you're up at it early, cranking out releases and dealing with the press, which is in feeding-frenzy mode.

I am at my desk by 8 A.M. I'm in jeans, an old black cashmere crew neck, and my hair's in a ponytail, but I'm here, writing my releases, reading the wires, and generally readying myself for the onslaught to come. Suzanne is the first through the door.

"I know you knew about this," she says, tossing the *Times* business section onto my desk.

I glance up. "Yes, I read that. Last night. Picked it up at the newsstand on my way home. Interesting."

"*Interesting?* Oh, it's a lot more than interesting."

"Yes, it is," I say, looking up. "And we should probably have some sort of statement ready. Unless G's already prepared one."

She looks at me and shakes her head. "Why didn't you just come to me about all this? We could have handled it in-house."

I don't even bother challenging her assumption that I'm the "BIG-DWP publicist who insisted on remaining anonymous" named in the story. That I have broken the cardinal publicist's rule: Never tell the truth. At least not in print. As for why I did it, I could say that I did it for her. That she asked me to save her job and I did. Or I could tell her I did it to screw G. But I didn't do it for either of those reasons. In fact, I'm still not sure why I did it.

"I don't know," I say. "I guess if I've learned anything here, it's that there are times when things really are wrong, and not just a matter of spinning it."

She looks at me like she's never seen me before. "This business is so different from when I started twenty-five years ago, I don't even know what's appropriate anymore," she says. "I don't know if I should thank you or suspend you."

"Well, if it helps you any," I say, turning back to the computer,

"G fired me last night, although God knows what that means. I mean, now."

There's a commotion outside my door. Steven, still in his tux, carrying a copy of the *Times* like it's on fire. "Jesus, I didn't know you actually talked to the reporter. . . . Oh, sorry," he says, catching sight of Suzanne.

"I suppose you knew about this as well?" she says.

Steven looks at me, then Suzanne, and then back at me.

"He's trying to decide if he's going to get blamed or praised," I say, folding my arms and leaning back in my chair. "Come on. Final answer."

Steven looks down, pulls his tie from his shirt, and then looks up. "Yeah, I did. I knew about it."

No one says anything for a minute. Down the hall, the phones begin to ring. It's already starting. The unraveling of BIG-DWP. Or at least part of it.

"So what happens now?" Steven says, looking at us.

"I couldn't tell you," Suzanne says, shaking her head and heading for the door. "I haven't a clue."

It happens fast, actually. As things do when the words *Hollywood* and *kickback* appear in a headline on the front page of the *L.A. Times'* business section. By tomorrow the trades will have it. Depending on what happens, if G pulls a Mike Ovitz and goes postal, blames the gay mafia, or in this case the girl mafia, it could make the national papers.

At the very least, he's finished here. There's a lot you can get away with in Hollywood, but not all of it. And not if it gets out. Last year, a CAA agent got the ax after the papers got wind of his kickback scheme involving a Beverly Hills real estate agent and the sale of his clients' houses. G's sins are bigger. A lot bigger.

In fact, everything Rachel, Steven, and I had suspected back at Tom Bergin's was there in black-and-white. It had started with my talking to the reporter about Troy and G and my suspicions about

G and Jerry, but the other break was finding a weak link in Jerry Gold's office. Another disgruntled employee who was more than happy to help connect the dots. How G had plotted with Jerry to bleed DWP dry before he even bought us out. How G had already paid Jerry a "good faith deposit" for taking Carla out of DWP. How G planned to revive the agency once Suzanne and the other original partners were gone and sell it to the highest bidder. Apparently, G had lined up an investment-banking house to drum up possible suitors. Opening bids were expected to be north of ten million.

"I had no idea we were worth that much," Steven says, after Suzanne leaves and he's reread the story for something like the fourth time. "Maybe I should go to business school."

"Maybe you should go home and change your clothes."

"I'm serious. There's a lot of ways to make money in this town if you just think about it the right way."

"Or the wrong way. Do yourself a favor. Go to law school. You've already watched so much *Law & Order* you might as well."

"Well, now that you mention it . . ."

"What?" I say. Assistants grow up to be publicists. Happens all the time. It's supposed to happen. Like the children of Mormons, because who in their right mind would convert? I guess I just thought Steven would always work here. He just wouldn't take my messages anymore.

"I have applications to USC, UCLA, and Stanford law schools at home. I'm thinking of filling them out and seeing what happens. I mean, it's late, but—"

"You'll get in," I say, shaking my head. "You'll make a hell of a lawyer."

"Well, they say it's always good to have a lawyer in the family," he says, balling his tie up in his hand. He looks at me and smiles a smile I can't really read. "Here," he says, coming toward me. He drapes his tie around my neck and wraps it loosely into a bow. "Okay." He stands back to admire his handiwork. "Now I'm going out for lattes. Like I always do."

I turn back to my desk. Take several congratulatory calls about Troy's upset win last night. And many more from the tabs and the fashion press wanting to know about the Phoenix's dress and if it is, in fact, on her website, www.phoenixgarb.com. Apparently, a few have already tried to find it. But mostly it's fallout from the *Times'* story. Everyone is shocked, shocked to learn gambling has been going on here in Casablanca.

Peg calls, sputtering about mistrust, miscreants, and men in general. "I never liked that guy," she says. "I always figured he was going to raise your rates."

I hear from the Phoenix. Or rather I hear from Tracy, who tells me I'm "on her call sheet" but that, due to the late night last night, "she will be getting to her calls later than usual."

I get an e-mail from Troy, who's on his way to some shoot somewhere. Some film offer he got at the last minute. *Daddy Madden would be proud. I am 2.*

Finally, Rachel weighs in.

"So you did it," she says.

"G did it to himself."

"If it were that simple, only the good guys would be running Hollywood."

"If it were that simple, this would be the smallest town in the world."

"So what are you going to do?"

"You mean, other than go to Disneyland?"

"I mean, I heard his final act was to fire you."

"Yeah, I guess I technically have thirty days."

"Seriously, what are you going to do?"

I sigh. "I haven't thought that far ahead. We still have the rest of award season to get through."

"I meant with your life. You were so Jean-Paul Sartre the other night."

"What do you mean, 'the other night'?"

"You're right, you're always hung up about your life. Like it hasn't even started and the rest of us have it all figured out."

"Don't you?"

"I don't think we're supposed to."

"Well, in that case," I say, "I guess I'm right where I should be." We make plans to meet later. For a drink. To celebrate. Or commiserate, depending on our moods. "By the way," Rachel says, "I heard G hired a publicist. Some crisis-management firm. I also heard that Sony is interested in the rights to his story. Apparently they think that with a few changes, it makes a good little thriller."

As for G, who knows if the rumor is true? He never even shows. The office is strangely muted. Lots of whispering behind closed doors. But then, what do you expect from publicists? They'll deny news even when they make it.

Finally, the blandest of press releases goes out: "regrettable actions," "resignation effective immediately." Suzanne sends a mass e-mail announcing an all-office meeting first thing tomorrow, but meanwhile keep our mouths shut and stay the course. We are still in the midst of award season. Everyone seems relieved to go back to work.

Except me. I've been here since eight, since time began, and all I want to do is go home and sleep. For about three years. Or at least until award season is over. But I still have a ton of e-mails to return and a meeting tomorrow morning about some client's movie I should prepare for. I check my watch. Coming up on seven. Everyone in the office has bailed. Even Steven. God knows why I'm still here. Maybe I know that if I leave, I might never come back.

I decide to give it another half hour. Tops. But even that's going to require some stimulants. One of the muffins in that basket somebody sent over for something earlier today. I head down the hall to the kitchen. The kitchen that is its usual charming self. A pile of dirty coffee cups in the sink, napkins, and crumbs all over the counter. A spilled, empty container of vanilla soy milk. And the looted muffin basket. Just another one of our messes for the cleaning crew.

I wipe up the worst of it, root around the basket of muffin remains, and find a whole one. Or most of a whole one. Poppy seed, I think. Oh well. I hop up on the counter and start tearing the top off, bit by bit. You never want to rush this. I'm just pondering the idea of a second muffin, when the kitchen door flies open. Suzanne with an armload of flowers—lilies, irises, and roses. I'm so startled I immediately hop down.

"Alex, I didn't know you were still here," she says. "I was just looking for a vase."

"Nice," I say, nodding at the flowers. "Who sent them?"

I expect her to rattle off the name of a client's manager. Or a studio publicist. The usual post-awards graft.

"My parents, actually," she says, sounding embarrassed.

"Your *parents* sent you flowers?" Somehow it had never crossed my mind that Suzanne had parents. Not now. Not ever. She didn't seem to need them.

"Is it your birthday?"

"No," she says, turning toward the cupboards, looking for a vase. "They wanted to congratulate me."

"For our Globe winners?"

"No." She turns to look at me. "For keeping my job. For hanging on to my company."

"They knew about that?" I say, stunned. Who tells their parents about their job? Who tells their parents about anything?

"Yes, they did," she says, still looking at me.

"Wow." I nod. "Lucky you."

She looks at me for another long second. "You know, it is okay to trust people once in a while."

"Really? I guess that's something I haven't learned yet," I say, matching her gaze. I've worked alongside her for three years, put my own job on the line to protect hers, but I realize I don't know her at all.

She pulls a vase from one of the cupboards, turns to the sink, drops in the flowers, and starts filling it with water. Over the rush of the tap, she says something I can't hear.

"I'm sorry," I say.

"I said, you could learn," she says, turning back to me. "And you can start here." She hands me the vase.

"No, no," I say, shaking my head. "They're yours. Why should I—"

"Take them. I want you to have them. You deserve them. You're the reason I'm still here. Why we're all still here. Besides, I owe you a thank-you and I'm sorry I didn't say so before. I guess I was just so shocked to find out what had been happening here that it took me a minute to sort through it all."

"Oh, I don't know."

"Trust me," she says, thrusting the vase, heavy and slippery with water, into my hands. "These belong to you."

I take the flowers, breathing in their cold, damp fragrance. "Thanks," I say, giving her a smile. "Thanks." We're just heading out into the hall, so quiet now you can hear the buzzing of the fluorescent lights overhead, when there's a noise from the direction of G's office. "Oh my God, did he come in?" I whisper.

"Probably his assistant cleaning out the crypt. Come on," she says, heading down the corridor. Still carrying the flowers like some overburdened flower girl, I follow her.

Suzanne all but kicks in the door. G, in a pair of jeans and a sweater and glasses—glasses!—rummaging through his drawers. He looks up, startled. Nobody says anything for a minute.

"Doug—" is all Suzanne gets out.

"Ah, the good-bye girls," he says, shutting drawers. "You know, I had my doubts about you, about this agency, right from the start."

"Doug, I think it's a little late for that kind of—"

"Do me one favor," he says, looking up. "Don't 'Doug' me. Not now. Not," he says, nodding at the flowers, "in your little moment of triumph."

I'm tempted to back out of the room. Let them have their showdown in private. They started this without me. They can finish it.

"I don't know," Suzanne says, turning to me. "I don't think it's so 'little,' do you, Alex? Seems to me it's a pretty damn big moment of triumph."

"Oh, you would," Doug says, coming around the desk toward us. "You would think hanging on to this stupid agency is worth celebrating. Never made a dime. Never dreamed of making a dime until I came along with an idea how to turn this has-been into a cash cow. You just couldn't see it."

"Oh, she saw it," I say suddenly. "She just saw it happening with her here."

"I actually saw it happening for all of us," Suzanne says. "I'm only sorry you didn't."

Down the hall, the sounds of the cleaning crew, their laughter, voices, hit the office. A vacuum cleaner roars to life.

"Spare me," G says with a wave, turning back to his desk. "This is a small town. And as everybody knows, you only fail upward in Hollywood."

The vacuuming grows louder. It sounds like the end of the world.

"You know, it's really too bad you're giving up on publicity," I say, raising my voice over the noise. "Because you really can spin anything. You did what you did, nearly destroyed this place, and you still act like you're the winner. That's a real skill, lying like that," I'm all but shouting now. "I can't do it."

Suddenly, the office door bursts open. A cleaning-crew guy pushing the roaring vacuum noses in. "Oh, sorry," he says, looking up, startled to find us here. He reaches down and fumbles with the switch. Silence settles over the room. I look down at the flowers. "I can't do it," I say again, handing them back to Suzanne. "I don't ever want to do it."

And then it's finally over. Just a half-burnt broom and a smoldering witch's hat. And the requisite mopping-up by the lawyers.

Or it would have been if the day had ended there. With me

staring out my window at the last of the rush-hour traffic on Wilshire, the sea of lights in the growing dusk, feeling more sad than anything. We had done it. G was dispatched. Suzanne had been spared. I had been spared. We had restored the universe to rights. We'd even had our final showdown at the OK Corral. So why did it feel like an ending, not a beginning?

"Hey," I hear behind me.

I turn around. Charles. Looking the way one does after a cross-country flight, his tie loosened, a raincoat slung over one arm, and a look of utter exhaustion in his gray-green eyes.

"When did you get here?" I say, looking at my watch.

"Caught the first plane I could get this morning. Suzanne called me at home."

"I guess that's the beauty of flying east to west," I say, turning back to the window. This is the first time I've seen him since our aborted flagrante delicto before Thanksgiving, and a lot has happened since. Maybe too much.

"Look, I think I owe you an apology."

"Oh, let's not go there," I say. "I can't remember that far back."

"Okay, I suppose I deserve that," he says, looking down. "But for the record, I am sorry. I'm sorry I pressured you about taking sides against Doug. And I'm sorry I didn't respect your right to make your own decisions."

"I don't know," I say, still gazing out the window. "How could you be expected to respect my decisions, when I didn't?"

We stand there in silence for a minute. "But I'm mostly sorry about something else," he finally says.

I look over at him.

"I'm sorry we never got to finish what we started here," he says, running his hand through his hair, his silky forelock that I have touched only once.

I could say that I'm sorry as well. More than sorry. But it's not about him. Or even us. "You know, last night I decided I was going to quit. That if G didn't fire me, I was just going to quit. That I was finally finished with all this."

"And what do you think now?" he asks, taking a step toward me.

"That I honestly don't know."

"You know, Suzanne and I have talked and there's a much bigger role for you here now."

I shake my head. "It's not that. It's really not. It's just that so many people never know when to leave Hollywood. To just pack up and leave. I don't want to be one of those people."

"Look," he says, coming up to me and fingering Steven's tie. "Do you always wear this?"

I give a small laugh, shake my head, and reach up to undo the tie. In all the excitement, I'd forgotten I still had it on. But he catches my fingers in his fingers. "Look," he says, pressing his forehead to mine and closing his eyes. "I want to hear all about it. I do. Why don't we go to dinner tonight and talk about it. We can keep talking about it. Talking about it and everything else for as long as you want. As long as it takes."

For a minute, I feel like I'm in that scene in *Bull Durham*. Toward the end where it's raining and Kevin Costner tells Susan Sarandon he's quitting, but that he wants to hear all her theories about life and baseball. For as long as it takes. That's how I feel.

Except I'm not in a movie.

And I don't want to be.

"Okay," I say, closing my eyes and feeling the warmth of his head on mine. "We'll keep talking."

Acknowledgments

With particular thanks to Brian DeFiore, who first saw the light at the end of the tunnel—and figured out how to get there. Thanks, too, to Bruce Tracy and Ivan Held for their ardent enthusiasm, Tim Farrell for his unflagging and gracious stewardship, and Kate Garrick. Thanks also to Andrea and Dave de Vries, David Rensin, Lyman Leathers, the late Andre Dubus, Richard Sens, Nora Ephron, Leslie Peters, Stephanie Riseley, and, especially, as ever, to Michael Walker, who remains my best editor, for his inspiration and support. And finally, to my late mother, Gay de Vries, who taught me to always finish what I started.

ABOUT THE AUTHOR

HILARY DE VRIES is an award-winning journalist and author who has covered Hollywood for more than a decade. She is a regular contributor to *The New York Times* and has written for *Vogue, Rolling Stone, W, Vanity Fair,* and the *Los Angeles Times*. She lives in L.A. This is her first novel.